"A fun and engaging novel. The story sh
people face reconciling workplace dem
their own ethics and values. This is a bo
those interested in local government or a ~~~~~ ~~ ~~

Kevin O'Rourke, retired city manager,
Co-chair, CAL-ICMA Ethics Committee

"As entertaining as it is insightful. Thompson's fictional approach captures
the realities facing today's local government administrators as well as key
public issues that should concern us all.

Stephen G. Harding, retired city manager, Instructor,
Master of Public Policy & Administration Program, Northwestern University

"A highly enjoyable read, woven into a story of the city management
profession from a highly regarded retired city manager. The story provides
insight into development issues from the public and private perspective,
along with interesting stories about some little-known parts of California's
history. I wish I had read this before becoming a city manager."

Sean Quinn, retired city manager

"After serving as a city manager for twenty-five years and then working
in a consultant capacity with public agencies, it is encouraging to see a
leader in the profession translate his experience into an interesting book
featuring the city manager craft. Thompson has a thorough understanding
of the issues, concerns, and challenges faced by city managers everywhere.
Everyone should read it for entertainment and for the window it provides
into the exciting field of city management."

Jack A. Simpson
"Trackdown Management" Newsletter

"What a read! The diverse and complex challenges city management
professionals face on a daily basis come to life in Thompson's page-
turning story."

Nat Rojanasathira, President,
Municipal Management Association of Northern California

"Without Purpose of Evasion is much more than a fascinating novel. It is
an insightful and instructive primer on the day to day operations of local
government. Students of politics could learn a tremendous amount about
the inside workings of small cities from the experiences of Brad Jacks, the
city manager of the novel. Most enjoyable!"

Elizabeth F. Moulds
Professor of Government Emeritus, California State University, Sacramento

WITHOUT PURPOSE

of EVASION

OREGON

Mt.SHASTA

SACRAMENTO RIVER

SACRAMENTO VALLEY

SACRAMENTO

STOCKTON

Delta

STATE WATER PROJECT

SAN FRANCISCO

Pacific Ocean

SANTA YNEZ

SANTA BARBARA

|LOS ANGE

Map by
Vacaville High School Art class

Teacher- Donovan Clark
Anthony Acosta
Bianca Baron
Kirby Broughton
Cinthya Ceja
Lydia Edwards
Grant Ehlers
Tiara Gonsolis
Josephine Moseley
Elena Quintana
Cesiliya Yarrow
Principal Ed Santopadre

SHASTA DAM

TRACY PUMPING PLANT

e

NEVADA

Mono Lake
Moonscape

S VALLEY

ierra Nevadas

L.A AQUEDUCT

LA Aqueduct Cascades

lley

MOJAVE DESERT

COLORADO AQUEDUCT

ARIZONA

DIEGO

MEXICO

WITHOUT PURPOSE

of EVASION

A NOVEL

JOHN P. THOMPSON

NORTH LOOP BOOKS, MINNEAPOLIS MN

North Loop Books
322 First Avenue N, 5th floor
Minneapolis, MN 55401
612.455.2294
www.NorthLoopBooks.com

DISCLAIMER:
Without Purpose of Evasion is a work of fiction. Apart from the well-known actual people, events, and locales that figure in the narrative, all names, characters, places, and incidents are the products of the author's imagination or are used fictitiously.

ISBN-13: 978-1-63505-074-5
LCCN: 2016912910

Distributed by Itasca Books

Cover Design by Alexis Cooke
Typeset by James Arneson

Printed in the United States of America

NORTHLOOP
BOOKS

For our grandchildren with hope for their future.

I, [name], do solemnly swear (or affirm), that I will support and defend the Constitution of the United States and the Constitution of the State of California against all enemies, foreign and domestic; that I will bear true faith and allegiance to the Constitution of the United States and the Constitution of the State of California; that I take this obligation freely, without any mental reservation or purpose of evasion; and that I will well and faithfully discharge the duties upon which I am about to enter.

Public Officials' Oath of Office, Article 20 of the California Constitution

1

"Shit!" Brad Jacks stumbled over a rut in the decomposed granite track at the park. Why hadn't they ever fixed that thing? Well, because "they" was "he." As city manager of Santa Ynez, a small city on California's Central Coast, the buck stopped with him. There just weren't enough bucks stopping these days to make the bike/jogging track repair a high priority.

Of course, when it came to preventative maintenance, it was "pay me now or pay me a lot more later." As sidewalks and paths deteriorated, the city was vulnerable to trip and fall claims from average citizens. Even in the absence of a predatory sleaze ball attorney stirring up business for himself, the cost to settle those claims was typically more than regular maintenance. He stepped over another uneven patch of path raised by tree roots, noting the trip hazard. He pushed away the surge of frustration. When it was budget season there was always a clamor for more police, fire, and parks and recreation funding. In his thirty-year career, he'd never seen anyone toting a placard pleading "Save Our Preventative Maintenance." So the reality was that the bike path likely wouldn't rise in priority until after the tort claims started to mount unless somebody close to a key councilmember bent the right ears. It was the kind of government decision-making that drove his business friends nuts but passed for logic in Brad's world.

He sighed, as he always did when faced with a problem that he really couldn't solve, and continued with his jog. At fifty-four years old, he was well into his middle-age spread. Based on those ideal weight charts, apparently created by anorexics, he needed to lose thirty pounds from his six foot, two-hundred-fifteen-pound frame. The doctor's warnings about high blood pressure and his poor family health history had been a nudge. The depressing view of the aging pudgy guy in a department store's three-way mirror provided the final push.

While he didn't really like to jog, it was an aerobic activity he could often squeeze into his schedule. Listening to his eclectic music playlist was usually a good distraction from everything else going on in his life, but the stumble broke the mood and he was now fully into work mode. Even ZZ Top's "La Grange" and Benny Goodman's "Swing, Swing" couldn't bring him back to the moment. Screw it! He took out his earbuds, turned off the iPod, rubbed his throbbing left knee, and set out again to organize his thoughts for the day accompanied only by the soft squish of his cross trainers on the damp path.

The chilly gray November morning mirrored Brad's mood as he plodded along. It was going to be a busy day full of meetings with staff, councilmembers, and citizens. They would all want something from him. At any given moment, he might be requested to assign staff to work on somebody's idea, spend some of the city's money on a pet project, resolve a dispute with the city bureaucracy, or get someone fired. The city manager was the fulcrum point between the community, its politics, and the city organization. The city departments usually handled the routine day-to-day issues just fine. The out-of-the-ordinary found its way to his office.

Slogging around the damp path watching for more trip hazards, he spotted a long-haired Golden Retriever bounding across the wet grass right at him. The dog had the lumbering gait and dopey, tongue-waving smile that marked the breed. In other circumstances it might have been endearing, but right now he was in work mode and saw man's best friend as a violation of the city's leash law. "Goldie," or whatever clever name his owners picked, jumped up on him playfully as he tried to jog. Brad was not in a playful mood. He pushed the dog off and saw the streaks of mud on his jogging pants. Damn it.

The dog carried the odd combination of human shampoo, dog stink, and the outdoors that was indicative of a beloved pet. "Yah!" he yelled and flung his hands at the smelly canine. "Go on!"

Goldie gave him a hurt look with his big brown eyes. Then he dropped his haunches and deposited a steamy pile of last night's Alpo at Brad's feet. He took a mock swat at the dog, yelled "No!" then "Stay!" and started off again hoping he wasn't followed. He had nothing to clean up the mess with and it wasn't his responsibility anyway. He looked around for Goldie's owner and saw no one. He wasn't in a foul enough mood to sentence the dog to a visit from Animal Control.

An elderly woman with her dog passed him in the opposite direction. She had her Cocker Spaniel on a leash and a plastic bag in hand at the ready and scowled at him as they approached.

"Not my dog," he said defensively.

She still scowled. Her lotion, or whatever she had on, was more nauseating than Goldie's pile. How did her Cocker tolerate it with its keen sense of smell?

He was sure the woman recognized him and would likely be spreading the word about the public official who couldn't be bothered to enforce the city's leash ordinance. What was he supposed to do?

Pick up the poop in his hands and hogtie Goldie with his drawstring until Animal Control showed up? He sighed. Being unfairly judged was another occupational hazard.

He paused at the park entrance to remove the small baggie of soy nuts from his sweatshirt and popped them all into his mouth. They tasted like roasted sawdust but the crunch felt good to his teeth and the little bit of salt tingled the front of his tongue. It was as much pleasure as he was going to get out of the jog today.

He saw that the woman still had her eye on him as she walked her dog. He imagined just throwing the baggie on the ground and jogging off. Might as well give her a really good story to talk about. His good sense won out. He walked over to the garbage can and bent over to pick up a styrofoam cup and potato chip bag along the way. See, lady, I'm a diligent public servant after all.

He jogged out of the park into his older neighborhood trading the scent of leaves and grass for wet asphalt streets, car exhaust and chimney smoke. It was good to have some rain for a change. He breathed in the oak and pine that still hung in the morning's heavy air from neighborhood fireplaces. The smell reminded him of the blaze his grandfather always made in their huge stone fireplace on Christmas Eve; all the grandkids gathered around to hear him read *'Twas The Night Before Christmas*. The kids were always confused about how Santa could get passed the fire. The memory warmed him momentarily.

The dull gray of the morning suddenly glowed with a figure in the distance running toward him. "Excuse me," beckoned the hard-bodied young woman in lime green spandex stopping before him. "Aren't you Mr. Jacks, our city manager?"

He stopped his forward progress and jogged in place. She seemed friendly enough. "Yes. Brad. And you are?"

"Leslie Hitch," she said, extending her hand.

He wiped his right hand on his sweatshirt and met her firm shake.

"Glad to meet you, Leslie. Is there something I can do for you?" He hoped it wouldn't be much.

"Yes, you can get rid of all this smoke in the air. I know in other cities they've banned wood burning stoves and fireplaces entirely. This air is not healthy for running."

So much for the sweet memories of the smoke of Christmas past. People had different perspectives and values. He seldom found it productive to challenge them unless it required only a clarification of facts. He commiserated with her while continuing to bounce and told her how to write a letter to the City Council. She seemed satisfied with his response and they quickly parted company; she pranced, he trudged.

Not far away a car started up and backed down the driveway. He waved at his neighbor who had seen him and braked to let him go by. He saw the vapor coming out of the tailpipe in the cold morning air and grumbled to himself. Enjoy it while you can, pal, they'll probably be outlawing gas engines soon, too. We were all getting regulated to death in this country.

As often happened, his bad mood took a face - the controversial Green Valley Village "active adult community" being proposed by SoCal Communities. It was by far the biggest development ever proposed for his city of 5,000, and the biggest threat to his job security. Some people said it was too large and would blame the city manager if he supported it. Others saw it as a terrific opportunity for the entire community and would blame him if it didn't happen.

He waved again as his neighbor drove by and forced a smile but his thoughts rested on the meeting this morning with his fiery Planning Director, Megan Cain. What a perfect way to kick off a dreary Monday! He tugged at the t-shirt label scratching the back of his neck, trying in vain to rip it off as he continued down his street. Why the hell do they put those things on there? Do they ever wear the shirts they make themselves and see how irritating that stupid tag is?

Megan was young, smart, principled, courageous, and spirited. In short, she was a pain in the ass to manage. She had asked for the meeting this morning over some beef she had with the Public Works Department on the Green Valley project's EIR. He would spend his morning with her sitting across from him in his small office, twitching in her chair, all worked up, peppering him with complaints. Unless Brad took her side instantly, which wasn't going to happen, her words would come faster and louder, her bright blue eyes more penetrating. He fantasized about Megan getting so worked up that her auburn hair would spontaneously ignite. Pain in the ass.

He glanced at his watch and picked up the pace until slowing to a walk near his house. His next door neighbor, Lee Andre, was picking up the paper.

"Morning, Lee."

"I keep telling you, Brad, you only get so many heart beats. Don't waste them jogging."

He patted his belly. "Gotta do something if I'm going to live as long as you, neighbor."

Lee sneered. "Bah, I'm over ninety and haven't run since the army."

"Geez, Lee, I always had you figured for a Jack LaLanne kinda guy."

"Oh, I could pull a boat with my teeth across San Francisco Bay, too, if I used Gorilla Glue instead of Poligrip."

Brad hoped for that much spunk when he was Lee's age. He waved, went inside, showered quickly, put on his work clothes: gray blend slacks, white shirt with blue pinstripes, black loafers, grabbed his beige sport coat off the hanger and headed down to the kitchen. His son, Dillon, was wolfing down a stack of pancakes. My God, how that kid could eat! The hot pancakes, dripping with butter and maple syrup, smelled heavenly. He stared at them, his mouth watering.

"Don't even think about it," his wife, Marie, said, handing him his customary kale and fruit smoothie. "You got back a little early today," she said. "Did you run out of problems to solve?"

"Well, I just about had the finishing touches on those pesky Middle East problems, but I had to cut it short to focus on what I'm going to say to Dillon's government class this morning."

"Don't be boring," his son piped off through a mouthful of pancakes.

Brad glanced quizzically at Marie. As a former middle school English teacher, she knew that age far better than he. "Don't talk down to them," she said, glancing at Dillon then back at Brad.

"Yeah," he replied, "I get that. So I guess I shouldn't hand out those plastic firefighter helmets, police stick-on badges, or water conservation coloring books today?"

She ignored him. "And just be yourself. They can spot a phony right off the bat." She added a small smirk that did very little to calm his nerves.

Dillon shook his head. "Just don't be boring."

"I know! I know!" Brad said excitedly. "I could do the whole city organization chart in rap!"

Marie rolled her eyes.

"Forget what Mom said about being yourself," Dillon taunted with mock disgust. "Be somebody cool."

"Hey, who's cooler than a city manager?" Brad asked, leading with his chin.

"That would be everybody, Dad," Dillon said, shoving the last bite of pancakes in his mouth, getting up from the table, and giving his dad a fist bump. "Gotta go!" he said, jingling his car keys. "See you at school, Dad."

*****

Brad made the short drive to City Hall constantly scanning from side to side. That illegal banner on the real estate office was still up. The mayor, a Realtor himself, complained about it a week ago. Better see where Planning was on that. A few blocks later he noticed that somebody had run into a stop sign the previous night. The metal pole was bent nearly to the ground with just a sliver still connected to the base. Better report that to Public Works. The developer was finally starting construction on that junior anchor department store. It was controversial, but he knew the city needed the sales tax. It was satisfying to see something he'd worked on come out of the ground.

He turned onto State Highway 246, the two-lane east/west arterial at the south side of the city. Passing the Chumash Casino reminded him about the petition circulating to name this section of Highway 246 after the farm labor reformer, Cesar Chavez. That didn't sit well with the Chumash Tribe who felt that it should be named for their tribe, especially since much of the road passed through their reservation. Brad felt the small squeeze in his gut. Hopefully he could duck that issue completely.

He switched the car's satellite radio to the old-time radio classics hoping for a snippet of *Dragnet* before getting to City Hall. Better yet, *Gunsmoke* was just coming on. The baritone voice of the macho lawman Marshal Dillon, played by William Conrad, concluded the show's opening with, "It's a chancy job, and it makes a man watchful, and a little lonely." That always elicited a wry smile. Brad could relate.

He guided his politically correct, locally-purchased white Ford Fusion into the parking lot of the small single story City Hall building off Highway 246 and walked into the lobby at 8:20 a.m. Kerry Smith, Executive Director of the Santa Ynez Tourism Bureau, was right behind him with a box in both arms. Brad held the door.

"Hi, Kerry. Bringing us doughnuts?"

"New brochures, hot off the press, Brad," she said, lifting the box slightly as if to emphasize her point. "Your public dollars at work."

"Good going, Kerry!" he cheered and started walking away in case there was another request to do something in the offing. But seeing Kerry straining a few paces was too much for him. He turned back and took the heavy box from her over to the tourism racks.

"By the way, Kerry, if I haven't told you before, I just wanted to say that you are doing a helluva good job."

She smiled, "Well, thanks, Brad."

Emboldened he continued. "You've really found a way for us to capitalize on *Sideways*. Loved that movie."

"Yup. The adventures of Jack and Miles have done great things for our wineries, hotels and tourism in general," she observed.

"Well, don't sell yourself short in that. I know how hard you've worked to make that happen. Before *Sideways*, if people stopped at all at Santa Ynez, it was usually for gas to get somewhere else."

"Hah! You're forgetting that we were home to the Leader of the Free World." She gestured at the mountain range to the west. "When the Reagans lived up there, we'd see motorcades right here in town with people like Queen Elizabeth, Mikhail Gorbachev, or Margaret Thatcher."

"Maybe so, but I know that since you took over the Visitor's Bureau our motel tax revenue has jumped to $1.6 million, 25 percent of the city's total General Fund. I give you credit for a large chunk of that."

"Thanks again, Brad. It's a team effort, as you know."

"Sure. See you later." He turned to walk away and had an impulse. "Oh, I didn't mean to imply that I'm going to support a big increase in your budget. Just wanted to let you know you're appreciated even if we can't afford to pay you more."

"Oh, God forbid you should be so reckless with the public's money," she laughed. "I know. Thanks for the nice words, Brad."

"Well deserved. And, since you brought it up, how about giving Marie and me a tour of Rancho Del Cielo? I read that Reagan said the panoramic view of the Pacific fed his soul. My soul is really hungry!"

"That would be fun. Let's email some dates."

"Great. Gotta go. I have urgent, unimportant things waiting for me."

Mission accomplished. Kerry was someone Marshal Dillon would have watched. She was Public Works Director, Dipak "Dee" Sharma's sister-in-law, and tight with several councilmembers. There was a back-channel pipeline between City Hall and the mayor's supporters and, even if he had no proof, he suspected Kerry was a coupling. Add to that all the rumors about her being seen with Green Valley's Scott Graves. A person couldn't get away with anything in a small town like Santa Ynez. Regardless, Kerry had some political influence and was worth courting.

He paused outside the glass wall panel off the lobby with the words "City Manager's Office" painted in gothic gold lettering. His assistant, Jane Stanar, was busy on her keyboard. It had been two years since her husband had died in a car accident leaving her and their two young daughters in dire financial straits. It couldn't be easy for a woman in her mid-forties to raise kids, hold down a job, and have much social life in a small town. Jane deserved better cards than she'd been dealt.

She had some kind of new hairdo—yes, he had noticed—with gold streaks. He also noticed Jane's turquoise turtleneck and remembered a Rotary program on color analysis. He and Jane had fun deciding their "seasons" using a color chart handout. They concluded that with her strawberry blonde hair, hazel eyes, and pinkish skin tone, Jane was a "spring." Turquoise must be one of her colors. He glanced down at his camel hair sport coat and smiled, anticipating the grief she'd give him again about it. "Winters" shouldn't wear beige.

He put his hand on the chrome door handle and paused to take in the Spartan waiting area. The four aged, but sturdy, dark walnut-stained wood chairs on the left side of the door and a brown cabinet on the right side looked like refugees from an insurance office remodel. A small copy machine and coffee pot sat on top of the cabinet.

"Morning," he said, heading to the swinging half door to the left of the light walnut veneer counter that ran across the entire room. Jane's walnut veneer desk and beige filing cabinets filled up all of the space behind the counter leaving a passageway from the swinging door to Brad's office.

"Oh, my favorite sport coat," Jane teased. "You know if that had a burgundy lining you should wear it inside out."

"I picked it for you. I know how much you love it."

"Yeah. Why don't you hang it out here? It will give me something else exciting to look at."

He scanned the lobby. The right and rear walls of the small room were filled with locked glass cases crammed with official postings, many of which were faded. The only real adornment in the entire space was a framed painting, this year's City of Santa Ynez Award winner at the art show. He nodded toward the painting. "Did I ever tell you this picture is much better than most years? You picked well."

"Thanks. I like the broken down old wagon rusting away in a golden brown field. It seems lonely but not alone," she said, sounding more cheeky than reflective. Brad, on the other hand, could see something more in the picture. It could have been on the Green Valley Village site or many other spots in the valley. He sighed again thinking of his upcoming meeting.

He looked at his watch as he walked into his office, set his things down, sat at his desk, and grabbed a handful of paperwork from the top of his in-basket to kill some time. Megan was late for their 8:30 meeting, as usual. He started tapping his gold Cross pen on his desk and launched into a mental bitch session about his young department head.

She was a planning purist who didn't live in the real world. Her only professional experience during and after college had been in Santa Ynez. She didn't seem to care about the city's precarious financial position and all the benefits the Green Valley project offered. Didn't she understand that there was plenty of support for this project? Maybe, but she was young and more driven by her ideals. She had to know how much heat she was creating for him personally with her known criticisms of the project and how that could ultimately affect her. Couldn't she be a team player for once and find a gentler way to temper her strident opinions with Brad's desire to get this project approved?

At 8:49 Megan Cain, Planning Director, strolled into his office. "Hi," she said as she took a seat, not bothering to apologize for being late.

He didn't return the greeting. He just pivoted around his cluttered desk to his customary chair at the coffee table across from her. She plopped her pile of papers on the table. Her movements were quick and stiff. Her auburn hair was pulled straight back exposing her pale forehead. She wore no discernable makeup or fragrance. Her black slacks and canary yellow sweater accentuated her bright blue eyes and athletic body. She looked ready to pounce.

Brad had some leadership training years ago on how to communicate with different people. He took a clever profile test that really pegged his personality and leadership style. It went on to describe his preferred communication approach and how to adjust to people with different styles. It turned out that among the department heads, Megan's preferred communication style was the closest to his own. No need wasting time with small talk. Get on with the business at hand.

"What's up?" he began.

"I've got a real problem with Public Works on this Green Valley review."

"What's your problem with Dee now?" he asked. Megan Cain and Public Works Director, Dipak Sharma, were like fire and ice, sparring all the time. They were both competent and hardworking but they had far different styles. Megan was fire.

"I don't know, it's like he is deliberately understating the impacts for the Green Valley EIR," she continued.

He flinched at such a serious accusation. "Come on Megan, why would he do that? Explain what you mean."

"Well," she continued undaunted, "people think Dee is in Scott Graves' pocket. He sure acts like SoCal's interests are a higher priority than the city's. The fact that SoCal's biggest community donation so far was to Dee's pet cause makes me wonder."

"Now hold on, Megan. I want all the department heads to be active in the community. Dee happens to be really involved with his kids in youth soccer just like hundreds of other parents. I think he's even a vice president on their board. It's great that the board got SoCal to donate the new fields. But I'm sure Dee was careful not to make the 'ask' to Scott himself or give any indication that there would be any sort of quid pro quo regarding Public Works' review of Green Valley."

She sneered. "I'm glad you defend your department heads . . ."

Brad interrupted before she could get to her "but."

"*You*, of all people should be, Megan! All of us take shots from our critics, deserved or not. You do know people call you Megan 'Cain't,' don't you?"

"Yeah," she said, softening her demeanor.

"You know," he continued, "a city manager is like a boxer. We can only take so many shots before we go down. I've taken more body blows over you and your relationship with Kay Nance than all the other department heads combined. I'll continue to do that so long as you do your job well. It's part of my job to shield department heads from political pressure. You don't make that easy for me but I'll keep at it, at least for as long as I can keep getting off the canvas." He managed a quick smile, hoping to ease the tension.

She leaned forward slightly. "I know that, Brad. All of us appreciate how much you protect us and let us run our shops. But as to Councilwoman Nance, I happen to think that she is right about a lot of her views on community development and environmental protection; a lot more so than Mayor Buddy and his 'let's-break-some-ground-today' cronies."

He winced again.

"I've never compromised my integrity for Kay Nance or anyone else. And I've never been disloyal to you, Brad. I'm not so sure you could say that about your public works director."

"You need to have more evidence than a soccer field to back that up."

"Well, take a look at this." She leaned over to pick up two reports from the table.

He looked back at the pile of paperwork on his desk. "What's all that?" he asked weakly. "Just summarize for now."

For the next twenty minutes, Megan shuffled through the stack of reports. She focused on two prepared by the Department of Public Works and one by her own Planning Department. She went back and forth between them describing apparent inconsistencies in factors used in recent traffic reports compared to prior studies. She contended they showed an unrealistically high "level of service" for several intersections that will be affected by the Green Valley Village traffic.

He made a point of looking again at his messy desk. She picked up the cue.

"Give me just a couple more minutes, Brad. There's an even more serious problem with the draft Water Supply Assessment Study. It's a report required by state law for a project the size of Green Valley. Take a look at this table."

He sat impassively for the next five minutes as she pointed from one table and chart to another. He'd been in this business long enough to know that there are few absolutes in planning the city's infrastructure, or most other public issues, for that matter. People with different backgrounds and interests can fairly arrive at different conclusions using the same data.

"And, as you can see here," she droned on, "the average residential demand here doesn't jibe with what we had in this other report here."

He nodded and continued to look at the pages with unseeing eyes.

"I can see I'm losing you," she said. "I'll cut to the bottom line. I'm seeing a lot of problems with Public Works' analyses of Green Valley traffic and water impacts. I think it's fishy, like somebody is deliberately glossing over major issues. And my choice for 'somebody' is Dee Sharma." She sat back, jaw set.

"I'm listening, but you are making a lot of charges and dumping all kinds of stuff on me. I assume you haven't shared this with Dee."

"I tried and he blew me off."

He pondered a moment. "Did you even try to use the communication training to talk to him in a way he'd listen? You and I tend to be pretty abrupt. Dee is hypersensitive to criticism so you can't go right at him and expect him to engage."

"Oh, but it's OK for Dee to treat me like I'm some unstable girl right out of college who doesn't understand anything? Is this about my age and gender?"

"Of course not! You have a habit of trying to cast any legitimate disagreement someone might have with you into some epic battle between good and evil."

It was Megan's turn to flinch. Good. She needed a course correction for her own personal and professional development before she took them both down.

Brad leaned back in his chair and laced his fingers. "Look, from the time we first got wind a couple years ago that SoCal had optioned Hubie's land, people have complained that you have been sniping at the project."

It was Brad's great misfortune that SoCal Communities wanted to build Green Valley Village on land adjacent to the city owned by Hubie Nettler. Hubert "Hubie" Nettler was the surviving octogenarian patriarch of the Nettler clan that first settled in the valley more than a hundred years ago. Hubie and his sons, Hal and Hank, all lived on the family cattle ranch in the hilly land to the northeast of the city. Brad knew Hank the best. They were friendly enough although Hank had too much of Hubie's DNA for Brad's tastes, including the same deep raspy voice that made him want to clear his throat whenever Hank talked.

"For your information, Megan, there are a lot of people, possibly including a majority of my bosses, who think it's a great project." He felt building annoyance. "Now, I'm willing to look more into the information you talked about today but you need to lighten up a little. Stop parroting Kay Nance's anti-growth biases. People question your objectivity."

She scoffed. "I don't care what people say about me."

"*You* might not, but I do. I have college tuitions to pay and plan to retire in this town even if you are long gone. I'm not going to let you turn Green Valley into some personal crusade, especially not at my expense."

She recoiled slightly and stared at him with wide blue eyes. The reaction startled him. He'd never seen her look vulnerable.

"Megan," he said pacifyingly, "You're a smart person. When it comes to city planning, you know your onions, as my grandfather used to say. I admire your tenacity and courage. But dial it down a little, would you? Everything isn't as black and white as you make it seem. Public policy comes in shades of gray."

She sat quietly for a moment, looking more serene. "I know that, Brad. And I also know that I'm in a lot of gun sights in this town. I'll let you worry about what your public works director is or isn't doing. My main concern is with the environmental assessment. That's my responsibility."

"It's the *city's* responsibility to lead the environmental assessment," he corrected. "Not yours alone. There are a lot of other city departments and agencies who have a responsibility, too. Everyone might not see things the same way you do."

Megan didn't miss a beat. "True, but CEQA has been interpreted by the courts many times. The environmental review process is pretty detailed. There's not all that much gray in it, Brad. And with Green Valley Village sprawling out on pristine rolling range land and jumping the city's population by some 60 percent, you know there's going to be formidable opposition. They are going to be all over the EIR, so we better not give it a wink and a nod or the courts will throw it out."

Brad shook his head. "I understand that the legislative intent behind CEQA was to give the public good information on a project's impact before the legislative body makes a final decision. But I don't have nearly the reverence you do for the whole process. It has morphed into a multi-billion-dollar playground for biologists, archeologists, geologists, traffic engineers, civil engineers, civil service bureaucrats, and lawyers. It's hard as hell for anyone, including the city itself, to build something these days without undergoing a NIMBY attack."

"Well," she argued more calmly, "if I were about to get a big project like this in my backyard, I'd want to make sure I understood the likely impacts. And I'd be pretty pissed if it looked like the city hadn't done its job to study and mitigate those impacts."

He sighed and tossed the report she gave him on the table. "You know as well as I do that the real fight is over the project itself, not the environmental impacts. The EIR is just a battleground. A developer will spend a half million dollars or more, and a year in the analyses, to produce a document that few people will even read, let alone fully comprehend."

She narrowed her eyes. "I grant you that few will read the EIR, but that doesn't make it less important."

He sneered. "What makes the environmental assessment important isn't the information that comes out of it. It's that smart opponents know it's the best place to attack a project. They may not be able to convince the elected councilmembers to kill the project even with picketing, tears, anger, and threats of recall. But challenging the EIR gives them access to the courts. The threat of a delay is the weapon, not the environmental impacts."

"Exactly!" she replied. "And that's my point. The more thorough we are with the environmental assessment, the better the chance of getting a quick summary judgment to throw out a legal challenge. Leave too much unstudied and the court will be more likely to send the EIR back. You know Scott and SoCal won't like that."

"Sure, they'll want to see a good EIR. But you can study things to death and opponents will still sue. I'm not going to stand by and watch a project that is clearly in the public interest bottled up in an endless, futile process." Brad felt his building defiance. "Not on my watch!"

She jerked to attention. "I don't know how you can say Green Valley is 'clearly in the public interest' when we haven't fully studied the impacts yet."

He sighed again. "Look, we have different roles. Yours puts the emphasis on process. And that certainly is important given how litigious society has become. My role requires me to consider other realities including the Council majority's policy position and, yes, the city's financial situation, notwithstanding your disdain for those factors."

Her eyes narrowed more. "I care about those other things, too, but you're right, my primary function is to follow the law."

He leaned back and looked to the ceiling with exasperation. "What I'm trying to say is that sometimes the process runs amuck from common sense. Let me tell you a little story."

She slumped but he was determined to continue whether she was interested on not.

"Years ago the assistant city manager of Santa Rosa and I were selected by UC Berkeley to go to Mexico City for a week to give a class on how we do community development in California. There were about twenty high-ranking federal, state and city officials in the class who were really interested in what we had to say."

"That must have been interesting," she said neutrally.

"It was. The highlight was when the guy from Santa Rosa gave a lecture on his city's attempts to build a new wastewater plant to clean up their discharge into the Russian River. It was an important project for the whole region and Santa Rosa was trying to get it done. He concluded his talk with a picture of himself standing next to a five-foot-tall stack of boxes filled with CEQA-related reports."

"Wow!" she said. "Must have cost them millions."

"It did. You should have heard the gasp from these Mexican officials. Some of them came from cities that didn't even have sewer systems in all their neighborhoods. They thought it was complete nonsense. They talked about how much they could have accomplished in their cities with just the money Santa Rosa was spending on the studies."

"What's your point?" she challenged.

"Maybe the Mexicans figured they dodged a bullet in 1848 when they ceded California to US control."

"So, you would prefer that California cities developed like they did in Mexico?"

"Oh, lighten up, Megan, for chrissake. That's a joke." He shook his head. "What I'm saying is that we in government can get way too hung up on process and possible litigation. Sometimes we have to keep charging ahead with a project we know benefits the public, despite hard-core opposition."

"Well," she countered, "we better nail down the traffic and water numbers if you want this project to survive legal scrutiny. Everyone else hasn't decided already that Green Valley is in the public interest."

"Touché. But we also shouldn't conclude it isn't in the public interest either. Got it?"

"Message received," she said. "But you better make sure Dee gets it, too. Look at these reports yourself. They don't add up. People think he is too pro-project."

"I've managed to spend my entire career without having to verify everything in an EIR. I don't intend to start now. I depend on staff to be competent and fair. If you and Dee can't get on the same page, I'll set up a meeting and listen to what you both have to say."

She shrugged. "If that's what you want to do. But if you are going to stay on the schedule we set with SoCal, we better meet soon to complete the IS pretty fast."

"IS?"

"Initial Study. It's required by CEQA. It's a notice to the public and responsible agencies describing the basics of the project, anticipated environmental impacts, and potential mitigations. It gives them a chance to comment about what should be included for study in the DEIR, sorry, Draft EIR."

"Ok, I'll ask Jane to set up the meeting ASAP." He raised his finger for emphasis. "Oh, that means, As Soon As Possible," he said smiling.

"I know," Megan said, not smiling back. He guessed she didn't appreciate the attempt at humor.

He re-grouped. "While you're here, can you give me a quick rundown on the entitlements Green Valley will have to get before it can build? I've got to speak to the Chamber Wednesday." He settled back and felt the tension in his jaw muscles begin to release now that the discussion moved off her arguments.

Megan also seemed more placid and less defensive. "Well, let's see," she said, holding up her left fist then raising her thumb as if her fingers held all the answers. "We've started on the Specific Plan. It will have all of the land use and design regulations." She held up her index finger. "We'll need to amend the General Plan and all of the affected elements of the plan to sync up the General Plan to the Green Valley Specific Plan." She held up her middle finger and looked to the ceiling for assistance. "We'll need to process some variances to our existing regulations and probably approve some conditional use permits depending on what comes out of the plan." She held up the fourth finger. "We'll have to make findings to approve the Development Agreement we are still negotiating with SoCal." She shook her left hand slightly to get another step in the process dislodged, then pointed her little finger. "Of course, we'll have to get the EIR certified since it encompasses everything else."

"Whew!" Brad whistled.

Megan still had her five fingers in the air. She was wagging them and still looking upwards. "Oh, and don't forget the site isn't in our Sphere of Influence so we'll have to go to the Local Agency Formation Commission to get it annexed. That's actually the first hurdle before we can do the rest. But LAFCo won't accept the annexation application without all the other land use plans ready to be approved."

"I haven't had the pleasure yet," he said. "How's the LAFCo in this county?"

"They are very thorough. We'll have to amend our Municipal Services Report in addition to finishing most of the other entitlements before they'll even accept the application."

She was now smiling. Or was it a smirk?

"So, realize what you just said, Megan. SoCal is going to spend years and hundreds of thousands of dollars on plans, EIR, and the rest, then jump through all sorts of hoops just to get in front of LAFCo to see if the city will be able to exercise jurisdiction over the site?"

"That's the way it works," she said.

His jaw muscle twitched. "But LAFCo is completely independent and has their own staff. They could reject our request to annex it for their own reasons and then this project is dead on arrival. It doesn't matter what the city wants to do."

"That's possible," she acknowledged. "But LAFCo would have to adopt findings to back up the decision."

He sighed deeply and rolled his eyes. "I don't share your abiding faith in independent, fair process, Megan. It's also possible that LAFCo could deny the Sphere amendment and annexation for reasons that have nothing to do with whatever findings they adopt for the record. Remember four of the five commissioners are politicians who represent other constituencies. There might be political rivalries or allegiances that come to bear on our application. Or maybe some other city wants to see us fall on our ass with Green Valley so they can make a play for it."

"That's pretty far-fetched," she said with a skeptical expression.

"I've got a lot more experience with these sorts of things, and I tell you it can happen. My point is to not get too wrapped around the axle over all of the minutiae in these reports. At the end of the day, the politics at all levels will decide whether the project will get built, whether or not all the t's get crossed in the EIR."

"So you want me to just pencil-whip our environmental assessment, Brad?"

He pounded the arms of his chair. "Of course not. Stop making this black or white. Sure, we need to follow the steps and prepare all the required reports. But there probably won't be more than two or three people who will read all of that crap. Make it a fair, objective analysis but don't get so stressed out about making this the best ever EIR. What will happen will happen regardless. Move it along."

"I'm not stressed, Brad," she snapped, clearly stressed. She sat up and moved forward in her chair. "I have a responsibility to follow the law with our review of this project or any other. I'm not doing anything on Green Valley that isn't required."

"Maybe nothing that's not required. But it's a question of what level of analysis is sufficient. We can study things to death and still find more things to study. At the end of all this process we will end up where we already are."

She shook her head seeming to be disgusted. He felt a little sleazy. "Look, Megan, like I said, you know your job. But all of your training has been from the classroom or what has come across your desk here in Santa Ynez. And, as you know, that ain't been much. Maybe if you had worked in a consulting firm or had been in charge of getting something approved you'd be a little more sympathetic to how arduous the trek is for a developer."

She stiffened and bore into him with her bright blue eyes, a tiger ready to spring.

He struck first. "In fact, let me make this easier for you. Yes, Green Valley's 3,000 senior citizens will generate more traffic, require more water, and add some air pollution and run-off. Some people won't like it at first but will get used to it. But it will also be an attractive project with nice homes for people who will contribute their cash to the city, including your own salary by the way, and contribute their energies to community causes. There, I just saved you a ton of work!" He crossed his arms over his chest, leaned back in his chair, and gave her a big smile.

The planning director rolled her palms up, then dropped them and fell back in her chair heavily. "I'm sorry you have so little regard for the work I do."

He slumped. He hated bullies and he had acted like one. Back pedal quickly. He forced a smile and folded his hands casually.

"OK, Megan." Call her by name, tone it down. "Like I said, it's a matter of degree. I want us to do a fair and reasonable job on the studies but not overkill it. Let the politics sort themselves out. Avoid making yourself part of the politics. I'll call Dee and set up a meeting when we can all be in the room together and get to the bottom of your concerns."

"Fine," she replied abruptly, gathering her reports and getting up to leave.

His mind raced searching for a more positive note to end their meeting. "And thanks for studying all the traffic and water so closely." She tossed him a strained nod on the way out.

He was left alone in his office with his regrets. He needed a friend and went out to talk to Jane under the pretext of giving her some of the finished paperwork off his desk.

"Here's some of the pile," he said flatly, hoping for some validation from his loyal assistant.

"It's none of my business," she volunteered, "but from the look Megan had when she stormed out, it must have been a rough meeting."

"It was. Not a career highlight for me. She made me lose my cool and put her down."

Jane smiled. "Well, you didn't put her down like Hubie would one of his cows. She *did* walk out, after all."

"Hah! Truth is I admire Megan. I'm trying to protect her, whether she wants me to or not. It's my nature to try to shield my staff from the political winds. But she seems to go out of her way to make herself controversial."

"And you know Hubie and SoCal aren't going to sit by and watch the project get torpedoed by her. I mean, Scott Graves is a great guy and all, but he has bosses, too. And they'll roll right over you to get to her if they think it's necessary."

"I know," he said, dropping his head.

Neither said anything for a few moments. He glared through the glass wall in the direction of the lobby where two men were laughing loudly.

"Damn it, I feel for the developers' plight. They go through hell these days in order to bring people jobs, places to live, shop, or play, and keep the local economy afloat."

"The average citizen has no idea what it takes to get a project approved," she agreed.

"I've dealt with a lot of developers in my career. Some were jerks with no appreciation or finesse in managing the public processes. Others, like SoCal, hire good people you can trust, like Scott, and are more win/win. SoCal is in the upper percentile for community generosity."

"You're right, there," she said. "Scott must get hit up for donations all the time. In the two years he's been around and, especially since he started renting that house, he has really made himself a popular guy."

"Yeah, nice house. It's convenient to his other projects in Ventura County and Santa Maria, too. But the poor guy must entertain stakeholders from someplace every night."

"He's good at it, too," she observed. "Really personable!"

"And good looking!" he added. "He dresses so nicely, and that blond hair is never out of place."

Jane grinned. "Is this a budding bromance?"

"OK, OK. He's just so polished. I'm more like George Gobel when he described himself on the Johnny Carson Show, 'Did you ever get the feeling that the world was a tuxedo and you were a pair of brown shoes?' Now, don't you agree, Scott's got to be the most eligible bachelor in the area?"

Jane shifted her eyes to her computer screen. "He does throw a nice party," she said, still looking at the screen.

"I've been to a few," he said. "There's nothing wild and crazy that goes on. Just classy. The backyard is right out of a design magazine with a free form pool and spa, outdoor kitchen, and a killer view of the valley."

Jane smiled. "I know someone, who shall be nameless, who desperately wanted an invitation to one of his events. She went up to Scott at a Chamber mixer and said, 'What's it take for a girl to get an invitation to one of your parties?' He was so gracious about it and invited her to the next one."

"So, did you have fun?"

She laughed, but he noticed she didn't answer.

2

Brad busied himself with emails and paperwork until it was time to leave for the high school to do his annual "City Government 101" talk to the government class. He turned into the high school parking lot and smiled, remembering the fear and nausea he always felt each time he had to give a formal presentation in high school.

He took a spot in the faculty lot and just sat in the car a moment organizing his thoughts. A shrill buzzer went off and the benign scene erupted in an explosion of noise and movement. The corridors were jammed. Girls screamed somewhere. A couple boys wrestled in an apparent noogie attack.

Thirty-five years ago he would have been just another face in that crowd, hoping to get through the day without being picked on or doing something embarrassing. He had been late hitting puberty and one of the smallest boys in his class. He would have gladly traded a full point from his GPA for some height, a deeper voice, and a girlfriend.

He walked through the parking lot in a fantasy about returning to high school with his adult confidence and abilities. Oh, to have those high school years to do over now! He spotted his son, Dillon, walking and talking freely with some friends, both girls and boys. Thank God Dillon got his mother's genes. His son was roughly the same size as his friends, had been shaving since his junior year, and had a steady girlfriend. Dillon was nearer the in-crowd than Brad ever dreamed of getting. He felt a little chink in his armored confidence thinking about his son's plea not to be boring.

Brad made his way through the bustling hallways to the classroom, eyes straight ahead. He held open the door to the classroom for two girls behind him. They were in an animated conversation and walked past him as if he was part of the door frame. Being ignored by the girls in high school. Déjà vu.

Mr. Heldt, Dillon's Government teacher, met him at the door, shook hands, and said, "Congratulations for running the gauntlet. I sometimes lose guest speakers at the parking lot."

Brad laughed. "The whole scene *is* a little intimidating. It reminded me that high school wasn't a fun time for me."

Mr. Heldt nodded. "You're not alone. I've heard it said that most of us spend our adult years either trying to live up to, or down from, whatever we were in high school."

"I guess I'm in the latter category," Brad said. "I'm just trying to get through this without embarrassing my son."

Mr. Heldt nodded. "Don't worry, I got your back." The teacher turned to greet the students.

Brad watched the teacher engaging and fist bumping with the students as they arrived. *"I got your back."* Shouldn't a high school teacher rise above the students' level of jargon? Or maybe it's more important to him to be worshipped by these acne-faced impressionables than to impart any sense of adult authority. He scanned the teacher's outfit critically. He could put on a pair of slacks and a dress shirt, for God's sake. High school was no beach party, even if the teacher was trying to look like a Beach Boy.

He paused. Had he really become so old that his thoughts sounded like the cranky men he rebelled against? He envied Mr. Heldt's connection with these kids. Jealousy was ugly.

Brad busied himself loading his thumb drive into Mr. Heldt's laptop and shuffling through his notes at the lectern while students trickled through the door. He took in the commotion and competing odors of Right Guard, Clearasil, and what must have been buckets of drugstore perfume wafting through the classroom. He felt gas building up in his lower GI and regretted the third cup of coffee. The numbers on the digital clock ticked closer to 10:05. He gave himself a pep talk, woke up his monitor again, and scanned the classroom. The buzzer went off, but the students continued their conversations.

"Ladies and gentlemen," Mr. Heldt said, "we are honored to have Mr. Jacks, our city manager, with us this morning."

Brad saw several students turn to look at his son but the rest of them turned forward and looked between the teacher and himself.

"Yes, he is Dillon's father," Mr. Heldt continued. "And he's a very important and busy man so I want you to give him your fullest attention."

Brad put his right hand in his pocket and leaned on the lectern, the coolest stance he could come up with. Dillon gave him a quick but encouraging thumbs-up. He relaxed…a little.

Mr. Heldt continued. "We talked a little about city government last week and we are lucky that Mr. Jacks is here to tell you more about what he does and what is going on with the city." The teacher picked up a stack of papers and moved toward his desk gesturing to Brad that the floor was his. "Mr. Jacks?"

There was no applause. He squeezed back a gas cramp and stared out at all the young faces. Most of them were staring back at him with blank expressions. A few were oblivious to his presence. They were too busy flirting or clowning around with each other. One lanky, acne-covered young man in the back row seemed to be asleep already. Dillon looked nervous. Had kids been this disrespectful when he was in school? Probably.

"Good morning," Brad began. Not the snappiest opening, but he was trying to be himself, as Marie advised. Two or three of them returned the salutation.

"I would like this to be a conversation with you rather than me standing here and lecturing you for the next fifty minutes. So please feel free to ask questions as we go along." He glanced at Mr. Heldt for his approval and got a head nod. All righty, then, an endorsement from Mr. Popular.

"I'd like to start with a short quiz." Someone moaned. A chubby, acne-faced boy on the left side of class shot his hand up. Brad acknowledged him.

The boy leaned to address Mr. Heldt. "Does the quiz count for our grade?"

The rest of the class groaned at the question. Brad suspected he had uncovered the class dork. He rescued him.

"No, it's not really a test. I just want to ask you a few questions. If you know the answers, shout them out, OK?"

A few head nods. The lanky boy in the back row now had his head all the way back with his mouth open and his legs splayed into the aisle. Brad pressed on.

"Who is the President of the United States?"

"Barack Obama!"

Most of them answered eagerly.

"Vice President?"

"Joe Biden," said a smaller number.

"What is the term of office for a US Senator?"

"Six years," said several students in unison. Dillon was playing along.

"Very good. What branch of the US government is responsible for making laws?"

"Congress," said several kids.

He started to add a clarification, "What I was looking for…"

"The House of Representatives makes laws," interrupted a boy near the front.

"The House is the same thing as Congress, idiot," teased another boy. "I've met our congressman. He's cool."

A cute girl in the second row shot her hand up. After Brad called on her, she added his intended clarification. "Actually, the question was about the branch of government. That's called the Legislative Branch which is another term for Congress. And Congress consists of two chambers, the Senate and the House of Representatives." She sat back smugly.

"Why, that's absolutely correct, young lady!" Brad turned to Mr. Heldt. "You have a smart group here." Mr. Heldt made an odd face. What did that mean?

"Let's try a few more questions." He was feeling more confident. "Who knows the name of the mayor? You're not eligible to play, Dillon."

"Buddy Murray," several answered correctly.

"Do any of you know what he does for a living?"

The smart, cute girl in the second row was the only one to respond. "He has a real estate office on Edison Street."

"Right. Who knows the name and vocation of the vice mayor?"

The same girl in the second row was the only one to respond. "His name is Tim Mullikin and he used to be a cop." She sounded bored.

"Right, again. How did you know that?"

"We talk about politics all the time in my family," she said casually.

He felt guilty. He should take more time explaining important things to Dillon before he went off to college. This girl seemed to be way ahead of him.

"Good for you." He was hoping to draw in more students. "How many people are on the City Council?"

He looked past the raised hand of the girl in the second row and called on an eager boy with his waving hand in the air.

"Seven?" the boy guessed.

"Close. Others?" There weren't any others willing to try, except for the girl in the second row. Brad took a closer look at her. She was dressed in denim jeans, a red and white plaid long sleeve cowboy shirt, and boots. Brad had taken his children to all of the *"Toy Story"* movies. This girl could be Jessie in the flesh.

"OK," he said, reluctantly nodding at her.

"Five," she answered correctly. "Do you want their names?"

"That's OK. I already know them," he laughed. Only Mr. Heldt joined him. What was with this girl? He looked again at Mr. Heldt who shrugged as if to say "good luck with her, pal."

He pressed on. "OK. How about this one? What is the term of office for the city manager?"

Silence. Even the cute girl didn't have a ready answer. Dillon looked up with a puzzled expression.

After a few seconds, Brad broke the silence. "That was a trick question. The city manager isn't elected at all. I serve at the pleasure of the mayor and City Council. That means I don't have a specific term. Some city managers serve the same city for twenty years and some don't last a year. It all depends."

He scanned his audience hopefully. Oh, God, he was boring them. He clenched his gut and ran his hand across his forehead. Where was he going next? Ah, his "importance of local government" shtick.

"I'm not surprised that, except for the young lady over here, most of you seem to know much more about the federal government than you do about the one down the street. And to be fair, the federal government is in charge of some really important things, like national security, Social Security, the Post Office, and the overall economy. And the state government does important things, too, like prisons, highways, welfare, and, your favorite, the DMV."

Some energy. Whispering. A minor score.

"But when people are surveyed about which government services are most important to them, they will normally list services provided by *local* government, not federal or state. Think about it. You got up this morning and nobody burglarized your house and it wasn't on fire partially because of the Police and Fire departments. You showered in water the city treated and delivered to the faucet. When your shower drained or you flushed your toilet, you got rid of the waste so that the city could treat it in a healthy way that won't hurt the environment. You drove here on streets built and maintained by the city and some of you will play soccer or swim at the city pool right here on campus before the day is out."

A couple of head nods. They got it. More energy.

"Whether you know it, or not, your lives are affected every day by local government. And yet local government is hardly touched in high school or even college. It's a pet peeve of mine and why I'm here."

He hadn't expected shouts of "the injustice of it all!" He had hoped for more reaction than the boy in back digging into his nose. Don't they care about anything besides what's on *Entertainment Tonight*? He watched Mr. Heldt as he moved stealthily to the rear of the room, came down the center aisle, gave Sleeping Beauty's huge sneaker a kick, and gestured to him to sit up.

"In the time we have left, I want to give you some information that will help you understand the level of government that you will most likely need and be able to influence at some point."

He clicked through a few slides describing the origins of the council-manager form of government, beginning with George Washington's proposal for managing Federal City that became Washington D.C.; the corruption found in big cities like New York City under Boss Tweed and Tammany Hall in the late 1800s; and the Progressive Era leaders like President Woodrow Wilson and California Governor and US Senator Hiram Johnson who campaigned for professional city management to reform corrupt local government.

He really liked his little history lesson. But as he looked from the slide back to the class he could tell he was a cult of one. He did notice a few of the kids were writing. He started to feel excited that they found his comments noteworthy until two boys in the back giggled. Then he remembered himself drawing a caricature of a guest speaker in one of his high school classes. He had written "BORING" on it and showed it to his buddy across the aisle.

He stifled another gas cramp and leaned on the podium faking confidence. "OK, I've got fascinating stories about the council-manager form of government we use here in Santa Ynez and now in many places all over the world." The joke didn't go over. "But I really want to get to the Q&A and hear what's on your minds."

He clicked to the next slide and got a whiff of his own deodorant. "Only one more picture left of an old guy, I promise. This is Charles Ashburner who is considered to be the first true city manager. He was appointed to that position by the City Council of Staunton, Virginia in 1908. In the early 1900s, the country was growing rapidly and needed roads, water lines, and things built. So, most of the early city managers of that era, like Ashburner, were engineers."

Silence. Fewer students making eye contact. "A funny story: Ashburner came to the City of Stockton, California in 1923. The local paper heralded his arrival as the man who would get things done. He's quoted in his first interview saying, 'By God, I go into a town to build! When I can't build, I get out!' The same excited newspaper would soon nickname him Charles 'Cashburner' because he was building too much. Sometimes you just can't win."

"Jessie" smirked. The others either didn't get it or didn't care.

"Like Ashburner, building things like streets and parks or helping to bring in new restaurants or stores is my favorite part of the job. And, like Ashburner, the local newspaper picks on me, too."

Some grins. They're still listening. He clicked to the next slide feeling momentum. It was a picture of the logos of six companies that he was certain the teenagers would be able to identify. He pointed to a logo.

"What company is this?" Most of the class responded quickly, "Apple."

"And this?"

"McDonald's" was the loud response.

"OK, I can see you know about these companies. But did you know that they each have a board of directors who set broad policy direction for the company and hire a qualified Chief Executive Officer, or CEO, to run the company?"

Again, they didn't seem to care. They're probably thinking about a Big Mac.

"Well, the City of Santa Ynez and cities all over the USA are organized similarly to these corporations, except we have a City Council instead of a board of directors and a city manager instead of a CEO. Of course, a board member for Apple or McDonald's makes a lot more money than a councilmember. And I'll bet Dillon wished I made closer to what their CEO pulls in. Maybe he'd be driving a nicer car."

A few chuckles this time. The boy behind Dillon gave him a slug on the arm.

He clicked to the slide showing the growth of the council-manager plan since the 1920s.

"The voters elect who they want to represent them on the City Council. The Council sets the big policies and the Council hires a city manager with the education and training to carry out their policies. The system provides the citizens with two big benefits. They get political accountability from the people they elect to the Council and more efficient government operations from having objective, nonpartisan management in the form of a city manager."

He thought they were still with him. Mr. Heldt gave him a nod. He liked this guy after all.

"Remember, we said that our mayor, Buddy Murray, who is like the chairman of the board of a company, works in real estate. A lot of people who have a problem with the city call City Hall wanting to speak to him and are surprised to learn he isn't there. Besides that, in most cities, the mayor is a political leader of the community but has no more power than the other members of the City Council. When there is a problem, the Council expects the City staff to fix it. Only the city attorney and I are appointed by the Council and serve at their pleasure. If three out of the five of them don't like me anymore, for whatever reason, they can fire me."

Dillon looked up again apparently surprised to learn of his father's precarious position. Brad was surprised Dillon was surprised. They needed to talk.

"Jessie" raised her hand as she said, "So, you are a bureaucrat? My dad said if you want something out of City Hall don't waste your time with the bureaucrats, talk to the politicians."

Brad cleared his throat. "Well, that's sure what some people think. And, yes, I'd be considered a bureaucrat because I manage a bureaucracy. But I don't consider that a pejorative term." He noticed Mr. Heldt shake his head slightly.

"I mean, yes, a bureaucrat is an appointed official of the government, so that fits me, but some people also use the term to mean somebody who is all hung up on procedures and maybe uses the power of their office to make life difficult for people. I hope that doesn't describe me. If it did, I'd expect the Council to fire me and hire someone who can get things done."

Apparently his desire to serve the city with excellence didn't impress these students much. He continued. "Councilmembers get reelected when the citizens think their city is doing good things for them, not just processing paperwork."

"How much money do you make?" "Jessie" asked unabashedly.

The question caught him off guard. He had been on a roll. He looked at Mr. Heldt who merely shrugged again.

"You have a right to ask that question, young lady, because it's public information, but don't try asking that same question to the guy who runs the casino or the Chevy dealership. They'd consider it rude to ask." He smiled. She did not. Charming girl. "My annual salary is about $138,000."

That got their attention. There were some oohs in the crowd. Mr. Heldt said, "I picked the wrong profession."

"Jessie" continued her assault. "My dad thinks city employees are overpaid and that their pensions and healthcare will bankrupt the country."

Geez! Who is this kid? He launched into a hurried justification of his salary and compared his responsibilities to the Apple and McDonald's CEOs. She stared at him, unimpressed. He got the impression that this girl made a practice of eviscerating authority figures. Most of the other students seemed more interested in what she would do next than what he had to say. Brad defended his pension pointing out that it was in lieu of stock options and other programs available to private sector CEO's. He lost them. He talked about reforms underway to better control pension and healthcare costs. He sneaked a glance at his son who seemed unfazed. Maybe he was over-reacting.

As soon as he finished his counter-punching, the girl raised her hand again. He braced himself for the next blow.

"Now Jenny," Mr. Heldt broke in, "let's let someone else ask a question." Then to the class, "Remember, ladies and gentlemen, we will have a quiz on what Mr. Jacks told us today which will count for three-quarters of this lesson. The other quarter will be based on class participation. So let's have some other questions."

Jessie, AKA Jenny, sat there smugly.

"Where did you go to school?" asked Sleeping Beauty.

"I got a bachelor's degree in political science at UC Santa Barbara…"

"Yes!" Sleeping Beauty cheered with a quick fist pump. It was hard to imagine him hoping to get in to such a desirable institution. More likely he had crashed the annual Halloween street bash in Isla Vista and tossed his cookies all over the street.

The rest of class went as expected. The questions were more benign as the students worked down a checklist of topics that Mr. Heldt had likely prepared for them.

Brad showed his slides of the organization chart, starting with pictures of each of the councilmembers and added a short bio and their remaining terms of office. He reminded them that the Council appoints the city attorney so as to have legal advice that is independent from the city manager.

"The city manager is the Council's only other appointee. The manager oversees all the other departments like Police, Fire, Parks and

Recreation, Planning, Public Works, and Administrative Services that includes Finance, Human Resources, and Information Technology. Anyone interested in IT?" Brad asked.

Blank faces. Shuffling feet. Another loud yawn. He still had three slides to cover. Screw it.

"OK, like I said at the beginning. I'd like this to be more of a conversation. Let's go back to your questions or comments about the city."

With what must have been his last ounce of energy, Sleeping Beauty raised his hand ever so slowly. "Would you please describe a typical day?"

Other students turned from the boy to Brad as if they were actually interested to hear his answer.

"That's a good question," Brad said enthusiastically. God bless Sleeping Beauty. He started down his daily routine and the questions came rapidly after that.

What's being built in the lot next to the Shell station?

Why does the water taste funny?

Why don't you heat the swimming pool?

Do you get free backstage passes at the casino to meet the performers?

When are we going to get an In-N-Out?

He fielded them all crisply and even occasionally with humor that hit its mark. Gone were stomach pains and trepidation. He was in his element fielding questions like he would in his own office. The questions started to slow and he checked the clock. A few minutes until wrap-up.

Jenny suddenly shot her hand up.

"Yes?" he said warily.

"You didn't say anything about the Green Valley Village project. It's a lot more important than a stupid In-N-Out. Aren't you in favor of it?"

This kid had to be a narc posing as a student. Her questions reeked of an agenda that went beyond a grade.

"Well, yes, young lady, Green Valley is very important. It's still early in the CEQA process. We're just starting the EIR, so it's a little premature to talk about."

He saw nothing but blank faces.

Mr. Heldt stepped in again. "Mr. Jacks, we haven't talked about city planning. Maybe you could give the class a quick overview on what you mean by CEQA and EIR."

"Oh, sure. We use lots of acronyms in government." Brad began.

"Maybe first you should tell them a little about the project," Mr. Heldt interrupted.

"Oh, right," Brad said, casting a glance to Jenny. "Green Valley Village is being planned as an active adult community for residents fifty-five and older. SoCal Communities is the company trying to develop it. They do high quality, large residential projects all over Southern California. Green Valley will have about 1,200 EDU's…"

"EDU's?" Mr. Heldt interjected.

"Oh, sorry. 'EDU' means 'equivalent dwelling units,'" Brad explained, moving away from the podium and pacing before the class. "The project will have mostly single-family homes. That means, like most of you probably live in, a house that isn't attached to another one. It will also have some duplexes, two houses that share a common wall, and some multi-family. Those are rental apartments and for-sale units built in clusters. There will actually be about 1,400 living units built, but, because the multi-family units won't use as much water and sewer capacity, we convert utility demand into what a single-family home would use." He looked around the class and again saw blank stares. Too much detail, Brad.

Mr. Heldt must have reached the same conclusion. "Maybe you could just summarize the main features of the project, where it is proposed, some of the benefits, that sort of thing."

"Sure. Well, on top of about 1,400 housing units, there will be seven acres of neighborhood commercial; things the residents will want nearby like a small market, beauty shop, coffee shop, bakery, that sort of thing." He saw some head nods. OK, stay at that level of explanation.

"There will be a community center, pool, and other meeting and activity rooms, an RV lot and storage lockers, a park a little smaller than Sunny Fields, and an eighteen-hole golf course." At the mention of the golf course, Sleeping Beauty slugged the guy to his left and let loose another fist pump.

"It is being planned on 550 acres just on the east side of town off Highway 246 as you head toward Lake Cachuma." He noticed Jenny smile and others in the class look her way.

"Why did you ask them to build that project there?" asked a girl from the back row innocently enough.

"I didn't," he said. "By the time I first heard about SoCal's plans, they had already optioned the property."

He saw Mr. Heldt shake his head slightly.

"Oh, in real estate development, the developer doesn't want to purchase property until he or she is sure they can build what they want on it. So, they'll pay the landowner a smaller amount of money for the right to purchase the land at the agreed upon price later on, usually after they get their entitlements." He saw that they didn't know that term. "I mean once they have all of the approvals they need from the city and other agencies to start construction."

He looked around. Better. So far, so good.

"Earlier I mentioned CEQA and EIR. CEQA is the California Environmental Quality Act. It's a state law that lays out what cities and counties have to do to analyze and disclose the environmental impacts of a proposed project. An Environmental Impact Report, or EIR, is a very critical document in that process. The EIR for Green Valley is in process now. It could take as much as two years to know how that all goes and if the project will be approved."

The classroom sat silently. His son didn't seem quite as confused as the rest.

"Are there other questions about Green Valley?" Brad asked, being careful not to look at Jenny.

"Why did SoCal pick Santa Ynez for that kind of project?" Mr. Heldt asked when no other hands were raised.

"They did very thorough studies of all sorts of factors. Santa Ynez has some advantages for a senior citizen development. We are far enough from the high land prices of the more urban areas which is good for people on a fixed income. Yet we're convenient to a lot of attractions that would appeal to seniors like art galleries, wineries, museums, community theatre, boutique shopping, Solvang, golf, fishing, and boating. And the beaches and ambience of Santa Barbara are just over the hill."

"And the weather is so good," Mr. Heldt added.

"It sure is and that's a major attraction as well." He thought a few more students were showing an interest in the topic.

"Being ten miles inland from the Pacific and protected by the California Coast Range mountains, we get cooling breezes in the summer and moderate temperatures in the winter without as much fog as more coastal areas get. And, like the rest of the Central Coast, it doesn't rain much, so most of the days will be fine for all of these active adults to golf, swim, bike, and whatever."

"It sounds good," Jenny said, without being called, "but you didn't say if you were supporting it."

"I would rather share with the class information about the project so that you can understand the impact of it—good and bad—on the community. That is my job."

"If the landowner wants to sell to some other company for this kind of project shouldn't they be allowed to?" she continued, completely ignoring his comment. "You *do* believe in private property rights, don't you?"

What the hell? What seventeen-year-old cares about private property rights? Or even knows about what that means?

Heat burned up his chest and neck. Normally it was only belligerent constituents or unreasonable bureaucracies that could evoke this level of frustration. In a couple of years, she could be one of his bosses. He should be pleased that there was a teenager so interested in the workings of local government, but she was more on a gotcha mission than a quest for knowledge.

"Of course," he finally responded.

"'Of course' you support Green Valley or 'of course' you believe in private property rights. Or both?" Jenny pressed, her face hard.

He stared at her trying to formulate a response and thought of an out. "Yes, I believe in property rights. I own a house myself. And, yes, Green Valley offers a lot of benefits to the city and the citizens. But it also has some controversial elements that I don't have time to get into right now. Our time is about up and I want to get to this last slide."

He looked away from Jenny toward the screen and clicked through listings of various city jobs and the qualifications required. He urged them to come to Career Day when city employees will tell them more about their jobs.

"Will you be there, too, Mr. Jacks?" Jenny asked with a grin. It seemed more like a dare than a plea.

"Absolutely!" he responded, not letting her chase him off. He scanned the classroom. "If you want me back, I'm happy to help you."

The class applauded. Even Jenny joined half-heartedly. He beamed and gave them a little wave. He had connected. He was popular in high school.

The students filed out, most thanking him politely for his talk. Mr. Heldt shook his hand. "Sorry about Jenny, I should have warned you."

"You did fine, Dad," Dillon said as he walked up.

"Thanks, son. Who was that girl anyway?"

"That's Jen Nettler," Dillon said. "She lives out at that big ranch past Meadowvale near Highway 154. Her dad owns the rental yard."

Brad grimaced.

Dillon must have read his expression. "He's a good guy. He gave us a flatbed for our homecoming float."

And now it made sense.

3

The stress of high school behind him again, Brad drove back to City Hall in a reflective mood. He took in the panoramic views of the Santa Ynez Mountains to the south, the San Rafael Mountains to the north, and the rolling, oak-studded hills and meadows in between. While he knew he had let Marie down on the move to an inferior house, being reminded of the area's beauty and the fact that Santa Barbara and the Pacific Ocean were only thirty minutes away was worth something.

Funny how things work out. Thirty something years ago he was working on his degree in Political Science at UC Santa Barbara. A roommate had tipped him off to a secluded spot overlooking Lake Cachuma less than ten miles from where he now lived. Brad sometimes thought about the times he and his first love drove his little blue VW from the student community of Isla Vista southeast to Santa Barbara, then north on Highway 154 to the parking spot above the lake. After the windows were sufficiently steamed up, they would complete the loop back to Highway 154 west on Highway 246, stopping for something cheap to nibble on in the quaint Danish replica village of Solvang, then over to Buellton to catch Highway 101 south back to Isla Vista.

He passed a gas station and his mind drifted to a memorable stop there many years ago during a sudden downpour. He pictured his girlfriend and him straining and laughing as they crawled around the cramped interior of his VW digging for coins to feed the Coke machine. He remembered their contorted hug when she dug the last dime they needed from under the seat. He felt warm thinking about his first love. It had been the greatest joy and excitement of his young life. The reverie dissolved into a deep sigh as he recalled the way it had ended, still one of his biggest life regrets. A distant siren brought him back. Funny. And now here he was, living a good life, hopefully until the end of his days, in this same idyllic region. That thought triggered his anxiety about the Green Valley project. He was still reliving the earlier meeting with Megan Cain as he approached City Hall.

"How'd it go at school?" Jane asked. "Standing O?"

Her voice pulled him from his thoughts. He put his thumbs to his armpits and puffed out his chest. "None of the boys picked on me and only one cute girl rejected me. So, I'd have to say *this* high school experience was a lot better than thirty-five years ago."

"Please tell me you didn't try to hit on those young girls. I was just getting you broken in," she teased.

"Nah, I got sandbagged by a cute little girl who looked like Jessie from *Toy Story*. Dillon says she's a Nettler."

"Oh? Which branch?"

"Hank's daughter. She must have had a full glass of Hubie's Kool-Aid for breakfast."

"Hank's daughter, Jenny?" Jane seemed surprised. "She's a sweetie. I always thought Hank's family was the best of the Nettler clan."

"Let's say it's a low bar," Brad cracked. "I've never had any real problem with Hank. We're in Rotary together. And he's always been generous supporting local causes. But he comes at you pretty hard sometimes."

"I suppose. But he's not as bad as his father," Jane said. "Hubie donates to local causes, too, but he makes you grovel for it. I've known the family all my life and went to school with the boys. They're a lot more bark than bite."

"From the stories I've heard, they were all brawlers. Wasn't Hubie pushing seventy when he punched that building inspector less than half his age? I'm glad I wasn't around when the city tried to acquire a patch of his property for the well."

"I was," Jane said. "A lot of that hassle was Hubie's attorneys. They are a hard-nosed bunch."

"Hubie has plenty of money and I'm sure he hired the meanest pit bulls he could to fight the city over that well. It's like only an acre or so. No big deal. But I heard they put the city through hell finally settling at an extortionist price."

She laughed. "I guess Hubie can get his back up if he gets pushed, especially by government."

Brad struck another pose, now sticking his thumbs in his belt and standing ramrod straight. "Now listen, and listen tight. We got no use for your fancy law books in these parts. We settle our fights with guns."

Jane laughed. "You do a horrible John Wayne. It *was* John Wayne, wasn't it?"

"My daughter likes it," he protested. He thought of the times watching *The Man Who Shot Liberty Valance* with Kristen and trying to best her Jimmy Stewart impressions with his of "Duke" Wayne.

"Well, I hope Hank's daughter didn't burn you too badly today."

He shook his head. "I'll survive. But I can tell you that the crab apples don't fall far from that family tree. She basically called me a worthless bureaucrat, and grilled me about my salary, pension, health benefits, and private property rights. Cute kid."

"That will teach you to volunteer some time to help our youth. Aren't you the guy whose favorite slogan is, 'no good deed goes unpunished?'"

"If I only had a competent assistant who would remind me of that ahead of time."

He turned back to pour himself a cup of coffee and went into his office. The day was rushing past him and he worked best in the mornings. His burgeoning in-basket was like a claxon that couldn't be ignored. He thought of his comment to Kerry Smith about having too many urgent, unimportant things to do and the management training he conducted based on Stephen Covey's *The Seven Habits of Highly Successful People*. Covey had it right. Managers are bombarded with issues that are urgent to someone. Nobody ever said "if you get around to it in the next couple years, would you consider fixing this pothole" or "there's no rush approving my building permit." The trick was to carve some time away from everyone else's agenda, hopefully every day, to work on projects that you know are truly important for the long run but not urgent to others. Like flossing, it was a wise practice but a hard discipline to maintain.

Brad knocked out a few calls and email messages to staff about problems he spotted in his travels this morning. He took another stack from his in-basket, sorting them quickly, tossing many of the unsolicited vendor brochures, writing the name of the appropriate staff member to follow up with quick notes like "let's discuss," "pls handle," or "fyi." Jane would take care of everything from there. She would put anything that needed follow-up into a tickler system to make sure it was.

He whizzed through the League of California Cities weekly legislative report. More bad news for cities. Amazing how many state legislators, most of whom had cut their political teeth as local government electeds, forgot their roots when they made it to Sacramento. He made some notes on the report for Jane to forward to various departments for a heads-up. He reached over to grab the next paper on the pile of his desk, glanced at the two inches of additional paperwork in his in-basket, and let out a long sigh. He threw down his pen, leaned back in his high back leather chair, and stuck his nose into the large mug of the dark roasted black coffee.

He studied the mug, a gift commemorating the completion of a tots play area at the same city park he jogged around this morning. The white mug had a fairy flicking a wand with stars coming off and the words:

"THANKS FOR CREATING THE MAGIC"
City of Santa Ynez Fairytale Town – 2010

Brad had been on the project committee shortly after he came to town. He accompanied Mayor Buddy and Councilwoman Gretchen Schmitz to meet tribe leaders at the Indian casino to ask for a big donation. He also went to several other clubs to get them to sponsor the Rapunzel slide, "crooked mile" concrete path, and other features. The whole community came out on the build weekend to donate their skills, equipment, and muscle power. Contractors barked orders, restaurants dropped off food, and youth bands entertained the volunteers. Brad got to check an item off his bucket list when Hank Nettler let him play with a Bobcat tractor. It was a fun project and a good introduction to the community. He loved seeing young families now enjoying the fruits of his labor.

He took a few more sips of coffee and looked down at his large walnut veneer desk chockablock with work, reminding him he had important responsibilities. He examined the silver-framed family photo. A lucky man. He shifted to his left to take in four firm, beige upholstered chairs next to a floor-to-ceiling window surrounding a dark walnut veneer, round coffee table. The table and chairs made his little office even more cramped looking, but he preferred the more casual touch of sitting around a table. He had heard of another city manager who made visitors sit across his desk in low, hard wooden chairs that forced all but the tallest visitor to look up at him and clearly signaled "don't stay long." That didn't fly with Brad, which was fortunate, because it certainly wouldn't fly with Santa Ynez, either.

The far wall was lined with open bookcases jammed with books on community development, modern personnel practices, organizational development, and the like. He paused over the decorated hardhats and other mementos of groundbreakings and ribbon cuttings from his career. There was the clear water in a champagne bottle from a water plant dedication so many years and miles from here, and a photo of him and several other city dignitaries from a prior city all dressed in full-body swimsuits out of the 1920s, simulating a dive into a new city pool. He remembered each project and ceremony as if they happened last week. Building things was definitely more exciting than this damn paperwork.

He looked at the top of the bookcase to the framed certificate showing his membership in the International City/County Management Association and the Rotary Four-Way Test plaque. He had accumulated plenty of other plaques and honors over his career, but opted not to display them. Some of his colleagues filled their walls with their college degrees and probably every certificate or plaque they'd ever received. Brad knew some of them required nothing more than paying dues, the professional equivalent of fogging a mirror. He thought it better to underplay his "ego wall." Maybe people would think he had more honors than he really did and give him credit for humility.

He thought of an excuse for abandoning the in-basket. He poked his head out the door and handed Jane some of the paperwork.

"Merry Christmas. I forgot. Would you set up a meeting with Megan and Dee for some time tomorrow to go over the Green Valley reports that Megan has a concern about? An hour should do."

"Will do," she said, hitting some keys on her computer. "You're pretty open tomorrow. I won't let that out or you'll fill up again."

He turned and went back to his office in a better mood. As soon as he sat down, he cringed, remembering that he'd failed again to inquire about Jane's mother. Or was it her former mother-in-law? He didn't make time for inter-personal niceties as often as he intended, even though he knew from their personal profiles that some of his staff needed a little TLC from the boss once in a while. Jane was one of those.

He sighed, threw down his pen and rose from his desk to deliver some TLC. Just as he reached his doorway, he saw Councilwoman Kay Nance coming to the outer office door.

Kay Nance. There she stood in her customary loose fitting, floral moo-moo dress that, thankfully, concealed most of her considerable body. Her name evoked a stream of associations from everyone, whether they had ever met her, or not. She looked, acted, and probably was a 1960s Hippie throwback. Her unrestrained, sagging breasts swayed as she flowed into the outer office. He marveled at the braid of gray hair stretching to the small of her back. While you couldn't say Kay was pretty, she had a pleasant, open, and unwrinkled face that radiated quiet confidence and made her seem younger than her sixty-two years.

Kay was Brad's polar opposite. He dressed conservatively, chose a house and car that wouldn't raise eyebrows, was careful about who he was seen with, and tried to be everyone's friend or to at least reduce his list of enemies. By contrast, Kay's personal mantra could have been "Here I am. Deal with it!"

She was just entering the outer office lobby when Brad caught the first whiff of her musk oil scent. The scent reminded him of his college years. It had been sexier on a twenty-year-old. He kept a bottle of air freshener in his desk and used it discretely after a long meeting with Kay. Otherwise, the olfactory memories of her would linger through the day. While often frustrated with Councilwoman Nance's politics, and feeling dull in her presence, Brad liked Kay personally and enjoyed their banter.

"Jane, when is my moat going to be installed?" he asked his assistant, pretending not to notice the colorful councilwoman dressed like a flowerbed a few feet away. "Oh, hi, Kay. What can I do for you," he opened.

"Many things, my friend," she said, her confident smile painted plainly on her face.

"Well, I mean that wouldn't clash with my Puritan ethics." He took shallow breaths through his mouth.

"Won't stay long," she said. "Just wanted to drop off our League talking points for you to look at."

"Good," he said, smiling insincerely.

"Do you mean 'good' that I'm not staying long or 'good' that I brought our League materials?" Kay teased.

"Yes," he smiled again, leaning on the counter. "How goes the battle? Any hope of getting the Environmental Quality policy committee to endorse your proposal to the board?"

"Slim to none. Got a few votes, but most of the other committee members can't get beyond the notion that maybe having 482 cities, 58 counties, and nearly 5,000 single-purpose special districts, all trying to maximize their own provincial interests, is ruining this state. Their city staffs poison them with all the talk about the virtues of local home rule and demonize any attempt at statewide or regional coordination."

"'Poison them' you say? You trust the state to make decisions for Santa Ynez residents?"

"Don't be so black and white, Brad."

He stiffened, having recently accused Megan of the same kind of limited thinking. He glanced at Jane sheepishly.

Kay continued, "Sure, local decisions should stay local. Home rule was a strong value back in the 50s when the emphasis was on expansion. But with thirty-nine million people now in California, it doesn't work to have so many agencies doing their own thing, at least not if we want to keep the state from becoming a cesspool of pollution, stripped natural resources, and driving up costs for everybody."

"I agree there should be better coordination of development in this state," Brad responded, attempting to recover some standing. "It's pretty much a hash right now. But you're bucking strong inertia."

"I know," she said. "We're expecting to get shot down by the committee so we're taking our proposal directly to the League board with a big petition from councilmembers across the state who care about our future and are willing to fight for it."

He looked at his watch unintentionally and saw her annoyance.

"OK, I get the message, Brad. I'm on my way."

"What do you mean?" he asked innocently, panicked by his boss's sudden annoyance.

"I shouldn't have expected you to care about our petition drive," she huffed.

"I do," he lied. Kay could become confrontational if provoked. He didn't need that.

"No you don't. You'd be drummed out of the city manager corps for even suggesting that it may be time to consider stronger regional planning." She turned to leave.

"No, no, no," he said hastily. "Don't hurry off, Kay. I've got a lot going on right now. But I can always find time for one of my five favorite councilmembers. Can we get you some coffee?"

"No thanks, I don't do stimulants, at least not this early," she laughed, walking past him into his office, a contrail of musk oil scent in her wake.

Brad looked back at Jane and rolled his eyes. She simulated spraying an aerosol can. He walked slowly back into his office, his mind racing to find something to talk about to feign interest in Kay's latest windmill tilt.

She sat on her crossed legs, yoga style, in the chair to the right of where Brad usually sat instead of across from him. She raised her head to accept the late morning rays streaming through the open vertical blinds.

"So, how many petition signatures do you have so far?" he asked.

"Oh, Brad, you're such a linear thinker. It's all about numbers for you. An artist sees a deeper reality."

"Hah! Not doing too well, huh?"

"We have close to thirty. It's a good start. More importantly, we have key mayors and councilmembers from all over the state. We're also reaching out to some county supervisors who are taking the proposal to CSAC. And I just heard that we have a meeting in Sacramento coming up with the leadership of the California Special District Association." She handed him the papers.

He accepted the stack but immediately tossed it on the table.

"I can see you're not impressed, Brad. But this idea is going to result in a legislative proposal, with or without the League and CSAC support. And if we can't get it done in Sacramento, we'll take the fight directly to the public and put it on as an initiative."

"*I* wouldn't want to get in your way," he smiled.

"Why don't you join us then? We could use some help from a seasoned city manager. We're not talking about cutting cities' balls off with these regional land use plans. You and Mayor Buddy will still have your share of groundbreaking ceremonies to strut around at."

"Whew!" he said, wiping his forehead with the back of his hand sarcastically.

"We just want local development decisions better tied to preservation of the natural resources of the nine planning zones. That includes promoting infill of the urban areas instead of sprawling on ag land and open space, more efficient long range infrastructure planning, and sharing the costs and benefits of development more fairly across an entire region."

"Oh, that's all?" he scoffed. "You are up against a century of local government tradition and a huge power base that will fight to the death to protect the status quo."

"I know it's an uphill fight. But what else do I have to do but stock my gallery with sculptures for the tourists and show up at Council meetings pretending to have read all the junk you sent us?"

"I'm shocked and deeply saddened!" he joked.

"It really is a fight worth joining, Brad. You should give it some thought. Back when you woke up every morning hoping to find some armpit hair, I was marching for civil rights and peace. It's in my blood. It's fun. But you have to be willing to accept setbacks and realize you're in it until you win it."

"Yeah, but voters could understand racial inequality and people dying in Vietnam. How are you going to explain the fiscalization of land use resulting from Proposition 13 and how development regulation in California is an absolute mess of bureaucracies? It's too complicated for a campaign sound bite."

"We're going to take a page from Howard Jarvis and Paul Gann. They kept the message simple, 'Everyone knows the property taxes in California are too high but you can't trust the government to constrain itself. Prop 13 returns power to the people.' Power to the people, Brad. Can you hear John Lennon's song playing over the TV ads?"

"Wait a minute, Kay, how does 'power to the people' equate to moving more control out of the local citizens' hands into nine regional agencies?"

"Again, Brad, you're too linear. Initiatives are won by appealing to the public's sentiments, not with hard facts. How many people bother to even read their ballot pamphlet?"

"Not me," he admitted. "Not completely, at least. And I have a master's degree in government and a personal stake in some of it. But it's too much to absorb. Where's your hook?"

"It's just like it was with Prop 13. They tried to get legislative reforms at state and local levels. The politicians and bureaucrats knew the system was broken but nobody stepped up to lead a more reasonable reform. Jarvis/Gann grabbed the flag and ran with it."

"Sure," he began, "but that was a simple pocketbook appeal. Who wouldn't want their taxes cut 65 percent? What you're talking about with development and natural resources is too tough to get across on a campaign poster."

Kay shook her head. "The public may not know all of the facts or have the answers. But they know at a visceral level that California is in deep trouble. They spend hours every day fighting freeway congestion to get from their homes in the suburbs to jobs fifty or even a hundred miles away. They see ag land converted to more housing and know that will make the commute worse. And they don't have any faith that it's going to get fixed because of all the special interests. They're right."

"Ah" he said. "So, like with Prop 13, the message is 'you know it's broken and you can't depend on the people in power to fix it, power to the people, stop the madness, shake the system up, take control away from the politicians and government bureaucrats.' I can see how that would appeal to the public these days. They have so little confidence in their government anymore." He felt some sadness that such a cynical strategy made sense. Were the pundits right that California had become ungovernable?

Kay saw the opportunity. "We are failing the people of this state on the growth issue like they did in the 60s and 70s on the property tax problem. Our proposal for stronger regional coordination of development is sensible. History shows that we either deal with our problems sensibly or the public, courts or federal government will eventually take control. That's where you come in."

"Go on," he said warily. He thought about all of the other matters on his plate.

"Relax. All I want you to do is look at these talking points and give me a city manager's take."

He frowned. "Not an easy sale. Those of us who've been in this business a while remember how bad things got after the feds took away our ability to regulate cable TV. Just moving decision-making up a level or two isn't necessarily an improvement in governance. The devil's in the details."

"Well, then, you tell me how we can convince fair-minded, concerned officials that the status quo isn't working and they have a professional and moral responsibility to engage on the issues, not just hide behind the home rule veil."

He maintained the frown, thinking he wasn't up to the task she had dropped on his lap.

"Hey, look at it this way, Brad, would you rather have me working on a statewide campaign like this or applying all of my time and energy on city business. . . with you?" She let loose a hearty howl.

He opened his arms widely. "Putting it that way, I'd *love* to help you with your talking points."

"Great, can you get back to me tomorrow with any suggestions? I need to send this out to the group right away."

For a split second Brad imagined himself shouting "Noooo!" He might as well have some fun with it.

"Like I said, I'd love to work on it for you, Kay. But you know the Council's policy on that. It takes a majority vote of the Council to direct the city manager. Should I call the other councilmembers to make sure they're OK with me working on your statewide land use issue?" He grinned.

Kay didn't bite. "Yeah, right. And while you're at it, tell them that you intend to have the staff spend as much time on projects that will protect the public's interest, like my proposal does, as you do on projects like Green Valley that don't. You *are* supposed to be neutral, right?"

He ducked his head behind raised arms in a fighter's protective pose. "OK, OK, Kay. I'll have time tonight to work on it. Sleep is over-rated. I'll just have to tell Marie that I can't take her out for dinner like we planned."

Kay didn't buy it. "Tell her she can come to my house for dinner tonight while you work on this. I guarantee she'd have more fun. My 'no stimulant' policy ends at five." She turned to leave. "Thanks Brad. I owe you. I'll be a good girl and won't give you, Buddy, or Scott any grief about Green Valley." She gave her braid a flip and added, "for the rest of the day."

*****

Brad's afternoon was mostly filled with a tense meeting with the top officers of the largest city employee union over a grievance about a scheduling change in street maintenance affecting overtime. He finally came up with a compromise that he judged as being good enough for reducing costs while avoiding an appeal to the City Council. He didn't need the employees challenging his leadership of the organization to his bosses.

He had just enough time to scan and comment on a technical study to consolidate countywide communications and safety records management being led by a city/county task force. Santa Ynez was too small to have its own police and fire operations, so it contracted with the county and argued every year about the city's fair share of the costs. His city was a minor player in public safety compared to other agencies in the county. Because the draft report was thick and filled with technical jargon, he would make only a token effort to review and comment.

Halfway through the Executive Summary, he noticed similarities with this countywide communication consolidation effort and Kay's cause; both sought better results for the public by ceding some local control in favor of shared authority. A joint powers authority would be formed to finance and operate the new communication system with every agency having input. Still, he scoffed with the complexity of getting this off the ground once the inevitable provincial inertia kicked in.

He learned early in his career that he could never become technically proficient in all the issues that came his way. He was a generalist. He had to depend upon the staff to do the right thing. His approach was to ask penetrating questions, primarily just to satisfy himself that they were on top of things. He had developed a sensitive "bullshit meter" that alerted him to probe further if he sensed that his staff's knowledge of the issues was only superficial.

He typed some questions on nontechnical aspects of the study, mainly to show his colleagues that he was participating: *Is the JPA going to guarantee jobs to all of the dispatchers from all the other agencies? If so, how will the salaries and benefits be set? Will everyone go up to the highest level now being paid? Or will those who are currently making more be grandfathered until the JPA scale catches up? What about the different retirement plans? Will there be reciprocity? Will everyone convert over to a single reporting protocol for records management or will there be room for variation? What if an agency opts out of the JPA?*

Jane poked her head through the door. "Your four o'clock is here. And he's quite handsome."

He got up from his desk to greet his guest and did a double-take. His son stood in the lobby dressed in a long- sleeved white dress shirt, black slacks, and dress shoes that he had at least cleaned, if not actually polished. Brad flushed with pride.

"Mr. Jacks? Please come in," he said, reaching out to shake his son's hand. "Let me introduce you to Ms. Stanar. She can also supply you with information for your term paper."

Dillon rolled his eyes and screwed up his face. "I already said 'hi' to Jane, Dad."

"Come on in. You look very professional. Good job, son."

They sat down at the coffee table and Brad began. "Now pretend you just met me and this is a real interview. Start by telling me why you're here."

"Do I have to call you Mr. Jacks, Dad? That's stupid."

"Dad will do. Go ahead."

Dillon went on to describe his government class assignment to do a ten-page paper on some current issue being discussed at public meetings. He explained that he had to list the major players and interview at least one participant in the debate.

Brad knew all of that from their prior discussions. He and Marie made several topic suggestions Dillon determined to be too boring. Marie suggested the Green Valley project, noting her son's golf interest and the opportunity to be in on the ground floor of planning a golf course. Brad volunteered to make the introduction to Scott Graves, the SoCal development rep, but only after Dillon met with him first to get some background on the project and practice his interviewing technique.

Dillon sat up straight, looked down at the tablet on his lap, and then up at his father, his pen poised. "Will you please summarize the Green Valley Village project?" Brad's heart melted.

Brad pulled out conceptual drawings of the project and walked his son through the housing areas, parks and landscaping, golf course, neighborhood commercial, and community meeting areas. Dillon asked appropriate questions and kept busy writing notes.

"As city manager, what is your position on the project?" Dillon read.

"Well, I'd have to say I'm supporting it. There are a lot of benefits included in the DA."

Dillon looked up. "DA?"

"Development Agreement. I'll call it a DA from now on 'cause it's shorter, OK?"

Dillon nodded.

"A project like Green Valley Village will take years to completely build out. The developer will have to front millions of dollars of planning, entitlement, and infrastructure work to even start construction on the initial phase of the project. Usually, they won't start seeing a decent return on their investment until the later phases. However, it's not uncommon with a large, controversial project for things to change between project approval and completion. A new Council majority may be elected with a mandate to overturn the project approvals, for example. A DA is a contract between the developer and the approving city or county that restricts the public agencies from making changes to the project down the road. It gives the developer some protection for what is already a very expensive and risky venture."

Dillon put his pen to his lips and stared at his tablet before looking up. "Do all projects have DA's?"

"No, just big ones like Green Valley that will be built over a long period. It's too expensive and time consuming for a developer of a small project to mess with it. Besides, cities get some benefit, too, that can cost the developer big bucks. There are laws that limit what cities can require a private project to do in order to get a building permit. With a DA, there is more give-and-take. The city can give the developer some protections and special benefits and in exchange get all kinds of goodies we wouldn't be able to require otherwise. It's a negotiation."

"And are you the one who negotiates for the city?" Dillon asked.

Brad puffed out his chest. "I'm in the meetings when I need to be. But mostly I meet with other city staff to discuss everything and give them direction."

Dillon looked impressed. "What are some of the things you are getting out of Green Valley?"

Brad felt proud. His son was asking good questions and going with the flow of the conversation, not just reading off a prepared script.

Brad picked up the file on the table and pulled out the latest draft of the DA. "I'll ask Jane to make a copy of this for you. There are all sorts of benefits for the community from the development. For example, SoCal will use one of their home sites for a Fire Department substation. And they'll set up a special taxing district so that the residents and businesses will pay the cost of keeping two firefighter/ paramedics there 24/7. You know 85 percent of Fire Department calls are medical-related, not fires. Having this substation out there will provide a quick first response to the residents until back-up arrives from the city fire station downtown. Plus, the entire community would benefit by having two more professionals on duty 24/7 to assist the main fire station on calls outside Green Valley."

"That's cool," Dillon said. "What else?"

"We got them to front the cost to widen and signalize two intersections to improve traffic circulation in the general area of the project."

"But how is that a community benefit, if it's just for their own project's traffic?" Dillon asked.

"Good, Dillon! You're asking good questions that flow from the discussion."

"I'm not a moron, Dad," Dillon said, sitting up a little straighter.

"I know, I'm just being a proud father, give me a break. On your question, yes, the project will produce more traffic and we have lots of detailed studies about that. But the DA calls for SoCal to make street improvements that are far beyond what we could require them to do based on their fair share of the traffic that uses the area of improvements. Got it?"

"Got it. Anything else?"

He flipped the page. "They are dedicating the ridgeline for equestrian and hiking trails and installing a big water tank up there. The tank will serve Green Valley and also be sized to eliminate chronic low pressure problems at some houses in other parts of the city that are at the higher end of the main pressure zone."

"Like at our house? I'd be able to take a shower that doesn't just trickle out when the sprinklers come on?"

"That's the idea."

"I'm for it already!" Dillon exclaimed.

Brad flipped another page of the DA. "There are a lot more benefits. Of course, the city will get property tax revenue from the project that will help overall city services. However, the residents out there will be assessed for all the landscape maintenance, plus the project will be gated and have private security so our police won't have to patrol it all the time. And, because of the gates, the streets will all be private and the residents will be assessed to pay for the maintenance not the city. It's a good cost/benefit ratio for us. That's why I like it."

Dillon held a finger in the air as he finished writing in the tablet. "I think that gives me enough."

Brad flipped the page again. "Wait, I almost forgot the mayor's and Councilwoman Gretchen Schmitz' favorite part of the DA. SoCal will buy an existing 10,000 square foot office or industrial space and master lease it to the city for a dollar a year for ten years."

"What for?"

"We'll sublease the space to local nonprofits that would be responsible for all building operating costs in exchange for free rent. The museum has first dibs on half of the space. You've seen their big carriage collection. They have a lot more artifacts to display than they have room for in their downtown location. The new space will include a roll-up door and high ceilings to accommodate storage and work areas for the collection and offices. It will free up the more valuable space downtown for exhibits."

"Why is that so big to the mayor?" Dillon asked.

"His wife and Councilwoman Schmitz are both on the board for the museum. SoCal was really looking for something to put in the DA package to appeal to some movers and shakers in town and that was what I proposed. Of course, I asked for more space and a permanent donation, not just ten years, but remember, it's a negotiation. The museum folks are thrilled."

"Good job, Dad. I haven't heard you talk about Councilwoman Schmitz much. What's she like?"

"Gretchen Schmitz is an eighty-year-old dynamo. She retired as a high school nurse a long time ago and has been involved with every type of social service issue for decades. She knows everybody. She's on all kinds of nonprofit boards and has been plugged into Democratic Party politics since Adlai Stevenson. She was a founding member of the Historical Society, Soroptimists, and League of Women Voters."

"She's a Democrat? Aren't you a Republican? Is that a problem for you?"

"No. Local government elections in California are strictly nonpartisan. People often know the candidates' political party but they don't run on a party platform. Gretchen is too liberal for my tastes on social and environmental issues. But I like her. She usually tries to do the good government thing even though I don't always agree with her take on that. She and Kay Nance are usually on the losing side of a 3-2 vote but sometimes Councilman Al Landon, a minister, joins them. He is the swing vote a lot of times."

"Does she like you?"

"Sure. I got a lot of strokes from Gretchen by getting that nonprofit space in the draft DA. Plus, I got SoCal to build a 2,000 square foot 'Santa Ynez Room' next to the Green Valley Village community center they'll build for the residents. SoCal will manage the space and give it free, mostly for the museum for its rotating displays. Two smaller partitioned areas will be set aside. One is for the Tourism Bureau to promote regional events and attractions and the other for the city to advertise recreation classes, fire prevention week, and stuff. Gretchen likes that, too."

"Good to have your bosses like you, Dad, especially after what you said at school about how easy it is for you to be fired."

"Sure is, Dillon. I get along with all of them. That wasn't always true in other cities. I've had some real difficult bosses in my career. The councilmembers here are all different people and I have to deal with them differently. But so far, nobody is after me."

Dillon glanced at his notes. "Oh, yeah, you know how whacked out my friend, Bruce, is about golf? He wanted me to ask if we'll be able to play the Green Valley golf course."

"Yes. It'll be privately-owned, but the DA requires that for at least the first ten years they have to open it for public play at least after noon on weekends and anytime on Tuesdays at rates comparable to other courses in the area. They said they'd probably sell annual golf passes to nonresidents to bring in more outside play."

"Cool. We'll be able to play when we visit from college." Dillon set his pen down and began fidgeting. "By the way, Dad, about college. . ."

Brad furrowed his eyebrows. "Yessss?"

"Yeah, well," Dillon said haltingly, "I've been thinking lately about Colorado State."

"What?! Where the hell did that come from?"

"Yeah, well, that's where Bruce is going now. Sounds pretty good."

"I thought it was all set for both of you to go to Sacramento State. What happened?"

"It was. But Bruce always really wanted to go to Colorado. You know how he's always wearing Colorado State clothes with the ram on it? He has relatives in Fort Collins and has been to the campus a few times."

Brad had no clue what his son's best friend wore.

"Bruce didn't think he could afford Colorado with the out-of-state tuition. But he got a football scholarship so his parents can afford it now. Plus, he's going to live for free room and board with his aunt in Fort Collins. He wants me to come with him and his aunt said I could live with them, too.

"When did all of this happen? Does Mom know? How much more is the tuition than Sac State?" Brad asked, holding his breath.

"Only about $20,000 a year more," Dillon said happily, as if he were still twelve trying to talk his dad up from the small to the medium bag of popcorn at the movies.

Brad gasped. "Twenty thousand?! More?! For a state college? So we pay taxes in California forever, and, rather than getting a break by going to a state university here, you suddenly want to go out of state and pay more? What's wrong with starting at Sac State and transferring to Cal Poly like we planned?"

"Nothing much, I guess," Dillon said looking down. "It just doesn't turn me on. Bruce says Colorado State is a great school and the skiing is phenomenal."

"What are you talking about?" Brad protested. "It's only a little more than an hour to the slopes from Sacramento."

"Yeah, but the season is so much longer in Colorado. And they have that nice dry powder that I love."

"So this is all about snow conditions?!" He threw up his hands. He was just starting to look at Dillon as a budding man and now his son was acting like an over-indulged pre-teen.

"No, Dad," Dillon protested. "Their engineering school is awesome. I'll show you the ratings when we get home."

"Geez, I've built our family financial plan around you attending a California public college. "I just don't know about suddenly having to spend over $40,000 a year."

"I know it's a lot of money, Dad. And I can't get an athletic or academic scholarship. But I'll get a part-time job when I get there to help cover costs and I'll work full-time this summer and every summer. Besides, it will be a lot less than what you are paying for Kris at UOP. I checked that, too."

"Good one!" he thought to himself, remembering his last tuition payment to the University of the Pacific. He needed to stall. He looked at his watch. "Our time is about up. Let's finish up on your term paper and talk more about this college stuff later."

He gave Dillon another few minutes' briefing on the process the Green Valley project would have to go through, some of the main problematic issues, like water, and a few of the key players. Dillon was back to being businesslike again.

When they concluded, Brad gave him a hug instead of a handshake. "Good job with this interview. We'll talk some more about Colorado."

By the way his son left the office beaming, Brad guessed that Dillon figured he was already at least a lamb if not yet a ram.

Jane stuck her head in the door. "I'm taking off. Need anything before I go?"

He looked at his watch and was surprised to see it was 5:30. "A few more hours in the day, if you can swing it. Kay just dumped something in my lap that I'll have to work on tonight."

"Better watch that working at home stuff. You can be an absentee husband and father even sitting in your family room with a pile of work."

"Is marriage counseling in your 'other duties as required'? It's not that bad. I have a system."

"Why am I not surprised about that?" she teased.

"I try not to do any work at home until after about 7. That gives us time to sit together for dinner. After that, everyone goes their own way anyway. The other rule is that anyone can interrupt me up until 10. If I'm still working that late, they should try to leave me alone so I can finish up before it gets too late."

She made a face like she'd just had a whiff of limburger cheese. "So do you have this written into a notarized Memorandum of Understanding? Do you issue your family reprimands if they violate your adopted policies?"

"All right," he grinned and shrugged. "Maybe too structured for some people, but it works in our family."

She shook her head. "God bless Marie. You're a lucky man. Most women wouldn't put up with that kind of structure at home."

"Yeah, I know. She tolerates me pretty well by now, except for when it's time to update the family budget. She hates that."

"I can imagine," she said.

"Speaking of tolerating me, if you have a couple minutes, why don't you have a seat? Just want to check in with you."

Alone in the locked office after hours, he started on safe ground asking about Jane's satisfaction with work. He eventually moved the conversation to more personal issues. He asked about her daughters and how she was getting along since Alex's death.

"I'm guessing that quality male companionship is hard to come by in Santa Ynez," he said, probing.

Jane gave a short, nervous laugh, looked at her watch, and jumped to her feet. "Got to pick up the girls." She walked out and began putting on her coat next to her desk and shouted into Brad, "By the way, why don't you add an addendum to whatever you are working on for Kay with tips for getting organized? I went into the co-op gallery she shares in Solvang to do some Christmas shopping. What a mess!"

He noticed but ignored her change of subject. "Kay's a piece of work herself, I'll grant you," he agreed.

"And her car! Have you seen that lately? That dinged up old green Prius? It's filled with boxes of papers and God knows what else. I think the only time it's ever washed is when it rains, and you know how seldom that is."

He smiled and nodded agreement. "I don't think she has any time for cleaning. She lectures in art history at UCSB two days a week, does her sculpting on the off days, sells it in the gallery on weekends, and is plugged into state and regional political issues. She's pretty amazing, actually."

"OK, I give, Boss," she said, reappearing at his door. "I'm not going to get you to say anything bad about a councilmember. I'm outta here. Don't forget that Scott Graves is your program for Rotary tomorrow. Don't work too late tonight so you can be alert for that."

He said goodnight and heard his guardian angel close and lock the outer door. Jane had a point about work stress that was worth keeping in mind. Too many of his colleagues were making alimony and child support payments. That, along with out-of-state tuition, was not in his spreadsheet.

4

When Jane left, Brad picked up his homework with Kay's materials on top and drove home. He saw that Public Works had already fixed the stop sign he reported. He forgot to tell them about the trip hazard on the jogging track. The illegal banner the mayor mentioned was still draped across the real estate office's parking lot. Megan hadn't responded to his request this morning to have her staff follow up. Brad made a mental note to shoot her an email about it before bed.

Rounding the corner of his block, his house came into view. Even after living there for six years, his heart sank a little every time he approached. Not that there was anything wrong with it. The two-story ranch house was large and stylish enough and the neighborhood was well-kept. It was just so much less house than what he and Marie left behind in West Sacramento to take the job in Santa Ynez.

West Sacramento had been Brad's second city manager job. He and Marie bought a brand new house in a subdivision paying $395,000 in 2003. It was almost 3,500 square feet, with four bedrooms, three baths, and a large lot, at least by California subdivision standards. They put a ton of time, money, and sweat into it, adding landscaping, a pool with spa, and furnishings selected by a professional decorator. He smiled thinking about the one-and-only time he and Marie tried to wallpaper together. The marriage nearly ended on the spot.

They saw their investment grow in the up-market, only to see it come crashing down in the recession, when in 2010 they ended up selling for less than they had in it. Marie had mentioned that fact only once, but it was enough. The $70,000 loss was a hit to his carefully crafted financial projections, and his wife's comment stung his pride. He rationalized, noting friends who lost their houses entirely when the values dropped. He pointed out that their investment portfolio was down only 15 percent when friends admitted to 50 percent drops. He patted himself on the back for being broadly diversified in inexpensive index funds covering a variety of market segments, both internationally and in the USA. It could have been much worse if he hadn't been so prudent. Marie understood his explanation but he still felt like he'd let her down. He prided himself on managing money, both the city's and his own. He wasn't cheap, just careful.

Taking the loss on the West Sac house wasn't on Brad's spreadsheet at the time. But he had to leave. The city was emerging from the shadows of the much larger City of Sacramento, just across the Sacramento River. There were huge office, commercial, and high-density residential projects being planned that would give a much-needed upgrade to the city's image and continue the population growth from its 47,000 at that time. Brad was in the middle of all of it, schmoozing with the developers considering major investments, working with staff to ensure that infrastructure like water, sewer, streets, and parks was coming online, and helping the City Council navigate the inevitable growing pains and public discord that comes with rapid growth.

After six years of the breakneck pace, he knew he had to get out for his own health. He was working too many hours, feeling unrelenting stress, drinking too much at night to relax, putting on weight, and setting off more red flags at annual physicals. Both parents had died quite young of heart attacks. As he approached his late 40s, he tried to take solace in the fact that they were heavy smokers. Still, the gene pool is master and his wasn't very robust. He and Marie talked about it and she kept saying that health was more important than his spreadsheet.

Marie was wonderful through all of it. She loved their new, large home in West Sacramento, had made close friends, and liked being close to her family, most of whom still lived in the nearby Sacramento River Delta area where she had grown up. Her biggest worry about moving away had been being so far from her mother, who was getting feebler and needed her more since Marie's father's death. But she knew the job was killing Brad and supported him when he started sending out resumes.

They took their lumps and started over in Santa Ynez in February, 2010, hoping for a less stressful lifestyle in a smaller town. It was their fifth move. The biggest complaint came from their daughter, Kristen, who was finishing up her senior year in high school. Fortunately, Kris was invited to live with her best friend's family so she could graduate with her class. Then she would join the family in Santa Ynez for the summer before starting her freshman year at the University of the Pacific in Stockton.

House prices were a lot higher in Santa Ynez. The best they could manage, after selling in West Sac, was a nine-year-old four-bedroom, two-bath, two-story tract house of 2,400 square feet. Compared to their old house, it felt like everyone was on top of each other when Kris joined them that first summer. Teenage girls take up an inordinate amount of physical and emotional space, anyway. But when Kris left for UOP, Marie, Brad, and Dillon settled in for the last time, Marie and Brad hoped. Marie had been such a good sport, he owed her some stability. They would get Dillon through high school here, then through college, and spend their retirement years in the beautiful Santa Ynez Valley. His spreadsheet showed that would work.

Pulling into his garage, his mind shifted from work to the promise of his waiting leather recliner and the bourbon and water he would sip while watching the nightly news with the family. He walked through the garage door into the house, through the laundry room, and into the kitchen where Marie was making a sandwich. He took a moment to enjoy the view. His wife was curvier than she used to be, but still looked great in a pair of pants. He didn't say it very often but Brad knew he'd made a good choice marrying Marie twenty-eight years earlier. She had been a Personnel Technician in the medium sized city where Brad started his career after grad school. He'd been an administrative analyst in the City Manager's Office. Since employee salaries and benefits were as much as 85 percent of some of the city departments' budgets, Brad reasoned it was important for him to learn the details. At least that was his cover for all the hours spent with Marie in the Personnel Department doing research. Of course, if Marie had been a hag, he would have spent more time analyzing vehicle maintenance or utility costs instead. He felt a familiar jolt of excitement in his loins.

"Howdy. Sandwiches for dinner?"

"Don't get too comfortable," Marie warned, breaking the mood before it had a chance to get going. "Lee called from the hospital. Lilly fell."

Lee and Lilly Andre were good neighbors. They weren't close friends but they had always watched out for each other, as good neighbors do. Brad had treated Lee to a round of golf a few months ago to celebrate his 90th birthday. They spent five hours together, but Brad failed Marie's interrogation afterwards about how Lee and Lilly were doing.

"What happened?" Brad asked. There'd be no evening news, no bourbon and water, and no anything else anytime soon.

"I don't know. I just got home from the store and heard the message on the machine. Lee was at the hospital and asked if we'd double check that the oven was off and the door locked. I did that," she said, cutting the thick sandwich in half and then putting it on a paper towel. "He sounded pretty shaken up. I made you a sandwich for the road. I'm sure he could use some company."

He took a bite out of the sandwich and headed back to the bedroom to put on more casual clothes.

*****

It didn't take long for them to find Lee Andre in the waiting room of Valley Community Hospital. It was a small community hospital boasting a new emergency room. Lee sat alone staring straight ahead, paying no attention to the news broadcast on the small TV in front of him. Lee slowly rose when he saw Brad and Marie. He accepted Marie's comforting hug. Brad added his version of the guy hug, a quick embrace and a couple light back slaps.

"What happened, Lee?" Marie asked. It always bugged Brad that this was usually her first question when he came into the house with a bleeding leg or yelled in pain from smashing his finger. Brad always thought something more along the lines of "are you OK?" would be more appropriate. It put the emphasis on her concern about his condition rather than on her curiosity. Just one of the many things couples adjust to without making an issue of after years of marriage.

"She fell," responded Lee.

"Where'd she fall?" Marie probed further. Brad ground his teeth.

"She was putting up Thanksgiving decorations and tripped on the fireplace hearth. She said she heard a snap and just went down.

She has osteoporosis, you know."

"I didn't know that," Marie admitted. "My mother has it, too. Pretty common in older women. It must have really hurt."

"Lilly doesn't complain much about aches and pains. But she sure yelled this time. I called 911 and didn't move her. The ambulance got there fast but it really hurt getting her on the gurney."

"How's she doing?" Marie asked. Ding, ding, ding, thought Brad.

"They think she broke her hip. Her left leg was shorter and turned at a weird angle. She's in for x-rays now. They gave her an IV that I think is just salt and sugar and a little morphine for pain. She has settled down some. Just waiting for the doctor."

They all sat down to wait it out. Brad and Marie offered up a little small talk about how nicely Lee's chrysanthemums looked this year, asked about their family, and were they all coming for Thanksgiving? Anything to give Lee something positive to think about. Mostly there was silence.

After twenty minutes, the doctor entered and confirmed that Lilly had broken her hip. She advised that the best course of treatment would be to transfer Lilly right away to the larger regional hospital in Santa Maria for surgery tomorrow. She explained that, especially with older patients in pain, they want to get them into surgery within twenty-four hours if the patient's EKG, chest x-ray, and labs indicate they can handle it.

"They've had good results with repairing broken hips, even in patients of Lilly's age," the doctor continued. "It mostly depends upon the patient's temperament and whether they have the will to get up and get going again."

"Oh, you don't need to worry about Lilly, Doctor," Lee said proudly. "She's made it through tougher scrapes than this. She'll take whatever you have to do to her to get better, Doc. She's a survivor, you know."

Brad debated about asking Lee what he meant.

"What do you mean, 'she's a survivor,' Lee?" Marie asked.

Brad smiled, grateful that she did the prying.

Lee looked down and shook his head. "It was something that happened when she was little. There was a big dam that broke and flooded everything. It killed hundreds of people. She just barely survived it." He looked toward the doors leading to the Emergency Department. "Lilly doesn't like to talk about it much. The family knows the story."

"Where did that happen?" Marie asked. "That sounds terrible."

"You know where Castaic Junction is at the bottom of the Grapevine on I-5?"

"Sure," Brad interjected, "just as you drop down the mountains on southbound I-5 into the Los Angeles Basin."

Interstate 5 was the main north/south freeway running through California's inland area stretching all the way from Canada to Mexico. The Grapevine was the section of freeway that went over the Tehachapi Mountains separating the San Joaquin Valley on the north from the Los Angeles area to the south.

"You know where that big amusement park is just down the road from Castaic?" Lee continued.

"Sure," Brad said again. "Magic Mountain, right along the west side of I-5, just past the turn-off to Highway 126. I've driven through there many times. Did it happen there?"

"Los Angeles built a big dam in the mountains to the east of where that amusement park is now," Lee said. "It was back in the 1920s. The dam broke and a wall of water came down, flooded Castaic, then it turned west toward Santa Paula along Highway 126. It wiped out everything in its path all the way out to the ocean at Ventura. Dead bodies from miles away washed up on the beaches of the Pacific Ocean. Lilly was in the path of the flood but was one of the lucky ones who survived."

Brad was bewildered. He had grown up in Camarillo,

just over the hill from the valley where this flood was supposed to have happened. His father, Spike, took Highway 126 east from Camarillo to State Highway 99, before that section became part of Interstate 5, to visit family in Sacramento. His father would talk about historical sites along the route of the family's travels all over California. Brad later drove 126 himself many times coming and going between Camarillo and points north. He even took California history while at UCSB. Through all of that he had never heard anything about such a major disaster.

"I never heard anything about that. What happened to Lilly?" Marie asked.

Lee suddenly stiffened. His words became more measured. "I shouldn't have said anything about that. Lilly doesn't like to talk about it. Maybe she will tell you some day." They both got the message and reverted to small talk and watching the TV news.

Ten minutes later, Lilly was wheeled back to the ER to await transport to Santa Maria. She was groggy but not complaining of pain. Brad and Marie offered to go with them. Lee declined, saying his son was on his way down from Salinas to meet them. They waited a bit longer until the ambulance came, hugged Lee, patted Lilly's hand, and promised to check in.

They walked out of the hospital into the evening air. The sun was down and the air was damp. He saw an ambulance turn in to the hospital blinking red strobe lights noting another life in danger. Brad reached over and took Marie's hand. She responded by interlocking her fingers with his. It felt good that she still loved him so much.

"Poor Lilly." Brad said.

"I know. I'm a native Californian, too, and I never knew about that dam break."

"It sure got my curiosity going," he said. "I'd like to look into it but have a bunch of stuff to do tonight."

"I'll Google it and let you know what I find out," she offered. With that decided, they walked the rest of the way to the car in silence.

They got home around 8 p.m. Brad finally got his bourbon and retreated to his black leather recliner with his homework and turned on a basketball game to run in the background. His first priority was to comment on the report Councilwoman Nance had asked him to review. He wasn't going to spend a lot of time on what he regarded as a fantasy flight. Since its admission to the Union in 1850, there had been attempts to divide the over-sized state of California into smaller states or regional entities. The last push came in a 1996 report by the California Constitutional Revision Commission. The Commission came out with some progressive ideas for improving alignment of responsibilities between the state and local governments, especially in the area of finance. One of his city manager colleagues was involved and was sure that, this time, changes would be made. They weren't. No reason to believe they would be this time, either.

Brad skimmed Kay's talking points looking for a few spots in different sections of the report where he could write some pithy margin notes. He wanted her to see that he'd put in some effort, much like he had with the countywide communications study.

Marie sat on the couch across the room with her laptop. "I just Googled 'California dam break.' On the top of the page there is a link to a Wikipedia article with a blurb saying '…failure of the St. Francis dam near Saugus, California.'"

"Saugus? Yeah, that's in the area Lee was talking about."

Marie started reading the Wikipedia article out loud. He looked back and forth between her and his own screen, tapping his fingers on the laptop.

"What you're reading is more interesting than this. But I promised

Kay I'd look at this tonight. So, let me get through it first, then I'll take a break and see what you got. OK?"

He concentrated on the councilwoman's materials, looking up occasionally at his wife's inadvertent "oh my God" or "huh." She was playing the part of someone quietly reading, but they'd been together long enough to recognize when she was trying to get him to ask her what she'd found. He focused harder on Kay's missives, trying to find a place for a meaningful note. After forty minutes and another interruption, he'd had his fill. He glared at Marie, plopped the laptop down loudly on the table, and stomped to the bathroom. He took an indirect route back, going through the living room, into the kitchen, and quietly began to make another bourbon and water.

"Back for more?" Marie grumbled. She had rabbit ears.

He gave up trying to be quiet and changed the subject. "I take it from all your 'oh my Gods,' you found something."

"Plenty," she responded, seizing the opening. "It says that the St. Francis Dam break was the second worst disaster in California history, second only to the Great San Francisco Earthquake and Fire of 1906. And it was the worst US engineering disaster of the 20th century. It happened in 1928. Some 450 to 600 people were killed. Just like Lee said, the flood washed people, livestock, and everything else all the way out to the Pacific Ocean between Ventura and Oxnard."

"Holy crap! How have I never heard of this? Tell me more." He looked back at his laptop and added, "quickly."

"The dam was built under the direction of the Chief of the Los Angeles Department of Water and Power, a man named William Mulholland."

"Sure, Mulholland. There's a windy street in the hills above LA named after him. It's a popular place for couples to park. Great views of the city lights." He stopped short of mentioning the time he and his girlfriend drove from UCSB to park along Mulholland Drive, just to be able to say they had done it. He opted to share a different memory.

"I remember a lecture in my California History class about how Mulholland and other Los Angeles officials secretly bought most of the water rights from the Owens Valley on the east side of the Sierras, hundreds of miles from LA. When the locals realized they had been conned and had no water left for their farms, it started the water wars. Did the locals blow up the dam?"

"No, it just gave way," Marie said clicking her keyboard. "It was built in 1926 and burst just as the reservoir was reaching the top of the dam around midnight on March 12, 1928."

"Then what?" he asked, reluctantly picking up his own laptop.

"I was just skimming some other sites about that. It was a huge concrete gravity dam, which, I think, means that the water in the reservoir was held back by the sheer weight of the thick concrete. I read something about the possibility of a landslide causing the hill next to the dam to give way. There was something wrong with the rock the dam was anchored to." Marie punched a couple more keys. "Here it is. It was called 'schist.' Apparently not a stable material for a dam."

"No schist?" he smiled, proud of himself.

"Very funny," she replied.

He glanced at the mantel clock. "I have a few more minutes on this report. Why don't you do a search to see if you find any mention of Lilly's family?"

"I started to but we don't know her parents' last name. I'm going to bed to read." She put her computer down, closed the screen, and walked over to his recliner to give him a peck on the cheek. She motioned to his glass.

"Remember, you have Rotary in the morning."

"Night, hon," he said, deflecting the admonition.

After what seemed to him a reasonable attempt to help his

councilmember with her project, he got up and went into the kitchen again. The two bourbons were doing their job. He was relaxing. A third would really mellow him out.

With Marie in bed and Dillon in his room doing homework, or, more likely, playing on his computer, he had the room to himself. He took a sip of bourbon and began doing his own Internet research on the dam disaster. He watched a video simulation of the dam break made by engineers and discovered a wealth of information on the Santa Clarita Valley Historical Society website. He watched some video interviews of octogenarians who had witnessed the flood. The worst carnage took place along a railroad siding close to the Los Angeles and Ventura County borders. Southern California Edison power company had a construction camp there, a tent city, with 150 men and their families living there for months while building a transmission line through the valley. Eighty-four people were killed when the wave hit that camp.

He sat staring at the screen following the interview of a construction camp survivor. His father, Spike, came to mind. He remembered his grandmother showing him the old family photo album. There were pictures of his grandparents, father, and aunts and uncles living in similar construction tent camps. His grandfather had worked for the state as a surveyor so the family went anywhere the work was. That could have been his ancestors in the path of the flood. He shuddered and finished his bourbon.

The piercing chime of the mantel clock activated his constant time pressure stress. He pushed it aside and typed "usa disasters" then "worst engineering disasters." Surprisingly, St. Francis made the lists.

He whizzed through summaries of some of the other engineering disasters and compared them to the St. Francis Dam. The worst on the list was the Johnstown Flood of 1889. A dam burst above the town of Johnstown, Pennsylvania releasing 4.8 billion gallons of water. The flood killed 2,209 people and was the first major test of Clara Barton's new American Red Cross. Brad noted that the website put the St. Francis Dam release at 12.5 billion gallons, over two-and-a-half times more floodwater than Johnstown.

He knew something about the other engineering-related disasters. He remembered the news coverage of the collapse of a walkway at the Hyatt Regency Hotel in Kansas City that killed 114 people in 1981.

He had seen newsreel footage from the 40s of the Tacoma Narrows Bridge, vibrating from heavy winds, in giant rhythmic spasms that eventually brought the structure down. Fortunately, the only loss of life was a Cocker Spaniel.

The St. Francis story was so much more compelling, yet mysterious. He was totally absorbed in the topic until startled by the clock chime on the quarter hour, 11:45 p.m. He closed the laptop, and trudged off to bed, determined to learn more.

*****

Six fifteen a.m. Tuesday morning came too early for Brad after being up until midnight the night before. He might have been tempted to blow off the weekly Rotary Club meeting but Scott Graves was scheduled to speak about his Green Valley Village project. He had to be there.

"Good morning, sunshine!" Marie said when he came downstairs, making a beeline to the coffee pot. "You put quite a dent in the bourbon last night."

"Yeah, I stayed up a little too late reading about the dam disaster," he said, shifting the conversation away from his hangover and a potential "I told you so." He made a show of looking at his watch. "I need to get going." He gulped down the rest of his coffee and took his cup to the sink.

As he put on his sport coat he said, "You know, what really kills me, besides the fact that I had never heard of this, is how fast the dam was done. Mulholland personally selected the site and his staff designed the dam and began construction with no outside oversight from any other government agency. The entire project was completed a year-and-a-half later. Hell, the process would take twenty years now before you put a shovel in the dirt. That was definitely the golden age for city managers and engineers."

"Hmmm," she said.

"I told Dillon's class about the first city manager, an engineer named Ashburner, who said, 'By God, I go into a town to build!' That guy would have hated managing today. It was so much easier to build things back then." He shook his head, grabbed his keys, kissed Marie on the cheek, and turned toward the garage.

"Maybe so," Marie called after him, "but I'll bet Lilly wished it hadn't been *that* easy back then."

5

He rolled through two neighborhood stop signs trying to get to the Red Barn restaurant before the 7:30 a.m. start of Rotary. He imagined a headline resulting from his haste, "City Manager Cited for Reckless Driving," and slowed down. City managers have been fired for lesser offenses than a moving violation.

Brad was proud to be a Rotarian for all the good the club did internationally and locally. He exchanged "good mornings" with many of his club friends as he moved through the receiving line to pick up his badge, pay for his meal, and fill his plate. He willed himself to pass up the fried potatoes but went extra heavy on the scrambled eggs and bacon; a questionable diet trade-off. The bacon smelled so good. He stopped at the coffee urn and stared at the pastry tray as he filled his cup. Screw it. He opted to take just one bear claw, started to walk away, then turned to grab a small cheese Danish. After all, it was small and cheese was protein.

He walked slowly toward the main room, perusing the framed old photos of riders on horseback lining the walls. He liked bringing guests here and telling the history depicted in the black and white photos. The Rancheros Visatadores social club goes back to 1930. Seven hundred prominent people from all over the USA converge on the Santa Ynez Valley every year for a sixty-mile horseback ride to honor the Old West and raise money for charity along the way. Clark Gable and Ronald Reagan participated. Walt Disney rode his horse, Minnie. The ride lasts a week with campfire cook-outs and partying along the way and ends with a parade to Mission Santa Ines for a blessing. It was part of the local color Brad always enjoyed learning when he arrived in a new city. Knowing that dignitaries from all over chose his adopted city for this celebration was another source of pride and reason for retiring here.

He stood there with his plate, scanning the crowd as he always did in any social gathering where there were community movers and shakers. He spotted the mayor and two councilmembers, noting who they were talking to.

"Morning, Brad."

Brad flinched and turned. Behind him stood Scott Graves, the Green Valley Village developer, without a plate. He glanced at his own impressive mound of food and sucked in his belly. "Welcome to Rotary, Scott. Not eating?"

"Have to work the room a little first."

He saw Scott glance at his full plate and felt a wave of shame. "These are good people. They won't ruin your appetite."

"Yeah, maybe someday when I'm settled like you, I'll join Rotary, too."

He sucked his gut in a little tighter. "I'd offer to sponsor you to our club but I know the mayor would want that honor."

The developer nodded his head quickly in the direction of a small group to their left. "The opportunity to meet more often with Hank Nettler? I'm all in!"

"You think Hank is tough, you should meet his teenage daughter. The cute little girl tried to castrate me in her government class yesterday."

"I can imagine," Scott said. "Did I ever tell you about what it was like to negotiate with Hubie and the boys? It was quite a career experience."

Brad saw the coast was clear. "Tell me."

"Hubie always wanted our meetings to take place at his house with Hank and Hal there. I'd sit on one side of their huge oak dining room table. Hubie, the boys, and their attorney, a frothing bull, all sat on the other side, snarling."

Brad shook his head. "Doesn't sound like western hospitality. I guess Hubie never watched *Bonanza*."

"Nope," Scott laughed. "They really kept me off balance. Hank and their attorney did most of the talking, but Hank was always looking over at his father. Hubie mostly leaned back in his chair, scowling, with his hands crossed behind his head and eyes closed. It was like he wasn't interested at all but he was tracking every word."

"I'll bet," Brad said. "I'm surprised Hubie ever agreed to sell. The Nettlers have a reputation for always trying to buy more land, never sell."

"Tell you the truth, I was never sure we'd make a deal either. Hank and the attorney and I would go back and forth and make some progress. A few times, when it looked like we had a deal point decided, Hubie would open his eyes, lean forward and say something like, 'bullshit, Hank, here's how we're going to do it.' He'd completely undercut his son and the attorney. I actually felt sorry for Hank."

Brad wasn't convinced. "Maybe that was just their negotiating strategy."

"Maybe. It sure was frustrating. And it was the most convoluted option I've ever done. A whole schedule of milestones we were required to achieve by deadlines and hard money deposits with each one. They gave me the impression that they really didn't want to sell their land, but, if we were interested, we had to jump through a bunch of hoops. We're already in the deal pretty deep with all the progress payments we've made."

"How did you ever get it done?" Brad asked.

Scott smirked. "After our fourth half-day meeting, and, after Hubie reneged on a previous deal point I had with Hank, I left in a huff. Hank called me the next day to see about another meeting. I bitched about the way Hubie was undercutting the negotiations. I told him my boss, you've met Jeff Simpson, was ready to throw in the towel. And he was. We agreed to have one more 'make or break' meeting, but this time it would be Hubie and Jeff leading things."

"I've met Jeff. He comes on like a Sherman tank. Must have been an epic face-off."

"It was. Hubie met us at his front door and right off the bat, it was like two boxers sizing each other up. Hubie's entry hall walls are lined with heads of deer, wild boars, mountain lions, and other game he and the boys killed and stuffed. As we walked toward the dining room, Hubie points to the animal heads and says to Jeff, 'If we don't get this deal done today, there's a spot up there reserved for you.'"

"Wow! What did Jeff do?"

"He told Hubie to go fuck himself and turned to leave. Hubie gave him a big slap on the back, let out a belly laugh and said, 'now here's a son-of-a-bitch I can make a deal with.'"

"I can picture it."

"Jeff and Hubie cussed their way through the final points of the agreement until they both finally stood up and shook hands on the basic points. They went off to drink Tequila while Hank and the attorney and I worked on the final language. By the time we were done, both of them were smashed and arguing over recipes for tri-tip rub."

"City boy Jeff arguing with a cattle man on barbeque?"

"Hey, he held his own. Jeff said he'd send him a bottle of his rub and Hubie promised to try it. Hank grilled steaks for everyone and we were there most of the night eating, drinking, playing poker, and smoking cigars."

Brad laughed. "I'd love to have the Norman Rockwell painting of that scene. The Nettlers can be the best of the good ol' boys. Unless you cross them."

"So, don't cross them, Brad. Gimme a building permit and nobody gets hurt."

"Sure, Megan will have it at the counter waiting for you."

Mayor Murray walked up to them with Vice Mayor Tim Mullikin in tow. "There's the man of the hour. Welcome, Scott," the mayor said extending his hand.

"Good to see you, Scott," Mullikin echoed. In fact, Mullikin was known to echo most of what the mayor said. He was a retired sergeant from the Santa Barbara Sheriff's Department and used to patrol the Santa Ynez area. Mullikin lacked the mayor's political skill but he had lived in the community all his life and had stories about many of the people in the room. His discretion about the tales from his law enforcement career made him a popular person in the club as well.

"Come on, Scott," the mayor said, "let me introduce you to a few people." He grabbed the developer's arm and led him off with the vice mayor on their coattails.

Brad stood there a few moments longer watching Scott work the room. He easily moved around glad-handing all the people he knew and introducing himself to new friends. Scott was good at this sort of thing. Brad saw himself as the type who blended into the background at social gatherings.

Scott looked like one of those suit models in the Nordstrom ads. He was in his early forties, just over six feet tall, trim, thick blond hair with a little gray peeking through at the temples, clear blue eyes, big smile with perfect teeth, and an air of confidence. Brad noted that Scott had on his business casual uniform for this occasion. No sport coat or tie, but a well-fitted plaid dress shirt and slacks. He must have been shooting for the "I'm-successful-but-still-one-of-you" look.

Brad spotted the third councilmember in the club, Al Landon, sitting at a table at the other side of the room. He made his way over. "Can I join you, Al?"

"Please do, Brad," the councilman said, gesturing to the chair next to him. "I saw you talking to Scott over there before the mayor whisked him away. Everything going OK with Green Valley?"

Brad was preparing to answer the question when the mayor, vice mayor, and Scott Graves approached the table.

"Al, say hi to Scott," the mayor ordered.

"Welcome, Scott," the councilman said. "Looking forward to your program." They shook hands. In contrast to the mayor and vice mayor, Al Landon held his cards close. He was cordial enough to Scott Graves but Brad noticed the councilman remained seated until the trio moved to the next table.

"To answer your question, Al, yes, the project is moving along." He waited expectantly.

"Hmmm," was all the councilman said.

Brad exhaled and slumped slightly. Councilman Landon was too tough to read. He could count on Mayor Buddy Murray and Vice

Mayor Tim Mullikin to take the pro-business, pro-growth perspective on local issues. Councilwomen Kay Nance and, to a lesser extent, Gretchen Schmitz had a left-leaning bent. More correctly, Schmitz leaned, Kay Nance fell over. This often put Landon in the powerful position of being the third, majority, vote. And that was Brad's problem. You never knew which way Landon would go until the vote was taken. He seemed to delight in being inscrutable. To his detractors, Landon was mercurial and wishy-washy. To his supporters, he was thoughtfully independent.

Brad had sought out the councilman this morning specifically because of the program on Green Valley. It would help him to navigate the troubled waters if he had a stronger feeling about the pivot councilman's thoughts. He had to try again. He nodded toward the head table and snickered, "Looks like the mayor isn't going to let Scott sit down and eat."

Al Landon shook his head and leaned in. "Buddy wears his positions on his sleeve. I can see a lot of benefits from the project, too. But I can give you a lot more bargaining power if Scott doesn't think he's got enough votes already lined up."

Brad felt a jolt of excitement. While it wasn't a manifesto, it was the clearest indication he'd had that Landon might be a Green Valley supporter.

"Gents?" said Hank Nettler, as he pulled out the chair across from Brad and Councilman Landon. "Hand me a program, would you, Al?" he added with a voice as rough as his big, calloused, cracked hands.

"Morning, Hank," said other members at the table in unison, more out of protocol than sincerity.

"I forgot Scott was the program today," Hank said, tucking his napkin into the collar of his flannel shirt. "You got the votes all lined up for Green Valley, Brad?" Hank asked, scooping up a mouthful of potatoes.

Brad blanched. What a stupid question to ask right in front of Councilman Landon. "Well, Al can certainly speak for himself. But the answer to your question is 'no.' It's actually illegal for me to poll the councilmembers or try to work a majority on something that has to be decided in public."

"And I suppose you never do that, right? How do you know what to recommend then?" teased Hank.

Brad squirmed. Hank had blundered into one of his core challenges, his obligation to carry out the policy wishes of a majority of the elected officials while also being responsible for conducting municipal operations based on sound management practices. Politics and management can be strange bedfellows. That's why, for many years, the logo of the International City/ County Management Association reflected this dichotomy, a square peg in a round hole.

Maybe in Charles Ashburner's day, the city manager was expected to call them like he saw them, politics be damned. Maybe. Nowadays, a successful city manager has to show political savvy to survive. It's made even more difficult by so-called "sunshine laws" which limit interaction among city elected and appointed officials outside of public forums. Brad supported the concept of the public's right to know. But it's tricky to divine the Council majority's will when they meet only twice a month and there are other limitations on bringing matters to the Council for discussion.

"Well, Hank," Brad said with a wink, "like I said, there are laws about this. My official answer to your question is that a city manager has to learn to read the tea leaves."

"That's a bullshit answer, Brad," Hank snapped in his raspy, bass voice. "You can't tell me you make all of your decisions or recommendations in a vacuum." Hank looked at Al Landon. "He's got to be talking to all of you all the time outside Council meetings, right, Al?"

Brad jumped in. "Sure, we can talk outside the meetings, and we do. But I can't legally try to build a consensus position. Like I said, you learn how to read the tea leaves and when you can go hard on something and when to back off." He tried to change the subject. "My wife says I drive the same way; constantly alternating between the accelerator and brake. She calls it 'city manager foot.' I argued with her about it until I rode with another manager and got car sick from his driving."

That elicited some chuckles from most of the breakfast mates. Hank brushed them off, pressing his point. "What a horrible way to run an operation. We'd go bankrupt in the family businesses if we had to operate with those kinds of rules."

Brad thought of the badgering he'd taken from Hank's daughter. "It's not that bad," he argued. "You get your cues on what the Council majority wants based on how they dealt with similar issues in the past. If it's a totally new issue, I make a recommendation based on what I think is best for the city. Sometimes the majority disagrees. Then my job is to do it their way, unless what they want me to do is illegal or unethical."

"Then what?" Hank wouldn't let it go.

"I either make a stand or try again to talk them out of it. Or I could resign. It's happened to friends of mine," Brad continued, "but I've never been put into the position of being told to do something I couldn't live with. I've always been able to argue for a better way."

Hank pointed his fork at Brad. "Or, you just went along because you know where your bread is buttered, right? So, what do your tea leaves tell you the Council will decide on Green Valley?"

"You tell me, Hank," Brad grumbled. "I'm not allowed to poll them, remember?"

Hank looked confidently at Landon. "I'll do your job for you, Brad. We think the majority are smart enough to see Green Valley is good for Santa Ynez. Of course, we'll never get the bitch, but we have a shot at Schmitz."

Brad smiled and said, "I know you are referring to Councilwoman Schmitz, but I have no idea who the other reference applies to."

"Keep lickin' them boots, Brad. I'd hate to have your job. I'd probably punch somebody out on the first day."

"Yeah," Brad replied, "I get that a lot." He tried again to change the subject. "This bacon is awesome. Is the Red Barn still buying your family's meat?"

"Yup," Hank said proudly. "We supply most of the restaurants in the area. A lot of Rotarians are in our meat club. It's a lot fresher and tastier than the crap you get at the store, and cheaper, too, when you buy in bulk. Why don't I set aside some steaks, roasts and ribs for your family to try?"

He noticed that other members at the table were listening in. He wasn't sure if Hank was offering him a gift or looking for business. He punted. "Thanks anyway, Hank. I'm thinking of going vegan." He took another big bite of bacon and grinned.

"You're missing out. Our family has been in the beef business for generations. Whether or not this Green Valley project goes, we'll stay in it. In fact, we're planning to expand into dairy, also."

"Well, good luck, Hank." Brad said, looking away.

"It's not a matter of luck," Hank persisted. "We'll get the votes for Green Valley. It's your job to get the paperwork done fast. SoCal has some milestones to hit. But don't worry, Brad, we have some ideas for helping you get that done, too." Hank Nettler shoved a whole piece of bacon in his mouth and smiled mysteriously.

Brad picked up the weekly club bulletin, feigning disinterest in whatever scheme Hank may be hatching. Fortunately, the club president, Lynn Waslohn, rang the bell to begin the meeting.

Brad paid no attention to President Waslohn's announcements as he mulled the conversation with Hank. Was he right about three, or even four, votes for the project? What was he cooking up?

He stole a glance at Councilman Landon. Brad liked him, despite his peccadillos. Landon was the senior minister of a medium-sized Protestant church in the nearby city of Buellton. Landon was well-educated, thoughtful, and moderately attentive to his Council role. His day job made him the leader of his organization, which Brad expected would make him more of a supporter on the organizational issues Brad faced. But he was often disappointed in that regard. Landon, like everyone else, looked at things through the filter of his own experience. The minister's organization was small, collegial with loose policies, and dependent upon volunteerism. Brad's was larger, procedurally based, more legalistic, and authoritarian. The problem for Brad was that Landon often thought that his experience as the CEO of his organization made him an expert on Brad's. He could feel himself getting annoyed as he thought about the times when the minister tried to tell him how the city should be managed.

The President finished her announcements, gave another pitch to everyone to invite new people to the club, then turned it over to the finemaster, Terry Comerford, a dentist and legendary extractor. The fining or "recognition" period was usually a highlight of the meeting if the finemaster was decently prepared and witty. Members were fined for all manner of trumped up offenses. It didn't matter. There was no escape. Comerford nailed a female florist for $10 for having her name in the paper. Then he fined a chiropractor on a rumor that he'd been spotted in a new car. The finemaster bumped it to $20 when the doctor was forced to reveal that it was a luxury import.

"Brad Jacks," the finemaster announced as his next victim. Brad was easy game. He stood up grudgingly.

"Brad, I know I just fined you last week. But then your city does something truly stupid. In accordance with the Four-Way Test, it wouldn't be 'Fair To All Concerned' to let you off the hook." He held up a piece of paper. "I have here my city water and sewer bill. Just came in yesterday's mail."

Brad knew where this was going. He was embarrassed already.

"Now Brad, I know you do things a little different in government. And I appreciate that you include a return envelope with the water bill. But wouldn't it be a good idea to have the return address part of the bill that you send back actually line up with the little window?" The finemaster put the detachable portion of the bill into the return envelope to demonstrate that the city's return address was halfway outside the clear window.

The room exploded in hoots and claps. Many people must have already discovered the colossal screw-up. Brad was busted but not going down meekly.

"Well, Terry, we contracted for a new print shop and got a heckuva deal from the low bidder, a local business by the way. It was an add alternate to have the full return address appear in the window. We passed. Always looking to save you taxpayers some money, you know."

More laughs.

Comerford played along, "You aren't going to get a lot of checks delivered if the Post Office can't see where they're supposed to go. Isn't that what they call 'false economy'?"

"That's the genius of it, Terry," Brad protested. "See, if we don't get their payments, we'll shut off their water and collect penalties to turn it back on. We'll make a killing!"

The room erupted in boo's. "Twenty bucks!" the finemaster ordered. Brad took it in stride. It was fun to joke around with these friends.

At 8 a.m. sharp, the club's program chair went to the podium to introduce Scott Graves, reading what had obviously been prepared by

SoCal Communities. The bio mentioned Scott's degree from USC in business and his experience building high quality living environments around Southern California. It covered his charitable activities and closed with a short statement on the Green Valley Village project that was being reviewed by the City of Santa Ynez.

Scott Graves approached the podium to hearty applause. "Thank you for the nice introduction. It's almost like I wrote it myself." A courtesy laugh. The members had heard that one before.

"I'm happy to be here this morning and I want to tell you how excited we are to be working on such a great project with your outstanding mayor, City Council, and city manager. I can assure you our company's interests line up a whole lot better for this community than Brad's envelopes." Real laughs this time. Brad gave Scott a little salute.

The developer went on to tell everyone how much he loved Santa Ynez and how it reminded him of his hometown outside Austin, Texas. Score. Most people are proud of where they live and happy to hear an outsider envy them for living there. The object was to not seem like an outsider. Brad imagined Scott pitching his Santa Maria project a half hour away; a community dubbed by Sunset Magazine as "The West's Best BBQ Town." He'd probably be talking about his boss's beef rub by now. Once again, Brad acknowledged that Scott was a capable representative for his project.

Scott spent twenty minutes walking everyone through a PowerPoint presentation showing the lay-out of the Green Valley Village project, attractive renderings of the streetscapes and buildings, and the amenities. The last slides had deal points from the draft DA that proved Green Valley would be a valuable partner for Santa Ynez.

"We have received a warm welcome from *most* of the members of the City Council and city staff." Scott added with a smirk. There were some more chuckles and whispered conversations about who would not have been included in that comment. Most knew.

Brad looked to his right at Al Landon who was smiling and nodding, then to his left to see the mayor and vice mayor who seemed to be sitting up straighter, hoping eyes were upon them.

"But I can assure you," Scott continued, "that just because they are friendly, they aren't pushovers. They are representing the public interest very competently. There are times I leave City Hall feeling like Jack, from *Sideways.* You remember the scene when his new girlfriend beats the stuffing out of him with his motorcycle helmet?"

More laughs. Hank, seated next to him, leaned over and said a little too loudly, "I hate hearing that, Brad."

Brad nodded, keeping his eyes on the speaker.

After his presentation, Scott opened himself for questions from the audience. What would the houses sell for? Who's designing the golf course? When would they start construction? Brad recognized some of the questions as "softballs," lobbed to Scott from members who could be expected to support the growth or from representatives of organizations that had, or were destined to, receive donations from SoCal. There were also a couple of questions that were delivered politely in deference to Scott's status as a guest of the club, but which also evinced the questioners' problems with the project. Where was all the water going to come from? Why build such a big project in a small town like Santa Ynez? We like it the way it is.

Scott handled all of the questions adroitly. He cited statistics about projected growth statewide, in Southern California and in the region. He then covered a few facts about the aging of the Baby Boomer generation, the market demand for adult-oriented communities, and how desirable the senior residents of Green Valley will be in terms of their sizable net worth, positive impact on the local economy, and the value they would add to all sorts of worthwhile community activities.

Brad noticed President Waslohn get up and move toward the podium. Scott was about to get the hook. Mayor Buddy also noticed it and rose to his feet hastily. "I'd like to add something."

"Make it quick, Buddy." The president told him. "Time to adjourn," she added. The mayor was a big shot in the community but merely another member in this setting.

"I just wanted to pick up on Scott's last point. I've got other mayors and councilmembers jealous because we are getting this project. SoCal is known as a builder of high quality developments. Other cities in the area have given them tours and offered incentives if they would build something like Green Valley Village in their towns. SoCal isn't asking us for anything special. In fact, the Development Agreement Brad and his staff are negotiating with Scott has them giving the community all sorts of extra benefits we wouldn't ordinarily get from a new development. We are lucky to have Scott and Green Valley here. I think I speak for the Council majority saying we should expedite the approval process."

"You bet," blurted Vice Mayor Mullikin.

Brad glanced at Councilman Landon who merely smiled and raised his coffee cup to his mouth. Inscrutable to the end.

The mayor, vice mayor, and Scott stayed behind after the meeting was over to talk with the half dozen Rotarians lined up to shake hands and wish Scott the best in getting the project approved. Members introduced themselves and exchanged cards in hopes of drumming up some business for themselves or a donation. Brad joined the line.

"Good job, Scott and Mr. Mayor."

"You heard what the mayor said, Brad," Hank Nettler barked hoarsely, walking over. "Don't let Megan Cain't chase this project away."

"He won't," Mayor Buddy assured the small group. "Brad

will take care of city staff. We need to make sure we have Landon committed, then we can nail down Schmitz."

Brad was uncomfortable being included in the strategizing. "I have to get back to the office," he said lamely. "We're meeting with the water bill printer to see if they want to take over paramedic services, too."

Everyone laughed. Except Hank.

6

Back in the office at about 8:45 a.m., Brad returned
some phone calls and dictated a short letter and two memos for Jane to
put in final form. He was grateful that Jane knew shorthand, a dying
skill. He gathered up the stack of papers he needed for the staff meeting
at 9:30 and walked the short distance to the main conference room
down the hall. This was a standing weekly meeting with his department
heads to exchange information and, because of the scheduled Council
meeting next week, go over the agenda for the meeting and discuss
revisions to the draft reports that had been sent in so far.

He looked forward to staff meetings even though he had to be
"on." He had to diligently track the substance of the discussion to give
appropriate direction, while also being attentive to any signs of conflict
within the group; either directed at him or to another department
head. Resolving problems with inter-personal relations wasn't his
favorite task. Like Ashburner, and likely Mulholland, he would much

rather spend his energy getting things built. New parks, streets, stores, and restaurants added to the citizens' quality of life. They also helped his bosses get re-elected and bookmarked his career. He always enjoyed driving through cities he had once worked for and seeing projects he had contributed to building. Every one of them held a story. Driving by, twenty-five years later, evoked memories of perseverance, triumph, and celebrations. Few other jobs offered such an enduring legacy.

During the staff meeting, he paid special attention to Megan and Dee. Thankfully, they behaved cordially and kept their differing opinions about the Green Valley project to themselves; probably waiting for their upcoming meeting with him. He hadn't even thought about that meeting since they scheduled it. He'd have to wing it.

Megan and Dee were already in his office when he arrived after the staff meeting. They sat stiffly, mutely across from each other at his coffee table. The tension hung like accumulated adolescent body odor in an old locker room. He walked across the room trying not to let the feeling stick to him. Brad put his materials from the staff meeting on his desk and sat between the department heads in his normal chair.

"Thanks for coming in," he began. "Megan spoke with me yesterday about some concerns she has about Public Works' reports related to the Green Valley Initial Study. I think she's especially concerned about water impacts. I wanted us all to get together to discuss the concerns."

Brad looked between the two of them and noted the tension rise a bit. He should have taken the time to practice the opening comment. He had already used the word "concern" three times, thinking it helped to minimize the degree of conflict. However, overusing it, as he had, made it seem more like the attempted manipulation that it was. He had deliberately glossed over the full breadth of Megan's attack yesterday on Dee's competence and ethics.

"Now, it's Megan's job to coordinate the EIR," he continued. "Public Works is an important contributor to that study. I value you both and want us to all be on the same page." That was as touchy-feely as he was going to go. The only way to stop the infighting would be to get into the substance of the disagreement.

"I'll start with a basic question about the Initial Study," Brad began. "I know it's based on SoCal's detailed application and some further studies that were mostly done in Dee's shop. Megan's staff is going to send it out to other government agencies for their comments about likely environmental impacts and potential mitigation measures."

He looked between the two of them. Both stared at him with the controlled intensity reserved for those moments when a person's anger was near boiling. He continued.

"But I thought the main purpose of the Initial Study was to give agencies and the public the chance to comment on the city's proposed environmental assessment and see if a full EIR is needed. Since we already concluded that SoCal will need to do a full EIR, why circulate an Initial Study at all? Why not just launch the EIR?"

"We *could* skip the IS step, you're right, Brad," Megan said, with measured pleasantness. "But it's good insurance to go ahead with it. It puts the other regulatory agencies on notice that they need to pay attention. If they have some killer issue they think needs to be studied, they can let us know up-front so we can get it resolved with them rather than raising it after they get the Notice of Preparation."

"Gotcha," Brad said, going for casual. "So we want a thorough and accurate IS to make sure the EIR covers everything it should." He knew he was stating the obvious.

"Yes," Megan said, sounding bored.

"Of course," Dee added impatiently.

"Good. We're all on the same page," Brad said in a chipper voice, a futile attempt to create momentum. "I want to give you each the opportunity to express any concerns you have about water, traffic, or anything else with the Green Valley study." Damn! There's that word again.

"*I* don't have any concerns," Dee said abruptly. "We've done our review and sent our reports over to Planning. I don't know what *her* problem is. She didn't bring it to me first."

The engineers in Public Works tended to look down their noses at their closely-related colleagues in Planning. Engineers lived in an objective world of math, physics, and computer models. In their view, planners haunted the back alleys of aesthetics and political policy. Brad was used to dealing with the professional differences and was only hoping to keep it from becoming personal. He hated when that happened. It was like fighting within the family. Dee's opening jab at Megan was a bad start.

Brad looked over at Megan. She was sitting straight, her fingers tightly laced in her lap. She was actually restraining herself quite well. Dee was the unprofessional one in this round.

"OK, we are going to keep this professional. I'm OK with the reality that sometimes department heads will have different opinions on things. That's OK. But I want the disagreement to be on the facts, not personal. OK?"

He winced, but saw that his point made it through the "okay" redundancy. Dee shrunk back a little from the scolding, and Megan held back from a counter-offensive.

"Megan, why don't you start out by explaining your concerns?" Damn. Sometimes Brad even bored himself when he became aware of using the same words or phrases all of the time. The image of Scott Graves' smoothness popped into his mind. He frowned, knowing he could never measure up.

Megan shuffled her papers and began. "I'll start with traffic. You probably know that cities plan their street networks based on current and projected peak morning and evening trips. Public Works does traffic counts for existing conditions and uses manuals provided by national professional organizations to project peak trips for different land use categories that may build out in the future, like retail, office, or residential."

"Yes, what LOS does our General Plan call for?" Brad asked Megan smugly.

"Oh, good, so you understand about the Levels of Service. As is common for smaller suburban communities, Santa Ynez sets LOS 'C' as our policy standard. Traffic would be expected to flow fairly freely most of the day, but in peak commute times the motorist may have to wait for a traffic signal to cycle once or twice to get through an intersection."

"LOS C, got it," Brad said. "What's the existing and 'with project' LOS for the study intersections around Green Valley?"

Megan smiled. "I can see you've been through this before. The Public Works' model shows it will stay at Level C with a few mitigation projects required of Green Valley, like minor intersection widening and lane striping."

"All right," Brad said. "Where's the issue?"

She walked them through several tables and exhibits before summarizing. "In the new report, the existing counts and base General Plan build-out projections, without Green Valley, don't tie with the prior reports. The trip counts are much lower in the new report without any explanation."

"Thank you, Megan," Brad said. "Dee, can you comment on Megan's concerns?"

The public works director leaned back in his chair, folded his hands on his stomach, and let out a huge sigh as if having to once again correct a petulant teenager. Brad braced himself for something ugly to come out of Dee's mouth. Then Dee seemed to resolve some internal conflict and relaxed visibly.

"No big thing," he said. "Had she asked me, I could have told her that there is a new manual out now. ITE publishes updates regularly and can use different assumptions."

"ITE?" Brad asked.

"Oh, that's the Institute of Transportation Engineering. ITE is the neutral professional body that traffic engineers rely on for objective information on engineering factors like trips and parking factors for all sorts of land uses, intersection queuing, and LOS."

"Right," Brad remembered. "You think the new ITE manual accounts for the differences Megan is concerned about?"

Dee Sharma looked confident. "Most likely. SoCal's engineers did the report and I can't cite all the differences off the top of my head between the factors they used and what *she* is pointing at. If I'd known that was an issue, I could have easily been prepared to discuss it today."

"I see, makes sense," Brad said, glancing at Megan who looked somewhat deflated.

Dee wasn't finished. "We also got that grant last year to update all the traffic counts along Highway 246 and several adjacent intersections. We used the data to calibrate the computer model and do some signal optimization. And I can think of two street projects that have been done since those earlier studies so we have more room for additional traffic than we had before. So, I'm not surprised if the current studies actually show better LOS than the prior ones *she* cited despite our growth since then. We are always trying to do things to improve service levels. *We* don't just sit back nitpicking.

Brad tensed. Megan leaned forward, her unspoken tone unmistakable. She started to poke first at one argument, then the next, pointing at pages and arguing numbers. Brad let them talk it out, only occasionally inserting a comment. Dee responded to each question with ample details but a little too much smugness. Finally, she sat back, apparently having nothing further to argue about.

Brad felt emerging relief. If Megan capitulated on her traffic arguments, he wouldn't have to read the cryptic reports and try to make sense of them. The computer model used complicated formulas that might as well have been written in Sanskrit. He didn't understand logarithms when he was sixteen and he wasn't about to try forty years later.

"Thanks for those clarifications, Dee. That's very helpful," he said, turning to Megan. "Did you have any other concerns you wanted to talk about?" Oops.

He saw her quickly come back to life, ready to do battle anew. She pushed aside her stack of traffic-related reports and picked up two others from the table. One was entitled "Green Valley Village Water Supply Assessment Report – DRAFT," authored by Western Planning Consultants.

"I'll take another look at the traffic numbers myself," she said. "But my bigger issue is water." Looking at Brad, not Dee, she continued. "This is a report required by state law to ensure that water and land use planning are integrated. It will be cited in the EIR and submitted to LAFCo with the annexation application."

Brad slumped at the mention of the countywide planning agency.

"Take a look at these tables," Megan said, flipping to paper-clipped pages in the report. "They're from the Water section of our Municipal Services Review report adopted by LAFCo four years ago."

Brad exhaled deeply, leaned forward, and squinted trying to see the small print. Dee sat back looking bored, not bothering to look.

"As you can see," she said directly to Brad extending the page closer to him, "the tables in this four-year-old report show a factor for average residential demand for potable water of 160 gallons per person per day." She paused to pick up another report from the table and flipped to a clipped page. "Dee's report used a lower average of 132 gallons per day for Green Valley residential. Why?"

Brad saw the numbers she cited and turned to his public works director. "Can you speak to that issue, Dee?"

Dee Sharma motioned to Megan to hand him the two reports. He looked at them impassively for a couple of minutes when a look of recognition came to his face. "I remember now," he said. "The MSR used a citywide average for all residential units. Newer houses use less water than the older ones because of the conservation measures we've put into our standard specs. Green Valley will be required to install high efficiency dishwashers and washing machines and low-flow showerheads and toilets that will bring down usage way below the citywide average. Plus, we now have limits on lawns, which is where much of the residential water use goes. And, by the way, Megan, it wasn't *my* report. The estimated water demand was worked out between SoCal's engineers and our consultant."

Megan nodded. Brad thought her expression was more, "I hear you, but will check it out for myself." She moved on to her next point.

"And where did you get the golf course demand?" she asked. "Two acre-feet per acre per year seems way too low for a nice golf course. Our studies used a higher factor even for a city park."

"Again, *I* didn't come up with that factor, the consultant did," Dee snapped. He uncrossed his legs and threw the reports on the table in Megan's direction.

She continued. "Well, the planning standard I've seen for a golf course in our climate zone is more like 3 acre-feet per acre, per year."

"Help me out, how big a difference are you arguing about, Megan?" Brad asked, trying to mediate.

"Well, an acre foot of water is about 326,000 gallons, the amount of water required to cover an acre of land to one-foot depth. The difference I'm talking about is a hundred acre-feet which would amount to nearly thirty-three million gallons of water a year. It's a big difference, Brad, considering our limited supply."

"Oh," Brad shrugged with disappointment. This wasn't a trifling issue.

"And I'm not sure I agree with your conversion of peak demand to annual acre-feet, Dee," Megan added. "You are assuming that maximum daily demand is only double the average demand. That may be OK where you come from. But it doesn't work here."

Dee bolted up in his chair. "What do you mean by 'where you come from?' You think I used Bangladesh factors or something? My last job was in Monterey!"

"I know that," Megan said hastily. "I just meant that our climate is warmer than Monterey. People use more landscape water year around and a lot more during hot spells. There will be more variance between the max and average demand here which needs to be planned when sizing water facilities for the project. I understand that there are already times in the year when our storage runs too low. I'm worried that we should be requiring more from the project in the way of pipe and pump sizing and storage to cover ourselves for higher peak demand."

Dee bristled. "I thought you were the planning director. You want to be public works director, too? Why don't you worry about signs and flowers and let me take care of streets and water?"

"OK, OK," Brad jumped in. "Everybody simmer down. Let's keep this on the facts, not personal."

"Here's a fact," Dee seethed. "We are requiring the project to build a storage tank to handle peak demand. It was sized by their consultant and approved by Western. We have also upsized some old mains this past year and beefed up two pumps to fill our tanks and the reservoir faster. It's not a problem."

"God, yes," Brad intervened, trying to lighten the tone. "We can't forget about the water tank. That almost cost me one of my lives." He remembered his failed attempts to purchase a water tank site from the Nettlers when he first came to town. The saga included Hubie's citizen's arrest of two city staffers for trespassing. The Council majority refused the staff recommendation to pursue an eminent domain action against the Nettlers to acquire the site. Hubie knew that and upped his demands so high, Brad abandoned the effort. Some residents continued to live with low pressure ever since. He thought of how quickly William Mulholland built a 230-mile aqueduct and huge reservoirs in comparison. Oh, to have managed in Mulholland's era!

Dee exhaled loudly. "Yes, the tank is important, but back to the golf course demand. Again, I didn't come up with that, Western's engineers did. From what I remember, they talked to SoCal's golf course architect who told them about design techniques they'll use to reduce water demand. I think they had to do with better moisture-sensing irrigation systems, chemicals to reduce grass growth, and larger unirrigated native areas." Dee glared at Megan. "Western is in a better position to decide what's reasonable." He thankfully left off the "than you." "Why don't you talk to them yourself?"

"I guess I'll have to, since you don't seem willing to dig too deeply yourself," she retorted.

Brad squirmed in his chair, searching for something to deescalate the building tension. "Ought to be easy enough to get more information on those issues, right Dee?"

"Yeah, Western has been our water and wastewater consultants for years. They've done a good job for us. I'm sure they can help Megan understand this." Dee smirked again.

Megan didn't miss the dig. "It's not about educating me," she said sharply. "It's about having solid, objective information. I've heard that SoCal uses Western on other projects. True?"

Dee bristled again. "It's a big firm. I'm sure they do work for developers all over the area. But the point is they aren't working for SoCal on this project. They are working for us."

"Well," Megan continued, "I question how neutral and objective they are being with this report."

"That's a cheap shot," Dee barked.

Megan reached over to pick up one of the reports from the table, right in front of the public works director. "Look at this table. It has our groundwater reliability at 100 percent and reservoir at 90. Shouldn't we be using a lower percentage for a multi-year drought since the groundwater table and reservoir will be dropping? It sure seems like somebody is overstating the available supply and understating the Green Valley demand."

Dee Sharma was now clearly pissed off. He had been educated in the top engineering school in India. He got embarrassed and angry when his colleagues in the USA made jokes about the ability of Indian engineers to apply their book learning to real world situations. It didn't take much for Dee to get hot if he felt his competence was being questioned. Megan was questioning his ethics, too. The debate continued to get hotter as the two department heads argued about the water demand factors used in the report, the reliability of the water supply itself, and the objectivity of the consulting engineer Dee hired to prepare the report. The whole time Brad racked his brain for a resolution of the conflict.

He looked at his watch. "We've been at this for over an hour. I can see how there could be some professional differences of opinion on these study factors." He looked at Megan. "Based on Dee's responses, the traffic reports seem OK. But it sounds like Megan has some legitimate concerns on the water side." They both remained stony in their silence. "Since that is going to be a big issue, we need to make sure we have it right. So, Dee, why don't you hire another consultant to do a peer review of Western's report?"

Dee Sharma's eyebrows shot up. "It's a waste of money, Brad."

The city manager cut him off, trying to lighten things. "No, paying the guy to wipe down your already-clean clubs at the end of a golf round is a waste of money." No reaction from either combatant.

Dee looked agitated. "Western has done our water planning for years. It's a good company. They'll be offended if we bring in somebody now to check their work. They have all our modeling on their proprietary software. It's going to be a big setback if they quit and we have to start over with somebody else."

Brad considered that for a moment and said, "SoCal would pay, not us. They should want to be sure that we have bulletproof data since they will be taking fire. It's that 'abundance of caution thing.' And Western shouldn't be offended. Peer review is common in their business. I'll bet you the doughnut I wish I had right now, that Western has done peer review of other engineering companies themselves."

Megan chimed in. "How do we know another firm Dee hires is going to be any better? They all have a pro-growth bias. They aren't going to make it tough on SoCal. And there's that whole 'professional courtesy' issue. They aren't going to be hard on Western, either."

Brad started wagging his foot. The conversation was going nowhere. He pounded the sides of his chair with his fist. "Look, you know how I feel about department heads dumping their monkeys on me. We're not doing that, anymore." It felt good to vent a little.

"The two of you don't seem to be able to resolve these issues yourselves. All I'm hearing are gotcha's from both of you, not teamwork. So, here's what we're going to do. Dee is going to hire a qualified, independent firm to do a peer review of Western's report. He'll handle the contract and be the liaison. Megan will be an equal participant in the selection process. I want the two of you to agree on the firm. If you can't, each of you will give me your recommendation and I'll pick one. I'd rather you two get together rather than bringing this problem back in here. My office is filling up with monkeys."

Touchy-feely time was over. If they were going to push him into authoritarian mode, when they both knew how much he hated it, he was going to go all the way with it. They talked briefly about the details of the peer review process. Brad was more directive than he'd usually be.

He tried to salvage a positive wrap-up to the meeting. "Thanks again for coming in. Like I said, I value your opinions. Peer review is the best I can come up with to resolve things. I know neither of you like it. Maybe that's what makes it a reasonable compromise."

Alone in his office, Brad took a moment to reflect on how he had handled the meeting and gave himself a B-. He spent the rest of the morning reviewing and tweaking staff memos headed to the City Council for their meeting next Tuesday night. He insisted on reviewing anything that went out to the Council or public over his signature and was not bashful about sending the same report back to the author several times, if need be, until it passed his inspection. It wasn't his favorite task but he felt more competent in this task than mediating peer conflict. Thankfully, Jane often caught mistakes and had them corrected by the offender before the drafts even got to Brad, so he could focus on content.

It was already nearing lunchtime. He was burning through a myriad of administrative tasks, feeling productive.

"Hey Brad."

He looked up from his paperwork, grateful for the distraction.

"Hello, Mr. Mayor."

Buddy Murray was easy to like. He was in his early 70's, above average height, with thick wavy gray hair parted on the side and perpetually sprinkled with dandruff. Despite being thin, he had a penchant for looking sloppy in anything he wore. The mayor was gregarious, up-beat, and had a ready smile that you sensed even over the phone. He was a Jimmy Stewart, "aw-shucks" kind of guy whose self-deprecating manner endeared him to people who didn't realize they were being played.

Buddy was the top real estate professional in town. Some of that, no doubt, was due to the business he received because of his public stature. Brad and the city attorney, Henry Fitzhenry, were constantly alerting the mayor to potential conflicts of interest if he were to vote or advocate on behalf of someone who had paid him a commission. The mayor wasn't crooked and always followed their advice to recuse himself in order to avoid a conflict charge from a political opponent, or, worse, a criminal charge.

Despite popular sentiment that most politicians are corrupt, in his long experience working with scores of councilmembers, Brad suspected only two of them of selling their votes. Mayor Buddy wasn't one of them. In fact, Brad and others suspected the mayor of being too careful about declaring a potential conflict of interest as an excuse to duck controversial votes. The mayor was happy to sit those out while claiming the ethical high ground. Mayor Buddy didn't have a hard ideology to promote. He just liked being mayor. Whether selling a home or settling a neighborhood dispute with the city government, the mayor's focus wasn't on getting his way, it was on getting a deal.

"I see the banner is still up," the mayor complained.

Brad's heart sank. "Yeah, I noticed that, too, on the way in from Rotary. I sent Megan a note about it yesterday but haven't heard back from her yet. I'll give her another nudge."

"She's a tough person to nudge, Brad. You may need to give her a boot in the butt," the mayor advised. "And that goes for the Green Valley project, too. I hear she has it in for Scott."

Do the walls really talk? Brad wondered again about the mayor's sources. "She's just doing her job, Buddy," Brad responded. "She wants to make sure the project is well- analyzed. I think we both know it's likely to go to a referendum challenge if the Council majority approves it. It's better to have Megan finding the weak points up-front instead of the opponents afterwards, right?"

"Just don't let her drive SoCal off by creating so many extra hoops for them to jump through that they decide to cut their losses and move down the road. We need this project, Brad. Agreed?" It was more of a final word than a question.

"It sure has a lot of benefits," Brad said. "Let's make it as bullet-proof as possible." His use of "let's" was Brad's attempt to signal to the mayor that they were in this together without actually committing himself.

"Got a meeting," the mayor said, turning to leave. "Get that banner down today, will you? Otherwise, I'm going to put one up. And keep pushing Green Valley ahead from your end. I'll get the votes. Don't let Megan screw this up. This is your highest priority," the mayor ordered.

"There's a flash!" Brad said under his breath.

*****

Brad quickly scanned a draft agreement in preparation for his lunch meeting with Deborah Downey, the newish superintendent of schools. While schools were typically separate governing entities from cities, they share constituencies and many issues.

Brad had always made it a habit to try to build a personal relationship with the local superintendent, hoping it would lead to cooperative efforts to share information, cut costs, or at least reduce instances of open political struggle among the elected officials.

The city manager before Brad had worked with the recently retired superintendent to construct a swimming pool on the high school campus that was shared by both agencies. It was a source of local pride and enjoyment. Each agency received awards for their cooperative work. The pool had been open a few years now and the bloom was off the rose. Bickering had developed at the front line level over the details of the joint-use agreement. Staffs from the city and school district were lobbing accusatory emails back and forth.

"Off to lunch," he told Jane, as he emerged from his office, carrying a folder.

"Oh, how delightful!" she teased. "A bonding session with *Doctor* Downey, AKA Debby Downer!"

"Yeah, if I accomplish nothing else, by the time this lunch is over, either she'll be 'Debby' or 'Deb' or she'll be calling me 'Master Jacks' if she insists I call her 'Doctor Downey.'"

"Well, in that case, enjoy your lunch, Master Jacks!"

"Pessimist!" he snapped back. "Geez, I miss Paul. He was so much more easy-going and trusting. We could have worked out these sharing problems over the phone."

"Well, I've only met 'Doctor' Downey once but I can see why you'd miss Paul. It's not a good sign that rather than calling you about the problems, she sent you a formal letter, attaching the District Counsel's memo and copying the entire school board."

"Yeah, that's not how to build a bond. Maybe I'll go for broke right off the bat. When she walks in I'll give her a big hug and say, 'lemme buy you a beer, DeeDee.'"

7

"So, how was lunch?" Jane asked, as Brad walked into the office.

"Not very good," Brad said rubbing his stomach. "Gave me gas."

"But you love Moreno's," she said.

"Oh, the enchiladas were good. The company churned my stomach. I was hoping to connect with a new kindred spirit." He set a pack of papers on the counter. "Paul and I got a lot done because we got along so well. Not going to be so easy with Deborah. She and Paul are as different as they could be."

"Sounds like you at least are calling her by her first name. But still a little stiff, was she?"

"Stiff? You'd need a whole can of WD-40 to get her to stiff. I tried to order some wine, or something, to loosen her up but she made it seem like some cardinal sin; she made a big deal out of being a non-drinker. Made me feel like Otis on *The Andy Griffith Show* when I ordered my Tecate. And she had this annoying way of looking at me with her head tilted and squinty eyes. I was my usual dazzling self, trying to warm things up between us, but she acted like she didn't believe anything I said."

"Well, she's new and it's her first superintendent job so she's probably cautious to begin with, or maybe awed by being in the presence of your radiance."

He smirked and rubbed his stomach again. "I never ate Mexican food so fast in my life. I felt like saying 'check please' as soon as the plates hit the table."

Councilwoman Kay Nance walked through the outer glass door.

"Hi, Kay," Brad said, picking his papers back up from the counter. "I was just updating Jane on my meeting with the new school superintendent."

"Really? I haven't met her yet. What's she like?" Kay asked.

"Not me, that's for sure. You wouldn't like her, but you sure could help her."

"How so?" the councilwoman asked.

"She's even more uptight than me, and you know how much you always loosen me up."

"Yeah," Jane added. "He's usually happy for hours every time you leave his office."

They all laughed at her double entendre as Kay and Brad headed into his office.

Despite her pungent musk oil scent, Kay was a welcome breath of fresh air compared to his lunch partner. They talked a while about her petition drive. Brad offered some arguments for selling her concepts to city officials who are steeped in the tradition of local home rule and consider state or regional planning anathema.

"Thanks, Brad," Kay eventually said. "You've made some good points. I think we can make some minor modifications to our proposal without sacrificing our goal."

He simulated a tipping of the hat. "Glad to be of service, ma'am."

"I heard Scott Graves charmed them at Rotary this morning," she said. She had missed the cue to leave.

"He's very good." Brad wasn't the least bit surprised that Kay had received a report from someone in the club.

"Did he talk about where the water is coming from?" she asked, narrowing her eyes.

Brad tensed. Had she been talking to Megan? "That's going to be a main topic of the EIR. Dee says we have plenty of supply to serve it but Megan has concerns," he responded. There's that word again. He figured she already knew this and was hoping his candor about the disagreement between his department heads would earn him credibility.

"We can't keep approving sprawling development in this state. We don't have the water," she added.

That was another of those 40,000-foot elevation perspectives that Brad couldn't handle. His responsibility was right here in Santa Ynez, not statewide issues. He tried to bring her back to home. "I've told staff to hire an independent water consultant for the EIR to be careful," Brad said, hoping that would satisfy her.

"Good," she replied. "But they should evaluate the reliability of our State Water Project supply, not just use the contract amount we have," Kay persisted. "We are writing checks that we can't cash all over California. New development is being approved based on contracted water that the state will never be able to deliver. You remember your Oglethorpe, don't you? California started as a myth and we are still living it."

Brad got the Oglethorpe reference, a popular professor at UCSB who taught a California history class they had both taken. It was one of the few things he and Kay had in common. He saw an opportunity to show off.

"Sure, California was named by Spanish conquistadors in the early 1500s after a mythical island from a popular novel of that time. Queen Califia ruled the island of giant Black women warriors who rode their griffins, part lion and part eagle, to support Muslims trying to take back Constantinople from the Christians."

"Very good," she said. "*You* must have actually gone to your classes."

Since that impressed her, he'd show off a bit more. "The virgin Queen was stunningly beautiful. Her warriors used weapons and armor of gold, the only metal they had," he added. "If I remember correctly, Queen Califia ends up being taken in battle, falling in love with her captor, and converting to Christianity."

"Bravo! That's the way I heard it, too. Back in the Middle Ages, myth and fact blended in popular wisdom."

"Kind of like my kids did when they were little," he noted. "They had no problem moving between fantasy and reality in the same sentence."

"Well," she continued, "the Spanish had no problem with that either. They came to believe that California was a land of beautiful giant women warriors covered in gold and waiting to be converted to Christianity. That belief funded a lot of Spanish expeditions. And that mindset has been played out for over half a millennium. We still are living the California myth. Only now the myth isn't about gold, it's about water."

His chest slumped. Kay was about to launch into one of her anti-growth tirades. He took a deep breath.

"Have you ever heard that in California, water doesn't flow downhill, it flows to money?" she asked. "Too much of Queen Califia's treasure has been spent on big water boondoggles."

"Don't know about that," he responded, not wanting to appear too meek to his tough-minded boss. "There's no denying that water has always been a huge issue for California. But we wouldn't be the 8th largest economy in the world without the State Water Project. It made the state bloom. My father idolized Governor Pat Brown for building it."

"Hmmm. What did your father do?" Kay asked.

"He was an engineer. He started with the old Department of Highways and Bridges, like his father. He got disgusted with the waste and inefficiency he saw in government and joined a big construction company."

He felt a wave of sadness thinking about his father and shifted the topic. "By the way, I got my name from his nickname, Spike. He got that from his boxing days in the Navy during World War II. When I was born, my uncle suggested they call me Brad, a little version of a spike."

"Clever," she said.

He forced a smile but still felt some sadness. "My father never had anything good to say about most politicians or government bureaucrats except for Pat Brown because he got things built. He wasn't into process." He suddenly realized there was a lot of Hubie Nettler in his father. "I really disappointed my dad by choosing a career in government."

"Hah," Kay laughed. "My dad wanted me to be an accountant like him. Can you imagine that?"

He repressed an emphatic NO! "My father used to talk about what an exciting time it was for California after World War II. So much growth and opportunity. His construction company got in on plenty of jobs that Brown pushed through to keep up with the state's expansion. Brown was responsible for building a lot of the infrastructure we are still wearing out today: state highways and bridges, state colleges and universities, and tons of big office buildings. But my father always said the State Water Project was Pat Brown's biggest legacy."

"Humph," Kay responded. "I can see why your father would love Pat Brown. The State Water Project is still the largest public works project in the nation. Back then, everyone wanted growth. We didn't put much thought into the environmental consequences of these huge projects until the late 60s and early 70s."

He sighed again.

She picked up on it. "Sure," she continued, "the state water project was massive. But you used the word 'bloom' to describe its impact on California. I wouldn't use that term. If you read up on any objective summaries of the project, you'll find that it was built with lies to satisfy the big-moneyed interests. You can trace a lot of the state's problems today to that project."

He began to fidget. He often found Kay's perspectives interesting, but they were beyond his scope of responsibility and he had some pressing work to get back to. The phrase "not my monkeys, not my circus" came to mind. He'd play along for a few more minutes.

"Lies?" he asked.

"Absolutely!" she said. "I can see you are pressed for time but give me five minutes to educate you on some history that will help you understand where I'm coming from now."

"Sure," he said reluctantly.

Kay settled in. "During the Great Depression, the federal US Bureau of Reclamation began building what was called the Central Valley Project or CVP for short; large dams in northern and central California to create Shasta, Folsom, Friant, and Trinity lakes, and a huge network of canals to bring the water south to irrigate California's Great Central Valley. Big corporations like Southern Pacific and Standard Oil bought up thousands of acres of the San Joaquin Valley for farming and blocked the Bureau from enforcing its regulation that limited its taxpayer-subsidized water to small family farms of 160 acres maximum. You know, California's water laws go back to the 1850's when the state was admitted to the Union and the emphasis was on encouraging settlement. The laws no longer make sense in a complex state with thirty-nine million people, but the state government has never mustered the ability and desire to bring reform. There's too much money fighting it."

He saw an opening to derail the lecture. "I think it was former Assembly Speaker Jesse Unruh who said that 'money is the mother's milk of politics.'"

She nodded. "There's so much money at stake from how water laws are interpreted that I can imagine there have been decades of legal battles with highly paid law firms duking it out in the courts. The money is so influential that there aren't many politicians willing to stand up for meaningful water management reform."

"I see," he said, feeling restless. "But what's the CVP got to do with the State Water Project we were talking about?"

"Relax, Brad," she grumbled. "I was just getting to that. If you are going to manage a city in California, you should know that water has always been the key issue in how the state developed and will continue to be."

"It *is* interesting," he said reluctantly. "But not my problem," he wanted to add.

Kay Nance continued her history lesson. "The big corporations in the Central Valley and Southern California wanted more water for development and were worried about the 160-acre limit of the Federal CVP. They devised a similar project, the State Water Project, to pick up where the CVP left off at the south end of Fresno County. But they were fighting a tough opponent: gravity."

"Gravity?" he asked.

"Yeah, you might not notice it driving south on I-5, but the southern end of the San Joaquin Valley slopes up hundreds of feet from north to south, heading toward the Tehachapi Mountains.

Water from the Delta would have to be put into aqueducts at sea level, then pumped uphill to get to the arid lands at the far south of the San Joaquin Valley. It's very expensive to pump that much water so far uphill."

"True, he acknowledged, "but look at the value of all that ag land that would be opened up."

"Well, back then, the main crop in the area was cotton. With CVP-subsidized water, the northerly portions of the valley could successfully compete with cotton grown in the South, where rainfall provides the water. But the marginal soils on the south end of California's Central Valley couldn't compete if they had to cover the tremendous costs of constructing new dams and reservoirs in Northern California, along with hundreds of miles of aqueducts, and hydroelectric and pumping plants. Especially not for low value crops like cotton."

"And?" He sneaked a look at his watch.

"The big corporations that bought much of the southern San Joaquin Valley teamed up with the public agencies and developers in the greater Los Angeles area. They came up with a solution; make the project even bigger and get the water to Los Angeles where they have always been obsessed with getting more water for growth, even if they would never use it all. The property tax base in the urban area would make the entire project more affordable to the growers. Plus, Southern California had the voting bloc that would be necessary to swing a statewide bond election to finance everything."

"Pretty slick," he said. "Bring all of that land into ag production, have the urban areas of Southern California pay most of the debt, and get the whole state to front it with a bond measure."

"You're learning, Brad. Where water is concerned, it's always about money and power. Public interest and environmental stewardship are nuisances that sometimes get in the way. The big water contractors will do whatever they can to block reforms that threaten their current deliveries and to get even more water. They'll use every legal maneuver they can think of and deceitful public relations tactics to serve their purposes."

"That's pretty cynical, Kay, don't you think?"

"Cynical? Take a look at Pat Brown's interview for UC Berkeley's Oral History program at the end of his political career. He admits that they lied about what the State Water Project would cost to get the initial construction bonds approved. They felt that demand for water would always overshadow cost. That's the way the water game has always been played. I'll email you an article about that. It will be good reading for you tonight."

He sat up in his chair. "Great, Kay! I was afraid I was going to have to just go home and relax."

She narrowed her eyes. "You are a major player in public policy around here and you should know more about the implications of what you're doing."

He back pedaled. "Just teasing, I'd love to read your article. In fact, I was just reading about how Los Angeles conned everyone back in the 1900s to build the LA Aqueduct from the Owens Valley by creating a phony shortage. I suppose there's so much money to be made if you have water in this state, that all sorts of shenanigans go on."

Kay shook her head in disgust. "It's been that way for over a hundred years. Big government and big corporations have always colluded to exploit water for economic gain. Do you know that we use more electricity just moving water hundreds of miles around the state than the total consumption of several states?"

"Hmmm," was all he could come up with.

"What's really galling to me is that despite all this exploitation of the environment and all the money we've spent, the state puts almost no restrictions on how this publicly- subsidized water is used."

"But, Kay, we've had lots of governors since Pat Brown. They've had different political bases. You're telling me that none of them has pushed back against the water contractors?"

"Yup," she said. "Look, they all needed money and political support to get elected. Do you think they could get elected on a platform to truly reform water policies? They'd get slaughtered by the PR campaign the water contractors would fund. Remember, there are twenty-five million people who use the State Water Project water alone. And the issues are so complex. The public would be easy to spook against any proposed change. Who wants to buck that?"

"You may be right about that," he offered, "but there are also scores of government agencies that have authority over water and the environment. There are tens of thousands of career civil servants in those agencies who care about protecting the public. In my experience, the bureaucracy itself exerts a buffering effect on the political winds that blow."

She shook her head. "I'm sure the vast majority of the state employees want to do the right thing and probably get pissed off with the politics from time to time. But state agencies are directed by Governor appointees who will march to the Governor's beat or be replaced."

He squirmed. "I don't know. You make it seem so one-sided and conspiratorial. It just seems like today there are so many interest groups out there that are able to instantly get their arguments out to millions over the Internet. It should be harder to put one over on the public like they did with the Los Angeles Aqueduct or the State Water Project."

"Oh, I think it is harder now for sure. But it doesn't stop them from trying. It's still going on today. Your daughter is studying the

Delta, right? Ask her about the Bay Delta Conservation Plan, BDCP. You mentioned the LA water grab of Owens Valley. This is the modern version of the same story. Let's ruin one region of the state so that an area that God didn't want to have water can use it wastefully."

"I'm not an expert on the BDCP," he admitted sheepishly. "From the little reading I've done, the plan came out of a lot of study with every possible interest group involved. Isn't protecting the Delta environment a co-equal goal of the plan, along with improving the reliability of the water delivery?"

Kay scoffed. "That's how it was pitched, but that's not how it has evolved. The plan has drawn so much fire by public agencies and groups that are concerned about the Delta that the state and water contractors backing the plan keep revising it. Now it's been divided into 'California Water Fix' and 'Eco Restore.' Same game, different name. The one thing that has stayed constant is the gigantic tunnels, thirty-five miles long and forty feet wide each, to pull water around the Delta."

"It's a re-do of the Peripheral Canal Jerry Brown tried to sell during his first term as California's Governor in the 80s that got trounced by the voters, right?" Brad asked.

"Pretty much the same thing. It's a horrible plan and has been discredited by anyone who is cares about preserving the Delta. Yet state government is trying to ram it down our throats on behalf of the water contractors. Do you know that the State Department of Water Resources even has a group of water agencies and private contractors embedded within it designing the project today?"

"No, hadn't heard that," he said skeptically.

"It's called the Delta Conveyance Facilities Design and Construction Enterprise. It's actually part of the state government now. They are simply ignoring the arguments from the fishing industry, Delta area local governments, and environmentalists, not to mention the horrible economics of the project. They want to just jump ahead to construction."

He strangled back a yawn. "Like you said, water has always been a controversy in California. Was it Mark Twain who said 'whiskey is for drinking; water is for fighting?'" He tried again to bring her back to his reality. "We are fortunate to have plenty of contracted water here so that shouldn't be a big problem for Green Valley," Brad dangled hopefully. "And since we're at the end of one of the state's pipelines, I'm glad there are projects being planned that will protect our deliveries."

"You think you have a state water commitment now because it's in your supply contract? You may be surprised," Kay warned ominously.

"What do you mean?"

"It's in that article I'm emailing you about how the state has participated in this game with the big water contractors allowing them to make millions of dollars trading the state water they contracted for but have never received. It's called 'paper water.'"

"Paper water?" he asked.

"That's it. To make the State Water Project look more feasible when they were designing it, they sold contracts for double the amount of water the system has ever been able to deliver. The rest exists only on paper but has been allowed to be treated as if it were real. Water contractors have been allowed to sell the water that exists only on paper to other water suppliers who then show it as a firm supply to accommodate new development or irrigation. But it's not real and everyone knows it. It's a big money game with the state a partner with the major water contractors."

"Interesting," he said, daring another furtive look at his in-basket.

She leaned forward and wagged her finger in the air. She didn't miss much. "Now this is important, Brad. What do you think is going to happen when long-term drought, climate change, over-pumping of groundwater, pollution, endangered species, degrading water quality in the Delta, and everything else, further reduces water supplies around the state?"

"I would have to say I never really thought about it," he said guiltily.

"Well, you should! What really worries us is what's going to happen when all of the people who are moving into new communities in semi-arid regions that supposedly have a firm supply of state water find out they don't. The water their project was approved with isn't real. They'll have to let their lawns go brown, no more swimming pool permits, and severe rationing on a permanent basis, not just like we have during our periodic droughts. At that point, the populace will link arms with the water contractors and demand more dams and other projects that will further ruin habitat and cost the taxpayers through the nose. The people will vote to protect their own comfort and property values. They'll get hustled because they'll be told California has a water problem. We don't. There's plenty of water to serve reasonable agricultural use and projected population growth for many decades, *if* we use it wisely."

He felt smothered. "I see your point, Kay. I just don't know what you expect me or the city to do about this whole situation. Santa Ynez is such a small player in all of this."

"And I'm sure every other sprawling development could say the same thing, 'Let me have my water. I'm just a little guy in the whole scheme of things.'"

"I suppose," he said.

The councilwoman ran a hand down the long braid of hair falling over her breasts to her lap, her countenance serious. "We all share a responsibility for the environment. We owe it to future generations. We need to take a stand somewhere and Green Valley is as good a place to start as any. We aren't convinced that there will be enough water available for Scott's project without putting the rest of the city in jeopardy."

Brad's antenna twitched with that comment. Who is "we?" Did that include his own planning director who may be working hand-in-glove with Kay and her crowd? He knew better than to try to get Kay to reveal her sources. He was sure she viewed him as backing the Green Valley project and therefore in the enemy's camp. He tried to calm things and end on a more neutral, professional tone.

"I'm sure the EIR will fully address that concern," he said, that word indelibly etched into his voice today.

"I doubt it, but we'll see," Kay said, rising from her chair. "Well, Brad, I know you'd love to sit here and talk water policy with me all day but I need to get going."

"It's always interesting to hear your perspective, Kay. And I will talk to my daughter about the BDCP."

"Thanks for your help on the petition," she said, heading to the door. "Tell Scott to gird his loins. See ya."

That parting shot was unnerving. Councilwoman Nance was sending a message that she fully expected Brad would relay her conversation to Scott. And yet, she was friendly, as though everyone was just playing out their predesigned roles in the unfolding drama. While Kay's politics and lifestyle were very different from Brad's, he respected her and appreciated that she could disagree with people, including him, without being nasty about it. Not all councilmembers had that maturity.

He waited until Kay left the outer office then sprayed a few bursts of his gardenia-scented air freshener. Her assault on big government and corporate greed exhausted him. Her arguments were interesting, but he had a city to run, not a futile battle to wage against money and political muscle. What he mainly cared about regarding water, right now, was ensuring there would be enough for Green Valley Village. A majority of his bosses seemed to want that.

He finished the afternoon with several scheduled monthly meetings with department heads. These were normally interesting sessions to update progress on a list of high priority projects and resolve potential obstacles. The sense of being part of a team accomplishing good things for the public was a favorite part of the job. He was distracted today. He kept mulling the meeting with Kay. Something was nagging him about it, but the problem wasn't obvious and he didn't have time to dig too deeply in self-reflection. He pushed the feeling down every time it came up and got through the rest of the day.

8

Brad got home early at about 5:30 p.m. to pick up Marie and drive to the hospital in Santa Maria to visit Lilly. She was recovering from her surgery that morning. He hadn't had time to ask Marie about it yet.

"I have a sandwich, apple, and Diet Coke for you for the road," Marie said as he entered through the front door. "Ready to go?"

"Can't you at least let me change my clothes first?" he barked.

"Bad day?" Marie asked.

He tossed his keys in the wicker basket on the entry hall table and turned right to go upstairs. "Sorry. Let's talk in the car. I'll be right down."

They drove off in silence with Marie at the wheel. He had been gruff, so it was up to him to initiate the conversation. He had to sort things out himself, first. Marie drove quietly giving him time. After a few miles and sighs, he was ready to bring his wife into his inner world.

He summarized his meeting with Councilwoman Kay Nance, since that was at the root of whatever was eating at him.

"So was it her warning shot about Green Valley Village that bothers you?" she asked.

"I thought that was it at first. She made it sound like the opponents have some tricks up their sleeves. As I've thought more about it, that really isn't it. I always knew she'd be an opponent. No surprise there."

"Even still," Marie continued, "you also know Kay's smart and creative. I could see you being worried about what she'll do. I would be."

"Oh, I am," he admitted. "But I don't think that's what is mainly bugging me. I haven't been able to figure it out yet."

"Maybe you are thinking too much. You know that's what you do. Why don't you give your brain a rest and listen to your body like you used to? Didn't that usually help?"

With her permission to break off the conversation, he closed his eyes and focused on his breathing and, gradually, the sensations in his stomach, chest, and throat. The sounds of the car and outside world became white noise. Eventually, he opened his eyes and said, "Huh. That was a good idea."

"What did you come up with?" she asked, encouragingly.

"I went through the meeting with Kay again and felt the kind of tension in my body that I associate with fear. I sat with it a while and the feeling shifted to more like sadness."

"Sadness?"

"Yeah. Some of it might have been the way she bashed former Governor Pat Brown over the State Water Project. My father loved him. At first I thought I was just sad about being reminded that dad's not around anymore or that I didn't defend Brown for my father."

She smiled at him with soft eyes.

"But I wasn't done yet. The sadness settled into a sense of confusion; like I was losing my direction."

"For a guy who is always planning and tries so hard to control everything around him, I could understand why Kay could cause some confusion. But what's the lost direction about?"

He pondered that a moment. "Well, maybe 'lost direction' isn't the right term. It's more like I'm questioning what I believe after listening to Megan and Kay. I never had much use for the environmental assessment process. It was always a hurdle to jump over to get a project approved. And I never really thought about water policy like Kay has, but I have to say, she makes good points. I want to talk to Kris tonight when we get home to check out some of what she said. It was unsettling."

Marie glanced at him quickly then back to the road. "So Megan and Kay said some things that caused you to think. Why should that be so upsetting?"

He closed his eyes for a few moments. "You remember that slogan from the 60s, 'if you're not part of the solution, you're part of the problem?'"

"Sure. It was groovy," she smiled.

"I always thought of myself as being part of the solution. Maybe because I bought into the old adage 'if you aren't growing, you're dying.' Early on, one of my city manager mentors told me, 'this job is a lot easier if you keep the budget balanced, the reservoirs full, and don't try to regulate cats.' I've always seen having enough water to grow as a measure of my success. I haven't worried as much about the nature of that growth or managing water resources for the long term."

"Isn't that what the Council majority wants you to be doing?" Marie asked.

"Yes, and because it fit with what I had drilled into me, I never really gave it another thought. But, after talking to Megan and Kay,

I'm starting to wonder if I'm part of the problem after all." He paused a moment, the sting of saying those words burning a hole in his chest. "Maybe those two aren't quite as whacked out as people around here believe. Maybe I should be paying more attention to the consequences of that growth. Or, am I just another wimpy bureaucrat responding to money and power over the public interest? What *is* the public interest anyway? I'm not so sure all of a sudden."

Marie turned back to him. "You're not wimpy. You just got some new information that has caused you to be open to re-thinking what you believe. That's one of your strengths. You always credited your Coro Foundation training for some of that. You talk about all the different internships you did that gave you an appreciation for the role big corporations, labor unions, the media, nonprofits, and others play in public affairs. Don't you think being able to understand different perspectives has made you more effective?"

"OK, you win," he said, letting her assessment give him a small measure of comfort. "But sometimes I wish I held stronger opinions. It would make decision-making so much easier. It's like my favorite scene in *Midway*."

She rolled her eyes. "Oh, God. You watch that movie every time it comes on."

"My favorite scene is when Glenn Ford, as Admiral Ray Spruance, visits Admiral "Bull" Halsey, played by Robert Mitchum. Halsey is hospitalized by a rash and Spruance has taken over his command just before the big battle. Spruance confesses to Halsey that when the battle comes he worries that he might not call things the way Halsey would. Halsey blasts back, 'When you're in command, command!'"

"If you say so," she responded. "I've never actually sat through the whole thing."

"I just wish I had more Bull Halsey in me."

"Or William Mulholland?" she dangled.

"Yeah, maybe," he replied warily. "They were macho leaders who made things happen; damn-the-torpedoes types."

Marie frowned. "There is a time and place for strong-willed leadership. Commanding the fleet in the most important naval battle of the war would be one. But, as we've learned from Lilly, in other cases it would be better to have a leader who wasn't so sure of himself, who reached out to get other opinions."

"Good point." He looked out the windshield watching the buildings move toward them. "Thanks for boosting my ego."

"You're just too hard on yourself, Brad. You never give yourself enough credit. Your staff likes you because you aren't a Bull Halsey. You are open to their opinions and try to find compromises that will resolve conflict rather than just asserting your own will. Instead of seeing that as a plus, your mind distorts it to a negative, like you aren't measuring up to some fictional, macho standard that wouldn't be as effective in your situation anyway."

"Geez, you're not just a pretty face, are you?"

She smiled and sneaked another quick look at him. "I wish you could relax more and stop worrying so much about everything. You work way too hard attempting to control everything. Of course, that's impossible. But you stress yourself trying anyway."

He smiled back at her. "You're right. I see the pattern. I don't need to have all the answers all the time. Being open to new information is a good thing, not threatening."

"And when the situation calls for a command decision, you'll be a Bull Halsey. Right now you are struggling to do what is right in the midst of competing perspectives and pressures. There are too many people in leadership positions who wouldn't even consider challenging their own belief systems if it might jeopardize their own security. The fact that you are, I find to be macho. Better than that, sexy."

He felt a tingle. "I'm going to remind you of that when we get home." He reached over and turned on her favorite satellite station featuring love songs. Her smile confirmed that the message was received. He closed his eyes for a power nap.

*****

Marie and Brad were relieved to see that Lilly was awake when they entered Room 3 of the ICU. She looked frail but was awake and sitting up in bed with a dark pink housecoat over the top of her hospital gown. Lee was leaning over the metal side rail of the bed awkwardly trying to deliver a spoonful of chocolate pudding. They both perked up when they saw their visitors.

"Hey, you look great!" Brad opened cheerfully.

"She does," Lee responded. "They've already had her out of bed walking a little."

"I guess I'm a lucky girl, all things considered," Lilly said softly. "They were able to screw me back together. I didn't have to have a new hip."

"Yeah," Lee said, "she has more titanium in the plate they screwed in than I do on my three-wood. They said she had a simple fracture and, with the plate, she'll heal faster." He set the pudding on an end table. "They said she'd be out of here in a day or two and then moved to a rehab facility for a week or so before going home. Not bad, huh?"

"That's great." said Brad. "You really are a survivor, Lilly." Brad regretted his words as soon as they came out. He remembered how quickly Lee shut down talking about the St. Francis Dam break, saying it was a topic Lilly didn't like to talk about. He cast a quick grimace toward Lee that meant "oops, sorry about that."

Lilly caught the look. "It's OK," she said. "Lee told me he mentioned the dam break to you. It happened a long time ago. I don't talk about it outside the family and a few close friends mainly because I don't want to seem like I'm after some personal status from having been there. Too many people died in the tragedy. I'm not after any sort of fame from it."

"I understand. The important thing now is that you are going to be patched up and out of here," Brad said, changing the subject.

"We expect to see you out of here in a day or two," Marie said. "I'll have a plate of brownies for you to celebrate your release."

Lilly cocked her head slightly as though digging deep for a distant memory. "It's funny," she said. "I have trouble remembering what I had for breakfast or why I went into the other room. But every once in a while, I get memories of things I haven't thought about in a long time." She looked at Marie. "When you said 'brownie,' it reminded me of my favorite toy when I was little. It was a hobby horse. You know, one of those sticks with a horse's head on it that kids used to run around with, like they were riding a horse?"

"I had one of those, too." Marie said.

"My father made one for me out of an old broomstick. He painted it pink, my favorite color. Kind of silly now when I think about it, because I named the horse 'Brownie.' In fact, Brownie was pretty close to this color." She pinched the lapel of her housecoat. "Father had somebody burn on a brand and the word 'Brownie' in small letters on his neck. My father worked for Southern California Edison in the construction crews. That's what brought us to the Santa Clara Valley where the flood from the dam break went." She smoothed down her blanket and then laid her frail hands neatly on top of her thighs. "I didn't have many toys. I slept with Brownie. And I lost him in the flood," she said with a weak, trailing voice.

The area around her eyes turned red and she seemed to be near tears. "What a silly old lady I am!" she blurted, regaining her composure. "All those people who died including my own mother and father. And I'm getting mushy about a wooden horse."

Marie took Lilly's thin, nearly transparent hand etched, by blue veins. Lee caressed her shoulder lightly. Brad hated to see her sad, especially in her weakened condition. He'd been here only a few minutes and already regretted it.

"I'm OK." Lilly said, "a little tired maybe. But if you don't mind hearing an old lady walk down memory lane, I'll tell you what I remember about the dam disaster sometime. This little incident reminds me that I'm not going to live forever. And I owe it to the memory of the people who died to share their stories."

*****

As soon as they got home, Brad went upstairs to change into what he called his "lounging attire": cotton sweatpants and a nonmatching flannel sweatshirt. He settled back into his black leather recliner with a dish of chocolate peanut butter frozen yogurt and turned on the basketball game he had been waiting for all day. The local cable company covered the Lakers, but tonight they were playing the Sacramento Kings, his team. Life was suddenly good.

After a few minutes getting caught up on the game, he picked up the laptop next to his chair to check his emails, realizing he had fallen victim to the affliction of many people in this electronic age. He couldn't sit still and watch a movie or sporting event anymore. It just wasn't enough stimulation to hold his attention. He felt compelled to constantly check his cell phone and laptop for some further diversion.

There was the email from Councilwoman Nance attaching the article she mentioned earlier today. It was written by a nonprofit public policy advocacy group. Brad looked at the TV and saw that there were still five minutes left in the second quarter. That meant he had at least a half hour through halftime to look at what she had sent. Actually, he knew he could take an hour-and-a-half if he wanted to since it seemed like 90 percent of NBA games got decided in the last two minutes anyway.

He opened the attachment and began skimming while keeping one eye on the game. He whizzed through the write-up on the Central Valley Project and State Water Project which appeared to support what Kay had said about the cozy relationships that have existed between state government and the water contractors they are supposed to be regulating. His eye caught a paragraph about Governor Edmund G. "Pat" Brown admitting that he and his colleagues lied to the public in order to sell the State Water Project.

The article described how California was booming after World War II, with much more growth projected in Southern California in the 50s and 60s. Governor Pat Brown was obsessed with creating more water supply to avoid being blamed for stalling the welcomed growth. He was water development's tireless champion and he cracked the whip with the state agencies to deliver more water facilities immediately. His director of the new Department of Water Resources went around the state saying, "We must build now and ask questions later."

He saw the oral history quote from Brown near the end of his life that Kay referenced:

"I loved building things. I wanted to build that goddamned water project. I was absolutely determined I was going to pass this California Water Project. I wanted this to be a monument to me."

He read on about how Brown badgered the State Legislators to get the votes he needed for project approval and placing the bond issue to pay for it on the ballot. He wheeled and dealt, cajoled, and browbeat. Whatever it took for another vote.

Meanwhile, DWR did its part to cast the project in a positive light by deliberately understating the costs. The biggest project, the giant Oroville Dam, wasn't even included in the costing for the bond measure. Neither were the aqueduct branches to San Luis Obispo and

Santa Barbara counties which supplied Brad's region. And to make the cost per acre foot seem more reasonable, the state entered into contracts with water agencies all over the state for 4.2 million acre-feet of water per year to be delivered through the project. That dropped the cost per acre foot way down. The problem was the state knew full well that delivery of such a large quantity was not feasible. There just wasn't enough water being stored. And in fact, on average, the state had only been able to deliver about half the contracted amount all of these years. That resulted in the paper water Kay mentioned. Brown also convinced the Legislature to divert the tidelands oil tax paid by big oil companies to subsidize the water project. The oil companies didn't object since they owned so much of the southern San Joaquin Valley land that would be made quite valuable if the state-subsidized water arrived.

Then, to further make the cost of the water seem a bargain, DWR did a report comparing it to seawater desalination, a prohibitively expensive alternative at the time. The article had quotes from Brown admitting that they knew the project would cost a lot more than the bond measure placed before the voters. He figured they would get enough in the first bond measure to get the project going then go back for more later to finish it. Kay had the story correct.

He finally closed the document, surprised and slightly disgusted at the conniving between state government and the water contractors and at the federal Bureau of Reclamation for not enforcing its 160-acre limit against the big ag conglomerates it served via the CVP. It went on. Governor Brown acknowledged that the voters were given false numbers on the water project costs and capabilities. Where were the checks and balances on government? Weren't there courageous people with power somewhere in the bureaucracy who tried to get the truth out? He wondered what Kay expected from him.

He sighed wearily and looked for refuge in the basketball game. It was only halfway into the fourth quarter with the Lakers up eight points. Anybody's game, usually. However, the Lakers had achieved the 100-point threshold. If Ralph Lawler, the play-by-play announcer for the LA Clippers was right, the game was as good as over. "First to a hundred wins" was regrettably true 94 percent of the time. The Kings showed little threat of breaking the law tonight. He clicked the "Guide" button on the remote and began searching for an old movie when the phone rang.

He held his breath as Marie answered. He almost never took calls at home. He got too much phone time at work. It was either some emergency or other problem from work, or his daughter, Kristen. Those were the only calls they got after 9 p.m.

"Hi, hon," he heard Marie say from the kitchen phone. He relaxed and continued his movie search. Marie and Kristen were talking about something related to the cheesy potato dish Kris was supposed to make for the upcoming Thanksgiving dinner. He smiled. Kris was very bright but not much of a cook. As accomplished as she was, he knew she'd be all stressed out about the cheesy potatoes when the entire extended family gathered at the family ranch outside Stockton where Marie was raised. Kris lived rent-free in a small cottage at the ranch while attending graduate school at the University of the Pacific. He pictured the little efficiency kitchen at her cottage in complete disarray from her latest foray into the culinary arts.

He left them alone to talk for a few minutes then gave Marie a wave to get her attention, making a gesture with his thumb straight out to his ear and his little finger to his mouth.

"Just a minute, hon," she said to her daughter. "Your dad is giving me a hand signal. He either wants to talk to you or he's telling me to hang loose. Considering the source, I'm assuming he wants to talk to you." She brought the cordless phone to his chair.

"Hey there, you watching the Kings game?" he asked.

"It's on, but I'm not really watching. I study all night, remember? Lawler's Law strikes again, huh?"

"Yeah, but of course you wouldn't know that since you have been studying all night, right?"

She laughed. "It's called multi-tasking, Dad. My generation is better at it than yours."

"Tell you what, we'll trade places. I'll go to a few classes, party all night, and sleep 'til noon. Excuse me, I'll multi-task," Brad responded. "Were your ears burning today?"

"Yeah, right. My college life isn't anything like yours. I'm working hard up here! Why should my ears burn, anyway? Was it somebody wanting to give me a job for a hundred thousand when I get out?"

"I wish. One of my councilmembers was hammering me about state water policy. She emailed me an interesting report on how water has been mismanaged in California since the State Water Project. I'll forward it to you. Maybe you can use it someday. She knew you were doing some study of the Delta. And she said the Bay Delta Conservation Plan is the latest example of a corporate driven boondoggle. She said I should ask your opinion of it. I've read a little about it but, since it doesn't really affect me, I haven't studied it. How about an overview when we get together so I can get a little more up to speed? I know she'll talk about it some more and I want to hold my own with her."

"Well, Pilgrim, BDCP does affect you," Kris said in her best John Wayne accent, no better than her father's.

"How so?" he asked.

"Doesn't most of your water supply down there come from the State Water Project?" she queried.

"A lot of it. OK, that water comes through the Delta. I got it," he said.

"And what happens in the Delta ripples across most of the state. The Delta has been described as the Gordian Knot of the entire State Water Project. It's an absolute tangle of conflicting interests."

"So I gather. My councilwoman painted a pretty bleak picture about the current conditions of the Delta and how the state is promoting major plans on behalf of the big water contractors that will make it worse."

"That's true. Are you becoming a Greenie?"

"Hardly. I guess I'm just surprised and disgusted by what I'm reading. Looks like the state has always had a cozy relationship with the big water contractors."

"Hmmm," she said. "I wonder how many of your citizens feel like City Hall kowtows to developers' interests like your article says the state does for the water contractors?"

"Probably a lot," he said, without thinking. "People have been suspicious of government since the nation's founding. But I'd like to think that the city organization does a better job of looking after the public interest than it sounds like the state bureaucrats have done with water."

They eventually said their goodbyes, his daughter's query about his own interaction with the development community tugging at him. He thought again of his father's contempt for risk-averse government bureaucrats. Wasn't he better than that?

That night he dreamt of his father as a child astraddle a hobby horse in a tent city. He couldn't recall the details when he awoke in the middle of the night. The recurring theme of letting his father down kept him awake far too long.

9

The alarm went off at 6:00 a.m. No time to jog today. Brad had just enough time to shower and meet the mayor at City Hall before going to a Chamber of Commerce meeting at 7:30 a.m. He and the mayor were the featured speakers at the quarterly all-members breakfast meeting. They would be giving their annual city update. Typically, this was a big draw for the Chamber and helped to cement it as a major player in local politics.

The Chamber was Mayor Buddy's crowd. He knew everyone in the room and counted most of them as friends. Brad watched him move about the room shaking hands, slapping backs, and dispensing hugs. He saw him walk over to greet Hubie Nettler who was standing at his chair. Hubie towered over the half dozen men and women surrounding him who seemed to be competing for his attention. The rancher held up his hand to silence the woman talking to him and turned to accept the mayor's proffered hand.

As the mayor and Hubie did their bonding thing, Brad flipped through the hard copy of his slides. The mayor would take the upbeat items, like the new over-the-counter building permit process for minor projects, the youth soccer field nearing completion, and the recently arrived replacement fire engine.

He paused at the slide of the new 20,000 square foot junior anchor department store that had just started construction. "You can have that one," the mayor had said.

Brad understood immediately. The department store wasn't good news in all circles. Scores of residents, and even some business people from the Chamber, spoke against this intrusion of "big box" chain retail to their small town. They favored the smaller "mom and pop" stores and restaurants that contributed to Santa Ynez' charm. Brad and others in the room this morning had argued for the project and City Attorney Henry Fitzhenry advised the City Council that they were on thin legal grounds for denying a project that clearly met the General Plan and Zoning Ordinance. The Chamber leadership was looking for jobs, some spin-off business activity for its members, and a potential new corporate member that would be counted upon to sponsor all sorts of Chamber events. In the end, the Chamber endorsed the project and the Council approved it on a split vote with Councilwomen Kay Nance and Gretchen Schmitz dissenting. He hoped to breeze through this particular slide without any rancor this morning.

He looked up to see Santa Ynez's Grievant Laureate heading toward him. "Morning, Pat," he said, extending his hand.

"Mr. Jacks?" Pat said, taking the hand. "Looks like you have a genial group here this morning. Don't worry, I'll spice it up a little for you."

Pat Kirby, a seventy-plus-year-old former middle manager with the federal Government Accountability Office, was the local political gadfly. He was smart enough to be dangerous. He seemed to live to comment at public meetings, especially since the City Council and Planning Commission meetings started being aired on local cable TV. He always had a briefcase filled with paperwork nearby. Brad had been embarrassed on more than one occasion to find that Kirby was better prepared for an agenda item than he was.

Brad glanced down at the beat-up brown leather briefcase in Kirby's hand. "Looks like you're loaded for bear, Pat."

"Just trying to keep City Hall honest," Kirby responded, without a bit of malice. Brad noticed a moth hole in the lapel in one of the two dark business suits Kirby always wore to public meetings. He caught a whiff of what must be Old Spice and Brylcreem.

"Nobody does it better," Brad said. Pat Kirby was the consummate contrarian. No matter the issue, or its popularity, he could find something to squawk about. He generally got most of the facts right but sometimes missed something important that led him to some wrong conclusions. He wasn't mean, just skeptical and inquisitive. While most of the Council and staff saw him as an egotistical pest, Brad didn't mind him. Kirby's suspiciousness of government, willingness to stand alone for the truth, and curmudgeonly demeanor reminded Brad of his father.

Brad smiled watching Kirby make a beeline to an empty folding chair in the front row. He always sat in the front row at meetings in the Council Chambers where he could be seen by the primary camera shot of the speaker's podium. His facial gestures were legendary. You never had to guess if Kirby agreed with the current speaker or not. He could also be counted upon to say something during the Business from the Floor portion of the agenda. This was an opportunity for any member of the public to address the City Council on any item not already on the agenda. City managers likened this part of the meeting to open mic night at the comedy club. You never knew what was going to happen during Business from the Floor.

The presentation went as scripted. The collegial group even applauded a few of the accomplishments, especially the new minor building permit process that the Chamber had championed. Brad was relieved that there were only a few groans and some whispered conversations when he talked about the new department store under contruction. They closed with the mayor giving a status report on the Green Valley Village project.

The Chamber president, acting as emcee, conducted a question/answer session afterwards. It was also benign. The president said, "One final question" as they approached the customary cut-off time of 8:30 a.m.

Pat Kirby raised the only hand in the audience. The president couldn't pretend not to see him. There were groans as Kirby rose in place.

Kirby pulled out some reports from his briefcase and for the next few minutes asked detailed questions about Green Valley traffic, water supply, drainage, and budget impacts which the mayor deflected to the city manager. Brad did his best to answer factually and non-emotionally. Kirby kept probing for a soft spot. The mostly pro-development group started to mumble with restlessness. It was after the 8:30 witching hour. People started whispering and turning in their seats to glare at Kirby. He didn't yield the floor and asked yet another follow up question about water.

"Time to go, Pat," a woman from the back said, as she got up to leave.

Hubie slapped his thigh with the morning paper and bellowed, "Who the fuck let this guy into the Chamber?"

The president quickly interrupted Kirby and adjourned the meeting.

Notwithstanding Kirby's thrusts at Green Valley, the overall Chamber presentation had been positive. Mayor Buddy was particularly upbeat after the meeting, accepting congratulations from many in the room about the city's progress. They stood by the podium receiving atta-boys from people who came up to shake their hands. The mayor lapped up the praise. Even Hubie walked up and extended his huge paw to the mayor. He didn't offer it to Brad.

"Looks like we have the public behind us on Green Valley, Buddy," Hubie said.

"Well, at least some of the business community, Hubie," Brad cautioned.

"Oh, there's a lot more popular support besides the business community, Brad," the mayor claimed.

"There damn well oughta be," huffed Hubie, "with all the crap your city is making SoCal do to get the approval."

Hubie Nettler took the mayor's arm. "Come on over here, Buddy. I want to talk privately." The big man led the mayor away and the rest of the small gathering dispersed.

Scott Graves made his way to the front of the room. "Nice show, Brad," he said extending his hand. "Looks like you and Mayor Buddy have an adoring public. You are the Batman and Robin of Santa Ynez!"

"Day by day, Scott, day by day." Brad responded. "You should be happy with the reception Green Valley Village got."

"I am," Scott agreed. "Except for Pat, who I think most people discount anyway, people seemed supportive." He nodded his head in the direction of Hubie and the mayor. "And I think if Pat gets too heated up, Hubie and the boys will take him out back and show him how the west was won." He laughed.

"I'd worry more about Kay than Pat." Brad warned. "She has some big issues with water supply."

"Are they Kay's issues or Megan's?" Scott asked, looking around to be sure they weren't overheard.

"Hard to say," Brad said. "Kay was more into statewide water policy. She didn't get into anything specific about your project. But she pretty much seems to think that it's an example of how state water policy has promoted sprawl and destroyed the environment."

"Hah! So, our 1,400 homes will bring the state to its knees?"

Brad shrugged and shook his head. "She sent me this report I skimmed through last night about how water agencies are only getting about half of the water they contracted for from the State Water Project. They're making millions of dollars selling the undeliverable amount to other agencies that use it to show they have enough water for new development. It's called 'paper water.'"

The developer grinned and looked relieved. "Oh, is that what she's so worked up about? That 'paper water' stuff is a red herring," Scott sniffed.

"How so?"

"There was a court case, out of Sacramento, I think, a while back that basically said you had to prove that water supply is there if you're going to rely on it for an EIR. The court specifically rejected citing paper water. The Legislature followed up with the Urban Water Planning Act that requires detailed reports on current and future water supply and demand on big projects. In fact, we are working on a Water Supply Assessment report now as part of our EIR. Dee knows all about it."

"Oh, yeah, we just met on that report. I didn't connect it to the paper water issue," Brad said.

"If that's mainly what's bugging Kay," Scott continued, "we are in good shape. Long term water analyses are very well regulated. DWR reviews your water reports, and, to ensure everyone is working off the same assumptions, they tell you what types of analyses have to be included in your plan. And their own delivery reliability estimates under different scenarios get very close scrutiny by all sorts of interest groups. You'll have good, defensible data for the EIR. You should check with Dee. He's on top of it."

"Maybe not as much as you think," Brad thought. Still, he was impressed by Scott's grasp of the laws related to the city's requirement for water planning. In Brad's experience, most developers have only a smattering of knowledge about city policies and procedures, and even less interest in learning them. The good ones know the lay of the land from the city's perspective and help them to meet their objectives while achieving their own pro forma requirements. Scott Graves was not just a smooth PR guy. He had been well-trained. Brad felt a little sheepish about alerting him to the problem Kay had brought up since Scott was obviously on top of the issues and Kay had been exaggerating the paper water problem.

"I'll go back to Dee and make sure he has everything buttoned up for the EIR," Brad promised.

"I appreciate that, Brad," Scott replied, with all sincerity. "You and I have worked closely to create a really good project here. I hope you are as proud of it as I am at this point. We don't need any loose ends in the EIR for Kay and her folks to attack, right?"

It was Brad's turn to check for eavesdroppers. "She told me to tell you that you should 'gird your loins.'"

Scott laughed. "I'm not sure I like hearing that Kay has my loins on her mind!"

"Forgetting your loins for a minute, you better be sure of your water demand stats. Megan thinks they are too low. She's not convinced we have enough water for you."

"What's she saying now?" Scott sighed.

"She thinks the assumption on residential use and the factor used for the landscaped areas are both too low. She's going to talk to Western and I suspect your team will be quizzed some more. And, by the way, just to be doubly sure, I've directed that Megan and Dee hire another firm to peer review Western's report."

"Well, OK, if you think that's necessary. We need to be able to defend the numbers. It's the biggest environmental issue we have. I appreciate the heads up though, Brad," said Scott. "I just wish there were something I could do to get Megan to be a little friendlier. Boy, she's tough!"

"I know, Scott. She may be doing you a favor by looking closely from the get-go."

"Maybe that's her motive. I'm trying not to take it personally. I know they call her Megan 'Cain't' around here. It must not just be me or our project she's singling out. Just so you know, we've tried hard to accommodate her comments in revised plans all along the way. I can't tell you how much time, money, and compromising we've been through trying to get on her good side. And we don't seem to get any credit for that. I have to believe some of it is coming from Kay."

Brad felt himself getting angry. He suspected there was some truth to Scott's complaints about his planning director. "I'll talk to her again," he promised. "I'll make sure you get a fair and expeditious process."

"That's all we ask, Brad. It's a pleasure working with a good city manager. I wish we had more like you in our other cities." Scott shook hands with Brad then parted to say a few hellos to some of the other Chamber members still lingering after the meeting.

Brad was warmed by the flattery. He liked to think of himself as professional and helpful. Or was Scott just buttering him up, saying what he told every other city manager SoCal had to work with? He remembered Marie's comments in the car yesterday that he's too hard on himself. He quickly concluded he was just acting out his pattern and forced himself to take a moment to accept Scott's kind words.

When he got back to City Hall, he dumped off his briefcase at his office and walked across the building to see Public Works Director, Dee Sharma. He could have just called but he subscribed to the "MBWA" leadership strategy, Management By Walking Around. He made it a point to be out and about the city organization whenever time permitted. It was an adjunct activity related to his enjoyment of being part of a team working toward common goals. He said "hello" to the people he passed, calling them by name, and often chatting briefly.

On the short trip to Public Works, he was cornered by Stew Martin, the custodian, who always had a joke for him. Sometimes clean, usually dumb, but always good for a laugh.

"Hey, Brad, Dee called me into his office today," Martin began excitedly. "He said, 'Stew, we both know you're not the brightest spark around here. But over the last fifteen years you've never been sick or late and you do such good work. I think you deserve a reward. So, how does a brand new car sound?'" The custodian paused then scrunched his face like Lou Costello. "'Vrooom! Vrooooom!' I told him."

It was so stupid, but delivered with such zeal, Brad had to laugh. "Don't quit your day job, Stew."

He stopped to ask Cindy, the administrative assistant, how her husband's broken leg was coming along.

As he walked through the Public Works office, he glanced into the side cubicle of Associate Engineer Gene Lowe, a diehard Lakers fan.

"Ahem!" Brad grunted loudly.

Gene looked up and flashed Brad a big smile and two thumbs up. Brad paused briefly to look around to see if anyone was watching, then smiled back at Gene while rubbing the right side of his nose with his middle finger. A mock flipping off was the sincerest acknowledgement a Kings fan would give a Lakers victory.

"Hi, Dee," Brad said as he stood at the doorway. "Got a sec?"

"Sure," Dee said, putting aside what he was reading as Brad took a seat.

Brad passed along Scott Graves's confidence in the water numbers, mainly to give his public works director's bruised ego a little salve. Plus, he was starting to wonder if the peer review was really necessary. But he didn't want to express that doubt and get Dee's hopes up in case he decided to stay the course. He passed along a couple fix-it items he'd spotted on his travels around town, asked how Dee's son was doing in soccer, and left feeling like he had accomplished his objective for the pop-in visit.

He went back to his office and picked up phone messages from Jane's desk, then settled back to look at emails when Jane came in.

"Agenda reports," she said, handing him a stack of papers.

"Oh, crud," he said. "Tomorrow is Thanksgiving. I'm so used to having the agenda packet all done on Fridays."

"Nope," she said. "Got to get everything printed today since we're off Friday, too. Take all the time you need, Brad… in the next half hour." She twirled and left.

He found reviewing Council agenda reports to be important, albeit tedious, work. Some city managers want all agenda reports submitted to the City Council to be ghost written by staff members and issued over the city manager's name. That helped to solidify the city manager's authority and accountability to the City Council. Brad's preference was to have the reports issued in the name of the department head since they would be responsible for presenting the item at the meeting anyway. Brad didn't have time to be the expert on every agenda item. He wanted the staff members to take public responsibility for their reports. He found that most staff members liked it better that way since it gave them a little of the limelight. Brad's task was to read the reports, edit the writing, if necessary, or, once in a while, have the department head make major revisions. Ultimately, he would add his initials so that the Council could see he had reviewed and approved the report before passing it on.

After a quick read of the staff reports and a few minor mark-ups, he brought the stack back out to Jane who would get the changes made and assemble everything for copying and distribution later today.

"Pretty light meeting, huh?" he said.

She flipped through the pages to see how much he had edited. "Looks like it," she said. "I see that you moved a couple of the items to the Consent Calendar. You have a plane to catch next Wednesday morning or something?"

The Consent Calendar portion of the agenda was at the front and contained routine matters that weren't expected to necessitate any Council or public discussion. The proposed recommendations in the entire section would normally be approved by a single motion to expedite the meeting. A councilmember or citizen could ask to have anything on the Consent Calendar removed for separate discussion. That didn't happen often.

"Oh, I left a little fun for the Council under New Business."

Jane flipped through a few more reports. "There really aren't any 'killer' items on the agenda. I bet we'll be out in under two hours. For a donut." She would be attending the meeting, too, in her role as city clerk, official keeper of city records.

He scanned the agenda again. There was an update from the League of California Cities on some pending legislation with Brad's recommendations on official city policy positions that would be conveyed to their State Senator and Assembly member. Kerry Smith, executive director of the Santa Ynez Tourism Bureau, was scheduled to give a progress report on the Bureau's activities, a soft commercial for an expected future request to increase city financial support. The Council's Parks and Recreation Commission strategic plan for new facilities and programming would be presented by the director. The Council would hold open interviews at the meeting to fill a vacant seat on the same commission. The only matter on the Public Hearing agenda was a minor change to the Zoning Ordinance to add a blood donation center as a Conditional Use in a commercial district. This was to accommodate a proposed lease with the owner of the strip center, Hubie Nettler. Mayor Buddy was the broker handling both sides of the lease. He would step down and turn over the meeting to Vice Mayor Mullikin when that item came up.

The Council should dispense with the agenda items in less than two hours. But once they all get together, with the cameras on and nothing much else to talk about, a few of his bosses will become long-winded when they get to the Council Comments at the end of the agenda.

"Two hours you say? You're on," he said. "I'll take the 'over.' Make it a maple bar when you pay off. Come on in and let's crank out the transmittal memo."

He dictated a short blurb on each of the items as required by state law for public information. Jane would fill in the staff recommendations and other basics.

It was still before noon so he had time for a little more MBWA, this time to the Planning Department.

Approaching that end of the building he saw Megan Cain standing at the counter talking to Barry Stockwell, a local architect who was obviously upset. He stayed back to observe a moment. Megan was smiling and appeared to be trying to calm the man down. "Good job, Megan," he thought. He saw Stockwell eventually nod his head, gather his plans, and shake hands with Megan.

"Whatever that was about, looks like Barry left smiling," he told her.

"It's that over-the-counter permit. Barry was at the Chamber meeting this morning and got the impression the mayor had essentially said, 'You need a permit? Come on down. We'll have it waiting.' He came for a sign permit. He had a sketch of the sign showing the dimensions and colors. But no detail on materials or building elevations showing the sign in place. I told him we'd try to issue it in a day but we couldn't start 'til he gives us the info."

"Well, I guess it will take time for people to know what they have to do to help you do the one-day approval. Do you have a minute to talk in your office?"

She tensed and looked worried.

He jumped in. "Actually, it's no big deal. We can do it here."

She relaxed. "What's up?"

"Kay sent me a report that I read last night on the way the state manages water, mainly to benefit the water contractors over the general public interest. Have you seen it?" Brad asked.

As soon as he'd said it he realized that Megan might think his inquiry was a test to see if Megan and Kay were in cahoots. But since he had asked the question, he decided to pay close attention to her response. He remembered another Rotary program from years ago, featuring a self-proclaimed expert in reading body language. Brad figured there was something to it. He watched Megan closely trying to avoid looking like Larry David in *Curb Your Enthusiasm* who had a habit of staring down a person who had given him an answer he wasn't sure he believed, to see if the person would crack.

"Doesn't ring a bell," Megan said. Brad saw that there was no hesitation in her response and that she looked him straight in the eyes when she spoke, not down at the ground or off to the side first. She must be telling the truth.

"It talked about how big water contractors sell their unused state water entitlements to other agencies to cover new private development projects, but the water rights being sold aren't real," Brad explained.

"Oh, paper water," Megan said. "That used to be a big problem. Lots of new development got approved without any real supply of water because of how the DWR was allowing the water contractors to treat their unallocated supplies. But the State Supreme Court pretty much stopped that in the Vineyards case out of Sacramento years ago."

"That's what Scott said at the Chamber. He said water reliability is now very closely studied and regulated by the state," Brad said. "I'm wondering if we really need to have peer review of Western's report. Seems like it might be overkill."

She shook her head and scowled. "Yes, the state reviews and approves the Urban Water plans and they are copied on draft EIR's. But they don't get too involved in commenting about anything beyond the estimates of reliability used for state water deliveries. If you remember from our meeting, I wasn't objecting to what Western had for state water delivery; I think it was around 30 percent during an extended drought. But you should know, Brad, that there have been years when they didn't even deliver 30 percent of normal. I didn't even push that point."

"Oh," he said flatly.

She continued. "My bigger problem with the supply numbers was the reliability of groundwater pumping and our reservoir in a multi-year drought. The state doesn't weigh in on that. It's a matter of local discretion and I still maintain that Dee is leaning on Western to side with SoCal. Besides, I also think the demand numbers are being understated."

Brad's heart sank a little. He had hoped there wouldn't be a need to bring in a second water consultant. Maybe Megan was right about both Green Valley's water demand and the questionable reliability of the local water sources. He didn't know. He decided on the spot to stay the course with the peer review of Western's report. He reminded Megan to follow up on the illegal banner the mayor complained about, wished her a Happy Thanksgiving, and went back to his office.

Jane had already made the minor edit changes to the staff reports and had a draft transmittal memo ready to go for printing. He initialed the agenda reports and took them out to her for copying.

It was close to 1 p.m. and he was antsy to hit the road for the four-and-a-half hour trip to Stockton for the family Thanksgiving gathering.

He thought of his promise to Scott Graves to push the Green Valley EIR process along and had a brainstorm. Rather than waiting for Dee and Megan to try, and likely fail, to reach consensus on the consultant to be hired for the peer review, he took a few minutes to send them an email suggesting they hire Payton/Carlisle Associates. He disclosed to them that one of his city manager colleagues, Quinn O'Rourke, had retired and was now doing business development for the firm. He had been pitched by his friend and was impressed by the firm's size, breadth of services, and client list. He asked that the two department heads specifically consider that firm and get back to him Monday after the Thanksgiving break. He didn't mention his ulterior motive.

10

Brad's eyelids drooped as he drove home from work at 1:15 p.m. He had been looking forward to a nap while Marie drove the first leg of their trip to Stockton, however, Dillon pleaded to drive. They relented to his badgering. In exchange for his help packing the car, Dillon would be allowed to take the wheel for the forty-minute trip to Santa Maria where they would visit Lilly in the hospital.

Driver's training is one of those important, potentially frightening, rites of passage a parent has to help their teenager survive. Dillon and Kristen still laughed about their father's first lesson for each of them. He took them to a cemetery in the evening. There was nobody around who could be hurt or make the kids self-conscious. Brad liked the not-so-subtle message of safety the venue offered.

Approaching the hospital, Brad rallied in anticipation of hearing a little more from Lilly about the dam disaster. Dillon went straight to the cafeteria as Marie and Brad navigated the floors to Lilly's room, a regular room, not ICU. Not bad for someone her age who just had major surgery the day before. They embraced Lilly gently and got an update on her condition.

They exchanged small talk about Thanksgiving rituals, families, and hospital experiences. Brad stole a glance at his watch and tried to steer the conversation. He mentioned a bit more of his Internet research on the dam disaster.

Lilly picked up the prompt. "Listen, I know you want to get on the road so we can talk about my memories another time. You kids should take off."

"Not at all!" Brad blurted. "If you feel up to it now, we'd both be fascinated to hear from someone who actually lived through the disaster."

"Well, keep in mind that it was over eighty-five years ago. I was only four or five at the time. I only have bits of memories of the night it happened. Most of what I know I got from other people who were there or things people wrote."

"We're all ears," Brad said clearing a place on the padded window seat for Marie and him to sit.

Lilly took a long sip through the straw of her water and began. "So you probably know that LA built that big pipe to bring water from a lake on the east side of the Sierras that allowed the San Fernando Valley to be developed." Marie and Brad nodded. Lilly continued, "And that they built the St. Francis Dam to store some of that water in a canyon a few miles east of Highway 99."

"I-5." Lee interjected.

"It was 99, then. It's my story, don't interrupt!" Lilly scolded.

"OK, OK," Lee said. Then, to Marie and Brad, "You can tell she's her old self again. I'm going to take advantage of you being here to go to the cafeteria. Lilly is only going to get liquids. But can I bring you two back anything?"

They both declined and Lee walked out.

"So, Highway 99?" Brad prompted.

"Oh, yes, the Edison electricity company had a tent city with about 150 people along the Santa Clara River at a railroad siding called Kemp. It was maybe ten or fifteen miles to the west of the dam, right near the Los Angeles/Ventura county lines on what is now Highway 126 that connects the coast at Ventura to the San Fernando Valley and Los Angeles."

"I know the area," encouraged Brad. "I grew up just over the hill in Ventura County. And I read a little about that camp. Were you there?"

Lilly nodded. "The men were bringing power lines through the area. It was hard work. The families pretty much stayed in the camp all the time. But back then people didn't expect much. They were grateful to have a job and we kids got by. We had regular meals, a teacher who cracked a whip during the day, and lots of other kids to play with. I don't remember people griping about things. It was different back then."

"Did people at the camp worry about being downstream from the dam?" Brad asked.

"I heard that people used to joke about it," Lilly responded. "They'd say things like 'see you tomorrow. . . if the dam don't break.' But it wasn't a big issue everyone talked about. It was out of sight, out of mind."

"Was there any warning?" Brad wondered.

"None!" she said emphatically. "It was the middle of the night. Everyone was asleep. It was very cold and dark that night. The camp lights had all gone out for some reason. People said they heard and felt the flood coming before they ever saw it. They say the water was sixty feet high when it finally hit our camp."

"Wow," Brad said, "that's like a five-story building all of a sudden slamming down on you. It's amazing anyone survived."

"It made a roaring sound as it snapped citrus trees, houses, and anything else in its path. The only reason some people were able to escape is that the initial wave was so packed with debris and mud that it was moving slow." She looked between them, "I heard later they said it was moving about ten miles per hour."

"Still. . ." Marie added.

"Now that I think about it," Lilly interrupted, "the man who father got to paint my horse and burn 'Brownie' into him was Mr. Locke, the night watchman. He was the other reason some people survived. He was awake and must have heard the terrible noise and felt the earth trembling. He probably thought at first that it was a big freight train since the camp was right along the railroad tracks. They say that when Mr. Locke got his first glimpse of the water coming, he ran through the camp waking people up and yelling to run to high ground. He kept yelling until he got swallowed up by the floodwaters himself. He never even took a moment to remove his heavy topcoat. If he had, he would at least have had a chance to swim to safety." She paused, let out a long exhale, and stared into space. "He was a nice man."

"We don't have to do this now, Lilly," Marie said. "There will be other times." Brad nodded but leaned forward hoping that Lilly would opt to continue.

"It's all right. I feel like I'm honoring the memory of those who died by telling the story."

"Well, if you feel up to it, can you tell us what happened to you when the flood hit the camp?" Brad asked.

"Yes. I learned this part later on. Remember when I said it was a cold night? Well, father must have tied off the door flap of the tent we lived in to keep more warmth in. A lot of other families did the same thing that night. At first we were all swept away but then the water hit a big rock outcropping where the valley narrows called Blue Cut. At Blue Cut, some of the flood doubled back on itself and created a whirlpool. The tents that made it to that whirlpool and had their door flaps tied up had some air trapped inside. They bobbed to the surface and rode out the flood on top of the water."

"How scary!" Marie exclaimed.

Lilly nodded, paused again, and continued. "I don't know how much of this I remember and how much I imagine based on what I heard later. But I believe that after we bobbed to the surface of the whirlpool, my father pulled back the door flap of the tent and he and Mom both threw me into some brush on the the hill just above the water line. Another survivor who saw that said that right after they threw me out, water rushed into the tent and they went down again. Mother and father were found dead the next day, almost to the ocean, wrapped around each other inside the tent at the bottom of a huge plug of trees, pieces of barns and houses, cars, and all sorts of junk. They died saving me."

"Oh, my God!" Marie cried again. "I can't imagine. You were so little. You must have been terrified."

"To tell the truth, about all I can remember from the rest of that night was being freezing cold and being driven to some building for the night in the back of a truck. Everyone was crying. Some woman I didn't know, and don't think I ever saw again, wrapped me in a blanket and held me tight all the way there. I think she lived on a ranch in the area. She stayed with me all night and the next day until Dad came for me."

Marie and Brad looked at each other quizzically. She just said her father had died in the flood. Was she losing some of her faculties or was she just getting mixed up by the meds?

Lilly seemed to still be back to that dark night of March 12, 1928. "It took a long time before the authorities knew how many people had been killed. Bodies were turning up everywhere. Of course, we didn't have the kind of records or techniques to identify bodies that we have now. There were hundreds of people who were simply reported as missing and many bodies that were never identified. But I do know that of the 150 people at our camp, eighty-four were officially identified as dead. Many of those who died were found wrapped inside their tents. Some had literally torn off their fingernails trying to claw their way out through the canvas to get out as the water rushed in. I knew all of them. A camp like that is tight-knit."

"Horrifying!" Marie gasped.

"Yes," Lilly added blankly. "When I got older and started asking questions about the disaster, my dad told me about the Los Angeles Coroner's Inquest hearings afterwards. I'll never forget some of those stories."

Marie and Brad glanced at each other again at this second reference to her father whom she said had been killed.

Lilly didn't seem to notice their exchange. "There was a man named Ray Rising, a Los Angeles Department of Power and Water employee who lived at the dam's Powerhouse No. 2 with his family, a mile-and-a-half downstream from the dam. He heard the roar of the dam break but thought it was a tornado. He was from Minnesota. He ran to the front door just in time to see a wall of water and debris ten stories tall right on top of him. He was swept into the torrent and somehow was able to grab onto a rooftop racing by and climb aboard. He held on until it hit against the mountain where he was able to jump off and scramble up the mountain, out of the wave."

"Incredible," Brad said.

"He called to his wife and children from his perch on the side of the mountain but there was no answer. At dawn, he met a woman and her two-year-old son who had also miraculously survived. Of the twenty-eight workers and their families stationed at the powerhouse, these three were the only ones left alive. The powerhouse building itself, sixty-five feet tall of solid concrete, disappeared under the 120-foot wave of water and concrete from the dam."

Marie and Brad shook their heads, imagining the horror.

"There were some amazing accounts from other survivors," Lilly added. "There was a man named Chester Smith who lived a few miles down from Powerhouse No. 2. He had heard the talk about the dam's instability and had seen the leaks himself a few days before. He was nervous and decided to sleep up in the barn with the doors wide open despite the cold. I guess it was so he could hear anything coming, he was that nervous. Dogs barking after midnight woke him up. He heard the sound of trees and a nearby electrical pole snapping and instantly concluded the dam had broken. He jumped out of his cot and ran in the direction of the wave to warn his hired hand and wife sleeping in the main house. When he saw he'd never make it, he and another hired hand and his wife scrambled up the mountain with the flood nipping at their bare feet. They were cold and bleeding, but alive, because of his precautions."

"Whew, that was a close call," Marie said.

"I've heard stories of others who weren't so fortunate. A man and his wife were in their house when the wave hit. They felt the house move. He ran to the front door to see what was happening but the door wouldn't budge. The house lurched again. He grabbed his wife's wrist and smashed the door trying to get out. Water instantly gushed through the opening, knocking him over. He lost his grip on his wife's wrist in the rushing water. He never saw her again. For what must have seemed an eternity, he was swept along the top of the wave and sometimes below it. He swallowed so much water and mud, and got sliced open by tangled barbed wire, trees, massive concrete chunks from the dam, fence posts, and every manner of junk in the water. Finally, the wave deposited him on higher ground. He was all beat up, semi-conscious, and nude; barely alive, but heart-broken that his wife had slipped away."

"Oh, Lilly," Marie cried.

Lilly continued, seeming to not even hear Marie's shock, her only focus on finishing her story. "I also heard about a young boy who was grabbed by his father and floated to safety. He lived the rest of his life with the image of his brother being swept away. His father had neither the time nor the strength to save both of his sons."

"Geez," Brad cried, "that's like the movie, *Sophie's Choice*, with Meryl Streep. She had to choose either her son or daughter to save from the Nazis." He shuddered. "That scene was absolutely haunting."

Lilly nodded. "When the floodwaters hit the hill at what is now Magic Mountain, the water shifted north. Everything in Castaic Junction was gone. The owner of the café, gas station, and cabins was outside with one of his sons when the water hit and they were swept away. He was able to grab a utility pole sticking up through the flood water as they rushed by. He put his son on the back side of the pole at the water line and put his own back to the water to take the blows. He was smashed by debris as he tried to hold on. After a few minutes he cried, 'Oh, my God! I'm hurt!' Then just 'Goodbye' as he lost his grip on the utility pole. His son was the sole survivor of Castaic Junction."

"Good Lord," Brad said. His curiosity had been sated. "Lilly, this is all so terrible. Please don't feel like you need to say anymore."

She was looking straight ahead at the wall. "It does bring back horrible nightmares. But, like I said, at this point in my life, I feel like I owe it to the survivors to tell their story. People just don't know about this." She turned to face them. Brad felt she was looking directly at him. "Maybe there is some lesson to be learned."

He returned her look and they maintained eye contact for a few moments. He had the eerie feeling there was another dimension to her comment.

Lilly recounted a few other stories she had heard of the great tragedy that night in 1928. Of the seventy-five families living immediately below the dam in the San Francisquito Canyon, only one person survived by clawing his way up the sheer canyon walls just before the first wave hit.

She also told stories of great bravery. Volunteers plunged into the raging water to try to rescue victims, both human and animal. Some perished in the effort.

"At around 2:15 a.m., the alarms in Santa Paula started to go off, warning people of the coming flood. People came out of their houses half asleep in their night clothes to see what was going on. There was a California Highway Patrol officer named Thornton Edwards who rode his motorcycle at full speed yelling at people to get to high ground. But it wasn't raining like it always had in past floods so people didn't understand or react right away. There were about a hundred, mostly Spanish-speaking, gawkers congregating on the bridge over the Santa Clara River to see what all the fuss was about. Edwards yelled 'mucho agua' but the people were still confused. There was no water in the river below them. It isn't known what Officer Edwards said next but whatever it was put the fear of God in the people. They suddenly took off running. Some minutes later the flood hit the bridge and wiped it out, snapping the gas lines that hung from it. They say the gas explosions and noise from the bridge ripping apart were deafening."

"I can imagine," Brad said.

"Officer Edwards wasn't done. After the bridge, he continued his motorcycle dash through the streets of Santa Paula to warn people. He made a turn from one street downtown to another and found himself just yards from the wave, going too fast to get out of the way. He was inundated with mud, but lived, and became the first man in CHP history to receive a gold medal for bravery."

"Well deserved, I would say," Marie said.

Lilly nodded agreement. "There were other heroes; just common citizens. I heard about one rancher who put himself in the path of the flood to wake up a bunch of hoboes living under the Saticoy Bridge. He got eighteen people out just before the flood hit and washed half of the bridge away. A nineteenth hobo saw the dry river bed and refused to be bothered. His body was discovered in thick mud on the beach."

Lilly stopped and closed her eyes. Her energy was clearly flagging. Just when it seemed she might nod off, she opened her eyes and perked up. "So many tragedies and heroic actions and even some freak things like you hear about with tornadoes. You know, like a car that gets picked up and deposited five miles away, intact, and is able to be driven away. I remember hearing about a rancher up valley whose home was destroyed. Their free-standing cupboard was found on the side of the river ten miles away. None of the china was even chipped!"

Lee entered the room with a styrofoam cup of coffee. Marie and Brad looked at each other and Brad nodded his head toward the door. Marie nodded back getting the signal.

"Thank you for sharing all of these stories with us, Lilly." Brad said.

"I am so happy your surgery went well. You'll get stronger every day." Marie said encouragingly.

They each hugged Lilly and then walked through the door.

Brad signaled to Lee to walk with them outside. When they were in the corridor, Marie said to Lee quietly, "We really appreciate Lilly opening up to us about her experiences. But we are concerned that she seemed confused."

"Oh?" Lee said.

Marie nodded and continued. "She talked about how her father was killed in the flood while saving her but then later she talked about things her father told her years after the incident. I figured it would be normal for her to be disoriented about such a traumatic event early in her life especially when she's doped up on pain killers. Do you think she's OK?"

Lee smiled. "Her mind is sharp, don't worry about that. I think what she left out is that after her father was killed in the flood, his brother, her uncle, adopted her. She refers to her real father as 'Father' and to her adoptive father as 'Dad.' But I can see why that would be confusing."

"Oh, I see," responded Brad with relief. "What an admirable thing for her uncle to do. It must have been very tough for everyone involved."

"I never met him," Lee said. "I've heard he was a good guy and did a fine job raising Lilly. But there's more to it. Her uncle that she calls 'dad' worked for the LA Department of Power and Water and was involved in the dam design. He carried a lot of guilt over that. That's another part of the story that Lilly will have to tell you when she's up to it."

11

Marie was willing to take the next leg of the trip so that Brad could nap sometime during the hour-long trip from Santa Maria to Paso Robles. Marie was a competent, but nervous, driver and, while she didn't say it, Brad knew she'd like him to be awake when they exited northbound Highway 101 near the coast for eastbound Highway 46 to connect with Interstate 5 all the way north to Stockton through the Central Valley. Highway 46 could be slow and scary; its two lanes agonizingly slow if you get stuck behind a big rig or one of those families in a huge RV pulling a jeep piled high with camping gear. There were plenty of straight stretches where passing was permissible but it was dicey. The James Dean Memorial at the junction of Highways 46 and 41, near the site of the head-on crash that killed the Hollywood icon, was a grim reminder of the danger. Brad wanted to be awake to help her through that stretch.

"Good job," he said to Marie as they began to transition from Highway 41 to Interstate 5 near Kettleman City.

They crested the last hill before I-5 for a panoramic view of the southern San Joaquin Valley before them. The green agricultural lands, as far as the eye could see, were a stunning contrast to the still golden brown hills and occasional roadkill they had just passed. And there, quite close to I-5, was the Governor Edmund G. Brown California Aqueduct, the lifeline of the State Water Project. The aqueduct was a concrete-lined channel that, in most spots, was about forty feet wide and thirty feet deep. The channel had a flow rate of 13,100 cubic feet per second which converted to nearly 100,000 gallons every second. It was a mind boggling amount of water when considering that the aqueduct ran hundreds of miles from the Sacramento-San Joaquin Delta all along the west side of the San Joaquin Valley, up and over the Tehachapi Mountains, then down to the Los Angeles Basin.

They made a bathroom and burger stop. Brad took over the driving and, in accordance with their adopted policy, control of the radio. He switched it to Radio Classics just in time for *Tales of the Texas Rangers*.

"Do we have to?" Dillon whined from the back seat. Brad smiled in the rear view mirror at him. Dillon made a face and stuck in his earbuds. Brad soon realized it was a repeat of an episode he had heard last week. He touched the preset button to the 70s channel, always a reasonable compromise.

He looked out at the aqueduct and irrigated farmland with much more interest than he had on prior trips along I-5. It put him back into work mode.

"I'm looking forward to talking to Kris about all of this water stuff," he said to Marie.

"And Tanner may have a point of view on it too," she added.

"Gee, do you think your brother could be prodded to speak up?" he laughed.

Tanner McGuire was just a few years younger than Marie but still acted like a twenty-year-old. Over six feet tall and solidly built, he could still toss around 120-pound bales of alfalfa on the family ranch which he now ran since his and Marie's father's death six years ago. Tanner had been a starting linebacker on the University of California, Davis football team. That hadn't been enough physical contact for him so he also joined the university's rugby club. He continued to play rugby with a local club well into his 40s and now coached the team. Tanner was a man's man.

"You may have to speak up yourself when you talk to him," Marie advised. "Bridget says he's getting hard of hearing. Maybe one too many blows to the head. Hard to think of my brother as getting old."

A memory popped into his head. "Did I ever tell you that when we were first dating, Tanner invited me to one of his rugby matches?"

"Probably, but go ahead," she responded.

"As I was walking from the parking lot to the field I was surprised to see that some of the players were wearing helmets. I didn't think they wore any protection at all. As I got closer I saw that those silver helmets were actually duct tape. Tanner told me the players run a couple wraps of tape around their heads to keep their ears from being ripped off in the scrums!"

"I'm glad you got Dillon into golf!" she said, glancing in the rear view mirror.

"Yeah, just the pain of stripping the tape off afterwards would be too much for me. That's the only rugby match I've ever been to. Tanner and the other players smashed into each other at full speed for an hour-and-a-half. It was like a gang fight with halftime. But I'll say this, after trying to kill each other, when the match was over they all met in the center of the field, embraced, and went out for beers."

She chuckled. "Tanner used to claim that soccer is a gentlemen's game played by ruffians and rugby a ruffian's game played by gentlemen."

"How's he doing besides his hearing?" he asked.

"Sounds like he's doing fine. He's got a guy running the welding shop for him but he still drops in sometimes. Mostly he takes care of things on the ranch and plays."

Brad smiled. "He'll always be a big kid. I still carry a scar from that welding shop." He pointed to a burn mark on his right hand.

"I remember. That decorative iron lattice he was making that my dad asked you to pick up."

"Burned the crud out of my hand. I give him credit. He never teased me about it."

"He probably did the same thing to himself many times. I remember how much you whined when you got back to the ranch when I put on the cream and bandages."

Brad scowled at the shot. "Well, it hurt like hell!"

"I know. And you were *so* brave!" she teased.

He ground his teeth and drove on silently, thinking about his macho brother-in-law. After about ten more miles they passed a mileage sign to Coalinga.

"What do you hear from Joan these days?" he asked. Joan Ruiz, Marie's closest cousin, lived in Coalinga, a small town west of I-5 that got its name from a railway fueling stop, Coaling Station A, that was shortened to Coaling A.

"More trouble, I'm afraid," she said. "Mike lost his job a while back and, last I heard, hadn't landed anything yet."

Joan seemed to live under a perpetual dark cloud. In recent years, she had to deal with earthquake damage to their home, a car wreck, their teenage son's battle with drug addiction, and now her husband losing his job at the batch plant.

"Oh, God," he cried. "Not another problem. How are they getting by?"

"I feel bad that I haven't talked to her for a while. Last time I did, she still sounded upbeat. You know Joan."

"Amazing. Any one of the calamities she's faced could push another person into deep depression. I don't know how she does it."

He could feel her looking at him as he stared straight ahead at the road. "Oh, I think you know how she does it," Marie said. "She and Mike have a strong faith. Rather than stewing about their misfortunes, she always finds something to be grateful for. She'll talk about the wildflowers on the hills, the wide open spaces around them they love, a sunset, or the blessings of good health. They live modestly, but are happy."

Blessings. He sneaked a peek in the mirror at his son who was glued to his laptop. He smelled Marie's cologne. It was the fragrance he bought her for her last birthday. What was the name of it? He glanced over to Marie and felt the warmth of his wife's smile. Blessings, indeed.

Holiday traffic was heavy but moving at a decent clip. The weather was clear and they were treated to some beautiful sunset vistas of waterways and farmlands as they skirted the southeast edge of the Sacramento-San Joaquin River Delta in the upper middle part of the state, east of San Francisco Bay. "It really is pretty, isn't it?" Brad observed.

Marie seconded the observation. "I never appreciated it when I was growing up. It's nice to be back."

They drove the next half hour in relative silence, enjoying the views and music as they headed for Marie's family home in the rich agricultural area east of Stockton near the community of Linden. The family had 120 acres of walnuts, eighty acres of cherries, seventy acres of vineyards, and another thirty acres consisting of vegetable and herb gardens, various fruit trees, barn and stable areas, garages and out buildings, a rambling, single-story brick home, and two small, but tidy, guest houses. It was dark as they pulled off the asphalt county road onto the ranch's gravel driveway.

"Funny," Marie said, "just hearing the crunch of rocks under the tires makes me feel good." She busied herself by picking the things up around her seat and primping.

Brad pulled around the circular driveway and stopped under the porte-cochere. Their daughter, Kristen, was the first one out the front door. She walked briskly to hug Marie then Brad as they emerged from the car. Then, to Brad's surprise, and apparently Dillon's, she also gave her brother a quick hug. Brad had an instant flash of a Christmas morning when he sent the kids back up to their rooms for hitting each other as they scrambled for presents under the tree. The moment of melancholy was broken by the next person through the door.

"Hey, Scoot!" Tanner bellowed, plucking Marie off the ground for a bear hug.

Brad prepared himself for the handshake to come. The most important thing was getting good palm-to-palm contact. That engaged the larger muscles of the arm and gave him a chance of emerging unscathed. There had been times when Brad had undershot his arm extension and Tanner had caught just his fingers causing his hand to fold over onto Tanner's. It was a most unsatisfyingly weak shake like noblemen might have affected in the Victorian Era. Plus, taking the full impact of Tanner's grip on his knuckles was painful.

"And Crat Man!" Tanner had nicknames for everyone. "My favorite bureaucrat Super Hero." He liked teasing Brad for working for the government. At the same time, Tanner often made it clear that he respected his brother-in-law. He was the type of generous spirit who didn't feel diminished by propping somebody else up. Tanner was the prototype of a person "comfortable in his own skin."

Tanner bounded around the car, bulging arm starting to reach out for his brother-in-law. Brad braced for it and jammed his own hand deep into Tanner's. Good contact. No pain. A manly embrace. Tanner must have felt good about it, too. He put his big left hand on Brad's shoulder and gave him a couple thumps.

Brad nodded in the direction of the small cottage to the left where Kristen was living. "Well, I don't see any yellow tape around the house," Brad said. "It must have survived your cheesy potatoes."

Kris groaned. "Beat it into the ground, Dad."

Brad kept an arm around his daughter's shoulder as they walked to the door. The rest of the family was inside. Tanner's wife, Bridget, was in the kitchen. Their twin fourteen-year-old girls were lying on the carpet in the living room looking at magazines with the television blaring. Marie's mother, Beva, known to the family as Nana, was seated at a round maple table next to the kitchen working a jigsaw puzzle and giving instructions to Bridget.

After everyone had caught up a little, Nana called everyone to dinner. Marie and Kris helped Bridget serve the meal in the dining room.

Tanner walked in with two bottles of wine. "This is our latest Zin. You're going to love it," he said proudly. San Joaquin County was one of the top Zinfandel producing areas in the world. The combination of rich, fertile soil, and hot temperatures transformed the black-skinned grapes into a very robust red wine.

Tanner gushed about the wine like the father of a newborn. He deftly removed the cork and poured the juice into a decanter to "let it breathe" a little before serving. Then he poured a sample into the bottom of a large goblet, swirling it around, and raising the glass into the light. He showed the glass to his audience. "Good legs," he pronounced.

Tanner continued swirling and stuck his nose into the glass. "Ahhh, very fruity."

Finally, he took a sip and let it stay on his tongue a while before saying, "notes of blackberry, anise, and pepper."

He suddenly smiled mischievously.

"Who wants a belt?" he asked.

Tanner could pull off the transition from "Master Sommelier at the Ritz" to "Good Ole Boy at the bar" without seeming fake in either role.

All of the adults, including Kris, partook. Nana, whose personal longevity secret was two cigarettes and two shots of Scotch every night, indulged in a splash.

Brad wasn't much of a wine guy and he bored quickly with all of the chatter his oenologist friends seem to require before they could drink the stuff. Truth be told, it all tasted about the same to him. He preferred beer. At least Tanner played his role with good humor. And the wine did taste pretty good even if Brad never sensed the blackberry, anise, or pepper notes; well maybe the anise a little bit. Brad thought how satisfying it must be for Tanner to have used his own sweat to bring something out of the ground that was apparently so satisfying. Tanner was a man of the land.

The Sloppy Joes were good and filling. They all helped clear the table and Nana, Bridget, and Marie told everyone to leave the kitchen so they could clean up. That was code for "leave us alone so we can talk." Everyone complied willingly. Dillon went with the twins to watch TV. He enjoyed his status as the idolized older male cousin.

Kris, Tanner, and Brad migrated outside to the covered porch that ran the width of the front of the house, a glass of Zin in hand. They settled into the comfortable padded rocking chairs looking out at the walnut grove. A waxing moon played peekaboo with the scattered cumulus clouds. It was cold outside but they had coats. After starting the day early with the Chamber meeting, the long drive, big dinner, and a couple glasses of wine, Brad needed the invigorating air.

They engaged in a bit of small talk then Brad turned to Tanner.

"I have a councilwoman who is a big environmentalist and is all worked up about state water policies and especially protecting the Delta. If you don't mind, I asked Kris for her opinions. I'm interested in your take, too."

He knew Tanner would see that as a challenge. "Sure!" Tanner said. "Glad to hear it. We could use more politicians from south of Tracy to give a damn about the Delta."

"Great, feel free to add your two cents or just light a cigar and enjoy this great wine." Brad said.

Tanner considered his options as he made the redwood deck creak under his rocker. "Little Flea will be smarter on that. But I'll look for a gap in the line and charge in when I can." Then he jumped up. "I like the cigar idea, though. Can I get you one, Brad? Got some good ones in my truck."

"Absolutely!" Brad said enthusiastically. He really wasn't a big cigar fan either. Once in a blue moon he'd have one with the guys during a golf outing, but it was an opportunity to bond with Tanner in a mostly male activity.

When Tanner left, Brad turned to his daughter and said, "OK, let's see what a BA in Environmental Studies and two years of studying the Delta in grad school has taught you. Make me smart for my councilwoman."

"I'll try," she promised. "As I thought about our conversation, I decided to start with a little background. It will help you understand where we are today."

"I'm all ears, professor," Brad said.

She started with a quick introduction to basic geography. The Delta region bisected California's Central Valley, dividing it into the Sacramento Valley to the north and the San Joaquin Valley to the south. Much of the area is below sea level, gathering water from the north through the Sacramento River, from the Mokelumne River to the north and east and the San Joaquin River from the southeast. About 40 percent of all the run-off in California finds its way into those rivers. The fresh waters from the rivers blend with the saltwater from the San Francisco Bay on the west side of the Delta, creating the largest estuary west of the Mississippi.

"You like history, Dad. Did you know that before man came along and started to fiddle with the creeks and rivers, much of the valley was an inland sea and marshlands in the rainy season and golden grasslands in the dry periods? It was home to millions of ducks, geese, antelope, Tule elk, and thousands of grizzly bears."

"Hard to imagine that today," he said.

"Yeah. The Miwok Indians had a thriving culture in the Delta until the mid-1800s when American and European explorers and trappers in search of mink and beavers exposed them to diseases that nearly wiped them out. Then busted gold miners went back to farming and started damming and redirecting the waterways, changing everything."

"And Chinese laborers built the levees that really altered the environment," Brad chimed in.

"Good, Dad," she said. "Now, just a little enviro babble. Remember that the Delta is the low point of the Central Valley with all of the rivers draining there. With all of the gold mining dredgings washing down the rivers, along with just normal river flows and tidal action over millions of years, the Delta collected lots of upstream sediment. The sediment covered the tules and other plants in the region creating peat. That's a rich combination of silty soil and decomposed plant material. These organic soils reach depths of sixty feet in some areas of the Delta. It's great soil for agriculture but not a very sturdy foundation for levees. I had to read a book called *Battling the Inland Sea* for one of my classes. It describes the history of successful and failed efforts to keep flood waters contained and the levees shored enough to hold back the salt water from San Francisco Bay. It's a never ending battle that figures into what's going on today."

Tanner returned to catch the tail end of Kris' summary. As he held the torch for Brad and him to light their cigars, he added, "the big water contractors are trying to scare people about the levees to sell their water tunnel scheme to take water around the Delta to the pumping plants. It's bullshit!" Tanner took a big swallow to finish his glass of wine and re-filled his and Brad's before sitting down heavily in his rocker, blowing a giant smoke ring.

"Why is it bullshit, Tan Man?" Brad asked. "Aren't you worried that the levees could fail and the Delta would be ruined with salt water?"

"You say 'ruined', Dad," Kris interjected, before Tanner could respond. "Others would say 'restored.' Ever since the Gold Rush, the Delta and Central Valley have been exploited by people trying to overcome nature for their own purposes. You read about the federal Central Valley Project, CVP, and State Water Project. Cases in point."

"Yeah," Brad said. "My councilwoman thinks the state project was one of the worst things we could have done to California in terms of the environment and unsustainable development."

Tanner bristled. "She probably thinks we should let the levees go and give everything back to nature. Turn the Delta back into a swamp. When I was in Davis there were plenty of eco-freaks who wanted to do that."

Kris jumped to the defense. "Sure, you can find radicals on any issue, Unc. But environmentalists know that everything is a balancing act. The question is: what can *reasonably* be done to restore sensitive areas or at least reduce the damage caused by man's activities? There's too much invested in the Delta to turn it back to nature now."

Tanner exhaled another huge ring and picked up his prior

thought. "I said the levee scare is bullshit because we don't need the water tunnels to improve them. It would cost a fraction of what they want us to spend on the tunnels to shore up the levees. Those Delta peat soils you talked about produce over $500 million a year of asparagus, pears, corn, grain, hay, sugar beets, and tomatoes. And about two-thirds of all Californians, and millions of acres of irrigated farmland, get their water through the CVP and State Water Project by way of the Delta. Damn right, we have a lot invested here and we should be strengthening the levees, not stealing water destined for the Delta."

"No argument," said Kris, clearly hoping to appease her slightly buzzed uncle. Tanner was known to have strong political opinions that didn't pair well with Zin. "I think California's agriculture is worth something like $27 billion a year and the Delta is very productive. I'm not arguing that we can or should turn back the clock on what's already done. Remember, I'm going for my MBA now, Unc. I live in the real world."

"Well, all right!" Tanner slapped his knee enthusiastically. "And don't forget all of the tourism dollars and recreation that the Delta contributes for boating, fishing, and hunting." His speech was getting thicker and louder.

Kris continued her thought. "Beyond the economics, the Delta's ecosystem is a rich and productive habitat for more than 500 species of wildlife and supports twenty endangered species. It also serves as a migration path for salmon traveling to and from their home streams and the Pacific Ocean. And, during fall and winter, agricultural fields in the Delta provide habitat for large populations of migratory waterfowl. You know, Unc, those little birds you like to blow out of the sky!"

Tanner gulped some more wine and leaned forward to stop the rocker. "That reminds me, Crat Man, I have us all set up at the duck club Friday. You still in?" He polished off his glass of wine and picked up the bottle from the porch for another refill.

"Sure," Brad said with feigned enthusiasm. Yet another activity to bond with his brother-in-law which he'd prefer to avoid. It wasn't fair. Brad could never get Tanner out for a round of golf. It wasn't that Brad was such an avid golfer. It happened to be the only sport he had found that he was better at than Tanner.

"You're invited, too, Little Flea," Tanner said.

"Tempting offer, Unc, but I'll pass," Kristen said. "Mom, Bridget, and I are going to do some shopping."

Both men groaned.

"God, don't let Bridget buy any more shoes," Tanner begged. "I swear that woman is a centipede!"

Brad began tapping his foot on the wood porch. He had hoped that Tanner would either have left from boredom or fallen asleep by now. He felt himself fading and had a few more questions of his daughter before calling it quits.

"Back to water, Kris. Give me five minutes on the Bay Delta Conservation Plan."

"Five minutes?! It would take you that long just to lift it out of the boxes! The plan and EIR is over 40,000 pages."

"Forty thousand?" Brad cried with incredulity. "*War and Peace* was the longest book I ever read at about 1,000 pages of tiny print. It took me an entire summer after college to get through but I wanted to be able to say I read it. I can't imagine reading a government document equivalent to forty books that size."

"Yup, and it isn't even all coordinated in one place. There are hundreds of separate files you would have to download to see what is being proposed. It's a mess. I don't know how anyone could read and understand it."

"Maybe that's the whole idea," Brad observed. "Make it so

complicated and burdensome to analyze, people will just throw up their hands. I've learned lately that sort of obfuscation by government to help sell a big water project is not unprecedented."

Kris took a small sip of wine nodding her head. "One of the best classes I took as an undergrad was 'Water and Environmental Policy.' There's no question that since the very beginning, state policies and spending have emphasized making more water available for ag lands and urban uses over preserving the environment. There are just a lot more people who have a vested interest in using water than protecting the environment." She leaned back in her chair a bit and crossed her ankles. "Politicians and the state bureaucracy are responsive to those interests, so it shouldn't be a surprise that government has a pro-project bias, as BDCP is demonstrating. They have billions of dollars and thousands of employees on their side. People who want to see water used in a more sustainable way and to reverse some of the damage that has already been done to the environment are horribly out-gunned."

She paused, then nodded toward her uncle. Tanner's eyes were closed and his mouth open, but he still precariously held a cigar in one hand and a nearly empty glass in the other. "I guess my rant put him out," she whispered.

"I'm running out of gas myself. Can you just give me a quick summary of the BDCP before I join your uncle?"

"OK," she said. "It evolved from an earlier plan called CALFED that sought to reverse the decline of Delta water quality and endangered species resulting from the State Water Project. The feds required more water to be released to the Delta from the reservoirs and restricted exports from the southern Delta to protect the fish. As with other attempts to get a balanced plan, nobody was happy."

"Yeah, I remember CALFED," Brad said. "I was at a Mayors' Conference in Sacramento County when somebody from the State was there to talk about it. Poor guy took flak from all over the room. One of the small Delta town mayors threatened castration!"

"Woulda' been too painless," Tanner grumbled, opening his eyes and taking a pull on his cigar.

Kristen ignored him. "Well, it was a good try at bringing everyone together," she continued. "But they didn't have the money or clout to implement the plan and it fell apart. California returned to water litigation wars. There was a blue ribbon panel formed that created a strategic plan for the Delta in the late 2000s. It called for water reliability and restoration of the Delta's ecosystem to be considered as 'co-equal' goals. The Legislature passed the Delta Reform Act, which created the Delta Stewardship Council, with authority to manage the Delta. The BDCP is the planning effort that was supposed to negotiate all of the complex issues and competing interests with the stakeholders to achieve those co-equal goals. But it hasn't gone well, either."

"No shit!" Tanner sneered. "The governor's point man for the BDCP even admitted that the plan isn't, and never was, about saving the Delta. He said, 'the Delta can't be saved.' He was forced to resign for telling the truth." Tanner flicked ash into the sand-filled abalone shell that served as an ashtray and gulped down the rest of his wine. Tanner McGuire was no longer savoring the blackberry and anise tones of the Zin.

"Unc's right," Kristen said. "The BDCP has drawn so much fire that they have already moved away from that and replaced it with two separate plans. California Water Fix is the same idea to take water around the Delta in big tunnels instead of picking it up at the south end. And Eco Restore is the habitat restoration piece. However, the conservation portion went from $7 billion to just $300 million."

"Same ole, same ole," Tanner snarled. "They don't care about Delta conservation. They just want to grab the water. They aren't going to stop until they've completely destroyed the Delta. We can never let our guard down."

Kristen nodded. "It's not clear yet how the latest plans differ from BDCP which has drawn so much fire. I haven't read it yet. I heard it's another 8,000 pages. But it sure is evident that it's about the tunnels not improving habitat. In fact, most of the 30,000 acres left in the plan for habitat is already required to be restored under an endangered species agreement with the federal government. It's not new habitat."

Brad frowned and shifted in his chair to reach the abalone shell. "I'm sure it's all very complicated and there are multiple sides on all of the issues."

"I agree with that, Dad, but I'm afraid Unc is right about the motivations involved here. As an environmentalist, I applaud the attempt to develop a long range management plan that considers the Delta as an entire system. Sure, water supply reliability is hugely important for the entire state economy, not just the big growers in the San Joaquin and Southern California urban areas. But so are water quality, habitat restoration, levee stability, and maintaining the agricultural, recreational and tourism values of the Delta. It's going to require looking at everything as a system and making some compromises. But historically, the state and water lobby's approach has been to push for more water projects and do only what they were forced to do to address the impacts to ecosystems on a piecemeal basis."

"So I'm starting to understand," Brad said.

"My professor isn't optimistic that there can be a reasonable compromise solution. Too much money, too many unknowns, and too many people dug into their positions. In fact, I just read an article in the paper that LA water agencies are so desperate they are buying up land in the Delta and along the Colorado River to get control of the land's water rights. The Metropolitan Water District that provides most of the water in Southern California is now the biggest property owner in the Palo Verde Valley farming region at the Arizona border. The local farmers are worried they plan to dry it up in order to wheel the Colorado River water to Southern California for more development."

Brad sat forward and shot out a stream of smoke. "Really? Like they did in the Owens Valley a century ago? I hadn't heard that. I suppose it's the kind of action that arises when our political system doesn't take the leadership in solving problems," he added ruefully. "It's very tough to get anything major done anymore. And approval ratings for every institution in our society, whether politicians, government bureaucracies, big business, or labor unions are at all-time lows. The public doesn't trust anybody with the power to call the shots. Policy gridlock."

"I'll bet you see that a lot, Crat Man," Tanner slured.

"Way too much, Tan Man," Brad replied. "The media, and most of the big interest groups, make a lot of money fanning the flames of conflict. I don't know if we'll ever recover from the lack of civility and statesmanship in today's public decision-making." He finished his wine and handed his glass to Tanner for a refill.

"What are the big objections to the plan now?" he asked his daughter, settling back in his rocking chair.

"Besides the complaint that the whole plan is a 'document dump' intended to throw off informed opposition, the old plan converted thousands of acres of agricultural land to create new habitat."

"Stupid!" Tanner exclaimed too loudly. "We're supposed to give up farming on the best land in the state so that the big corporations can take our water to irrigate the desert? It's stupid!"

Kris pressed ahead. "There are also complaints about bad science being used to sell the plan. It doesn't describe how much existing habitat will be taken to implement the plan or what the mitigations will be. There is some expert opinion that putting the State Water Project intake on the north end of the Delta will cause reverse flows that will end up destroying fish populations rather than protecting them as the plan is supposed to do. It's just such a big project, it's impossible to be sure what the impacts are going to be and how to mitigate them up front."

"It sounds soooo complicated," Brad observed.

"It is, Dad. But this much we know. Every time man has intervened with the Delta since the days of the Miwoks, the water quality has suffered. Native Americans survived by living in harmony with their environment. Ever since the arrival of the Spanish in the 1700s, new settlers and their governments have viewed nature as something to be tamed and exploited. There are many who now believe the damage is irreversible."

"It's bullshit!" Tanner yelled again. "Anytime you hear the government talk about a plan for protecting the Delta, you should assume it's really about sending more water south or getting more control over what they already have."

"And we haven't even talked about the costs," Kristen added. "I'm part of a team helping a professor who is studying the plan's economics. BDCP had a chapter that pegs the total cost of the construction and operations over a fifty-year life at $25 billion. But when you factor in interest on the bond issues required to build the facilities and a whole bunch of other likely costs that aren't included in the analysis, recent estimates are closer to the $70 billion range."

"Holy cow!" Brad said. "This sounds just like when the state leaders deliberately understated the costs of the State Water Project to get it built. If the ratepayers are supposed to pay the load, that's going to be some very expensive water."

"There's also a problem with the demand estimates. The plan assumed five million more people in Southern California than the State Department of Finance is forecasting. It doesn't tie to the city and county General Plans on what the local communities are preparing for. Urban water demand is actually dropping because of local conservation practices and declining population growth. The cost of the water will be much higher if there isn't a bigger population base paying for it."

Brad sat up in his chair again. "Geez, again, just like when they contracted for twice as much State Water Project water as they knew they'd ever deliver to get the per unit cost down. 'Déjà vu all over again' as Yogi Berra said."

"The science behind the plan is questionable," Kris continued. "But the cost-benefit analysis used to promote the plan is downright vaporous. There are so many assumptions without adequate support that you could make any argument you want. Our team has tried to put numbers on some of the assumptions made in the plan and on other impacts that are likely, but not even addressed, in the plan. We've concluded it has a negative benefit-cost ratio. The state seems to be ignoring the cost evidence."

"It reminds me of the old joke," Brad interjected. "The CEO of a company is interviewing for a new Chief Financial Officer. He selects the candidate who, when asked, 'what is two plus two', looks around the room furtively, gets up from the chair to close the blinds and answers, 'whatever you want it to be.'"

"Liars figure and figures lie," Tanner added through closed eyes.

Brad nodded. "It's pretty shocking that our government would be a party to such a poor plan and what seems to be a deliberate attempt to mislead the public. I can understand that the big water contractors are focused on getting their water above all else; that water is money and money drives politics. But where are the state and federal civil servants who should be standing up to what's going on?" He stared at his wine and felt strangely discomforted by his own question and the question his daughter had asked him about his citizens' perception of City Hall.

"And the heck of it is," Kris said, "they want to spend $70 billion for a project that isn't even designed to deliver any new water. Yes, it is supposed to give more reliability for deliveries of water users south of the Delta especially in the event of levee breaches that could result in saltwater intrusion from the Bay. But it's at the risk of the ecosystem of the Delta, and all of the people who live, farm, recreate, or otherwise care about the Delta. It's back to pitting North against South in a win/lose power struggle."

Brad looked over the walnut trees to the moon and sky above, searching for an answer.

Kristen continued. "The communities around the Delta and the Delta watchdog groups feel like they have been given just a token effort at being heard. They made lots of suggestions when the plan was being developed and feel that they've been virtually ignored in favor of the big contractors. From the very beginning, the plan was developed to serve the water contractors' interest first. Even the governance structure that would be put in place under the plan's Implementing Agreement creates a clear conflict of interest. The water contractors, who should be the subject of the regulations by an impartial government agency, are themselves on all of the decision-making bodies but one. The Delta counties, and all the local agencies with jurisdiction over the areas that will be impacted by the plan, have no seat on *any* decision-making body at all."

"See? Bullshit!" Tanner said again.

"So, what *should* be done for the Delta and the rest of the state?" Brad asked sincerely.

Kristen shook her head. "I really don't know. It's complicated. One compromise is the so-called 'big gulp/little sip' approach. This would mean building more reservoirs and groundwater storage to capture more water in the wet periods. It could be metered out during the dry periods to reduce the impact on the environment while increasing delivery reliability. That kind of government spending should be coupled with better management of the state water, *and* groundwater, too."

"That sounds like where my councilwoman is coming from," Brad said. "She wants the state's water to be regulated more like we do air quality. Treat it as a public resource and use it wisely in support of stated public objectives."

"We are a long way from that," Kris responded. "California's water laws are an absolute hash and go back to the 1850s. But good luck trying to get reforms through the Legislature. Take a look at groundwater pumping. California has always had a 'pump-as-you-please' policy that hasn't served the state well as a whole. Every other western state has regulated pumping for years. But the water contractors have always had the money and votes to block true groundwater regulation in California. Remember, these are the same companies that have been given taxpayer-subsidized cheap water to use any way they want and make hundreds of millions of dollars on their otherwise useless land. They not only want that water to continue unimpeded, they also don't want anyone regulating how they use the water or how much they pump down the aquifer. They are even fighting legislation to limit how much Delta water can be used to extract more oil from their oil wells down the valley. It's called fracking."

Brad perked up with the mention of groundwater management since he had recently attended a session on the new law at a League meeting. "It took a horrible drought to get the California Legislature to finally start down the path of requiring local government to prepare groundwater management plans." He glanced at his daughter, hoping to see her impressed.

"Right, Dad, but it's too little, too late," Kristen complained. "We should be managing all of the water now. Today. That groundwater regulation Sacramento politicians are crowing about is so lame. It just calls for plans now. The law doesn't require the groundwater basins to achieve sustainability until around 2030. Meanwhile, the contractors can go right on pumping. With places in the Central Valley subsiding two feet a year from over-pumping, who knows how bad the state's aquifers will be by then?"

"Well, the new laws are a start at least. Maybe they'll be tightened up if things get worse," Brad said hopefully.

"Maybe. But we have a long way to go," she said. "There are still hundreds of thousands of homes in California that don't even have water meters and thousands of farmers who draw water completely unregulated. They can use as much as they like. The corporate interests in the Valley have things well in hand. Not a single Legislator from the Central Valley voted for even the wimpy groundwater planning law that was passed." She took a furtive look toward Tanner who, fortunately, was out for the count.

Brad felt the familiar shrug coming on. "I don't know how we are going to get California on track."

"The BDCP was an opportunity," Kris said ruefully. "It's like the plan sponsors just gave up trying to get a compromise and came up with their own scheme. They didn't want to consider any possibly better alternatives and thought they could muscle their way through. Maybe they figured they had enough votes in Sacramento and statewide to overcome the Delta stakeholders. But when the EPA weighed in with their opposition to the plan, because of concerns about water quality and impact on endangered species, that was a game-changer. They can't do the tunnels if the feds oppose them. I think the thing to watch is what our senators and congressmen are doing."

"There are a lot of smart people on all sides of this battle," Brad observed. "It sure looks to me that even with all of the money and time spent pushing this plan, the proponents must know it's not going to get the statewide traction it needs and the Delta folks know they aren't going to be safe until they become part of the Southern California water solution."

"Well, you're right about that, Dad. Nobody is winning from the way things are now. The fish populations are declining, the water quality is dropping, and water deliveries are being cut back."

"Unfortunately, it sure seems like the fixes aren't going to come from negotiation. Based on history, nobody trusts anybody. And government has a pro-build bias. I have to say that I'm guilty on that score myself. What's the answer, Kris?"

"I don't know, Dad. I did a paper on a book published by the California Public Policy Institute that seemed pretty level-headed. It had a bunch of recommendations for reconciling the opposing positions. It talked about regional plans for managing watersheds and reconciling them with local development plans, beefing up the authority of State Fish and Game to regulate water quality to support habitat, an independent state agency with enough funding to support other state departments with scientific research rather than relying on biased private studies, and specialized water courts run by judges and staff with expertise on water issues to adjudicate these complicated laws and public objectives."

Brad did a double-take. "Interesting. That's some of what my councilwoman has been promoting."

"Some reasonable concepts, Dad, but no slam dunk to get reforms done in this state through the normal legislative processes. Maybe the feds will provide the push."

"Maybe," he said quietly trying to appear hopeful.

He watched her closely as she lifted her glass and savored the last bit in the bottom, a serious expression on her face.

Through the haze of his cigar smoke, his daughter melted away and a colleague now sat before him.

12

Thirty plus of Marie's aunts, uncles, cousins, and their families descended upon the family home for the Thanksgiving festivities. It was the normal combination of noise, commotion, and exhaustion that creates family memories. Babies cried, little kids ran in, out, and around the house screaming; adults gathered around the dining room table drinking coffee, grazing, and catching up. Football and basketball blared on the TV all day with games few of the guests really cared about but tried to get excited about anyway. The elders held court in between naps.

Dinner was served kicking everything into an even higher gear. Plates and platters were passed around with mothers instructing children to take some Brussel sprouts and not so much cranberry sauce. The women talked over each other about the recipes and what minor change they were trying this time; "did you like it?" The men concentrated on eating.

Tanner was the MVP of the feast. He had raised the turkeys, smoked them all day, and did the carving honors to the rapt attention of the salivating crowd. He had also grown the squash, pumpkins for the pie, chrysanthemums for the centerpiece, and, of course, the grapes for the Zinfandel they were enjoying again.

After pumpkin pie when everyone was totally sated, the men moved to the living room and stared at the final football game of the day. Tanner brought out an expensive Port wine and tray of glasses. He gushed so much about it, Brad had to try it even though he was already fighting to stay awake.

At halftime, Tanner jumped up. "Come on outside, boys, I've got a surprise for you."

Brad sighed. Nappus interruptus.

All the men filed out to the porch where Tanner was already standing, his hands behind him. "Check this out." He brought around a rectangular wooden box of cigars. "Ta da! They're Cubans and they are the real deal."

Several of the men oohed and aahed and stepped closer as Tanner handed out the prized smokes. Dillon looked at Brad questioningly. Brad looked quickly toward the house then gave his son the OK nod. Brad didn't care for one but didn't want to be the only one out. They all stood around talking cigars a while.

"Smooth smoke, Tan Man," Brad said. "You can really taste the difference." Truth was, he didn't get any more enjoyment from the Cubans than he would have from a box of Roi Tans. He was always amazed that people would spend ten dollars or more on something that didn't taste good and left your breath smelling like a landfill.

When everyone had "enjoyed" a few puffs of the seven- inch cigars, Tanner sprung another surprise. "Follow me, boys. Come see my pride and joy." He led the procession to the side of the barn where his burgundy Ford F-250 diesel pickup truck was parked.

"Check this out," he said once again, moving to the bed where a large engine was sitting.

"You got it!" Tanner's brother, Red, said excitedly.

"Yup," Tanner said proudly. "428 Cobra Jet, boys! Been looking for one for months and just picked it up yesterday."

"Cool!" Red exclaimed. He and Tanner were "car guys." They exchanged tech talk while the other men looked from one to the other trying to keep up. Much of it was babble to Brad but he caught the high points. The engine apparently was manufactured in the late 60s, was rated at 335 horsepower, but Tanner said the true horsepower was over 400. It had special cylinder heads with larger intake ports and valves and heavier connecting rods. Blah, blah, blah. Brad got as much detail as he cared to know. It was a "big ass" engine designed for high performance racing.

"Let's see the Shelby," Red gushed.

Tanner led the group to the front of the barn and threw open the double doors. "Ta-da!" he said proudly at what looked to Brad to be a hopeless hulk of metal.

He escorted the group on a tour of the partially restored Mustang showing the best features, the work he'd already done, and the restorations to come. Tanner and Red must have been gazing upon a future Monarch butterfly that would soon take wing. Brad saw an ugly larva with primer.

Tanner and Red rolled the engine hoist over the concrete pad to the pickup and a couple of the others joined in to help transfer the apparently awesome engine into the barn. Brad looked for an opportunity to be useful. When everything was in place, he jumped in to grab the hydraulic lift bar and started pumping vigorously.

"Whoa! Whoa, now," Red yelled. "Not so fast. Here, let me get that for you." Red moved in to take the lever, leaving Brad to back away with his hands stuck deeply into his pockets.

Tanner must have seen his embarrassment. "Jump up here, Crat Man. Help me guide this bad boy out."

*****

When the last family said their goodbyes, Brad started eagerly toward the big leather sectional couch for his long-awaited nap.

"Before you go down for the count, why don't we lay everything out for tomorrow?" Tanner suggested.

Dillon leapt to his feet. Tanner had deemed that this year Dillon was ready for the big time, an outing at his duck club on Lower Jones Tract, a manmade island in the middle of the Delta due west of Stockton. On previous visits, Tanner had taken Dillon to a sporting-clay course to get him familiar with handling a shotgun and shooting at a moving object. Tanner was a patient teacher. He showed Dillon how to determine his master eye for aiming, to lead the target, keep his movements smooth with a slight forward lean, concentrate on the target with his head on the stock until after the shot, and take his time, don't jerk. Tomorrow was the big day.

Tanner brought in the shotguns and opened the breeches to be sure they were empty. He put two down and hefted one for Dillon's inspection. "Check this out," he said, for the third time that evening. "It's my new Browning twelve-gauge autoloader. Thirty-inch barrel. First time tomorrow." He let Dillon hold it and practice his shooting stance and motion.

Tanner handed Brad his trusty old Remington twelve-gauge and, for Dillon, Bridget's twenty-gauge Weatherby with a twenty-four-inch barrel, a better gun for a young beginner. Tanner supervised them both as they checked that everything functioned smoothly.

Tanner left and came back a few moments later with an armload of camouflaged waterproof pants, boots, jackets, and hats for Brad and Dillon.

"Try these on and inspect everything carefully to make sure there aren't any holes. It'll be cold in the morning and the last thing you want is to let water in."

Finally, Tanner pulled out a bag of duck calls and let Dillon try his skills. Dillon's first attempts were merely squeaks. With Tanner's patient instruction, he got better.

"Hey, you're pretty good at that," Tanner said. "I'm glad the door's closed or we'd have a house full of widgeons."

Dillon was obviously enjoying himself with his uncle. Maybe too much. Brad's mood soured a little thinking about feeling like a fifth wheel all day.

They piled all the gear next to the front door and cleared a spot in the cab of the F-250 to dump it all in first thing in the morning. With preparations completed, they went back to watch the end of a basketball game. Brad saw his opportunity to grab some of the spotlight. He pontificated about the recent Kings' trade as if he had personal insight on the matter instead of just reading a column in the paper that morning.

When the game was over, Tanner went to bed. Brad and Dillon decided to sleep on the sofas so they wouldn't disturb anyone else early in the morning. They compromised on an old black-and-white movie as a nightcap.

It was *Pride of the Yankees* starring Gary Cooper as Hall-of-Famer Lou Gehrig. A real tear jerker. Brad saw another chance to recapture his son's respect. When Babe Ruth appeared as himself in the movie, he pounced. "Did you ever hear about when The Babe called his home run shot, pointing out to right field?"

"Yeah, that's a classic, Dad."

Brad frowned then perked up. "Yeah, he did it with two strikes in the World Series against the Pirates. They were playing in Pittsburg and the crowd had been all over him. He got the last laugh."

"I think it was against the Cubs, Dad. And it was to centerfield."

He slumped. "Oh, yeah, that's right. Pretty cool, huh?" He was pushing too hard.

A few minutes later, when DiMaggio was featured in the movie, he tried again. "And did you know that Joltin' Joe DiMaggio, who batted just ahead of Gehrig, had a fifty-six-game hitting streak; a record that hasn't been closely challenged in over seventy years?"

"I heard about that. Actually, what impressed me more about DiMaggio was that he married Marilyn Monroe."

Brad was deflated. "She was a beauty. I'm surprised that you knew about her."

"I saw her spread in Playboy," Dillon said matter-of-factly, yawning and stretching.

Brad disregarded his internal warnings and stepped up to bat again. "And, did you know that DiMaggio was replaced in centerfield by Mickey Mantle?"

"I don't know that much about Mantle," Dillon said tiredly.

Aha! "Mantle was my favorite player. I read his biography when I was a kid. He grew up in Oklahoma where his father, Mutt, taught him to hit in the garage. He was probably the greatest switch-hitter of all time. I went to the Louisville Bat Factory in Kentucky when I was about your age. They had Mantle's original bat and his signed contract from when he was only eighteen hanging there in the plant."

"Awesome," Dillon said. "I'd like to go there with you sometime."

Mission accomplished. Take that, Cobra Man. He tossed the remote to Dillon with a smirk and snuggled into the soft sofa cushions.

*****

Brad was jolted awake by an annoying noise. Cell phone. He reached over to the coffee table and fumbled with it, trying to make it stop. "Hello?" "Hello?" It kept ringing. He finally figured out it was his phone's alarm. Was it 4:30 a.m. already? He shook Dillon awake and plodded to the hall bathroom. After donning his warm clothes and giving Dillon a "hurry-up," he joined Tanner who was in the kitchen pouring black coffee into a gallon thermos.

"Well, good afternoon, Crat Man!" Tanner said in a chipper voice as if he made it a habit to be up two hours before dawn and Brad was just a slacker.

"Morning, Tan Man," Brad replied. "Hey, before Dillon comes in, I appreciate you bringing him along and all. And I know you'll make sure he's safe today. But we don't want to mess up the experience for anyone else and have Dillon get all embarrassed. You know how teenagers are. So make sure you tell us if either of us is about to do something wrong. It will be important for him to fit in with your friends."

"No sweat," Tanner assured. "These are good guys. They come in all shapes and bank accounts. Out there everyone is just a duck hunter and a friend. They don't get all stressed out about making their limit. They'll make Big D feel welcome."

"OK," Brad said, "and I'll do my best to make sure the pointy end is toward the ducks."

Brad and Dillon loaded the gear into the rear of Tanner's truck cab while Tanner fetched his hunting dog, Blab, a Black Lab. Blab knew where they were going and nearly jumped out of his skin with anticipation. The four hunters climbed in the cab then drove slowly down the gravel driveway in the early morning blackness.

"Why don't you break out the coffee?" Tanner suggested to Brad. "And, Big D, there's a package of bear claws behind you."

They spent most of the forty-minute trip to Lower Jones Tract in relative silence just enjoying the coffee and pastry and the emerging views of the Delta as dawn heralded a cloudy, blustery morning.

Brad remembered his first visit to Tanner's duck club. He didn't expect anything lavish, like some swanky golf resort, but neither was he prepared for the rustic setting. The club was just a house that looked like what he might have drawn in the sixth grade. It was a simple, one-story rectangular building with inexpensive T-111 plywood siding and cheap composition asphalt shingles. There was duct tape securing aluminum foil over one of the window frames at the front. Several spindles in the wooden rail along the porch were either missing or hanging atilt. This was a place that got hard use by hardy men, not some prissy showplace.

They took a right on westbound Highway 4 and headed north on a narrow, rutted slough road until reaching the driveway to the club at around 5:45 a.m. It was still dark but the front door was wide open and provided enough light so that Brad could see that the building hadn't changed. They parked on the gravel, gathered their gear, climbed the three warped and squeaky wooden stairs to the porch, and prepared to enter the hubbub inside.

Somebody yelled "Tan Man!" as soon as Tanner hit the threshold. The club was where Brad first heard the nickname he had used ever since. Other men yelled their "howdys" and a few came over to shake hands and meet Brad and Dillon.

It didn't require Sherlock Holmes' levels of deduction to realize that they were late to the party. The large red picnic table off the kitchen was covered with cards, poker chips, crinkled cans of beer, spaghetti strands, half-eaten containers of dip, and open bags of chips and Oreos.

"Looks like the guys had a good time last night," Tanner said to Dillon and Brad.

"Come on, assholes. Get movin'. We gotta get out there," shouted a big burly man from the kitchen. He was frying bacon while shouting orders to his helpers who plopped down platters of scrambled eggs and toast for the dozen or so men who were slowly getting into motion.

One of the other guys, dressed only in a flannel shirt and boxer shorts, yelled back, "I'm already movin' quick, Doc. Your cookin's gave me the trots!" The cook smiled and flipped him off.

Tanner nodded toward the cook and whispered to Brad and Dillon, "that's Doc Tompkins, you'll like him."

"What kind of doctor is he?" Brad asked.

"Actually, he's a Superior Court judge in Calaveras County."

"Why do they call him Doc, then?" Dillon asked.

Tanner thought a moment and replied, "I think his real first name is David. The story I heard was that his parents wanted him to be a doctor not a lawyer. He graduated from law school with a Juris Doctor degree and his Dad started calling him 'Doc.' He's the most laid back judge you'll ever meet."

Under Doc's goading, the guys picked up their pace. Some attacked their breakfast while others started putting on their waterfowl gear. An obviously hung-over gentleman staggered out of a back bedroom wearing only his tighty whities and stood at the hall doorway trying to absorb the scene.

Doc motioned Tanner over to the table and said, "Welcome boys, grab some food and suit up. We leave in ten."

"Wind's comin' up, Doc," Tanner said. "So's the clouds. Should be a pretty good shoot."

They bolted down some breakfast, put on their gear, grabbed their guns, and walked down the levee in the pre-dawn light to a small pier where Tanner kept his duck boat. Nobody was worried about cleaning up the mess they left behind. That could wait. The ducks wouldn't.

They put their gear and themselves into the boat. Tanner yanked on the pull cord and the small outboard motor came to life. They putt-putted out to the farthest duck blind on the east edge of the flooded eighty-acre cornfield in a grassy area below the levee. The blinds, concealed shooting platforms, had been laid out in north/south rows on the east and west sides of the pond so the hunters didn't have to shoot into the sun in the morning or evening.

The club was located in a perfect spot along the Pacific Flyway, the path stretching from Alaska to the tip of South America that millions of migratory birds travel during the spring and fall. To attract some of the ducks their way, the club had shaved the corn stalks after the harvest and opened the levee gate to flood the field. Ducks prefer the high carbohydrate diet offered by grain fields to build their energy for the remaining flight. The problem was by the time the ducks reach them, they had already been hunted in Canada, Washington and Oregon for nearly two months and were warier than when they started. The hunters had to be skilled in their calling, blind construction, decoy placement, and camouflage to draw the birds in. Hopefully, at least Tanner and Blab would be up to the challenge.

"Good job with the decoy pattern, Sluggo," Tanner said to a man in the next boat, in a voice just barely audible over the motors.

"Thanks. We'll soon find out how good," Sluggo replied.

Brad started to ask about the nickname but let it pass, his fear of committing a faux pas with unnecessary chatter being stronger than his curiosity.

Tanner concentrated on mallards since they were good eating and scored a double in his first shoot. Blab bounded through the thick Johnson grass and corn stalks and returned the first duck. He stood on the platform looking at Tanner, his tail whipping like a metronome. Tanner stared at Blab holding up his index finger as if to say "wait for it, wait for it." Blab was raring to go. "Fetch!" Tanner finally commanded, pointing in the direction of his second bird. The retriever was off like a shot, returning with his prize carefully nestled in his soft mouth.

Tanner patted Blab and set his Browning down to focus on helping his guests. With his coaching and calling, Brad got a mallard himself and bagged a couple of teals twenty minutes later. Dillon had taken a few shots too but had nothing to show for them. Even Brad could tell he was shooting too jerkily. He could see Dillon's frustration building.

A cold wind was picking up out of the north as it started to drizzle sideways. The ripples on the pond were showing whitecaps.

"Won't need the Mojo today," Tanner said.

Dillon looked at his uncle quizzically.

"That's a mechanical duck we use on calm days to simulate duck movement," Tanner explained.

Brad felt water on his face and wasn't sure if it was the drizzle or just wave spray. Either way, it was bitterly cold sitting in the blind. Yes, Virginia, it was indeed lovely weather for a duck!

Brad's anxiety grew with each of his son's missed shots. The conditions were perfect. Sluggo's decoy pattern was proving enticing, and the ducks must have been really hungry. He worried that the other guys would be ready to leave soon. He made eye contact with Tanner and nodded toward his son. Tanner picked up the signal and leaned over to Dillon for a little more coaching.

"Remember, Big D, lead from behind, aim small, miss small, and keep the gun moving in front of him," Tanner reminded Dillon. "Relax, be smooth, stay on the gun," he added. Another hunter nearby blew his call. It got the attention of a gigantic flock of passing widgeons that came closer. Tanner pointed up, gave Dillon the "OK" sign, but waved his hands in the air signaling him to wait. The birds kept coming.

"EEEEEASY," Tanner said, barely over the cacophony of the flock directly above. Brad held his breath. The sounds of nature suddenly erupted in shotgun blasts all around them.

"Now SMOOTH, Big D, take your time," Tanner urged.

Dillon stood up, his twenty-gauge in perfect firing stance and, this time, slowed down his shot. KABLAAM! Then, a moment later, KABLAAM! The second shot scored. Feathers sprayed in the sky and a large widgeon fluttered into the stalks. Blab was up with the shot, tensed for motion. The Lab's eyes darted back and forth between the falling bird and his master. Finally, Tanner gave the command and Blab was off again.

When Blab returned, Brad gave his son a hearty pat on the back and pulled out his phone from the protective plastic bag. Dillon posed holding his trophy in the air with Tanner's arm on his shoulder and an ear-to-ear grin.

Dillon got off two more shots later. One missed but the other may have caught a wing. However, judging from the bird's flight trajectory after impact, Tanner suspected somebody in the next blind got the kill. Dillon was fine with letting it go. Blab was not so understanding. Brad suspected that's the way it was with a group of friends in a private club. People watched out for each other and shared the day's bounty. The legal limit was seven ducks each. With conditions like this, they could limit out just in the morning shoot if they wanted to. But these guys were in it for the sport. They didn't want to overshoot the flooded field and make it tougher for the evening hunters. They were content to harvest a little of what nature provided for their own use now and leave the rest for another time. It occurred to Brad how different this mindset towards nature was from the greed and exploitation he had been learning about that characterized California's water practices.

Brad took in the whole scene from his seat on a bucket in the duck blind. Despite the cold, windy conditions, he felt warm inside.

He studied his son as they all sat there in silence. How excited Dillon was about downing a duck on his first hunt. He noticed small, black whiskers sprouting from a face that was becoming more chiseled. Wasn't it just last year they were in the cul-de-sac playing Home Run Derby with whiffle balls? And soon he'd be off to college!

Brad shifted his gaze to his brother-in-law. Tanner had pivoted on his bucket ninety degrees to the right toward the harsh north wind. His face was becoming red raw from the wind that buffeted his thick brown hair sticking out from under his camo hat. The sun ducked in and out of the clouds, alternatingly shrouding the vista then bathing it in vivid color.

Tanner wasn't looking at anything in particular. He wasn't scouting to set up the next call or shoot. He was simply staring ahead with his chin raised to catch as much of the climate on his face as he could, the picture of contentment. His wife, Bridget, called it being in his "Puddy" mode, after a character in *Seinfeld*. Brad always joined the laugh when the Puddy crack was made. Now he got it. Tanner wasn't zoned out at all. To the contrary, he was completely in the moment.

In one of his many starts and stops into spiritual exploration, Brad had stumbled upon basic Buddhist teachings about finding inner peace by accepting what was in that moment. By being still and focusing on current bodily sensations, you were more open to connecting with the ever-present God Spirit and receiving His love and healing comfort. Or something like that.

Brad had tried to get to that state using different forms of meditation. But his "Monkey Mind" flittered from one random image to another and refused to be harnessed. He was so in his head and driven to achieve that it seemed like an unproductive use of time to sit and be still merely for its own benefit. He was much more accustomed to having his mind race constantly between the past and the future; reliving an encounter, regret, or memory, then, in the next flash of thought, worrying about something that might happen or fantasizing about something he hoped would. Usually, the hardest place for him to be was right where he was.

But at this moment, he, too, felt present. No more worries about his son getting his duck, someone getting hurt, blundering with some faux pas, or any of the other dozen negative thoughts that had crossed his mind. He simply sat, reveling in the peace and enjoying being in nature in a way he had never before experienced. He felt different somehow. He forced himself not to analyze it and just stayed with what might have been pure contentment.

"Thanks, Tan Man," he said, sweeping his hand at the view.

"Pleasure, Crat Man," Tanner replied, with a contented smile.

And it was.

The three sat there enjoying the sights until the intrusion of an outboard motor coming to life nearby. Others soon joined the chorus. The threesome, and Blab, loaded into the boat.

"Take us home, Big D. Or should I now call you Buffalo Dill?" Tanner started the motor then moved over to let Dillon pilot the boat from the blind to join the flotilla. Some of the guys held up their bounty for all to see as they chugged along on the pond. Tanner gave them a thumbs up then raised Dillon's hand and had him display his bird. Some of the guys returned the thumbs up or clapped.

With Dillon steering them home, Tanner took the opportunity to doff his hat and let the wind whip through his wavy hair. He leaned back in the boat with his head on a sideboard and raised both arms to the sky with a beaming smile as if giving thanks for the beauty they were enjoying. "It doesn't get any better than this, Crat Man," he said.

"Amen," Brad said, wondering where that came from. Brad couldn't recall ever having a serious discussion about theology with Tanner. He suspected he knew much more than Tanner about the Bible and the dogma of the world's leading religions, but that Tanner felt a closer connection to God.

The group finally sputtered up to the small dock by the house, tied their boats up, and passed around the iced beer that was waiting in the cooler at the dock. It was getting nastier outside and hot coffee might have been a better choice, but beer is the de rigueur quaff after a manly activity. The guys toasted each other's success. Brad could tell it wasn't his son's first beer.

Tanner took Brad and Dillon aside. "Hey, guys," he whispered, nodding at a man still in a boat, "Marty over there just got laid off and his family could probably use the meat. You OK with giving him some of the birds?"

With their quick concurrence, Tanner threw a can of beer to Marty and said to him, "I helped Big D here get his first bird. But you know I hate to clean 'em. Would you be willing to do the honors and give him a mallard to take home? You can have the rest."

Marty readily agreed. "I got my special marinade in the fridge," he said, "I'll throw some of that in and tell them how to cook it."

The men finished their beers and headed back to the house with the ducks to store their gear and guns and to relieve themselves. Many of the guys took care of the latter task from the levee rather than bothering to use the bathroom.

Inside, Doc Tompkins was already back wielding the whip. Some of the guys pitched in for a half-hearted attempt to clean up the mess. Somebody turned on the TV and found a college basketball game. Tanner and other guys were lining up at the large coffee urn. A bottle of Jameson Irish whisky sat next to it.

"Outta the way, assholes," Doc said gruffly. "I made it, me first." The jurist went to the front of the line, filled his mug, and added a healthy shot of whiskey before turning the bottle over to Tanner who did the same.

Brad held back. Better not have any whiskey. Early morning. Fresh air. It's warm in here. I'm already sleepy. Tanner will probably drink too much and I'll have to drive. Not wild about driving his over-sized truck on that narrow levee road. And then he caught himself reverting to pattern. "Loosen up!" he scolded himself. He got in the coffee line and added a generous shot of whiskey.

The trio took their drinks outside to keep Marty company as he cleaned the birds. The wind had died down and the light drizzle of the early morning was turning into a thickening ground fog. Brad knew from living in the region that the Tule fog could hang over the Central Valley for weeks at a time, sometimes causing horrendous car pile ups on the freeway. He worried again about having to drive home on the levee roads. He flashed on the image of a head-on wreck on the narrow, foggy roads leading out of the Delta. Once again, he caught himself, shook his head and took another sip of his spiked brew. Get out of your head!

The club had two large propane barbeques on over-sized wheels sitting on the packed gravel in front of the main house surrounding a big open fire pit made of mortared cobbles. One guy was cooking Italian sausage and warming up a pot of the leftover spaghetti. Marty had started a fire using manzanita for kindling and larger oak logs on top. The fire hissed, crackled, and popped. It was already providing warmth and an antidote to the grayness engulfing the area. Doc Tompkins and two other men came out of the house and plunked down on folding chairs next to the fire with their ducks, buckets, pans, and utensils.

The Irish coffee began hitting its mark. Brad felt himself relax deeper. He ignored the dreariness of the ground fog and the hazard it posed for the drive home. He leaned his head back on the red plastic mesh chair and felt his full breaths expand his chest and take tension out his nostrils on the exhale. It truly was nice to be here. In this place. Nowhere else. Right now.

He held up his cup to the other men. "Nice to be here, gents. Thanks for having us."

The men sat quietly for an hour or more, mostly staring at the fire. Brad had observed that when Marie was with other women, there was seldom a lag in the conversation and, more often, they talked over the top of each other. He, like most guys he knew, used words sparingly. He always found some truth in the jokes comedians told about the differences in the sexes. It was like women used spoken words as energy pellets, gathering strength the more they talked. Men seemed to have the opposite reaction, words sapping their power. It's like they have a finite amount of words they felt comfortable using in a day so they doled them out carefully. The guys were happy just sitting there watching the fire pop and enjoying the quiet camaraderie.

After a while, another man approached the seated group of duck pluckers. "This is Jack Kelly," Tanner told Brad and Dillon. "Crat Man, you'll have plenty to talk about. Jack's on the Lodi City Council. Brad here is city manager of Santa Ynez, down by Santa Barbara."

"Santa Ynez?!" Jack exclaimed. "The home of Kay Nance?"

Brad was surprised to hear his councilwoman brought up so far from home. "That's the place," he replied. "How do you know Kay?"

"We both are on the League's Environmental Quality Committee," he explained. "She's something! Can't say I agree with all her politics but she sure is one helluva lot of fun at a conference!" Jack had said it slyly, indicating that there was more spice to the story.

"Well, I'll take your word for that, Jack," Brad said, hoping to end it at that. Councilmembers were like siblings. It was all right for you to bitch about them, but you felt protective when others did.

He changed the subject. "How's my friend, Deni, doing?" he asked, referring to the city manager of Lodi. "Business acquaintance" would have been more apt. People working in professions like to feel connected to their colleagues. Besides, after a double-shot of Jameson, everyone felt like a friend.

"Deni's great," the councilman said.

The two talked a little shop as the other guys listened and plucked ducks or napped by the fire. Brad thought he would probably like having Jack as a councilmember/boss. He was happy to hear that Jack was pleased with Deni's performance. City managers are constantly aware of the tenuous environment in which they work. Every two years some of their bosses can turn over in an election. And any given day in between, they might make a bad move that would put them on the outs with the Council majority. It's comforting to hear when the relationship is going well.

The councilman's facial expression turned sour. "Yeah, Deni's fine," he repeated. "She's busting her butt rallying other cities to fight those tunnels around the Delta. Are you tracking that problem down there?"

"We were just talking about it the other night," Brad replied, taking another sip. "This really tastes good, Doc." He wasn't in the mood to get serious right now, preferring to enjoy his buzz and the crackling fire.

Jack frowned and looked toward the others. "I'm wondering if we should even bother spending money on repairs to the club? The Delta is going to pot."

The fire popped. Doc poked it with a long stick and looked up at Brad. "You should know, Brad, a lot of people and businesses up here are feeling discouraged. The Delta is in bad shape and getting worse. They're afraid the power and momentum is shifting to the big water contractors and corporations whose main interest is exploiting the Delta, not caring for it."

Tanner perked up. "That's what I was just telling him. They would let the natural flows drop, kill the fish, and destroy the best ag land in the state to squeeze some more money out of their crap land down south."

Brad really didn't want to be serious right now, but he was Tanner's guest and didn't want to leave him hanging. "Yeah, my eyes have really been opened lately about water issues in this state and especially the threats to the Delta. I'm afraid to admit that my city receives Delta water through the State Water Project. Don't lynch me!"

"Don't feel guilty, most of California does," Doc Tompkins said. The other men nodded without taking their eyes off fire watch.

Jack Kelly threw the remnants from his cup on the fire making it hiss and shoot up sparks. "Yeah, most everyone in this state gets something out of the Delta, whether they know it or not. Look at us. Some of our guys farm here. I sell marine insurance to clients with boats docked all over the Delta. And tourism employs a lot of people. Until recently, Marty here used to cook at a restaurant in Locke; food was good even if they only got the overflow from Al the Wop's," he laughed.

Brad had been to Al the Wop's. It was a local landmark in a small community on the Sacramento River founded by Chinese immigrants who were brought in to build the levees and stayed to farm. Locke looked pretty much like it did in the 1920s. That was part of its charm. Al's added more spice. Show up in a tie and they'd cut it off and hang it as a trophy. Stick a dollar bill and your business card into the ceiling in the bar. Take your seat at the indoor picnic tables and benches and they'd bring you peanut butter and jelly for an appetizer. Like much of the Delta, unique.

The men shared stories of the whore houses and gambling joints that used to comprise many of the small Delta communities. They did a brisk business from gentlemen heading to and from San Francisco and Sacramento on paddlewheel boats stopping over for some "entertainment."

Brad noticed that Councilman Kelly appeared annoyed with this banter. "Like I was saying," the councilman blurted, bringing them back on point, "millions of us in California get something valuable from the Delta."

Doc picked up the thread. "Here, here! There's no crime to use the water for good purposes. The crime is to waste it."

Jack Kelly nodded solemnly. "That's the biggest difference between us and the Big Ag conglomerates who take the most from the Delta. They don't care like the rest of us about not over-exploiting the resources of the area. I want my grandkids to still be selling marine insurance to Delta boaters thirty years from now. You think the big shots with the corporations who own most of the land in the south valley care about a thirty-year horizon in their balance sheets?"

Brad looked over at Dillon and was surprised to see that his son seemed to be following the discussion with interest rather that tweeting a friend.

Councilman Kelly was on a roll. "I'm not saying the radical environmentalists, like Brad's councilwoman, are right, either. If they had their way, we wouldn't even be allowed to farm, hunt, or boat out here." He swept the horizon with his right hand. "All of this would be protected habitat. That's too extreme. It's a balance. But, like Doc was saying, a lot of us are worried that the big water users don't care about balance or compromise."

"Look at how they fought fracking regulation," Doc added.

"What's that?" Dillon asked.

"That's where oil companies inject water and chemicals into their wells under high pressure to break up the shale and extract more oil," Doc said.

"What's wrong with that?" Dillon asked.

"It uses a lot of water, for one thing, Dillon," Doc responded. "About 100,000 gallons per well. There are thousands of oil wells in California and hundreds more being added every month. We are the third biggest oil producing state in the country. I believe they pump a lot of brackish water from the ground for fracking. Nobody knows how much potable water is being used since it isn't metered."

"It's a huge waste of water," Tanner huffed. "They could bring in sea water instead but that's more expensive. It's always about money, Big D, I mean, Buffalo Dill."

Dillon beamed.

Marty threw a handful of feathers into a bucket with authority. "It's not just the water waste from fracking. My uncle farms down by Bakersfield. With the cutbacks on state water deliveries through the aqueduct, he's pumping the hell out of the aquifer. He's really worried about all the wastewater from fracking getting dumped back into the ground. I don't think anybody has a good take on what that's going to do to the aquifers."

"He *should* be worried," Doc said. "The state is giving the oil companies a pass. They are approving new injection wells like crazy. They got their hands slapped by the EPA for allowing the wastewater to be injected into a federally protected aquifer. But even the feds didn't stop the process immediately. They are giving the oil companies a few more years to get into compliance."

Councilman Kelly shook his head. "Jerry Brown's backing of the oil companies is so out of sync with his support of solar, wind, and other renewable energy to fight climate change. I remember a quote from him when he pounded his chest about needing to maximize the state's resources, including drilling new oil wells. He said there will be screw-ups, indictments, and deaths. Then he said, 'But we're going to keep going. Nothing's going to stop us.' Pretty amazing stance for a supposedly environmentally-sensitive governor."

"And remember, Jack," Doc added. "He fired the top two state officials in charge of regulating the gas and oil wells after the oil companies complained that their environmental reviews were slowing down new drilling permits. State officials now hardly even use the word 'fracking', it has farmers and environmentalists so stirred up. They refer to it as 'well stimulation.' How's that for your government watching out for the public?"

"Geez, you guys are depressing," Brad said forcing a smile. "The Delta is being destroyed so that Big Ag can make billions planting the desert. And when they can't get enough water from the Delta, they pump the hell out of the aquifer without regulation. Meantime, Big Oil is dumping wastewater from fracking into the aquifers. State politicians and bureaucrats know all about it and let it happen because of the money and power involved."

"You got it, Crat Man," Tanner said, clearing his sinuses and leaning over to spit into the fire.

The other men nodded their heads in semi-sober agreement as they stared at the fire. Apparently they were approaching their daily word quota.

Brad glanced at his son who was studying him, not the fire. Brad felt compelled to act. He pounded his thighs with resolve, breaking the silence. "I never really considered it my responsibility to track all of these state issues. I've pretty much confined my sphere to the city I worked in. But it's beautiful out here. It would be a horrible shame not to take care of it. I don't know what I can do to help but I'm sure going to give it serious thought."

He saw Dillon set his jaw hard. Was his son truly interested in all of this chatter? Was he signing on to join his father in some piece of this fight? He again noted the whiskers on Dillon's jaw and felt both pride and sadness.

Councilman Kelly had a suggestion. "Here's a place to start, Brad. When you get back to Santa Ynez and get pushed in all directions like all you city managers do, I hope you'll just remember the beauty you've experienced today."

"I will," Brad promised. "This has been a terrific day. I want my son to have the same experience with his kids someday. I hate knowing that my generation is turning over such a troubled planet to the next one. I don't have much to do with what happens in the Delta but you've given me some food for thought."

Doc Tompkins shook his head. "But you have a *lot* to do with how you manage the piece of nature you're responsible for including how you use the water that comes from this place. All we ask is that you be a good steward of the natural resources in your area. Don't waste what you have. Think about the long-term impact of your decisions and don't be so quick to do the bidding of the powerful, like too many government officials have done, and are still doing. Can you do that much?"

He felt Dillon's eyes boring into him. "I will," he committed. It felt like a somber pledge, not just a throw-away, alcohol-induced line. Dillon's look suggested that his son also took it seriously. He felt connected to his son on a different plane than normal father/son love.

Once again, he forced himself to not overanalyze it. He sat quietly as the fire crackled, feeling the cold on his face, breathing in the aroma of the grilled sausages, and enjoying the moment, aware only that something had shifted within.

13

The Jacks family spent Saturday morning just kicking back at the family ranch. Around noon, Tanner took Dillon out to the barn to show him how to weld a metal floor panel into the Mustang. Brad took advantage of the free time to do Internet research on the St. Francis Dam disaster in anticipation of hearing more from Lilly about her dad's role in the project.

After hours of welcomed solitary confinement with his computer in the guest bedroom, he was ready to re-join the family. He opened the door to a quiet house. A note from Marie on the dining room table said: "didn't want to bother you – girls went to movie - chick flick, you wouldn't like - home for dinner." He opened the front door and heard clanging metal in the barn. He thought about turning back to find an old movie but grudgingly walked to the barn to check on the car guys. He never found an audience the rest of the day for his newfound knowledge.

They left for home right after breakfast on Sunday. Dillon was allowed to take the first two hours to Harris Ranch, a popular restaurant off Interstate 5. Brad noticed his son seemed to have a little swagger in his step following the duck hunt and welding experiences. Dillon was more confident behind the wheel than he had been driving up, moving easily from the slow to fast lane to get around the trucks. Brad relaxed a bit. With Marie as his captive audience, he kicked off his lecture.

"You know how I did some more research yesterday on the St. Francis Dam?"

"I know," she responded. "I wish we had gotten Lilly's dad's name to see if he was in anything you read. CHP coming up from behind, Dillon," she announced.

Dillon looked into the rearview mirror and nodded.

"Yeah, well, I'm hoping she'll tell us more about him," Brad said. "I wanted to get more background on why the dam was built to begin with before we talk to her again."

"Good," Marie said. "What did you learn?"

"Thought you'd never ask," he smiled. "Some of this about the LA water wars I heard in college, but forgot. I remembered that San Francisco really took off during the Gold Rush Era. I didn't realize that even thirty years after that, Los Angeles was still a dusty little pueblo of maybe 10,000. A man named Fred Eaton was superintendent of the private water company that served the area before the city bought the company. Eaton was close friends with the publisher of the *Los Angeles Times* and other big wigs. They were all jealous of San Francisco's growth and culture and wanted to see LA blossom into a major city, too. Eaton knew they had to have a lot of water to make that happen. Being surrounded by deserts and the Pacific Ocean, there wasn't a nearby source. Eaton had visited the Owens Valley. . ."

"Where's that, again?" Marie interrupted.

"It's on the Nevada side of the Sierra range up by Mt. Whitney. It's a narrow valley, maybe five miles wide and a hundred miles long. Eaton remembered the roaring rivers and streams coming down from the east side of the Sierras. He suspected that water could be channeled all the way to Los Angeles, over two hundred miles, by gravity. When Eaton left the water company and became mayor of LA, he pushed the idea of the city buying out the water company he used to work for, mainly because he knew it would take city bond measures to raise the money needed to acquire and transport the Owens Valley water. The water he was after wasn't intended for the city at the time. It would be needed to develop the thousands of acres Eaton and his buddies were secretly buying in the San Fernando Valley. But they had a problem."

"Brake lights," Marie warned urgently.

"I see them, Mom," Dillon huffed as he slowed.

"Are you listening, Marie?" Brad grumped.

"Yes, 'they had a problem. . .'" she repeated.

Brad leaned to his left and made a face into the mirror at his wife. "The problem was the federal Reclamation Service was already in the Owens Valley planning an irrigation project to open up more agricultural land. Los Angeles needed to kill that project in order to get the water for themselves."

"How'd they do that?" she asked a little too eagerly.

Brad felt that she was faking interest, but he went with it. "A guy named Lippincott was the Reclamation Service's employee in charge of the irrigation project. Eaton and William Mulholland paid him secretly to help them acquire property in Owens Valley at the same time the feds were organizing the locals for their project. He was an early day double agent. Lippincott gave Eaton and Mulholland all the Service's maps and land records. Eaton posed as a representative of the Reclamation Service and, with Lippincott's help, tied up enough land to make the city the controlling player in the future of the Owens Valley before anybody knew LA had any interest up there."

"What did the feds do when they learned about Los Angeles' plans?" Marie asked.

"Well, I skipped over some of that part. But I can imagine the feds weren't too happy to see LA messing with all their plans and work up there, especially when they found out their own employee was helping them on the side. I remember reading that at some point, Mulholland and other LA officials went directly to President Teddy Roosevelt and convinced him that the country needed a thriving Los Angeles on the West Coast a lot more than some more farmland. They got Roosevelt to kill the Service's irrigation project on the spot."

"I can see that happening at that point in our history!" Marie said. "Use your turn signals, Dillon."

Brad again caught his wife's eye in the mirror and shook his head slightly. "That group of San Fernando Valley speculators carried a lot of clout. It included Harry Chandler and Harrison Gray Otis, owners of the *Los Angeles Times;* tycoon Collis Huntington, part of the Central Pacific 'Big Four' who built the Transcontinental Railroad; and E. H. Harriman who owned controlling interest in both the Union Pacific and Southern Pacific railroads. These men had major influence beyond Los Angeles and they weren't going to let some federal bureaucrats at the Reclamation Service get in the way of their big land play."

Brad tensed seeing his son following too closely, his own brake foot pressing against the floor on a pedal that wasn't there. "Yeah," he continued, feigning composure, "and they weren't content to just kill the federal project in Owens Valley. From what I read, normally when the Reclamation Service dropped a project, the land got released to the public for homesteading. LA got Roosevelt to order that not be done so that LA wouldn't have any competition while they were tying up the surrounding land for the water rights. When the Interior Secretary squawked, Roosevelt fired him."

"Hard ball," Marie observed.

"Yup," Brad said. "And in the ultimate flaunting of their power, LA later even got the federal Forest Service to include the Owens Valley in the Inyo National Forest to ensure there wouldn't ever be any other uses up there that might compete for the water LA wanted to export. It was a cynical joke since there weren't any trees for miles. Some forest, huh?"

Brad was getting a headache trying to keep the story sorted out while spying on his son's every move behind the wheel. Marie's constant admonishments weren't helping. Brad could tell Dillon was losing the confidence he started with. He hoped his lecture would be soothing.

"With the feds out of the way, Mulholland finished the land acquisition and started designing the aqueduct to Los Angeles. Apparently, St. Francis Dam wasn't even part of the original plan. Eaton and Mulholland wanted a dam and reservoir up at Owens Lake, but that changed. Remember that Eaton was posing as a representative of the Reclamation Service and buying up options to land all over the valley. The deal he had with Mulholland was that the LA water department would pay him a commission for his efforts. But Eaton got greedy. He bought the best, most obvious, site for a dam for himself. He assumed he'd get his protégé to buy the site back from him at a huge profit. But Mulholland got his back up and killed the dam up there even though Eaton's land was the natural spot for it."

"I admire the fact that he didn't cave in to his friend and mentor," Marie said, "he was watching out for the city. Too close, Dillon."

An image of planning director Megan Cain came into Brad's mind. He shifted uncomfortably in his seat before continuing the story.

"It wasn't just his fight with Eaton that led to the dam at the St. Francis site. Owens Valley is a long way away from LA. About two-hundred-thirty miles. When word got out that the city had bought the water rights to the valley, the water department for years assured everyone they would only take surplus water after the locals had used what they needed. Of course, that was a lie, too. As real estate promoters and railroad companies touted the health benefits of San Fernando Valley living, the population boom outstripped even Mulholland's wildest growth projections. Soon, the aqueduct was running near capacity. The department extended it even farther up the valley to Mono Lake to capture more regional run-off then sunk hundreds of wells, too. There was nothing left for the local economy. When the locals finally realized they'd been had, and Los Angeles couldn't be trusted, some resorted to violence. They even dynamited sections of the aqueduct at different times."

"I remember reading a little about that when I was doing my research the night we first learned about this from Lilly," Marie recalled.

"Right," Brad said. "The city spent a fortune on its own police who patrolled the aqueduct through hundreds of miles of mountains. Mulholland wanted the reservoir closer to LA and farther from 'the dynamiters' as he called them. Besides, they were well aware that the aqueduct was going through all kinds of active faults. At any point, an earthquake could break the pipeline and LA would be out of water. Mulholland wanted all that storage on the LA side of the faults so that if the aqueduct did break or was dynamited, they'd still have all that water in the reservoir while they fixed it."

"Makes sense," Marie said. "Watch your speed, Dillon." Dillon sneaked a glance at his father and rolled his eyes. Brad shrugged back.

Marie missed it and continued. "I'm curious to ask Lilly if she knows why the dam was put where it was. Based on what I read before, it wasn't a stable area. Remember the schist?"

"What'd you say, Mom?" Dillon asked with a wide-eyed smile.

"Schist," she enunciated. "I think it was some kind of flaky rock that they built the St. Francis dam on."

"From what I read," Brad added, "Mulholland personally selected the St. Francis site because the way the canyon narrowed, it could hold back a lot of water. But Mulholland and others knew there were problems with the site from the start. The department knew the rock under the dam foundation wasn't good. Something about 'uplift' where water under intense pressure from the weight of all that water behind the dam seeps through the rock and the dam's foundation and side walls. The force from that seepage is high enough to actually raise and even break the foundation. They knew that was a problem when it was built but didn't do the drains through the foundation and other things they should have to deal with the problem. They were in a hurry to build it and Mulholland, the Chief, as he was known, prided himself on getting big projects built quickly and cheaply. To make things worse, they were constantly changing the original design of the dam as it was being built."

"How so?" Marie asked.

He reflected on Kay Nance's rant about the abuse of water for rampant growth. "Like I said, Los Angeles was booming back then and Mulholland was worried there wouldn't be enough water to keep it going. Twice he raised the height of the dam to hold more water, but they didn't also thicken it to withstand the force of the additional water. That was standard practice even then. In fact, when they measured the finished construction after the failure, they found that the dam's base was twenty feet less than it was designed to be, even before they raised it. That dam was doomed from the beginning by bad decisions driven by haste and greed."

"It will be interesting if Lilly can add to any of that," Marie said.

They were in the fast lane of an elevated section of Interstate 5, a few miles north of Harris Ranch, when Dillon looked to the left to gaze upon the vista of green fields. The car drifted with his gaze, left out of his lane, toward the center median, thumping over the bots dots in the road. Brad fought the impulse to grab the wheel. He gritted his teeth as his son eased the car back into the lane.

"Nice recovery," Brad said with a knotted stomach. "You remembered that if you run off the road, the worst thing you can do is yank the wheel back. The over-correction can put you in a spin. It's just like shooting a duck, don't jerk, make it smooth."

Dillon nodded quickly, both hands on the wheel in a death grip, visibly shaken.

"Relax, you're doing fine, Dillon. In fact, why don't you keep going to Kettleman City? I want to rest my eyes a while." He turned to Marie in the back seat and winked. He made a show of reclining his seat a little and resting his head on his left hand to shield his eyes from Dillon's view. His stomach stayed taut and his eyes open over the next thirty-mile stretch.

Brad paid more attention this trip to the big signs along the freeway in the foreground of fallowed ground, some of it with dead orchards. They said things like "Congress Created Dust Bowl" and "No Water = No Food = No Jobs." Some of the signs looked like they had been up a long time. The paint was faded and the signs partially shredded by the weather. Based on what Kris had said, he suspected those went up in the mid-90s after the feds forced cutbacks in Delta water exports to protect the salmon and smelt. He assumed that the newer signs were meant to sway public opinion in support of the BDCP, and other initiatives by the big water contractors that were under so much public debate these days. The signs had a homemade look to them. Brad was suspicious.

His mind strayed to his internship with a public relations firm during his training with the Coro Foundation, a seventy-year-old national public affairs leadership program. In his first week there, he was called into a dark screening room to view a movie about the history of brandy and how it is made. It was really a half-hour soft sell sponsored by the California Brandy Association. This was the client's first look at the firm's video. After it was played, the lights came on and a client big shot turned to twenty-four-year-old Brad and asked, "Did anything about that film stand out to you?" Dead silence. Brad could feel all the eyes in the studio turned to him. He glanced at the account executive he was shadowing, who was leaning forward with nervous anticipation. "Well, one thing was that I always thought of brandy as something you sip after skiing. I didn't know it was good in all kinds of summer drinks, too." The client was all smiles. He later learned from his mentor that Brad's reaction was exactly the message the viewer of this "documentary" was supposed to come away with in hopes of boosting year-round brandy sales. It had been a real- life demonstration of how an expert can get you to think his way. He wanted to check into those water signs along I-5.

They pulled into the driveway a little after 3 p.m. just as their neighbor, Lee, was walking to his car. They got a quick update on Lilly who was doing fine at the rehab center where Lee was headed. Brad suggested they all go over together as soon as they unloaded the car. Marie offered to bring a plate of leftover pumpkin pie.

The single-story rehab center had a Spanish mission style. It looked old but was nicely landscaped. They got directions to Lilly's room from a pleasant, plump lady at the front counter and found Lilly in the corridor with her walker, Lee, and a nursing assistant close by. They exchanged greetings and walked with them back to Lilly's small private room.

After catching up on Lilly's condition and talking about their Thanksgiving holidays, Marie served the pie using plastic plates and forks she had brought.

"You two have been so kind to Lee and me," Lilly said.

"We are lucky to have you as neighbors and friends," Brad said. "And that was before we knew Lilly had such an interesting life."

"Yes," Marie added. "And we want you to know how much we appreciated you telling us about the dam disaster. We know that wasn't easy for you to re-live.

"Yes, it was a horrible night," Lilly said soberly. "My life changed forever and so did my dad's." She sat up. "Oh dear, about that, Lee told me that when I was rambling in the hospital, I confused you about my father."

"Oh, right," Brad said. "Lee explained that you call your birth father who died in the flood, 'Father' and his brother who adopted you, 'Dad', right? And he said that your dad worked for the Los Angeles Department of Water and Power and even worked on the dam."

"Yes," Lilly said softly, becoming pensive. "I often wondered who got the worst of that disaster, my father, who died, or my dad, who had to live with the guilt of being part of killing him. I must have reminded him of it every time he saw me in the house. I imagine it was very hard for him especially after his own wife died so young. Cancer, I think. I was only eleven when she died. Then it was just dad and me. He didn't really know what to do with me. He managed with a little help from his sister, my other aunt, who lived close, and the lady next door who kind of became a surrogate mother."

"Yes," was all that Brad could manage, staring down at his pie. He thought about her comment about her dad's role in killing her father but opted not to break in.

"Oh, now, don't you go making sad eyes, Bradley," Lilly said. "A lot of other people had it worse. It was the Depression but we were in better shape than most people. The people who were really suffering were the ones living in the Dustbowl with no work and no ability to grow food. We lived in the nice Eagle Rock neighborhood of Los Angeles. The Depression didn't hit us as bad out here as in the Midwest. We had good weather and dad always had a good-paying job. We got by fine."

"What exactly did your dad do?" Marie asked.

"He was an engineer," Lilly replied, and became silent again. "He admitted to me when I was a teenager that he actually helped design the St. Francis Dam. That's why I say he felt some guilt about the disaster." Another pause. "Dad felt bad for not blowing the whistle about some of the things he knew were wrong with the dam design."

Brad perked up. "I was telling Marie about some of the design flaws I read about. I'd love to know more of the background if you are up to it."

"All right," she said, looking up to gather her memories. "I may get some of this wrong because my memory isn't so good anymore, especially after all the drugs lately."

"That's understandable, Lilly," Marie said. "Don't feel like you have to do this now."

"I'm fine," Lilly said. She seemed to ponder the story. "I think Chief Mulholland hired my dad soon after the city took over the private water company at the turn of the century. He was right out of college with a degree in civil engineering from UC Berkeley. He worked in Mulholland's office. Dad made it sound like he was one of the Chief's fair-haired boys. He got promoted fast and the Chief put him in charge of planning big construction projects."

"Your dad must have been very bright," Marie observed.

"He was but dad told me he always thought the Chief resented the college men he hired. The Chief didn't have a degree. He was a young Irish immigrant who jumped on a ship for America after his father beat him for bad grades in school. He started with the water company as a ditch cleaner. But he was no dummy. He studied all the technical manuals available at night and knew the entire water system inside and out. In later years, he had developed quite a reputation for getting big projects built on time and at budget. He kind of looked down on the younger men out of college with their degrees and no experience."

"Did your dad ever go to Mulholland with any of his concerns about the dam design?" Brad prompted.

"Yes, especially when the Chief raised the height and didn't build up the thickness. I guess the Chief blew up. You need to understand. The Chief didn't answer to anybody. He was very powerful and didn't tolerate anybody questioning him, especially someone like dad, fresh out of college."

Brad nodded knowingly.

Lilly continued. "Dad said the Chief told him that he would decide what was best and to do what he was told or keep walking out the front door."

"Wow!" Brad said. "I can't tell you how many times I've wanted to say something similar to my staff." He felt another pang of guilt about how he had treated Megan Cain.

"Oh, I doubt that, Bradley," Lilly said, pausing for a sip of water. She stared at the water in the glass and cocked her head. "Dad said that the rock in the canyon walls was unfit for a dam. He said that during a hearing after the disaster, an investigator actually dropped a piece of the rock from the canyon into a glass of water and it dissolved."

Lilly took another sip of water. "The whole affair was tainted by shady tactics from the start. Dad said they had legal advice that what they were doing to get the water rights was not illegal but that didn't make it right. There was no formal authorization from the city to do anything with the Owens project and the Chief didn't want to let the cat out of the bag by asking for it publicly. So, the Chief and Eaton brought a bunch of the San Fernando Valley speculators up there under the guise of being resort developers. The group saw the water, got excited, and ponied up all the money Mulholland needed to tie up enough land to control the valley's water rights. It all happened secretly and very fast."

"I read a little about that background," Brad noted again.

"Oh, and here I am carrying on about ancient history that you already know about," Lilly said.

"No!" Marie and Brad said in unison.

Brad swallowed his last bite of pie and set his fork down. "No, please Lilly, hearing your dad's take on things is fascinating. Please go on."

"Yes, please do, Lilly," Marie added.

"You know, Lilly," Brad prompted, "I have to admire what they pulled off with that Owens project, especially keeping it secret. You could never get away with such a scheme today." As soon as he said it, his mind drifted back to the Delta and the state's pushing ahead with the ill-conceived tunnels.

"It *is* incredible that the secret didn't get out about the whole scheme to bring the water to develop the San Fernando Valley," Lilly agreed. "The publisher of the *Los Angeles Times* knew all about it, of course, because he was part of the syndicate. He kept it quiet, at least until Mulholland gave the signal that he had enough water rights in Owens Valley. My dad kept a folder on the St. Francis. He saved an article from the *Times* bragging about how the city's representatives put one over on the unsuspecting residents of Owens Valley. It talked about how the country bumpkins had greedily lined up to take the land purchase money from these supposedly stupid out-of-town investors and how they were going to be surprised to learn that the water the land controlled would be sent to LA. The *Times* even admitted that the Owens Valley economy would be ruined."

"Boy, that's pretty brazen," Marie said.

Brad scratched his chin. "OK, I've read a little about how

Mulholland and Eaton got the water rights. Maybe you can fill me in on something else. They needed the voters to approve a bond issue to buy the land up there and then build the aqueduct, right? How were they able to get the citizens to vote for that, if the water was mainly to develop San Fernando Valley not for the existing citizens?"

"Well, Bradley," Lilly said, looking at her hands, "I'm afraid to say that the most honest answer is that they lied. My dad really felt dirty about his participation in that deception. The department was publicly issuing reports and giving speeches about a water crisis facing the city, but dad said they really had a big surplus of water. In fact, I've read that in the eight years the aqueduct was being built, before the Owens water even arrived, the city grew from 200,000 to 500,000, without any new water supply. There was no water crisis at all. And they were pretty cagey about how they went about getting the bond money. They first asked the voters to approve a small bond measure of $1.5 million that would only cover the Owens land purchases even though they figured the aqueduct would cost about $25 million. Then, after the first bond passed, they immediately pitched a second bond for the construction arguing it would be a waste of the taxpayers' money not to use the water they'd bought with the first bond."

"Interesting!" Brad exclaimed. "I'm seeing some parallels with how the State Water Project was sold to the voters in the 1960s."

"I don't know about that," Lilly said. "Dad said they really conned the voters to take care of the San Fernando speculators. The department even had their men dump water out of the city's reservoirs into the ocean to support the story of a water crisis. The *Times* was right on the spot, running pictures and scare stories about the dry reservoirs."

"Sounds like that movie *Chinatown* with Jack Nicholson," Brad said. "But there had to be a lot of people who knew the truth. Didn't anything come out to the public before the bond vote?"

Lilly thought a moment. "Yes, Dad kept a few other newspaper articles. One I think was from the *San Francisco Chronicle* and came out shortly after the LA *Times* story bragging about the Owens Valley project. The *Chronicle* story was the first to say publicly that the aqueduct was really linked to a land development scheme in the San Fernando Valley. The LA *Times* responded with an editorial a couple of days later dismissing the idea and suggesting that the *Chronicle's* motivation was keeping Los Angeles from reaching its own potential and grabbing some of San Francisco's limelight. Then the *Los Angeles Examiner*, another of William Randolph Hearst's papers, really broke the story. They had everything, including a list of the members in the San Fernando syndicate. In fact, they even reported that Harrison Gray Otis himself, the owner of the *Times*, had signed a check for $50,000, the first payment on the big area they optioned in the valley. That was the day after Otis had written the editorial poo-poohing that there was a land development scheme."

"Oops," chuckled Brad. "I wonder how Otis explained that!"

"Well," said Lilly, "that's the last *Times* article dad had clipped with the others. That one was a really nasty attack against Hearst himself for *The Examiner's* 'yellow journalism.' Otis basically said that Hearst was jealous that he didn't have the foresight to promote the Owens project. If he had, the *Examiner* would have dubbed it 'The Great Hearst Aqueduct' instead of attacking the project. Otis bashed Hearst for trying to discredit the civic-minded business people and the outstanding public servants who were bringing this much-needed water to the region."

"Ah," Brad said, "that's the old 'ad hominem' argument technique. When your opponent has you dead to rights on the facts, attack your opponent personally, not his arguments." He flashed back on his Coro experience and an evening training session with a high-profile developer at his home in the posh Pacific Heights neighborhood of San Francisco. The colorful character was a master at deflecting public criticism and showed the eager trainees how it's done.

"Add hominy?" Lee asked.

"Ad hominin. It's not important." Brad looked at Lilly. "You were saying that Hearst's paper broke the story about the valley development scheme before the bond election. But Mulholland and the syndicate still got it approved."

Lilly nodded and continued. "Dad said that some deal must have been made since Hearst told his *Examiner* editor to back off. Then Hearst personally wrote the editorial endorsing the upcoming vote on the LA aqueduct bond issue. That, along with the phony images of the dried up reservoirs, no rain for months, and a hot spell with days in the 100s just before the election, and the bond was approved by a landslide."

"Amazing," Brad said disgustedly. He thought of the trickery used to sell the State Water Project, the paper water scheme, and the BDCP.

"Yes," Lilly added. "But remember that back then Los Angeles was tiny, and people didn't have access to information like they do today. I think it only took 11,500 votes to get the first bond approved."

"Think about that," Brad said. "The second largest city in the country owes its standing to a handful of land speculators and a neighborhood-worth of voters."

"Pretty disgusting, if you asked my dad." Lilly responded. "He was right in the middle of it but didn't feel good about it. I think he wanted to quit all the time but my aunt would talk him out of it. It was a good job and they liked being invited to big events with the bigwigs of Southern California. Besides, I suspect that if Dad did quit, he knew the Chief would just find somebody else to do his bidding. He stayed on but wasn't happy."

"Probably right about that," Brad agreed. "Your dad was in a bad spot. It must have been a real ethical tug-of-war for him." His stomach tightened.

"He felt even worse about being part of building the dam even though the Chief took full responsibility for the failure."

"That must have taken some of the heat off of the rest of the department staff," Brad observed.

"Publicly, yes," agreed Lilly. "But Dad admitted to me that he and some of his workmates knew they shared in the blame. It haunted him all his life. Most of the other engineers who had been involved with the dam design eventually left for lesser paying jobs. Their careers were tainted."

"Seeing others leaving because of their involvement with St. Francis must have put even more pressure on your dad because he didn't." Marie observed.

"I'm sure it did," Lilly responded. "I think he stayed mainly for my benefit. Times were tough then and Dad wanted to make sure I was taken care of. Years later, I wondered if his staying on the job despite being miserable was some sort of self-punishment for his role in the dam failure."

"My goodness," Marie exclaimed. "I'm sure nobody did anything wrong on purpose. It must have just been that they didn't know as much about these things back then."

"That's pretty much what the general public opinion was at the time," Lilly agreed. "The Chief was viewed as a miracle worker who did great things for Los Angeles. Sure his image was destroyed by the dam disaster and he never did another project, but people forgave and even pitied him. But Dad never forgave himself for going along rather than fighting the powerful interests pushing the project ahead. He went to his grave with the guilt from that choice."

Lee pointed to Brad with his fork. "Government has always been controlled by the powerful. Right, Brad?"

While Brad saw the broad, wrinkled smile on his neighbor's face, he heard his father's contempt for government. He smiled but felt flushed and embarrassed.

"Dad waited until I moved out to start college," Lilly resumed softly. "I got the call one night at the dorms from the lady next door that he committed suicide."

"Oh!" Brad and Marie gasped in unison. Lee patted Lilly's hand.

"How awful," Marie said sadly.

"It was a shock at the time but, looking back, I should have expected it," Lilly said. "They found him in a bathtub full of water. He had cut his wrists with a razor blade and laid back to die. I'm sure he chose his method of death carefully. On the floor next to the tub was one of his favorite sayings, 'The only thing necessary for the triumph of evil is for good men to do nothing.' He used to say that all of the time."

"He must have lived with a lot of pain," Brad said, feeling another stomach cramp.

"I'm sure he did." Lilly continued. "He told me about having to drive the Chief to the Santa Paula area the day of the disaster. He saw a car in the middle of the riverbed covered in mud filled with the bodies of a family trying to get away from the flood. He saw the bodies of a little boy in his father's arms wedged upside down by debris in the fork of big oak tree. He talked about helping rescuers with a rope line retrieve a woman and her three children who had ridden out the flood on a mattress that was snagged at the top of a tree. They survived, thank God. But so many didn't."

"What did the locals do when they saw people from LA there?" Marie asked.

"Dad said there were signs that said 'Kill Mulholland.' But there wasn't any violence directed to the department officials who were on the scene right away trying to help. Unlike how things are today, Mulholland stepped up and took all the blame and the City of Los Angeles was credited, even by the victims, for how quickly they came to the aid of the people and paid restitution."

"Of course, there's even some speculation about ulterior motives with that." Lee chimed in. "The federal government was planning the Boulder Dam on the Colorado River. It was to be another big water source for all of Southern California. But it had a similar design as the St. Francis. The last thing LA wanted was a lot of publicity about that design failing. So they paid restitution fast and the whole story just sort of died away. Not many people know about it anymore."

"That's for sure. I still can't believe that I never heard anything about this," Brad said. "I'm so sorry, Lilly, about everything you had to deal with in your life because of the disaster. I can't imagine."

"Well, you never know what can happen to yourself and your loved ones. As bad as the flood was, the hardest part of this for me is thinking about the pain Dad lived with until he couldn't anymore. He was a good father to me but I don't remember him ever being happy. Every day he went to work he must have been reminded of his own failure to speak out about the dam design problems and then reminded again of the consequences when he got home and saw me."

"Too bad that, back then, people didn't seek out counseling when they had personal issues like that," Brad said.

"No, it wasn't done," Lilly agreed. "It wasn't just the design mistakes that tormented him, you know. He got my father the job with Southern California Edison that put him at that tent camp. Edison was the main competitor to the Department of Water and Power but people at the working level knew each other and were friendly. Dad used his contacts to help my father get a job with the construction crews."

"Geez!" Brad gasped.

"Yes, I've seen a lot of misery in my life. But one of my most painful memories is a night when I was a teenager. I came home from a dance and saw Dad sitting in his chair in the dark. There was a half-empty bottle of rye next to him. His eyes were wet."

Her words came slowly and her own eyes began to redden. "Dad told me that night that in the days just before the dam broke, he, and other department employees and residents downstream, saw leaks coming out of the dam face. People were getting nervous. The morning before it burst, the Chief himself visited the dam and announced that everything was fine. Father called Dad later that day asking if they were in danger. Dad could barely get the words out through his tears when he told me the last words he said to my father, 'Don't worry, Walt, the Chief won't allow the damn dam to fail.'"

14

Monday morning started with a department head
meeting organized by Jackie McCall, Director of Human Resources,
to discuss the first draft of a classification study that had been underway
for months. The study was agreed to in the previous year's bargaining
with the Santa Ynez Employee Association. A consultant was
reviewing the duties and skills required in the main job classifications
of the bargaining group, like the Maintenance Worker I, II, and III
series and Administrative Assistant I and II. These would be used
as benchmarks to peg salary ranges for other jobs in the bargaining
group with fewer people. The ostensible purposes were to ensure that
job descriptions for the classes reflected the work being done and that
there was appropriate alignment in pay and duties among the various
job classifications.

Brad approached the study with trepidation. He had warned
the City Council in closed-session bargaining meetings that such

WITHOUT PURPOSE *of* EVASION

studies usually stirred up more controversy than they resolved. Furthermore, they'd result in higher payroll cost, the expense that can be as much as 85 percent of some departments' budget. But the employee union had considerable influence in local elections. They contributed money to "their" candidates, made public endorsements, had members and their families write Letters to the Editor in the newspaper, and walked the neighborhoods handing out campaign literature. They earned councilmembers' gratitude and got their ears when it was time to negotiate a new labor contract. A city manager could find himself negotiating both with the employees' representatives and his own bosses to get an agreement that wouldn't break the treasury. The employees had obviously convinced several of the councilmembers to back the classification study over Brad's closed-session objections.

Brad entered the conference room, taking his customary seat at the end of the long walnut-stained table. Jackie McCall was about to kick off the meeting when he jumped in to set the stage. "Let me start by saying that these classification studies cause more problems than they correct. They raise the employees' expectations that there's a pay increase coming their way. Nobody ever said 'I don't think I'm doing everything in my job description and you should cut my salary.' We can't let this study get away from us and we can't afford to give everybody what they want. So let's not beat this into the ground and try to get out of here in an hour with as little damage to the budget as possible."

He gestured to his HR director to take it from there. Jackie wore what Brad's grandmother called a "spit up face."

The meeting followed a predictable path. A couple of the department heads were into it, asking good questions and clearly trying to contribute. They could be counted upon to be loyal troops when the Vigoro hit the fan with the bargaining group. Other department heads listened mutely. Brad eventually closed the meeting, reminding the department heads that they were a team, and they needed to defend the final study as best as they could. Still, he knew that when their own staff members confronted them about the study recommendations, some of the department heads would just blame HR. There were limits to what could be accomplished with team-building exercises. He swooped up the paperwork into an irregular pile, and went back to his office.

Councilwoman Kay Nance was at Jane's desk when he got back. "Hi, Kay," Brad said. "Have a nice Thanksgiving?"

"It was glorious," she responded with a smirk. "The Tofurky was especially yummy this year."

He stuck his index finger into his mouth in a gagging gesture. "What brings you in this morning?"

"Dropping off expenses for my League trip," she said.

Brad thought of Councilman Jack Kelly from Lodi sitting around the fire talking about how much fun Kay was.

"How was your trip north?" Kay asked.

"Interesting. I wanted to ask if you knew anything about those big water billboards all along I-5 that say things like, 'Congress Created Dust Bowl' and 'No Water = No Food = No Jobs.' I'm suspicious. Got a minute?"

She nodded and he led Kay into his office, plopped his paperwork on the desk, and joined her at the coffee table.

Kay was shaking her head. "Those signs are a mystery. I have a friend on the board for a nonprofit public interest group that is dedicated to protecting the Delta. They have been fighting against Astroturf groups."

"Astroturf?" he asked.

"It means a group that masquerades as a grassroots organization, but isn't," she explained. "Fake grass, get it?"

"Astroturf, huh? I gotta remember that one. Those signs look like they were made in somebody's garage, but I know what a good PR firm can accomplish," Brad said.

"My friend says these groups are really shills for the big water contractors. Their names and websites suggest they are all about protecting the Delta, but they are really fully funded and promoting big water. It's very devious. They did some digging on the billboards at the southerly end of the valley and traced them to a public relations firm in Los Angeles. Not exactly homemade."

Brad thought a moment. "It's pretty clever how they frame the issue that it's a choice between some lowly endangered species like the Delta smelt versus food and jobs for people. I get it that the smelt may not have a lot of commercial value but they are like the canary in the coal mine. My daughter, Kristen, says they're an indicator species, showing us by their near-extinction that the water quality in the Delta is in bad shape. That's why they're important."

"Good, Brad. Throw in a shot at Congress that has an all-time low approval rating of around 15 percent," Kay added, "and I can see people easily falling for the scam."

"Despite all their conniving," Brad countered, "the water contractors aren't getting their way on everything. Consider the cutbacks to state agricultural water deliveries."

"Sure," Kay said dismissively, with a wave of her hand. "We're in a serious drought and government deliveries have been cut. You'd think the growers would be fallowing their land for the time being. But you probably saw thousands of acres being planted in high-value, permanent crops like nuts, citrus, and grapes."

"Yeah, I guess I never paid attention to all that new planting before. I remember driving along I-5 and mostly dodging tumbleweeds. Now there are trees and vines as far as you can see. Might not be a good use of water but at least that worthless land is generating jobs and tax base."

Kay snickered. "You'd be surprised. Remember, in the southern part of the valley, we're mostly talking about huge corporations with thousands of acres, not small family farms. Everything is much more mechanized so there's not as much farm labor as you'd get with smaller farms."

"What about the increased value of all that new production?" he argued. He often felt obligated to play the independent thinker, especially with Kay.

"Oh, the land value *has* increased all right," the councilwoman countered. "But did you know that the total value of all the farm production and food processing in the entire state only amounts to between 1 and 2 percent of California's gross state product?"

"Really?" he exclaimed skeptically.

"Don't look at me with that tone of voice," she said smiling. "Isn't it weird how we end up saying the same stupid things our parents said to us? Anyway, check it out yourself, Brad. The vast majority of the water we spent billions of dollars to store and hundreds of millions to move around the state every year, mostly benefits a small number of the largest corporations in the world. Yet, it contributes only a small percentage of the state's economy."

"People have to eat, too. It's not just money."

"Don't fall victim to that 'jobs and food' spin, Brad. With all the new almond orchards planted in the Central Valley, California now has over one million acres producing 80 percent of the world supply. California is known around the world for its excellent wines. Almond value is now two-and-a-half times greater. But we aren't eating them here. Seventy percent is exported, mostly to China."

"Isn't that a *good* thing?" Brad persisted. "We need more exports to help our trade balance."

"Yes, but, like everything else, it's about balance. The California almond crop uses over a trillion gallons of water a year and walnuts are even thirstier."

"I can't relate to that," he admitted.

"Look, it takes one gallon of water to grow one almond and nearly five gallons for one walnut. You could flush your toilet five times with the water from a single walnut."

"Yeah, but I'd have to squeeze it really hard!"

She rolled her eyes. "Very funny. My point is that there's all this emphasis on conserving water in the urban areas while 80 percent of the water used by humans in California goes to agriculture. It's four times the urban use. And, like I said, all that ag water contributes less than 2 percent of the gross state product. Think of that, Brad. We've lost so much big industry in California. We have thousands of acres of abandoned industrial parks in the urban core that could be putting that water to much better use in terms of jobs, tax base, and community redevelopment."

"Not sure about that," he replied. "There are a ton of regulatory and global economic factors behind the decline of heavy industry. I don't think water supply is high on the list."

"Maybe with heavy industry," she conceded. "But we both know that many of our cities and counties have had to pass up opportunities to recruit wet industry because of their water constraints. We are missing out on high-paying jobs and a huge tax base so that a handful of big multi-national ag corporations can sell almonds to China. Almonds alone require 20 percent more water than all the indoor home uses across the state. You can't have a meaningful discussion about managing our water resources and leave out ag."

"But, Kay, the growers are conserving, too. I saw drip irrigation on all those new orchards. Besides, when I was talking to some guys a couple days ago about the Delta, one of the farmers admitted that dairy operations and row crops like tomatoes are worse than almonds in terms of water efficiency." He leaned back pleased to have come up with a counter.

"Oh, ag has conserved, all right. But instead of that conservation being used to reduce their dependence on Northern California water, they are using it to bring more land into production. In comparison, despite all the population growth in California in the last twenty years, urban water use is about the same. Per capita urban water use has actually dropped. Pricing and conservation measures have really worked. Where's the regulation on ag use?"

"So, let's hear it for good city leadership!" he joked.

"Not hardly, Brad. Cities are driven by their economic considerations just like the Central Valley ag conglomerates. Most cities that have been conserving haven't done so because of enlightened public interest. Stretching supplies means all you growth-oriented types have more water left for new development. Most cities don't have protecting our environment high on their priority list."

Brad frowned. "After Prop 13 and with all the other voter-approved tax limitations, and now losing redevelopment, new development is one of the only means left for a city to get its budget in shape. Can't do it without water."

Kay Nance shook her head again. "Again, Brad, your whole orientation is that water is a commodity; something that should be exploited to maximize economic gain."

He threw up his hands. "Well, citizens want good public services and amenities. That takes money. Sorry, Kay, that's a reality I live with. What would *you* have me do?"

"Back to what we talked about before," she snapped back. "Balanced public policy. Put some priority on the environment, not just on the budget."

He scowled. "You said yourself that the urban areas are already conserving on a per capita basis. How much more can we do without really affecting quality of life?"

She again waved her hand dismissively. "Cities have just been grabbing the low-hanging fruit on water conservation. We focus restrictions on residential water use because people expect it and won't squawk too much. I just learned at the League meeting I went to that there are trillions of gallons of potable water wasted in this state by big private buildings like factories, hospitals, supermarkets, and office complexes. We don't go after them, though, because they're more powerful."

"Wasted how?" he said, perplexed.

"Large buildings typically use cooling towers for their air conditioning, refrigeration, and manufacturing needs. These systems are more energy-efficient compared to other systems. But they waste an enormous amount of water through evaporation and, mostly, by diluting the chemical by-products in the process water so they can dump it into the sewer."

"I wasn't aware of that," Brad said, beginning to fidget.

"The more environmentally-sensitive firms don't dilute, they have automated systems to pretreat the cooling waste before discharging to the sanitary sewer. That cuts the amount of water they use by 85 percent."

"Impressive. Is that expensive?" Brad asked.

"My understanding is that it would cost about fifteen to twenty thousand dollars to retrofit the older systems. But if the typical supermarket did that, they'd save about a million gallons of potable water a year.

"Whewww," he whistled.

"Yes, it's a bunch. And supermarkets use a lot less water than the steam boilers in big buildings like hospitals and manufacturing plants. The estimate I heard is that if all these buildings went to automated pre-treatment, the savings statewide would be in the trillions of gallons every year. Cities should be requiring that conversion."

Brad was skeptical. "If it's that inexpensive to reduce their annual water bills, why wouldn't these supermarkets, office buildings, and factories do it as a good business move?"

Kay sighed. "From what I heard, many of these big private projects have deals worked out with their cities for their water and sewer that go back to when they were being courted. Some of them use water from the local irrigation districts for cooling and pay next to nothing. Some aren't even metered. Why should they spend twenty thousand dollars to save water if it's cheap or unmetered?"

"What about the potential wastewater savings?"

Kay shook her head again. "Same thing. We're talking about big projects that provide a lot of jobs and tax base. Many cities gave out discounted sewer rates or even flat-rated them as an inducement to build. There's little incentive to spend money to reduce their wastewater."

Brad felt embarrassed for being educated on this issue by his councilwoman, an artist. "I'm a little surprised cities haven't clamped down on this situation to conserve more water; maybe even financing the pre-treatment for them and collecting it over time in their bills."

"Like I said, most cities are only doing the easy, expected things for water conservation. It takes more courage to go after the big commercial and industrial uses. I heard that there are special districts that take care of just wastewater treatment and are running out of capacity at their plants. They've ordered these companies to disconnect their cooling tower discharge from the sanitary sewer entirely to save treatment capacity."

"So, where is that discharge going?" Brad asked.

"Good question, Brad. It's illegal for these buildings to discharge even that diluted wastewater into the storm system because of all the detergents that would end up in creeks and streams. But that's exactly what's happening because the special districts are focused on treating the wastewater that arrives at their plant. Water quality downstream is somebody else's problem. It's an untenable situation. I don't know if cities are doing this, too. By the way, that's another reason to broaden the scope of the regional watershed authorities like we're trying to do with our League petition so we are coordinating water conservation and quality. You won't have government agencies working at cross purposes."

"Interesting, Kay. I'll check with Dee to see if we have companies with cooling towers that fit your description. What else should we be doing to conserve?"

She leaned back and thought a moment. "Nothing too crazy. Just sensible planning. Emphasize infill and moderate or higher density development over sprawling out. It's cheaper to supply the infrastructure and easier to accommodate with public transportation. Fewer cars on the road, less air pollution, less drainage run-off, and more land left in open space or ag production."

"But, Kay, everyone doesn't want to live in an eight hundred square foot apartment or condo in the city. They want their own single-family detached house on a small lot in the suburbs. They're willing to commute several hours a day to give their families that sort of lifestyle."

"That's the argument Scott Graves, So Cal, and the other suburban developers use. Don't you see that we in local government are enabling that bad choice by continuing to approve projects like Green Valley?"

"It's what the homebuyer, the market, wants."

She shook her head. "What the market wants is a different issue. Listen, left to my preferences, I'd eat a whole bag of Fritos and drink two bottles of wine every day. But if I did, there'd be even more of me to love than there already is. So I substitute quinoa for the Fritos. The point is we don't get to do just what we'd like, without consequences.

It's not just about giving people what they think they want, it's about educating them about the consequences and giving them reasonable alternatives for making a better long-term choice."

He narrowed his eyes. "Ignore market preference?"

"Not entirely. You're being black and white again. If all the homebuyer has to pick from are single-family homes in the suburbs, they'll take it even if it means a long commute and too little family time. If, instead, you can offer them attractively designed, safe, higher-density communities closer to where they work, some, not all, I admit, will be swayed in that direction. A fifteen-minute bus or light-rail ride to and from work versus three hours a day in commute traffic means more time for family and leisure."

He wished, now, that he hadn't invited her in. "That's pretty idealistic, Kay."

"Maybe it is, based on how we have been doing community development since World War II. I'd argue that if we accept the fact that we are destroying the state with the status quo, and put more than lip service into sustainable development, gradual improvement will happen."

"Easier said than done, I'm afraid," he replied.

"Never said it would be easy, Brad. Add pricing mechanisms so that a single-family house in the burbs pays the true social and environmental cost of sprawl and you begin to drive more of the market to closer-in sustainable development. Cut back on how much low density development you'll allow in a watershed area, and the scarcity price will motivate others to higher density. It's a movement, not a quick fix. Why not do it right here in Santa Ynez?"

"Well, I'll do my best to make sure the Green Valley EIR is thorough," he offered, hoping to conclude things.

"It won't be. You'll throw a bone to those of us who care about the environment but, at the end of the day, Mayor Buddy and his group will push it aside. Whether you're talking about farming in the deserts of the Central Valley, the future of the Delta, or what we do right here in Santa Ynez, too much power tilts toward money and not to being good stewards."

Her "stewards" comment brought him back to the duck hunt and his commitment to the men around the fire. It was unsettling. He seized upon a new direction, exhaled deeply, leaned forward, and folded his hands. "Look, Kay, can I speak to you as a friend?"

"Yes, but be gentle. I'm fragile," she joked.

"I will. Thanks to you, and others I've talked to lately, I have a better understanding of the critical water issues we face in this state. I suspect there is a lot of truth in what you say, but there is also lots of complexity, too. I've been in this business long enough to also suspect that there are good counter-arguments that I am not knowledgeable enough to give. That aside, and with all due respect, your admonition about not being black and white goes both ways, you know. Beyond that, while you and I may not always be on the same page politically, I like and respect you."

"The feeling is mutual, Brad," the councilwoman responded with a mock tipping of the hat. "Say what you want to say. I can handle it."

He swallowed hard. "OK. It's not my role to give you political advice. So, as a friend, let me share my observation from thirty years of grappling with public policies and trying to help elected officials come to consensus."

She perked up and folded her hands in her lap like an obedient school girl. "Please do."

"This is just basic negotiation strategy. If people consider you immovable on an issue, they'll marginalize you. They'll dismiss your points of view and not put any effort into trying to work a compromise with you. You give up a lot of power by taking yourself out of the negotiation process. And a lot of the policy issues are just that, a negotiation among people with competing values and interests."

"So, is this about you wanting me to play nicer with the rest of the Council on Green Valley?"

Brad paused a moment for the right words. "Like I said, I'm not trying to give you political advice. Maybe you think you can swing three votes by digging in against Green Valley. Or, maybe, you are resigned to being on the short end of a 3-2 vote and that's OK with you."

"Hah!" she laughed. "Been there. Done that."

"I'd just ask you to consider what you want to accomplish in your role on the Council. None of you can get anything done without getting majority approval. And to get majority support, you have to be prepared to compromise sometimes. That draws people to you and makes them more willing to compromise *their* interests to stay connected to you. If you aren't willing to negotiate on anything, your colleagues have no incentive to give you anything *you* want. It will always be win/lose."

Kay was uncharacteristically quiet. He thought he saw her head nod slightly and pressed ahead. "One of my mentors used to quote a Persian proverb, 'the dogs may bark but the caravan moves on.'"

"So, I'm a barking dog, now?" she asked teasingly.

Brad was in serious mode. "I'll let you think about that in the context of what you want to accomplish on the Council. Remember, the barking dogs don't stop the caravan. You have to be in the tent, engaging with the leaders, to influence where the caravan goes."

"So do you have some ideas for me on where to compromise with Green Valley?" she asked.

"No, that's for you to decide," he replied. "You're a smart person. I'm just giving you a perspective to consider. Maybe you don't want to do anything other than let everyone know you are going to fight Green Valley to the bitter end. Or maybe you'll come up with some proposals for changing the plan that will make it more palatable than what it might end up being if you are on the losing end of a 3-2. Or maybe, if you send signals that you want to negotiate, just maybe, you'll get others to give you more of what you want on Green Valley or in trade-offs on other issues that are more important to you. Food for thought, huh?"

She sat still a few moments before gathering up her stack of travel receipts. "Very diplomatically put, Brad," she said, rising from her chair. "I appreciate the friendly advice and the spirit behind it. I'll think about it."

He stayed seated and watched her go out to the counter to talk to Jane about her receipts. After he heard the councilwoman leave the outer office, he went over to his office door and started to close it, giving Jane a wink. She nodded her understanding.

He turned his high, black leather chair around, leaned back, and put his feet up on the credenza made of wood veneer that matched his desk. He stared at the large framed photograph of Mount Shasta hanging on the wall over the credenza. It had been a gift from Marie many years ago. It was during his short-lived meditation phase. One of his favorites at the time was a mountain meditation on tape cassette. The speaker had him get relaxed then imagine himself as a huge mountain constantly undergoing forces it couldn't control like high winds, rain storms, and snow. Through the ages, the mountain just stood there, taking whatever came along, passively, stoically, unprotestingly. The mountain was at peace. Brad had a small photo of Mt. Shasta, a massive volcanic peak that sits majestically alone above the high desert of upper Northern California. The picture was taken just as a lightning bolt crashed against the mountain. It was a spectacular shot. Brad used the picture as a focal point to begin the mountain meditation. Marie had the photo blown up and framed for his office to bring him some relief at work.

Connecting with Mt. Shasta was like meeting with an old friend. Brad could level with the mountain about what he was feeling. He closed his eyes to concentrate on his body sensations. His breath was shallow and he felt tension in his shoulders, hands, and arms, like he was preparing for a fight. Sitting with the sensation for a short time, he came to understand that the underlying body sensation was fear. He sensed danger. From there it was a quick connection to the Green Valley Village project. He sat with it for a time and began to relax. Finally, he felt exhilaration and even a little hope arising from his candid conversation with Kay.

After ten minutes or so of quiet focusing, his restlessness took over. He opened his eyes, got up, stretched, and opened the door. "Good to go, now," he told Jane.

"You don't need me to bring you three envelopes do you?" she scoffed.

It was an old joke. The departing city manager leaves three envelopes behind in the desk drawer for his successor with notes containing advice for when things go bad with the City Council. The first envelope says "Blame your predecessor." At the next bump in the road, the second envelope suggests "Reorganize." After a third crisis, the advice is "Prepare three envelopes." It was the kind of gallows humor that pervaded city manager gatherings.

"No, not ready for that yet." He laughed it off going back in his office. But he recognized that Green Valley could well bring him to his third envelope.

Driving home after work he decided to shut the radio off and reflect on his day. This had been one of those days where he felt productive. The staff meeting in the morning was upbeat. Despite his anxiety about the classification study, most of the department heads took some ownership and contributed useful suggestions. He felt good about the frank discussion with Councilwoman Nance and allowed himself a feeling of hope that it might contribute to the Council becoming a more effective policy-making body. He had worked with the police chief to identify budget changes that would enable them to put more emphasis on traffic enforcement, knowing that citizens are far more likely to suffer injury or property loss from an accident than from crime. He mediated a dispute between a retail developer and the Planning staff regarding staff's design review comments that ended with both sides in agreement. He handled a couple citizen complaint calls and information requests from two councilmembers. He contributed some ideas on a conference call with other city managers around the nation who were planning conference topics of interest to smaller cities at the annual conference of the International City/County Management Association to be held in September. And he ended the day practicing MBWA, whistling as he walked around chatting with the staff.

It had been one of those days where he couldn't image a more fulfilling career.

15

6 weeks later; Thursday, mid-January

The Christmas and New Year's holidays passed easily and all too quickly for Brad Jacks. As far as he was concerned, the federal government may as well declare a national holiday period from about the third week of December through the first week of the New Year. Unless there is a December 31 looming deadline, such as a change in capital gains treatment or the tax- deferred exchange rules, which makes it imperative to close real estate deals by year-end, that time of year was usually very slow for cities. Many staff members took their "use it or lose it" vacation time in this period. Those who stayed on the job used it to catch up on paperwork or their year-long "to do" items. Everything slowed down. The phones didn't ring as much. The second Council meeting in December was usually canceled. Things were put on hold.

Not so, however, with the Green Valley Village project Megan and Dee had no objection to Brad's suggestion, just before Thanksgiving, about using Payton/Carlisle for the water analysis peer review. To Brad's great relief, both of them met with his friend and former colleague, Quinn O'Rourke. He had been given the title of Executive Vice President so that potential clients could feel like they were getting the "A Team." O'Rourke brought the Vice President who ran their Ventura office that would handle the Santa Ynez assignment. She, in turn, brought along the Senior Project Manager who would be doing most of the actual work. Dee and Megan were able to agree on the scope of work, timetable, deliverables, and fee to be paid from a deposit Megan collected from SoCal.

Brad really wanted Quinn O'Rourke involved. He trusted him to provide effective cover fire for Brad in the battle to come. Beyond that, he had shared with his former colleague that he would like some confidential feedback on the competence of his public works and planning directors from his firm's perspective, working with people in these positions all over the state.

Now, six weeks later, he was looking forward to the lunch meeting today with O'Rourke to get his friend's take. Brad got stuck on the phone with an angry resident and lost track of the time. Speeding over to Martellaro's, his favorite Italian restaurant, he jumped out of the car and walked quickly to the front door, his customary five minutes late.

"Sorry I'm late," he panted, as they shook hands in the lobby.

"Relax, buddy. You're going to blow a gasket. It's just me, remember? Besides, I was enjoying looking at all the autographed celebrity photos here."

"Yeah, judging by the clothes and cars, many of the visitors had probably been up to Rancho Del Cielo in the Ronald Reagan era."

"What about her?" O'Rourke said, pointing at the framed picture of Bo Derek sitting behind a plate of pasta. She had autographed it for the owners, "Lin & Ricky, your marinara sauce is a perfect 10!" "What a babe!" the consultant said.

"She lives just outside of town," Brad said matter-of-factly. "Has a horse ranch over there. We see her all the time. Lovely lady." Patting his stomach, he added, "Aged a whole lot better than some of us, huh, Quinn?"

O'Rourke was a little older than Brad, nearly bald and still had his prodigious gut despite his constant experimenting with fad diets. Weight control had been a topic of conversation between the two during lunch and dinner meetings over the years. They had started their careers at about the same time and even competed against each other once for a city manager job that O'Rourke got, and was fired from within six months. They had worked together on several task forces for the International City/County Management Association and on committees of the League of California Cities City Managers Department. They were comrades in arms.

Patting his own stomach, Quinn O'Rourke said, "Yeah, I really need to get back on the diet."

"Me too, Quinn," said Brad. "Let's just embrace our girth. I have a golf buddy who always gives me crap about jogging and trying to moderate my food. He keeps saying, 'all you're doing is adding a few more months on the back end of your life so you can spend more time in a nursing home.' Think he may have something there."

"Right," O'Rourke responded. "Enjoy the present, my friend. I've been out of the profession a few years now. I'm having fun but it's just not the same as running a city. There aren't many other jobs that can give you the variety of experiences day-to-day and the feeling that you're making a positive impact with your life. Don't lose sight of that or stress yourself over stupid stuff like losing a few pounds. Appreciate that you have an interesting job and enjoy the journey, even with all its craziness sometimes."

"Enjoy the journey," Brad said, "that's a message I keep hearing these days. Did God call your cell phone on the way over here and tell you to say that?"

"Might have. I was on the phone talking about your water report when He called, so I let it go to voice mail."

"Still full of bull," laughed Brad. "Let's go enjoy the journey." He led them to his favorite booth at the back of the dark room. The dining room was decorated with murals of Italian scenes, a wall-length painted map of Italy, tables with red and white checkered tablecloths, and waxed-over bottles of red wine with protruding candles. Martellaro's wasn't pretentious, just good.

As Brad's eyes adjusted to the darkness he spotted and said hello to people at several tables on the way back to "his" table that his favorite waitress, Twyla, was setting up for them. He had a special relationship with Twyla that started with exchanging wisecracks and went so far as her dropping a lemon meringue pie on Brad's head on his 50th birthday, all arranged by his assistant, Jane. Brad ate at Martellaro's all the time and Twyla was usually his server. They had become friends. Brad had helped get her grandson into the city's juvenile delinquency prevention program and to abate an abandoned house in her neighborhood that had been vandalized. He was glad to be able to help her and she became his biggest fan. Twyla doted over him every time he came in. She did her best to seat people away from him for privacy, she knew what to bring him to drink, and gave him attentive, but not invasive, service so Brad could talk business.

Brad and Quinn slid into the red, vinyl booth seats. Brad winked at Twyla. "All right, give him the show then get out of here."

Twyla opted for her flight attendant spiel for giving the daily specials. "In the event of a sudden drop in the booth's pressure, overhead masks will drop," she said, mimicking the motion of falling oxygen masks, "put the tube into your mouth and suck down the special Chianti at five dollars a glass until you don't care anymore." O'Rourke laughed.

With the specials creatively presented and drink orders placed, Twyla distributed the menus and left the lunch companions to themselves. They caught up on each other's lives, compared notes on what was happening with other city manager friends, reminisced about the old days, and talked about the pros and cons of the job. Twyla was back with the drinks and took their lunch orders. They both ordered the lunch lasagna which Brad recommended. In light of the "enjoy the journey" comment, he had resisted his normal guilt-ridden order of the small garden salad.

They chatted a while over their drinks and Martellaro's special fried bread. The aroma of garlic from the hot bread emanating from the red plastic basket was irresistible.

Twyla brought their heaping platters, staying in character. "Now, so that we can make an on-time start, please check that your belts are low and snug around your hips." And switching to the *Jaws* scene, "And by the way, 'you're gonna need a bigger belt!'"

Quinn clapped and Brad raised his glass to toast her performance. When she exited, stage left, Brad kicked off the purpose of the meeting. "So, what did you come up with on the water issues?"

"Before I go into that, do you remember Vern Graham?

"Sure, long time manager in Vacaville."

"Right," O'Rourke said. "Before that he was a city engineer. He used to say that unlike the precision of engineering, in public policy 'you measure it with a micrometer, mark it with chalk, and cut it with an axe.'"

"Hah, I've heard that one before," Brad said.

"Well, I work for an engineering company now. We take some basic concepts and assumptions, create some vocabulary around them, zero in on some data factors, run everything through computer models, and publish thick reports with lots of tables and numbers. It all seems empirical. But . . ." the consultant glanced conspiratorially over his shoulder, "the reality is that our conclusions are just estimates based on assumptions. There isn't mathematical precision to a lot it."

"I won't report you for blabbing that," Brad promised.

"I'm just giving it to you straight, Brad. All I'm saying is that a lot of this isn't Newton's Law. You can argue it up or down. Do I think our report is well-researched and presented? Yes. But we are working with probabilities here, not absolutes. SoCal, or your councilwoman, could take this same stuff and reach different conclusions."

Brad appreciated his friend's caveat. He doubted there would be comparable candor from another firm. And he was comforted by noting that Quinn was plugged into the political context of the study. He would make sure the study was both accurate and sensitive to the local dynamics. "I understand. What's your firm's best guess on the water?"

"Well, it's a mixed bag. A peer review firm is kind of in the same role as those instant replay officials sitting in New York. There needs to be solid justification for overturning the call that was made on the field. In this case, we didn't have much reason to change the Western's consumption estimates."

"I'm surprised," Brad said. "Megan really thought that the residential use was way too low."

"Maybe. Western used 132 gallons per day, per person. Yes, that's aggressive. It's way under your city's current average. On other projects like this, in this type of climate, we more typically would use something like 160 gallons. But is it a reasonable number to use? We think it could be if the city is going to require all the low flow appliances and xeriscape yard landscaping in the draft Specific Plan.

We didn't feel we should change that one. We want to support the water conservation measure required to achieve that factor. Of course, with 1,400 homes, you can't control it if the future residents change out their appliances or tear out their cactus and make rice paddies in the backyard. But the low-flow appliances like showerheads, toilets, and dishwashers have gotten better so people don't object to them as much as when they first came out. You might consider adding a condition of approval on the subdivision map that all the buyers must receive and initial a notice at escrow about not changing their low-flow stuff or converting to landscaping that takes more water than a typical xeriscape design. Then you can depend upon their neighbors to rat them out if they try."

"Oh, great," Brad groaned. "I needed another issue to pit neighbor against neighbor. So, no change on the demand?"

"Not on the residential or commercial side or for the common area landscaping demand. That all looked pretty decent. And, by the way, we didn't have a problem with the pipe or tank sizes based on peak demand. Another score for SoCal, Western, and your public works director."

"Good to know. Looks like Megan was off the mark."

"Not completely," O'Rourke added. "We are siding with her on the water demand for the golf course. Western used two acre-feet per acre, per year which is low for a golf course, even with their plans to use state-of-the art smart irrigation that adjusts for real time weather and plant conditions. Megan produced some information suggesting that 2.7 acre-feet is a more reasonable number to use in this climate zone. Like I said, there are good arguments on both sides. So, like Solomon, we went with 2.4. That leaves a little slack for the course designer to not have to create something that will look too stark or for the superintendent to have to sweat every gallon."

"And it makes your report seem more balanced by giving Megan a small victory," Brad said with a smile. "That reminds me, since we're playing 'do you remember?' Remember Warren Lavezzo from Vallejo? He retired and took that job as a shadow city manager for a new city being built in Saudi Arabia. He told me about a golf course they built called Whispering Sands. No grass anywhere. You show up for your tee time and they give you a square foot of Astroturf. You throw it on the desert, put your ball on it, whack it toward a flag in the desert, and putt out over finely ground sand. So, I suppose golfers can accommodate a less-than-lush venue. Where's that leave us on demand?"

"With our tweaks to Western's demand numbers, we are within about 10 percent of what they assumed. Given Vern Graham's saying, that's close enough."

"OK," Brad said, "what about the supply side? That's where I'm probably going to get the most push back from the anti-group."

"Also a mixed bag," said the consultant. "For your State Water Project water, Western used the reliability factor that DWR sends out for a multi-year drought scenario. If you use anything else, somebody or other is going to be able to challenge you since you don't have all the process and data the state used."

Brad shoved in a last forkful of lasagna saying, "I agree, but I think that is exactly what my councilwoman wants us to do."

"You'd really be opening up the city for attack if you second-guessed the state. Besides, maybe she'll be satisfied that we are using lower numbers for your groundwater than Western did. They used the full amount you are allowed to pump after the aquifer adjudication. Megan argued that the groundwater would be cut back in a drought. Your Public Works guy made a good case that if the State cut back its deliveries that bad because of a long drought, he'd probably actually be trying to increase his pumping since nobody knows for sure how much it holds. That's why Western didn't cut it in their report. We looked at the adjudication decision for ourselves. It basically says you can pump your full amount, up to the point where the water basin drops more than twenty feet, then you have to cut back. The problem is that your basin has never been tested under a multi-year drought so nobody knows if this restriction would kick in, or not. We decided to throw a bone at the issue and used 80 percent reliability. There, I just saved you hours of going through tables and learning stuff you'll forget anyway!" The consultant wiped his face.

"Megan was also arguing about our reservoir," Brad said, wiping his face, too. "What did you do with that?"

"Oh yeah, almost forgot," Quinn said. "This one is really a crap shoot. It's a relatively new reservoir. There just hasn't been enough study of the watershed over a long enough time and especially during a sustained drought to make a good estimate of how fast it will draw down in a multi-year drought. Western assumed 90 percent re-charge in a drought. Megan thought that was too high. We used 70 percent for that to have a little more margin of safety. Again, who knows? We thought a little more conservatism was warranted."

"I'll ask again, what's the bottom line?"

"Wait for it, Brad. There's one more variable you should know about. You and I know that if the drought gets bad enough, you're going to jack up your water rates. It drives the public crazy because they'll cut their own consumption way back and still end up paying a lot more on their monthly bill."

"You said it. They don't understand that water is a utility that has to pay its own way and there are fixed costs to treat and distribute water, regardless of actual consumption."

"There will be complaints," O'Rourke continued, "but people will conserve anyway because they'll know it's the right thing to do. So, it's fair to assume some reduction in normal consumption during a long drought. Western used a 20 percent cutback. For most of your water customers, that's no big deal. For the residents of Green Valley, where you're using a lower consumption factor already, that will be harder to pull off. It's not completely unreasonable, either. Hell, if things get too bad for too long, you'll get into even steeper tiered water rates that will have people letting their lawns go. You'll get way more than a 20 percent reduction. We didn't change that assumption but I'm letting you know there's plenty of wiggle room there. Lots of variables. Hard to predict too precisely."

"You're killing me, Quinn," Brad said anxiously. "Do we have enough water for Green Valley or not?"

"Yes," O'Rourke said, digging at something in his teeth with his tongue. "Some could argue it's too tight. The way everything shakes out, Western came up with enough water for existing uses plus some extra for the undeveloped lots in the city based on the General Plan, which isn't much, by the way, since you're pretty well built out, plus Green Valley. They had about 19 percent surplus of supply over demand. Our report, with the changes I just told you about, comes up with about a 12 percent freeboard. Your city, like most every other water supplier in this state, is going to want to keep looking for more supply and supporting any efforts to increase the reliability of the existing supplies so you don't run so close to the edge. But, yes, on paper, you have enough for Green Valley especially in the likelihood that, if it really hits the fan, you could adopt harsher water conservation measures and rates to stretch."

"Perfect," Brad said. "We can show enough water if the Council majority wants to. If they don't, we could argue that it leaves us too thin on water. Perfect!"

"Yeah," O'Rourke said laughingly, "and you and Public Works don't have to take the heat for killing the project off because you didn't plan ahead to have plenty of reserves."

"True, true," Brad agreed. "The general public doesn't understand how difficult it is to get more water these days. From what

I've been hearing lately, we'll be lucky to hang onto the supplies we already have. The Delta is a mess and that could reduce our current state water deliveries."

"Use what you have wisely, my friend," the consultant advised. "We'll never see more water at those prices again. There is some hope on new supplies. Desalination is getting better. There's a big new plant opening in San Diego County that will supply 9 percent of the countywide demand. They looked at tertiary treatment of wastewater but the whole 'toilet to tap' image was a political nonstarter. Desal is twice the cost and it has its own environmental impacts, but it sells to the public better. At the end of the day, nothing beats getting more out of conserving what you already have."

"Agreed. What's your assessment of the two department heads?" Brad asked.

"My guys said your public works director made it clear he didn't want us involved. He was very defensive toward Western. I understand that. In fact, I admire it. We consultants hope to build that kind of loyalty with our clients. Maybe he'll feel the same about us one of these days. My folks also said he seems to have a chip on his shoulder. It comes up when anybody asks him a question. It's like he takes it as an attack."

"Yeah, I've been working with him on that," Brad said. "He has actually improved, at least with responding to the public at Council meetings. Tell me more."

"As far as competency goes, my folks say he's better than average, especially compared to what we see in other small cities. He's probably more competent than he comes across. He's not as good as other directors with the give-and-take at a meeting, recalling facts, and that sort of thing. But he knows his business and did better when producing written reports. You could do a lot worse. He seems to be on top of things and watching out for the city. Plus, when you aren't appearing to challenge him, he seems like a nice guy."

"Yeah. Oil and water with Megan, right?" Brad asked.

"You got it, amigo," O'Rourke agreed. "Megan is very bright. And a bulldog! She latches onto an argument and doesn't let go. I'll bet she's a pain in the ass to you."

"Both cheeks!" Brad laughed. "But I have to say, I get a kick out of her, too. I love the passion and dedication she brings to the job. I wish I still had more of that myself. Been worn down, I suppose."

"Dedication, good. Passion, bad, Kemosabe," O'Rourke said in Tonto dialect.

"I hear you," Brad responded. "I just see her as more like the old time city managers, willing to call it like they saw it. That's changed. Too many times city staff wants to hire consultants, especially legal advisors, to do the heavy lifting when something is controversial. Not Megan."

"Yeah, well, be careful that she knows nobody anointed her to be Grand Protector of Santa Ynez. She needs to be reminded that she works for you and you work for the Council. If she responds too much to her own sense of what's right, it will end up being trouble for you."

"10-4," Brad said. His friend was right. He decided right then to have a heart-to-heart with his planning director. "My other problem with her is her relationship with Councilwoman Nance. Did you pick up anything about that?"

"No. Didn't hear anything about that. I did hear a little about your councilwoman. Sounds like a handful."

"A lot of people, me included, tend to dismiss her because of her lifestyle and radical views. But, lately, I've been thinking she might be right on some of the water issues. You know she's active with that petition heading to the League Board asking their support for legislation to divide the state into regional water agencies."

"It already is," O'Rourke protested.

"Not like this. We have nine regional boards that oversee water quality issues only. Kay's group wants to broaden that to include water supply, groundwater basin management, flood control, and fish and game preservation that now is done by thousands of entities, independently, with very little coordination. The idea is to look at the nine regional watershed areas and integrate local planning and development with these broader regional plans. I blew the idea off at first, but I'm now starting to believe it's a way to achieve some balance and pull some power away from all of the interests who profit by burning through our natural resources."

"Geez, Brad. You grew up like I did, nourished by the tit of local home rule." O'Rourke laughed. "They're going to take away your stripes for talking like this."

"I know." Brad said. "But don't you think we need to shake things up in this state? Don't you think we need to manage the water we have better? Do you think that's going to be done under the current system where all of us are focused on the buck?"

"Ok, Father Jacks, I got the sermon," O'Rourke said. "In fact, secretly, I've harbored some of the same sentiments. I'm worried for my grandkids. Of course, officially, I hate where you are going. Our company's business comes from those thousand agencies you mentioned who hire us to promote their own interests. A few companies will make a fortune working on those regional water plans. Most of us won't have as much work to do if regional watershed management becomes a limiting factor on city growth. But do I think our current approach is working? Hell, no! The water engineering industry knows that. Don't expect us to lead the charge to change it. The best you can hope for is that some of the bigger firms will write broad white papers on reforms, mostly fluff stuff that won't offend our clients."

Brad pushed his plate away. "That's the problem. I don't see the politics allowing major reform to come through Sacramento. More likely, it will be forced by a combination of federal agencies and the courts. The EPA is rattling sabers over the lack of progress with protecting endangered species."

"And you think turning the feds loose will be a good thing for California?" O'Rourke sneered.

"I don't know, Quinn. Sure, I'd be worried about the feds taking a stronger role in statewide planning. Some Congressional committee could go into a private room and come out with regulations that will be impossible for us to live with. God knows there's plenty of examples of that. The state and feds don't follow the same open government processes they make us in local government go through. But, like I said, many of us in local government know in our hearts that what we are doing now isn't working. Reform has got to come. I'd rather it be led within the region than Washington, D.C.." He paused to look for Twyla. "Oh, well, this is probably all a waste of time to talk about. The politics in Sacramento, and in all the hundreds of cities and counties, will never give that kind of power to regional agencies, at least willingly."

"It's not likely, I agree," O'Rourke said. "But if there's one thing we've learned in this business, you really can't predict the future. I never thought the state would kill redevelopment. That was the only effective tool we had for competing with other states for jobs and rehabbing neighborhoods. The governor got his knickers in a twist when cities started pushing back against state mandates and he decided to get even by killing redevelopment rather than supporting the modest reforms that the locals were willing to do. The state senators and assembly members who we could always count on to resist attempts to kill redevelopment because of the good it did in their own districts, didn't want to buck him. They justified it based on the state's financial crises, as if the relative pittance they got from killing redevelopment made a real difference in the problem."

"Yeah," Brad mourned. "It's been a mess for all those cities having to unravel years of projects. That's my point. I don't see good reform coming out of Sacramento."

"Like I said," O'Rourke continued, "you can't predict the future. Maybe we'll both be surprised and there will be a champion for good who will overcome all the special interests, including the cities, by the way, and do the right thing for the long term public interest. Hell, maybe you'll be the face of the sustainable development movement."

Brad waved him off. "The last guy who bucked the status quo that bad got crucified."

"Don't be so quick to dismiss the idea. Remember how involved I was with the California/Australia Exchange program? We'd send city managers over there for a month and they'd send their town clerks here."

Brad smiled, recalling a memorable night on the town with his Aussie colleagues.

O'Rourke remembered. "That's right, you were a host. One of the things you always hear from Americans who go over there is how much Australia is like we used to be fifty years ago. Well, think about all of the government reorganizations they've done. They are way ahead of us on adapting their government to changing conditions. We always had them talk about their 'amalgamation' progress at our annual conference."

"That was pretty interesting," Brad said. "One town clerk I hosted told me about literally having his city disappear by order of the state government. He had a picture of a company with a crane pulling his city's sign and logo off the City Hall building."

"I've heard those stories, too," said O'Rourke. "I still go over there at least once a year. There are different opinions on how the amalgamations are working out. The guys I talk to think it's like a lot of other reform movements. The benefits are over-hyped when reality finally sets in. But, in balance, most of them admit that government services are more efficient, less costly, and it's easier for the states and territories to manage the population and environment now that there are half as many cities to deal with as there used to be."

"I can see that," Brad said. "Each of us wants to control our own turf. Is the overall public well-served by having nearly 500 cities, each with their own staff and facilities that could be combined for cost savings? I know I'm speaking against my own job. At least we contract with the county for police and fire service instead of having our own small departments. We have cities all over the state where the closest fire and EMS response is actually from a fire station in the adjacent city. It's very tough to get services consolidated. It's happened and worked well in those places that have done it. But you're fighting lots of local politics, labor issues, and inertia."

"True," O'Rourke agreed, "and Australia is sure not California. Australia is about eighteen times larger than California but we have about one-and-a-half times the population. What works there may not here, and vice versa."

"Good point, Quinn," Brad said. "I'm not saying we should cut the number of local governments in California in half like Australia has been doing. I know it's heresy, but I do think there is something to be said for some consolidation. It won't happen if left to the individual cities. It's not in their parochial interest. Besides, the public likes the illusion of local home rule."

"'Illusion' is correct," the consultant agreed. "With so much local funding now going through Sacramento since Prop 13, hundreds of new laws coming out of the Legislature every year that either mandate or prohibit something at the local level, voter-approved initiatives, court rulings, federal, state and regional regulations, there really isn't all that much home rule left like in the old days anyway."

Brad sighed. "You can hardly scratch yourself anymore without either getting state enabling legislation or coming under fire from some state agency. Cities just don't seem to have the political clout to face off with Sacramento, certainly not like the big water contractors do. I don't know where this state is going, Quinn. All the areas of reform are obvious but they aren't getting through. Unfortunately, it reminds me of a former mayor's favorite saying, 'when all is said and done, more is said than done.'"

He glanced across the room. "Well, that's enough 'ain't it awful' for now. Let's get out of here. Twyla is giving me the stink eye." He set the napkin next to his plate. "She's dying to do her goodbye scene from *Romeo and Juliet* for you. Act surprised. Thanks for getting the water study done so quickly, Quinn."

Quinn O'Rourke tossed his napkin on the table, too. "You've obviously been thinking about bigger issues more than I have, Brad. You always were more of a policy wonk than I was. But, back to this Green Valley project that has you so wound up. I know you'll do your homework. Go ahead with that. I just encourage you to give your gut equal time with your brain. I was the 'ready/fire/aim' type who usually acted on instincts rather than following some drawn-out process to gather and weigh all the facts."

"My gut's getting bigger, Quinn. It's easier to pay attention to it these days."

Quinn chuckled. "I hope you will. Remember what we talked about earlier? Enjoy the journey. You can't control everything like you're trying to. You aren't God. You don't have the whole world in your hands. One more thing, amigo. I'm here for you anytime you need an ear to bend. No purchase order required. I know how lonely it gets at times and I'm a good listener who forgets everything I'm told."

Brad toasted his friend with the remainder of his Diet Coke. His gut was feeling quite good following Quinn's advice and Martellaro's lasagna. He resolved to calm down a little, right after getting Megan under control.

16

Brad walked briskly through the outer office door a little after 1:30 p.m.

"Well, don't you look chipper?" Jane observed. "I hope this doesn't ruin it for you." She handed him four phone messages.

He flipped through them. "OK, I've got to prepare for the meeting with that hotel developer, but Mom always said, 'eat your lima beans if you want dessert.' So, I'll start returning these." He reached out and accepted the phone messages in her hand. "Would you see if Megan can come over for a couple minutes to talk about the Payton/Carlisle report before my fun meeting?"

He handled the citizen complaint calls first, since they were probably the most upset. Jane's note said one was from a woman who had started with the mayor, requesting a stop sign at her corner and speed bumps mid-block, to slow down the speeding in her neighborhood. The mayor referred her to the city manager. As a veteran of these issues, the mayor knew placement of traffic control devices had to follow a careful analysis based on adopted engineering methods or the city risked further liability.

The conversation followed a predictable pattern. A nearly hysterical, angry mother demanding a stop sign to slow down traffic and a crosswalk at the corner. Brad patiently explaining the process the city has to go through before slapping up traffic control devices. Impatience on the other end and some statement like, "Does somebody have to die before you'll put up the stop sign?" Another attempt to provide factual information.

"I know this isn't what you want to hear," he began, "but accident studies show that if motorists, who by the way, are mostly your own neighbors, think a stop sign doesn't belong there, they are likely to run it or increase their speed in between the stop signs to make up the lost time from stopping too much. Worse, many will make a "Hollywood stop," rolling through the stop sign rather than coming to a complete stop. This is especially bad for pedestrians. As to crosswalks, studies show that's actually the most dangerous place for pedestrians."

"Huh?" the woman said with disbelief.

"Just look for yourself how people behave in a crosswalk. They may be chatting with each other or fiddling with their cell phones. Most aren't paying attention to the traffic at all. It's as if they think they have entered some zone of protection inside the lines of the crosswalk. Those lines won't hold back a five-thousand-pound vehicle driven by a motorist who doesn't expect a stop sign in that spot, or doesn't think it should be there, and exercises a bit of civil disobedience rolling right through it. The pedestrian has the right-of-way. But, as the old driver safety messages warned, 'you could be right, dead right.'"

"That's interesting," she said. Quiet on the line. His points had hit home. "So," she said, "do I have to get the whole neighborhood to petition the City Council to get the stop sign?"

He gave up and promised to refer her request to Public Works for further review, but he couldn't commit when they could get to it. He reiterated that having a study didn't mean she'd get what she wanted. There were regulations to observe.

The second complaint involved a property owner's objection to the building permit fee quote he received from Planning staff for his granny flat addition.

"Sir, it's a Council policy that the cost of processing a development application, a special benefit, should be paid by the applicant, not the taxpayers at large through their general tax contributions."

The man obviously couldn't care less about fee policy. "These costs are crazy. California is killing business. I'm building a spec house in Texas with my brother. The total permit fee was $200 for the city to inspect the connection of the driveway to the public street. That's it. No other fees. No building inspections. It's up to the contractor and architects to stand behind their work. They don't have big government watching over them and reaching into their pockets."

Brad tried to explain the rigor and legalities associated with setting those fees before concluding he wasn't going to satisfy the man. He walked him through the process for getting his issue in front of the Council to see if they were willing to consider the topic. The man hung up, saying he'd just talk to his friends on the Council one-on-one.

The third call to the school superintendent was more satisfying. Unlike her manner at lunch a while back, Dr. Deborah Downey was beginning to loosen up. She seemed less guarded with Brad in their subsequent phone calls about the joint-use agreement. She asked him to get some clarifying information so they could sign the latest amendment. Things were looking up.

Megan Cain crossed the threshold of his office ending moment of reverie. She didn't say hello, just stood there, a stack of papers in her arms. She looked even more agitated than usual. He sighed and got up from his desk to join her around the coffee table, each person taking their customary seats.

He saw she had the Payton/Carlisle report with her and made a preemptive strike. "I've already been briefed on the water supply report."

Megan plopped it on the coffee table with a look of scorn. It opened to the first page of the Executive Summary that had been all marked up with red pen. He let out another involuntary sigh.

"Your arguments were considered in the latest study," he reassured her. "Quinn O'Rourke told me that these are judgment calls and, just because they didn't side with you on all the points, it doesn't mean you were wrong."

He waited for a moment to see if her expression softened. It didn't.

"Megan, with peer review, 'the tie goes to the runner.' Payton agreed with you that that the golf course water demand was understated in the Western report and that a more conservative estimate of reliability was warranted for the groundwater pumping and the city reservoir."

He paused again. Still nothing.

"I really appreciate your thoroughness in going through the issues since water supply is such a pivotal issue with the Green Valley project."

Megan sat back in the chair and adopted a more relaxed posture. A nice change, even if she showed no indication of throwing in the towel.

"Well, Brad, I can tell you are fine with your friend's report. I still think Green Valley's demand will not leave us with enough water in a drought. It's my duty to make sure that a development project will mitigate its impacts and be a net benefit to the community. I'm not convinced."

He folded his hands and smiled. "I appreciate that, Megan. Like I said, Quinn O'Rourke admitted that this wasn't rocket surgery. Reasonable people could come to different conclusions."

Rather than accepting that as a face-saving out, Megan started pounding away again at why 132 gallons per resident, per day is too low, why there should be more conservative numbers used for groundwater pumping and the reservoir in a multi-year drought, and how the 12 percent remaining citywide water supply cited in the Payton report was too narrow a margin to rely on. She then advocated requiring the development to use tertiary-treated water, discharge from the city wastewater plant that is put through additional filtering, for the golf course, park, and street landscaped areas, as well as the front yards of the homes to save the city's precious supply of potable water.

As she continued to argue the report conclusions, he shifted his focus to his body. His breath was quickening and his muscles tightened. She was talking louder and faster, poking holes in the air with her hands and arms. She started to renew her attack on the public works director's ethics.

His hand shot up. "Stop!"

She recoiled with a jolt.

"Look, you're not the only one around here who feels a duty to make sure the project is a net benefit. I don't see anybody giving Scott or SoCal a pass on this thing, including Dee. Now, like I said, you can disagree with some of the findings on the facts and the pros and cons of Green Valley. That's OK. But you are out of line when you start attacking people's motives just because they don't agree with you. Knock that shit off!"

Megan Cain started to respond but he cut her off again, getting more exasperated.

"Look," he said tiredly, "what do you want from me? This project is controversial. I'm getting pressure from all sides and doing the best I can to be fair. That's why I ordered the peer review. I wanted to use Payton/Carlisle because I trusted them and thought they were well-qualified. I never talked to Quinn or anyone else with the firm about what their report should say. I think they would have resigned if I'd tried to influence them like that."

She sat, blinking.

He tensed, trying to keep his anger from running away with him. "And don't go carrying yourself as some sort of independent guardian of the public interest. You're not. You have some valuable input to offer to this process. I have, and will continue to, listen to it. But I'll make the call around here on the final staff positions, not you. Understood?"

She continued to just stare at him, blinking occasionally.

"Understood!?" he demanded again.

Awkward moments passed in silence until she finally nodded slightly. He saw the hurt in his young professional's eyes and resisted the impulse to soften his demeanor. Quinn O'Rourke's advice to get control of her rang in his ears. It was for her own good, and his.

"Here's what I'd like you to do," he said in a businesslike, nonthreatening way. He deliberately chose the "what I'd like you to do" phrase, instead of a more directive tone, in hopes of beginning to repair their relationship.

"I know you want to kick out the Initial Study soon. I would like you to use the Western *and* Payton reports, and Dee's input, as the basis for the water supply section. I'm OK including a short statement describing the difficulty of being too precise with some of these factors, particularly regarding the well and reservoir issues. And I'm OK if you want to ask the commission to weigh in on whether they think the 12 percent supply reserve from the Payton report is reasonable. That's fair, but I want you to have the Initial Study conclude that we have sufficient water for Green Valley."

Megan was still mute.

"When were you planning to circulate the IS?" he asked.

She thought for a moment. Brad wondered if she was thinking about the question or, more likely, whether she was trying to decide her attitude before responding to him.

"It's pretty much ready to go," she said sitting back again in her chair. "We were waiting for the Payton report to finish up the water section. I think we can get it to the Planning Commission tomorrow."

"Great," he said, pretending everything was hunky dory again. "Please let me see the final draft before it goes out."

"Will do," she said flatly, gathering her papers and leaving quickly. It wasn't "have a nice day," but the body language at least indicated acquiescence.

As he found himself doing more often these days, Brad stayed seated after Megan left and did a quick check on what he was feeling. He was remarkably relaxed considering the tension that still seemed to hang in the room. He had been appropriately direct to his feisty department head after she had left him little choice. He had attempted to honor her opinion and had made a concession to allow her to comment on the water analysis. He would have to spend the time to go through her write-up carefully to be sure she had complied with his direction.

He looked at his calendar for tomorrow morning. It would be a busy Friday. He walked out to talk to Jane. She was on the phone, talking very quietly and ended the call abruptly as soon as she saw him. He held his curiosity in check. He merely asked her to follow up with Megan tomorrow morning to get her final draft of the Initial Study for him to review before noon.

That accomplished, there was one more bite of lima beans to eat. He returned the call to the city's insurance claims adjustor. It wasn't good news. The elderly woman who had filed a claim regarding a slip-and-fall at the Senior Center was still complaining of back pain.

Or, rather, her attorney, who would get a big chunk of any settlement, was alleging back pain. Nearly impossible to prove or disprove. Brad thought of Lilly. Had she been the one to slip, she likely wouldn't have even complained. He okayed the adjustor's recommendation for defending the case and caught up with emails.

*****

The meeting with the hotel developer had been exciting. A fifty-room, three-star, boutique hotel with Spanish Colonial architecture and plenty of amenities, including a full restaurant, would be a game-changer for Santa Ynez. The Transient Occupancy Tax on the room rentals, along with the jobs, were reasons enough to compete for it. Beyond that, landing a classy project like that would be a big boost in the city's image. A Realtor in the mayor's real estate office had picked up the scent that the developer was looking at Solvang down the road and talked him into checking out Santa Ynez. Brad was pulling out all of the stops to entice the project, a far more difficult task without redevelopment money. The developer was savvy enough to know what the city could and couldn't do. He wasn't leaving any money on the table.

"I'd really be pioneering with this project here," he worried today. "What assurances can you give me that the Green Valley Village project is going to be approved? We need some other high-end projects like that to boost the city's image."

Message delivered. He, of course, could give no guarantees but joined the broker in listing all of the positives and political support Green Valley had already garnered. The courtship was going well. Brad could almost feel himself adding a feather to his cap. He called the mayor afterwards to give him a progress report on the hotel.

"Atta boy, Brad," said Mayor Buddy. "Don't we have your annual evaluation coming up? I really hope that you can nail down the hotel, along with showing good progress on Green Valley, before then. I'd like to get you a raise this year. You deserve it. You're doing a great job for us."

The mayor could be wonderfully charming, especially when he needed something from you. Still, he was warmed by the praise. Brad remembered basking in his father's praise when he presented him a lacquered oakwood tie rack for Christmas that he made in wood shop.

"Knock, knock," came a voice from the door. Human Resources Director Jackie McCall took a tentative step into the office, followed closely by Public Works Director Dee Sharma. "Got a minute?" she asked.

"They say you're in for a bad day when the *60 Minutes* crew shows up at your office. Why do I have that same feeling right now?" Brad asked grinning.

"Sorry about that," Jackie said. "I do sometimes feel like the grim reaper."

"What's up?"

Dee looked uncomfortable. He hadn't said a word.

They sat and the HR director started in. "We had the Skelly hearing this morning for Richard Stevenson. And, as these things sometimes go, it was like turning over a rock."

Stevenson was a water plant operator assigned to the graveyard shift. He had been arrested for driving under the influence two weeks ago. The arrest occurred near a bar between Buellton and Santa Ynez at 2:15 a.m. when Stevenson was supposed to be working. The Skelly hearing process arose from a California Supreme Court decision. It provides a public employee the right to a hearing and other due process measures prior to imposing discipline and a full evidentiary hearing to appeal any major discipline imposed.

"We won't go into too many details because you will probably end up getting an appeal and have to serve as the hearing officer," Jackie explained.

"Yeah," he groaned. "Tell me what you can." He hated being put in such a no-win position. Many cities turn the disciplinary appeal hearing over to a neutral third party, like an arbitrator, or a civil service commission. He had heard too many horror stories of truly bad employees being returned to work by an outside arbitrator who didn't have to live with the impact of their decision. As much as he dreaded it, Brad was old school and opted to make that decision himself despite putting himself in the hot seat with the unions and the employee's friends and family.

"In the course of conducting the investigation," Jackie continued, "through today's hearing, Stevenson basically ratted out the entire water plant."

"Here we go again," Brad groaned. "Doesn't anyone ever say 'yes, I screwed up and will take my medicine?' Does everybody have to try to scuttle the ship on the way out?" He thought of the way William Mulholland took immediate responsibility for the dam disaster.

Jackie ignored the rhetorical question and proceeded. "Again, without giving you too much information because there likely will be more people coming before you besides Stevenson, I'll just tell you that the investigation so far corroborates much of Stevenson's story. The water plant is a mess. Looks like most of the crew is a bunch of slackers."

Dee Sharma sat there looking down at his folded hands. He still hadn't said a word.

"How so?" Brad asked Jackie.

"We heard stories of employees playing poker on the job, while watching porn movies, and not putting down their vacation or sick leave time. Apparently, plant supplies and tools are routinely 'borrowed,'" Jackie said, making air quotes, "and never returned. One employee may actually be operating a pool service business after hours using city materials. We have PD checking on the theft issues. There was also a charge that some of the water quality reports have been faked."

Brad's heart sank. As if there weren't enough things stirring the pot right now. He glared at the mute public works director.

"Dee?"

"She's right, it's a mess," Dee Sharma said, shaking his head. "It comes down to lax supervision. As you recall, I've made budget requests the last few years for a utilities director to oversee both the water and wastewater plants. I'm kept so busy with development issues, capital improvement projects, and everything else here at City Hall that I just can't get out to the plants very often. I've had to rely on the chief plant operators."

"Oh, so this is all my fault for not approving that position?" Brad asked angrily.

"I didn't mean that, Brad," said Dee, backpedaling quickly. "The chief operators report to me and are my responsibility. I know that. I'm just saying that when you run with so little supervision like we do, things like this can happen."

Jackie's eyes darted from one man to the other and intervened. "Sure, in a small city like ours, we have to put more faith on a smaller number of staff. We just can't afford lots of layers in any of the departments. But we haven't had evidence of such severe mismanagement up until now. We have to deal with it aggressively to send a message."

Dee shook his head and cleared his throat, still looking down. "I don't disagree that we need to fix it." He looked up from his hands to Jackie. "But we need to be careful. The entire city could end up with a black eye if this whole thing becomes public." Then he looked directly at Brad. "And there could be ramifications up the chain of command."

Brad understood the threat.

"Tell me about the false water reporting," he said to Dee.

"Stevenson claims that the lab tech responsible for taking the daily samples, a guy named Chip Geis, has been dry labbing."

"Dry labbing?"

"Basically just faking the water analysis and plugging numbers into the water quality reports."

"Oh, great!" Brad moaned. "Jesus, Dee!"

Dee held up his hands. "It's not that bad. The accusation is that Geis hasn't been taking the samples just at one location. He denies the allegation so far."

"What location? Why wasn't he taking the samples?" Brad snapped back. "Come on, Dee, out with it!"

"Well, like I said, it's only an allegation. We don't know if the dry labbing charge is true and, if it is, why he would have done it."

"Where, Dee!"

"It's Well #2 on the site we acquired from the Nettlers."

"Nettlers again. I smell a rat!"

"I don't know, Brad," Dee said, quietly looking down again. "As to Chip's possible motivation, I'd only be guessing at this point."

"Then guess, damn it!"

Dee stiffened. "We had a tough time acquiring that well site from the Nettlers. This was before you came. We had to initiate eminent domain. Your predecessor was getting some political pressure to back off. We were told to do whatever we had to for an agreement without legal action. We ended up giving Nettlers unrestricted, unmetered water from the well for their agricultural use on the property and had to give them access through the gate to get to the well."

"Yeah, the same thing happened when you and I tried to get that reservoir site from them. But I dropped it rather than pay their extortionate demands. What's that got to do with not taking the samples?"

"Again, I'm only guessing here, but I know there have been problems with the gang lock on the chain link gate off the county road to the well. The city's lock sometimes was vandalized. One time it had been shot. City staff would have to track down one of the Nettlers to open their padlock so we could get back to the well. Maybe Chip got tired of hassling with the access and just entered data that was close to Well #1 right down the road."

He noticed the HR director shake her head slightly and sat back in her chair. "You seem skeptical, Jackie."

She leaned forward. "It *could* be as simple as that," she said guardedly. "But there could be more to the story. We heard, during the investigation, that Geis often threw big barbeques at his house, living way beyond his means. We also heard he has a roomful of expensive Scotch. A lab tech doesn't make that kind of money. Maybe Geis was getting free meat or money from the Nettlers to not take the samples, for whatever reason."

"You don't know that, Jackie!" Dee barked.

"You're absolutely right, Dee. I don't know. It could be as simple as Geis being just lazy and not wanting to leave his climate-controlled truck to open the gate. But, given everything we've found so far, I'm inclined to think there's a more sinister motive than laziness."

Brad felt the blood coursing through his body. "What if Geis, and maybe other city staff at the plant, knew there is something wrong with the water and have been covering it up. Why would they do that, Dee?"

The public works director slapped the arms of his chair. "There's no reason to suspect that. We don't have the facts. I have an independent lab taking samples now. I should have their report in a day or two and we'll be able to see how close their results at Well #2 match what Chip reported."

"Sure, let's get the facts," Brad agreed, starting to calm down. A pall suddenly engulfed him. "Dee, if there *is* something wrong with that well, what could that do to the water studies Western and Payton/Carlisle just did?"

"It shouldn't be a problem. Chip hasn't been with us that long. Even if he has been dry labbing, if his predecessor wasn't, it may not mean anything is wrong. Water quality wouldn't normally change that radically or quickly."

"Let me know as soon as you have that report. And, Jackie, let me know what you can as the investigation proceeds. I don't want to jeopardize my neutral status as a hearing officer but I also want to make sure we manage the information flow on this. I agree with Dee that it doesn't serve the city for this to get out right now."

*****

He squeezed in a jog before dinner, hoping to clear his mind, but the boredom of the jog was an open door for his anxieties. Top billing in the drama of his life was this new revelation of problems at the water plant. Would word get out? What would it mean to Green Valley Village? To him?

He tried to push work aside and fiddled with his iPod as he jogged, keeping one eye on the road. George Thorogood's *Bad To The Bone* came on. He recalled a small gathering of city managers at an overnight retreat when he participated in a parody of this song about a city manager who gets fired because the Council tells him he's "bad on the phone."

He thought of the retreat locale, the vacation home of a retired city manager on an island in the middle of the Delta. Les McLaughlin was one of the deans of the profession. Late in his retired life he volunteered to be a "Range Rider", traveling to cities around the San Francisco Bay Area offering city managers information, advice, and encouragement. He smiled thinking of McLaughlin, the skit, and enjoyable times with colleagues on McLaughlin's Delta island paradise. His feet slapped the asphalt road in time with the heavy beat.

His thoughts drifted to other colleagues he'd worked with over the years like Quinn O'Rourke. Dedicated, hardworking, caring people. As often occurred, the music improved his mood.

The iPod cycled to *In The Year 2525*. He reached across his chest to the iPod strapped to his left bicep and tried to hit the "Skip" button as he continued jogging. The song kept returning to the beginning. He ground his teeth, stopped his stride, yanked the iPod face around to see the buttons, and killed the annoying song.

He was oblivious to the next songs as he was sucked back into his anxieties. One tumbled into another. Green Valley. Kay. Mayor Buddy. The Nettlers. Megan. Dillon's out-of-state tuition. His retirement forecasts in jeopardy. Marie. Everything seemed to be spinning out of control. The run suddenly became forced labor. His right knee shot sharp pains with every slam to the pavement.

He slowly plodded to a stop, bent over, grabbed the bottom of his shorts, and panted. He shook his head in despair and tilted his head to the sky with his hands on his hips.

The Eagles' *Take It Easy* came on. Interesting! How often had he been in some sort of depression and been uplifted by the lyrics' reminder to lighten up? Was it mere coincidence? His logic said that it was just a popular song and he was under stress a lot, so no surprise when the song and a down mood aligned. But the last few times it had happened with this same song, he had been open to considering it a God moment. Coming so soon after Quinn O'Rourke's reminder at lunch to enjoy the journey, he hedged his bets and made a quick salute to the heavens.

17

Brad strode into City Hall Friday morning saying hello to everyone he passed, calling them by name.

"Morning, Brad," Jane said. "Megan said she was finishing up the Green Valley Initial Study draft and would have it over soon for you to look at before it gets copied for the packets."

"I've managed to go my entire career without having to read one of those. But anything associated with Green Valley is going to draw fire so I better take a look myself before it goes out. Keep after her if it doesn't come in by ten, OK?"

"Will do. You're clear until 9:30. You have that emergency plan exercise meeting." She rolled her eyes as she said the words. "Do I really have to participate in that again? It's such a waste of time."

"I suspect most everybody outside Police and Fire would agree with you," he responded. "I used to think the same thing. Then I took this really good course from FEMA back in Maryland. The fire chief dragged me to it, but I got a lot out of it. Of course, there's only so much you can do to prepare for a disaster. And you're likely to make some bad decisions in the heat of the moment. I sure did on my first disaster."

"Oh? Give me the dirt," she said eagerly.

"I activated our Emergency Operations Center because of a wildfire in the hills threatening houses in the city. A Fire Department battalion chief, acting as incident commander at the command post near the fire, received a damage assessment report from a fire captain at the fire line. To make a long story short, I hit the panic button when I was told nine houses had already been destroyed. I directed the opening of the community center for a relocation center, had them call the Red Cross, SPCA, County Emergency Services director, the whole shebang. It turned out that it was nine *structures*. Sheds, chicken coops, and fences. No houses at all. You could say we over-reacted."

"Oops, must have been embarrassing."

"It was. But I took more flack when the Monday Morning Quarterbacks found out we hadn't had any Emergency Plan training for years. I know it's a pain for non-safety folks, but these exercises are good to do once in a while, even if only to show the public later that you made a reasonable effort to be prepared."

Jane began to sing: "Paranoia strikes deep. Into your life it will creep."

"Yeah, I guess I do worry too much about job security. Especially lately. But remember the old saying, 'just because you're paranoid, doesn't mean people *aren't* out to get you.' Let me know when the Initial Study comes in. I'm going to make some Council calls."

He was able to catch all but Councilwoman Gretchen Schmitz on the phone. No matter, there was nothing urgent to report. He just looked for an excuse to call them all at least once a week, most often on Fridays, to check in. He mentioned that the Green Valley Initial

Study would be coming out so they wouldn't be surprised if they saw something in the paper over the weekend. He received a couple of complaints and information requests to follow up on that he gave to Jane to handle before leaving for the emergency planning meeting.

The meeting was productive, but too long. Police and Fire personnel went through agonizing detail laying out a hazardous materials scenario for a "table top" exercise of the emergency plan that would simulate, but not include, field level operations. He left the Police and Fire personnel to continue working on the details while he met with the finance director to go over the financial forecasts from the first six months of the fiscal year.

Having come up the ranks of city government through the budget and finance path, he was far more comfortable getting into the details of the numbers than reading an EIR Initial Study. The financials were mostly positive, tracking the budget. Nevertheless, he was distracted and called Jane twice asking if the IS was ready. She finally called him just after 11 a.m. to say it was on its way down. He cut his meeting with Finance short and headed back to his office.

Jane handed the report to him as he walked in. It said "City of Santa Ynez – Planning Department" with the city's logo at the top and "Green Valley Village Initial Study of Environmental Significance" at the bottom.

He looked at his watch and hefted the report. "About damn time." He settled in at his desk and began leafing through the twenty-seven pages to get familiar with what was inside. Then he went back to the beginning and read the first four pages containing the project description, environmental setting, list of potential environmental factors that could be affected, the summary determination to prepare an EIR, a listing of the main government approvals that would be needed, and the agencies responsible for those approvals. It all looked fine.

He skimmed through the sections devoted to the environmental issues, organized alphabetically. The first one was headed "Aesthetics." The questionnaire asked for a rating on four questions about whether the project would adversely affect a scenic vista, damage scenic resources or historic buildings within a state scenic highway, degrade the visual character of the site and its surroundings, or create substantial light or glare that would adversely affect nighttime views. Next to each question someone, presumable Megan, had marked a grid to show if that issue was expected to result in significant unmitigated environmental impact, significant, but mitigated impact, less than significant impact, or no impact. Below that was a Discussion section where the aesthetic issues were described along with a listing of mitigation measures. The mitigations were conditions the city planned to impose on the project approval to reduce environmental impacts. In the Aesthetics section they included requiring exterior lights to be shielded and directed downward, using flat paint on roofing, signs and buildings to reduce reflective glare, and parking lot designs to block headlights from spilling onto adjacent properties. Fine again.

He continued skimming through the list of issues: Agriculture, Air Quality, then Biological Resources. There were a lot of issues addressed but, when he paused long enough to read a bit, the issues and related mitigations seemed reasonable, at least by California development standards. He wondered if Scott Graves would agree.

Jane buzzed. "Don't forget, you have lunch with Scott in fifteen minutes."

"Geez, you're scary. I was just thinking about Scott."

"Sorry to nag but I need to get that report copied for the packets. Are you almost done with it?"

He looked at his watch and saw there was still too much report left to review. He picked up his skimming pace through the sections on Cultural Resources, Geology & Soils, Greenhouse Gas

Emissions, Hazards and Hazardous Materials, Land Use & Planning, Mineral Resources, Noise, Population and Housing, Public Services, Recreation, then Transportation and Traffic. Nothing jumped out. He was looking for Megan's summary of the water supply issues. He expected to find it under the Public Services section which he read more closely. Not there. He finally found it in the last section, Utilities and Service Systems.

He looked again at his watch. He had to leave for lunch. His heart raced until his eyes caught what he was looking for at Section XVIId:

> *Would the project have sufficient water supplies available to serve the project from existing entitlements and resources, or are new or expanded entitlements needed?*

He saw that the "Less than Significant Impact" box had been checked. There were two-and-half pages of small-font text and numbers in the Discussion section. Brad zipped over it and saw the references to the Western and Payton/Carlisle reports. He recognized a couple of the supply and reliability numbers from the Payton report and saw the phrase "the water assessment indicates sufficient water supply for the project."

Relieved, he dashed out and tossed the report on Jane's counter. "No changes. Let 'er rip!" He walked quickly to the car, looking forward to giving Scott the "all clear" on the IS and celebrating with an enchilada grande.

Scott Graves was already at Moreno's when Brad arrived. He had an iced tea in one hand and was checking his iPhone with the other. He rose slightly to shake hands as Brad squeezed into the booth opposite him.

Their relationship had always been collegial since SoCal first entered Brad's life. It went to the next level following a party at Scott's house; an annual fundraiser in early December to raise money to buy presents for needy kids in the region. It was always a popular, well-attended event. The entire City Council was there. Brad had asked City Attorney Henry Fitzhenry to advise the councilmembers that it would be legal for them to all be together at a social event so long as they didn't talk city business. With the prohibition on talking business, there was less tension in the air among the city officials. Any residual tension was washed away by the free-flowing liquor.

People got very drunk that night. Brad remembered how Scott watched out for him, cutting him off of the liquor after Brad chugged the last gulp of Mezcal and ate the worm on the bottom to the cheers of the inebriated group. Scott brought him strong black coffee and snacks and ended up driving him, Kay, and Mayor Buddy safely home. Brad's lighted breath could have started the BBQ, but, thanks to Scott, he was not nearly as far gone as his bosses by the time they piled into Scott's car. He owed Scott. Their meetings since then had been more like friends than business associates.

Brad noticed Scott's ice tea and guiltily dove into the warm, salty tortilla chips and hot salsa. "Salsa's vegetables, you know. Sorry I'm late. How's things on the dark side?"

"Just supplying the American dream," Scott responded.

They talked about Payton/Carlisle's review of Western's water supply assessment draft.

"Thanks for smoothing over some of the conflict between Dee and Megan," Scott said.

"Oh," Brad added, "and I got a look at the Initial Study Megan is sending out later. I wanted to check it out before it gets released. It's fine. It says we have sufficient water supply for your project and lists public utilities as a 'less than significant impact.' I'll make sure it goes out today when I get back so we can keep things moving."

"Thanks, again, Brad," Scott said sincerely.

They chatted some more about the project. Scott talked about an updated market study and some minor changes to their home designs it was prompting. They eventually got down to the main topic of the meeting, several deal points that separated them from a final draft Development Agreement.

Brad wasn't the main negotiator. He was the "behind-the-curtain" closer, but the city's legal consultant thought it would be helpful for him to intervene with Scott directly to see if there could be some movement to close the deal. They were able to leverage their relationship to have a candid exchange akin to "if you can do this, I can do that." In the more formal negotiating setting, representatives from each side had become reluctant to even put new break-through ideas on the table for fear they would appear weak. Scott and Brad were able to link a couple of tentative trade-offs between the menudo and the last bite of enchilada.

Brad spent the rest of the afternoon catching up with emails, reading memos, drafting a speech on economic development for the mayor, and returning phone calls. Just before five, Jane stuck her head into his office to confirm that the weekly packets had gone out for delivery and that the Initial Study was part of the Planning Commission's folder. After two-and-a-half years of behind-the-scenes effort, Green Valley Village was about to officially enter the public realm.

*****

Marie and Brad had Lilly and Lee over for dinner. Marie made a pot roast that hit the spot on the cold, foggy winter night. They had been seeing more of the Andres since Lilly's hip surgery. The ladies taunted them into a bridge rematch.

The card game supplied little drama for the evening until Lee asked how the Green Valley project was coming along. Lee was a supporter and had even attended one of the "Friends" receptions. Lee had asked Brad to pitch to SoCal the idea of including a neighborhood of single-story attached units somewhere in Green Valley. Even at their advanced age, they would be tempted to leave their large two-story home on one-third acre for a single-story, small lot, more energy-efficient house built with handicapped accessibility.

"You should move into one, too," Lilly threw out while sweeping up a trick after a deftly played finesse. "We could still be neighbors."

"Funny, Lilly, I've actually been thinking along the same lines," Marie said, looking at Brad.

His jaw dropped. She talked about looking at the floor plans Brad had brought home. She liked the ones that featured two master suites on opposite sides of the house with a granny flat and kitchenette over the garage. It would be perfect for guests and when the kids came home. The smaller lot with the homeowners' association handling the front yard maintenance would free them up for easier travel which was something she and Brad were looking forward to when Brad retired in a few years.

"You mean you'd be willing to move?" Brad said. "Again?"

"Well, hang on, Brad, because I was even thinking about taking up golf. It's something we can do in our old age together. I could take lessons and join a women's group at the Green Valley course."

He smiled and shook his head. "I've been trying for years to get you to take up the game. That's great!" He set his cards down and leaned on his elbows. "I hadn't even thought of us moving out there. I had no idea you'd even consider another move."

"I'd love to start over with a brand new house that better fits our needs. You know how I love to decorate." She raised her glass to toast. "And it would be so good to have our neighbors already pre-selected."

A surprising ending to a productive day.

18

Brad ran from the window to the bed and half -dragged Marie from her sleep to the front door. They had to get out. The wall of mud and roiling water slammed against their siding. Through the side living room window, he saw Lee and Lilly's house breaking apart from the impact of the wave. Their house was shaking violently, too. He grabbed Marie around the wrist and started to open the front door but hesitated. Should they ride it out inside the house and not let the water in? The living room window exploded as black muddy water spewed through. Marie screamed. The entire house was now being ripped from the foundation, jostling him from side to side.

"Brad, Brad! It's the mayor." Marie was at his bedside shaking him awake and holding the phone.

Brad didn't know what time it was but rallied enough to realize it was Saturday morning, much earlier than he would like to be awake. As with most people, when awakened early, he was hard-wired to sound like he had arisen early, observing Benjamin Franklin's prescription for being healthy, wealthy, and wise. He covered the receiver with his hand, cleared his throat, and practiced a "good morning."

"Good morning, Buddy," he said.

"Not so good, Brad. Have you seen the sign?"

"Not yet. What's up?"

"They have a huge anti-Green Valley sign right across the street from the site. Geez, Kay and her crowd aren't even going to give it a fair chance," the mayor fumed. "I want you to go take the damned thing down. Now!"

Brad's mind was just starting to engage. He stalled for time. "What does it say, Buddy?"

"'Don't destroy Santa Ynez' with NO written over Green Valley Village in big red letters," the mayor spat. "It's like the size of a billboard. They must have been at it all night. Why didn't PD stop them?"

Brad had revived enough to formulate a quick response. "Let me go out and take a look. If it's on public land I can have the weekend Public Works crew remove it right away. If it's on private property, I'll have to talk to the city attorney to see what we can do. It's probably a violation of our zoning ordinance either way but we are treading on Constitutional rights here and we don't want to be too heavy-handed."

"Like hell we don't! There's no reasoning with Kay and her groupies. The project deserves a fair hearing. This is America!" The mayor's sentences were delivered like the rat-a-tat of a machinegun. "You better call Scott so he doesn't hear about this from somebody else and tell him you are tearing it down."

"Well," Brad said carefully, "like I said, I'll go check it out myself and establish if it's on public right-of-way. I know we adopted a plan line for street and intersection widening in that area even before Green

Valley came along. But I don't know if any of the right-of-way has been acquired yet. We probably didn't because we wouldn't want to spend our street monies for it if we can make the land acquisition and widening a condition of Green Valley. I'll check it out right away but I can't promise we can get it removed today. I'll also talk to Henry to see what options we have if it's on private property." He held his breath.

"I've got a chain saw," the mayor threatened. Brad kept holding his breath. After a moment's pause, the mayor continued. "OK. Get on it right away. But call Scott first. Let him know these are just the fringe nuts doing this. Calm him down. We need this project."

Rather than calling the developer immediately as the mayor directed, Scott took a quick shower and completed his other normal daily preparations. He had a hard time functioning properly until he had showered, shaved, brushed his teeth, and been to the toilet. It used to drive Kris and Dillon crazy on Christmas morning, waiting to rip into their packages until Dad got ready for the day. As he was finishing off his routine with fluoride mouth rinse, the phone rang again. Marie answered it as usual, Brad seldom did when home. A moment later, she yelled upstairs, "It's Scott."

"Morning, Scott, I was just getting ready to call you."

"Brad?" the developer said brusquely. He was not his normal, upbeat self, either. "What the hell's going on?"

"Yeah, the mayor wanted me to let you know you shouldn't get too upset. This is normal stuff around here."

"Normal stuff?" the developer said incredulously. "I was completely sandbagged and you call that 'normal stuff?'"

Brad was puzzled by Scott's intense reaction. "You must have had the same thing happen with some of your other projects. Given the opposition from Kay, weren't you prepared to deal with these kinds of tactics?"

"Hell, no, we weren't," Scott seemed to be getting angrier. "This came out of left field, Brad. It's going to cost us millions. I never would have agreed to some of the terms of the DA with you yesterday if I thought this was even a possibility. Sure, things come out of the blue sometimes but I thought we could count on *you* to make sure it didn't here."

Now Brad was getting annoyed. "What do you think I could have done about it?" he snapped back.

"Well, for starters, you could have given me a heads up at lunch yesterday that it was coming. Based on your assurances that everything was fine, I sent my weekly report up the chain last night saying everything was coming along. I'm going to look stupid now."

"*I* didn't even know about it at lunch. I'll do what I can to get it removed, Scott," Brad said. "But I may not be able to kill it today and may need to get the city attorney involved."

"Why do you need the city attorney?! Why can't you tell her right now to remove it?"

"Hah!" the city manager replied. "I assume you're referring to Kay. You don't *tell* her anything. You know that."

"Kay?" queried Scott. "Who's talking about Kay? I'm talking about Megan!"

"Megan?" Brad quizzed. "What's she got to do with this? Are you accusing her of being involved?"

Scott paused. "Well I assume she's the one who wrote it. It wasn't *your* idea was it?"

Brad recoiled. "I can assure you, Scott, that I didn't know a thing about the sign ahead of time and if I find out that Megan was involved with it, I'll fire her."

"Sign? What sign? What are you talking about, Brad?"

Brad tightened his face and stared at the phone. "Let's start over.

Didn't you call me about the anti-Green Valley sign? I just heard about it a few minutes ago from the mayor and am on my way to check if it's in the public right-of-way so we can remove it."

"This is the first I heard about that," said the developer. "Tell me." Brad went on to summarize what the mayor had reported.

"So," Brad asked him, "if you weren't calling about the sign why did you call?"

"The tertiary treatment language, of course."

"Tertiary treatment?"

"You know, recycled water from your wastewater plant," the developer said.

"I know what tertiary water is," Brad said impatiently. "But what are you talking about?"

"The Initial Study language saying tertiary treatment would be studied as a project alternative with the EIR. Didn't you see that yesterday?"

"No. Where is it?"

"Page twenty-six. The write-up basically says that the studies by Western and Payton show there is sufficient water for the project and the rest of the General Plan build-out, but it goes on to say that the State Water Project is uncertain and the city may not even be able to count on the thirty-something percent reliability. So, the city should conserve its current supplies. It says that tertiary treatment for the golf course, common area landscaping, parks, and the front yards will be studied as an EIR alternative to reduce the project's demand for potable water. You said you read the IS."

"I skimmed the IS, didn't read every word," Brad said meekly. "I'm sure it wasn't in the draft I looked at before we met. I can't imagine that Megan added that after I reviewed it. I have my agenda packet right here, but the draft she sent over is at the office. I'll go in later and see if that language was in what she sent me. I promised the mayor I'd check on the sign first."

Brad heard the blender go off in the kitchen breaking the silence. "The sign is an annoyance for sure," Scott said. "But I'm much more worried about this tertiary treatment language. It will cost millions if we have to do it. I know already we can't make that work and keep everything in the DA that we have now."

"I understand," Brad assured. "I want to find out how that language got in the IS before I do anything else."

"We need to get it out of there, Brad. Tertiary could kill the project. I'll get more specifics from our folks and check back with you. This is a much bigger deal than the stupid sign."

Brad's next call was to the cell phone of Dee Sharma, Public Works Director. No response. Brad left him a voice mail about the sign asking him to call back immediately. He then called City Attorney Henry Fitzhenry to brief him on the problem and get him thinking about the legal alternatives if the sign is determined to be on private property, which Brad thought likely.

It was close to 8 a.m. on Saturday morning when he drove up to the sign. It was an attractively painted scene of the rolling hills across the street covered with box-shaped houses and proclaiming "NO GREEN VALLEY VILLAGE" in large, red letters over the top of the scene. He recognized the two women strolling in front of it waving pickets saying "Don't waste our precious water" and the word "NO" in red letters over "Green Valley Village" as it was on the billboard. Paisley Menezes, an artist who specialized in painting whimsical characters on rocks, and Kalo Debevec, a master gardener, waved to him as he pulled up. Common denominator: both friends of Councilwoman Kay Nance.

He recalled the advice he had given Kay about getting along with her colleagues on the Council and how he foolishly thought it had hit home with her. He sat in the car a moment and said to himself, "never let them see you sweat," and bounded from the car.

"Top of the morning, Brad," Kalo greeted him as if passing in the grocery aisle. "What do you think of our sign?"

"It's sure big," he said, trying to sound casual. "And well done, other than that typo."

Menezes and Debevec both snapped their heads around, scrutinizing the sign.

"Just kidding," Brad said. "Got to take a couple pictures to make sure it's not on public right-of-way. Do you want to be in or out?"

"We checked carefully," Kalo said, "we're on private property." The women posed proudly in front of the sign as he took pictures.

"Got to run," he said. "Heard there's a stray dog in the neighborhood and I'm on call this weekend. See you." He smiled, waved and drove off.

He hoped Kay was smart enough not to have done the sign painting herself or the proponents could force her recusal. No doubt she would know he had been out there within minutes.

He got to City Hall, rummaged through Jane's piles until he found his marked-up copy of Megan's draft Initial Study he'd looked at yesterday morning, and went immediately to the water discussion. This time he read the water section word for word. He hadn't noticed the subsection called "Special Mitigation Measures" below the main Discussion section. And there it was. The first sentence noted the difficulty of being too precise with water supply and demand forecasts and, therefore, suggesting that the Commission consider the adequacy of the remaining post-project water supply. Brad grumbled. It was close to what he had directed Megan to say, but she had taken some liberties that he didn't like. He read on:

> CEQA requires that the EIR consider alternatives for meeting the project's objectives while reducing environmental impacts. Tertiary treatment of the City's secondary-treated effluent for the Project's

golf course, set-back landscaping and common areas, parks and residential front yards will be analyzed as an alternative for reducing the Project's demand for potable water and, thereby, retaining a more comfortable water surplus for the future.

He gasped. How had he missed that? He remembered rushing to skim through the report before meeting Scott for lunch.

He called Megan at home and was relieved when her "significant other" live-in partner, Fred Buderi, a biology professor at the nearby community college, said Megan was in. He didn't know Fred well except that he seemed intense and smart. Buderi sometimes wrote Letters to the Editor or op-ed commentary pieces in the local paper on current events; always taking a liberal or environmental protection stance. The same people who called her Megan Cain't joked about her relationship with Fred. He recalled one of Scott's parties when Hank Nettler speculated that Megan and Fred sat around at home on Saturday nights getting stoned and gorging on fresh veggies and NPR broadcasts.

"Hi, Brad, you're at it early for a Saturday," Megan said in a neutrally friendly way.

"Yeah, the mayor woke me up early to tell me about an anti-Green Valley sign that went up last night across the street from the site. I'm trying to track down if it's public or private property and what, if anything, we can do about it." He resisted the impulse to ask if she knew anything about it. One issue at a time.

They talked briefly about the sign and the growing controversy the project would be receiving now that public comment was underway. Brad got down to business. He admitted that he had looked at the draft IS too quickly and was surprised about the tertiary treatment comment she had included. Megan assured him she wasn't trying to slip anything by him and defended how what she wrote was consistent with his direction. She had accurately cited the Western and Payton reports, noting their conclusions that there would be sufficient water supply for the project but raised the issue, as she had with Brad, that tertiary treated water for the golf course and landscaping was an option that should be studied for preserving more of the city's finite water supply. There was no remorse or defensiveness in her voice.

"Right now," he said, "my main concern is getting that tertiary language out of the IS. SoCal is having a fit. How do we do that?"

"But it's just an alternative to be explored. The law requires that we consider alternatives for meeting the project objectives, with less environmental impact, when we do the EIR. Besides, like I said before. . ."

"Megan!" he interrupted, "I'm not going to argue this with you. Now answer the question. Please," he softened. "How do we get that language out of the IS?"

"Hmmm. Not so easy, Brad. It already went out yesterday to the responsible agencies and public both electronically and with hard copies. It's a reasonable and common mitigation alternative. If we dropped it suddenly, it will raise a red flag. It would be obvious that the only reason for dropping it was pressure from the developer who didn't like the price tag."

She tried again to defend the study alternative and yammered on about all sorts of complex water issues involving the Delta and the State Water Project and why the city should be stingy with its water supply. He was only partially listening. He thought about those on the Council and in the community who will be angry about putting the project in peril with the tertiary treatment concept. He would look incompetent for allowing the language in the first place and weak if he couldn't get it out. City managers survive by helping the elected officials achieve what they want, not by delivering bad news that they can't.

"I have to deal with that sign now," he said, cutting her off again.

"I don't have time right now to debate that tertiary language with you."

"Can we at least meet on Monday to talk about it before you decide it has to come out?" she pleaded.

"First thing. Come prepared with a specific strategy for dumping tertiary entirely. I'm sure that's where I'll want to go."

He hung up with Megan and again tried and failed to reach his public works director. He pulled up the confidential on-line employee directory that included home and cell phone numbers and placed a call to Associate Engineer Gene Lowe, his Laker-loving buddy. Brad apologized for bothering him on a Saturday morning and explained that he needed him to go into the office and check the ownership on the sign location. He texted his photo to Gene's city cell phone.

There was nothing more he could do at the moment. He spent a few minutes tidying up the stacks of paper on his desk, locked up the building, stopped at Jiffy Lube for a long-delayed oil change and drove to the park for the soccer field dedication. SoCal had built two artificial turf youth soccer fields at Sunny Fields Park and he was tapped to be the emcee of the event. It was an honor he normally deferred to the mayor but Buddy Murray would be on the road for a wedding and asked Brad to do it. Brad suspected the mayor saw him as a safer choice than giving another local politician the limelight.

The day had become dark and blustery, sprinkling off and on. Nevertheless, this was a big event for his city and he expected a nice turnout. He felt himself slump a little at the wheel and sigh when he thought about Scott Graves and other Green Valley supporters who would surely jump him about the tertiary treatment study and the billboard. That worry tripped the "Play" button on the tape recorder in his head. He cycled through the familiar themes: his inadequacies, job insecurity, personal financial jeopardy, and general sense of impending catastrophe.

He suddenly became aware that he had been on automatic

pilot with no recollection of the last few minutes or miles of driving. His worry was palpable. The rain had progressed from a spitting sprinkle to a steady drizzle. He glanced down at the steering column to increase the rate of the variable speed windshield wiper. When he looked up again, his eyes were drawn to the sky to his left where there now appeared a break in the black, billowing clouds. A shaft of light illuminated his immediate surroundings showing off the beauty of the oak-dappled green hillsides.

He leaned forward against the steering wheel for a better view of the vivid winter scene displayed before him. OK. OK. I get it. He relaxed and again saluted to the heavens.

Pulling into the park's parking lot, he saw a large anti-Green Valley banner stretched across a section of chain link fence. It was a replica of the billboard-sized sign he was trying to remove. Gene Lowe had called him en route to confirm the billboard was on private property. Brad had relayed that to the city attorney who wanted more time to look at the Municipal Code to see what the choices were for abating it. Fitzhenry didn't volunteer to work on it over the weekend. No surprise there. That was City Attorney Henry Fitzhenry. There were times the city attorney was maddening. Like today. The man could not be made to feel a sense of urgency. Brad knew he'd be jumped about the legality of the sign in a few minutes and he didn't have any answers.

Brad had worked with plenty of city attorneys in his thirty-year career. His favorite had been Chuck Lemoore. Chuck was sharp, decisive, and quick with sound advice. Brad sometimes worried that he was winging it. He couldn't possibly be so sure all the time when there were so many issues flying at him. But there had never been a time when Lemoore's seemingly off-the-cuff opinion was later reversed by him or anybody else. What Brad really appreciated was that Lemoore was a problem-solver who liked to be in the middle of the fray rather than poring through legal publications. He sometimes stepped over the line of legal advisor into Brad's or the staff's policy role. However, it was good to have Chuck as part of the team helping to get things done rather than sitting back lobbing hand grenades at what the staff was trying to accomplish.

By contrast, Henry Fitzhenry preferred doing research in his office. With the door closed. When he was finally ready, he issued lengthy, carefully cited, opinions. Brad often thought Fitzhenry's opinions were overkill. He usually needed a quick and dirty opinion on the spot, or a paragraph emailed the next day, more than a three-page annotated memo next week. The phrase, "I asked you what time it is, not how to build a watch," applied to Henry.

Other staff members made jokes about Henry Fitzhenry's cautious, plodding nature. Some called him Bond, James Bond in exquisite satire. The city attorney was the antonym of swashbuckling. Brad got along with him well enough. Henry pretty much left him alone to run the city. He didn't meddle on policy matters and wasn't one to find prohibitive liability risk in every situation. Henry Fitzhenry was OK. Just slow.

Brad locked his car and walked to the park entrance. "Well hello, again," he said to the picketers he had photographed earlier at the sign. They, and a few others with pickets, stood behind a table under a portable canopy next to the big banner on the fence.

"Care to sign our petition?" Kalo Debevec teased.

"Oh, rats, I don't have a pen. Let me get back to you on that," he joked back.

He made a beeline for the portable podium under the tent where the event organizers were gathering. Scott Graves stood with his boss, Jeff Simpson, whom he had met before. His stomach tightened.

"Nice reception, huh?" Scott said nodding back at the banner and petitioners. "You remember Jeff Simpson."

"Hi, Jeff. Sorry about that. I didn't know that was going to happen." He shook Simpson's hand.

"Seems to be a pattern," Jeff said gruffly.

Scott quickly changed the subject to the weather and how pleased he was that so many people turned out for the dedication. Brad thanked Simpson for his company's generous donation and excused himself to make preparations for getting festivities underway. Simpson stood with his arms crossed.

Brad eventually made an announcement on the portable PA system for everyone to gather around. A Boy Scout group posted the colors under the tent and a sixth-grade girl sang the National Anthem to the shaky accompaniment of the Santa Ynez Valley Christian Academy band. He introduced Vice Mayor Mullikin, Councilwoman Gretchen Schmitz and Councilman Al Landon, moved on to the elected school board members in attendance, then to the State Assemblywoman's local representative. One speaker after another came to the portable rostrum to extoll the virtues of the youth soccer, the new fields and SoCal's generosity. It started raining harder as Brad invited Scott Graves to the mic.

Scott was his normal polished self. He credited his boss, Jeff Simpson, for approving the donation of the fields. "I have to tell you that Jeff has been giving me sideways looks all day. I've always argued that Santa Ynez has perfect weather for our active adult community and, so far, Jeff has been willing to write the checks to make it the first-class project we all want. He reminded me a few minutes ago that this is his fifth visit to the area. Two of the days it rained, one day we were socked in with fog, and another day it was so smoky from a wildland fire on those mountains you didn't want to be outside. I keep telling him it's usually perfect here but he's beginning to wonder." That brought some snickers from the crowd.

"I told him that the city arranged for the little rain today to demonstrate how good it's going to be for the kids to be able to play on these all-weather fields year around. Well done, Brad." More chuckles. "In fact Jeff's wondering if we should use artificial turf for the golf course just in case."

"Good!" came a sudden shout from the back of the crowd. Brad recognized Kalo Debevec's voice before looking. He recalled her yelling orders to all the volunteers who showed up to plant a rose garden on a small patch at City Hall last year. As everyone else turned, she started chanting "save our water, save our water." The chant was quickly picked up by Paisley Menezes then three other people braving the rain. The chanters pierced the air with their picket signs, punctuating each word. They did a few more choruses of "save our water" then stopped but kept their picket signs up to shield themselves from the rain. There was a moment of uncomfortable silence in the crowd.

Scott turned to his boss and said, "See, Jeff, I told you the Chamber's Ambassadors Committee would be here to welcome us today."

Even the protestors laughed. The tension was broken. Brad got the mic again and began to wrap up.

"Wait, Brad!" Vice Mayor Mullikin beseeched, walking forward. "I'd like to say something."

"Make it quick, Tim!" shouted the raspy voice of Hank Nettler, standing at the back of the tent with Hubie, Chamber Exec Brian Brando, and Kerry Smith.

The vice mayor grabbed the microphone. "Well, Hank, it's true it's all been said. But everybody hasn't said it yet." He got a laugh. "I know if the mayor were here, he'd want to be sure we tell everyone how thrilled we are to have SoCal Communities as a partner in the city." The vice mayor was doing his best to sound mayoral, but Brad thought he came across as a pretender, a sycophant heaping praise on the mayor and SoCal. The crowd was restless and wanted to get out of the weather.

After a few moments, Brad stepped forward giving the vice mayor his cue and called the dignitaries forward for the ceremonial first shots on goal. Cute little kids in every manner of brightly colored jerseys were in athletic stances at the goal and easily blocked the bunted kicks from the adults.

The rain induced most of the people to leave right away after that. Brad saw that the two officials from SoCal were huddled with Vice Mayor Mullikin under the canopy. Jeff Simpson was doing most of the talking, wagging his finger at the vice mayor. Jeff was a big man with a stern visage. Brad presumed Jeff was hammering his boss about tertiary treatment. He wished he could have briefed the councilmembers about this latest issue ahead of time. He waited for the group to break up and approached Scott and Jeff Simpson.

Simpson wasted no time. "What are you going to do about this tertiary treatment crap? We talked about it in the car on the way up here. Do you know how devastating that would be for our project?"

Jeff Simpson didn't seem to be the type who cared about building a relationship. He was all business so Brad responded accordingly. "It's been cited as an alternative to be studied in the EIR. It made its way into the Initial Study for the EIR without my knowledge. I'm trying to find out what we can do about it at this point."

"Let me help you with that one, Brad," Jeff said sarcastically. "Drive a stake through its heart. Right now!"

Brad felt his muscles tighten.

Simpson continued the attack. "I have our people working this weekend on a cost estimate. I don't have a good number yet. But from other projects we've done, I can tell you it runs about $100 a foot to run a twelve-inch line from the sewer plant to the project. That run is at least three miles so the line alone is around one-and-a-half million. The tertiary plant cost is based on gallons treated. At least another million-and-a-half. Then, if we have to run parallel potable and tertiary lines and meters to the golf course and all the landscaped areas, parks, and front yards, you're probably looking at an eight-inch distribution main at sixty dollars a foot plus two thousand for each one of the metered services. You're looking at over a million dollars just to connect each yard to the landscaping main in the street. We're talking at least a six-million-dollar hit."

"What we really don't understand, Brad," Scott added, with a less biting tone, "is that there's no need for it. Our engineer, your public works director, Western, who your city has used for years, and then Payton/Carlisle all concluded you have enough water to serve our project. Megan just couldn't let it go at that could she?"

Brad saw that Scott was giving him an opportunity to put all of the blame on his planning director; to make this about Megan's intransigence rather than his own ineffective oversight of the process. While getting out of Jeff Simpson's gun sights was appealing, he wasn't prepared to throw his young department under the proverbial bus. He recalled that he had agreed to give her a chance to pitch the tertiary alternative analysis on Monday.

"She's made a strong case that new water is going to be tougher to get in the future. From what I've been reading, we will be lucky to hang on to what we have now. She's just raising the question about whether we should be giving so much of our remaining supply to uses that could do just fine with recycled water. I'm meeting with her on Monday to see what we can do," he said noncommittally.

Simpson scowled. "That's not what I wanted to hear from you, Brad. Look, Green Valley is a big project for you but it's small for us. With everything we're giving away in the damn Development Agreement, it hardly pencils out at all. You throw this tertiary cost into it and the project is upside down. I've never lost the company money on any of the projects I built and I'm not going to start here. I'd sooner cut our losses now and take it down the road where we can count on the city leadership and we don't have people with closed minds." He nodded back towards the protestors. "I don't think that's what your Council wants, do you?"

"Neither do I," Brad said, his breath becoming short. "I think it's a great project and I'll continue to do my best to promote it. I don't know yet what I can do about the tertiary thing. It's just being proposed as a study, not a condition of approval, you know."

Jeff stiffened and put his fists on his hips, elbows straight out, ready to lash out again. "Bitch wings," Brad had heard the stance called.

Scott noticed too, and intervened quickly. "The problem is that, in our experience with government agencies, once something gets on the table it's hard to pull it off. And we don't face Megan Cain'ts in other cities. We're afraid that the tertiary will end up being imposed if it's studied."

"What the hell is this about pumping sewer water to Green Valley?" Hubie interrupted, as he and Hank walked up.

Brad felt like a piñata for the next few minutes as everyone took turns taking a whack at him. He admitted that he wasn't sure how to get rid of the offensive language now that the IS had been circulated.

"We're working on that, too," Scott said. "CEQA requires project alternatives to be considered in the EIR but the alternatives have to be reasonably capable of delivering the project's objectives. We know already that the cost of tertiary will kill the project's economic objectives so it won't qualify."

"There, Brad!" Hubie said. "Just use that argument and dump that language now so we can get on with the EIR."

"I already said I'd do what I could, Hubie," Brad snarled back. The big man glared and stiffened.

Scott jumped in again. "I think we can count on Brad to help us get rid of that study language. Right, Brad?"

"I'm meeting with Megan and the city attorney on Monday to see what can be done. I'll do what I can, Scott," he said looking at Jeff Simpson. "We've had a good working relationship and we'll get through this." He saw an opportunity to deflect their anger from him and mentioned the big billboard.

Scott said, "I heard it's already down. Got hit by a car or something."

"Or might have been a tractor," Hubie smirked. "What a shame. We should go out there and help them, Hank. It's the neighborly thing to do."

19

Planning Director Megan Cain sat channeling Tennessee Williams on Monday morning, fidgeting like a cat on a hot tin roof. She sat directly across from City Manager Brad Jacks, trying to act calm, but her slight, athletic frame seemed poised to spring up at any moment. Her normally flowing, straight, auburn hair looked ready to burst out from the tight bun constraining it. Her movements were quick, like she was trying to find an outlet for the adrenalin coursing through her body. He wanted to get this over with.

He looked at his watch and said, "I'll give you fifteen minutes to argue for that tertiary language."

As she had started to do on Saturday, she again expressed her skepticism about the Green Valley water demand and supply studies. She touched on a litany of daunting issues facing California water quality and supply. Speaking from notes in front of her, Megan described the age and deterioration of the statewide water infrastructure: the dams, aqueducts, pipelines, and pumping plants from the original State Water Project that are now over fifty years old. She then shifted to the threats posed by all the chemicals finding their way into the ecosystem and the immediate problems associated with accumulating salts, and the uranium contaminant in the soils and groundwater basins. She talked about the over-drafting of the groundwater basins, earthquake risk to the levees, loss of desirable aquatic and riparian habitat, and the resulting increase in endangered species listings. She cited studies about climate change, effects of water temperature changes, and rising tide and sea levels, with particular emphasis on how that is projected to further threaten future Delta water exports.

He sat mutely for close to twenty minutes, looking at his watch occasionally. She got the message and wrapped up.

"With all of these real threats out there, we should hang on to as much water as we can for the existing developed area for when the water reductions hit," she concluded decisively.

"Megan," he said, "you've made some good arguments for better water management. In fact, based on what I've been learning the last couple of months, I can't disagree with a lot of what you said. But these are huge, complicated issues. We are just a small city here. We can't hold the Green Valley project hostage over statewide issues that we can't possibly predict or influence anyway."

"So, where does that leave us, Brad? Should we keep on approving water-thirsty development without thinking about the long-term? Should cities just keep on sprawling because they can, at least for now?"

He shifted in his chair. "Again, you are talking about major statewide policy matters. Santa Ynez is a tiny player. I can only influence what happens right here, not statewide. Is this some personal crusade you're on? Are you trying to reenact *The Mouse That Roared?*"

She jerked forward, then sat back, dropping her chin to her interlaced hands, and looking down at the papers on the coffee table.

Brad sensed that he had struck a nerve. She was silent a bit longer, then shook her head as if committing to some unspoken thought.

"Well, Brad, maybe I am. I've been thinking a lot lately about how we plan our cities. It's mostly driven by finances and the political pressures of the day."

"Welcome to my world, Megan."

She continued, "I know it's the way it is. We review the impacts of the projects we approve, but we can't be certain about environmental impacts. Nature has a way of being unpredictable. Besides, there's a limit on how far we are willing to push a developer for environmental mitigation or better design. We end up with run-of-the-mill developments. Empty calories that fill up space in the General Plan."

"Wait a minute, Megan, you can't possibly be putting Green Valley in that category."

"It's really nothing special," she scoffed.

"I think you're selling yourself too short, Megan. The Development Agreement you contributed to has a lot of good things for this community, and the Specific Plan looks great."

She shrugged. "It's nothing too different from what SoCal has done in their other developments. That doesn't take any great creativity. And when you stand back and look at it, it's just another example of converting good ag land into low- density residential. It's sprawl. We already know that is the wrong way to provide for population growth. We are destroying our environment, and it's costing taxpayers and ratepayers too much to keep doing it."

He stiffened, feeling like he was under attack. "What would *you* have us do? You want us to reject Green Valley and change the General Plan so we only do high-rise residential from now on?"

"Well, frankly, if it were up to me, I *would* reject Green Valley. High rises in Santa Ynez is ridiculous, of course. But Fred and I talked a lot over the weekend about how boring and wasteful our community

WITHOUT PURPOSE *of* EVASION

development concepts have been for decades. Our subdivisions and neighborhood commercial areas look just like the ones in the cities down the road, which look just like the ones two hundred miles away. We could take a stand for something more special if the people around here had the vision and courage."

"Like what?" he snapped, feeling attacked again.

"Look at Solvang, right next door. A group of Danes founded it a hundred years ago, wanting to create a touch of home with their architecture. People love it because it's so unique for California. So, yes, I'd like to see us do something bolder than approve another sprawling, low-density residential project, like Green Valley, with very standard house designs and all painted in nice, safe, earth tones. Boring. Since I don't see the will to do anything special here, the best I can do is to try to reduce the project's impacts."

He bristled again. "Sure, downtown Solvang is unique, but most of their residential areas aren't. You want to one-up them by turning Santa Ynez into some sort of movie set? Maybe a blow up version of Disneyland, with one neighborhood in a New Orleans theme and another like a jungle? Come on, Megan. Get real."

She didn't flinch as much as she had to his prior scolding. In fact, he thought she was surprisingly calm.

"I didn't mean to upset you, Brad. I know you are under a lot of pressure with Green Valley. But the more Fred and I talked about it over the weekend, the more I concluded that I am being real. The reality is that we need a new paradigm for city planning that puts more value on preserving the environment and creating more intimate, pedestrian-oriented communities where people feel connected to their neighborhoods. Sprawling out into prime ag land, where people live behind gates and drive their cars to everything, isn't the answer. That's what's real to me."

"Well, like you acknowledged before, it isn't up to you. How Santa Ynez develops and what happens with Green Valley Village is a policy decision the public will make through their elected City Council. Not you, or me."

"I am well aware of that, Brad," Megan said with forced patience. "It's our job to provide professional advice to the Commission and Council. In my opinion, Green Valley represents the kind of sprawl that is ruining California. Like I said, I *am* being real and know that you, and probably the Council majority, want it. I'm not going to rail against it. I just think the policy makers should at least study the feasibility of tertiary treatment to make it a little less horrible."

Brad paused to consider that point. "The problem is that if tertiary gets into the EIR, it's going to be hard to not impose it as a condition. I have Dee checking with Payton/Carlisle today on the cost. The SoCal guys told me this weekend it would be in the $6 million range. That's a big hit on top of what we are already getting from them through the Specific Plan and DA. I think the Council majority wants all those benefits, more than saving some water, especially with the studies showing we have enough for the project."

Megan shook her head. "How do we know the project can't support that extra cost without dropping things from the DA? All we have is their argument that they can't afford it. Why don't we make them prove it by analyzing their pro forma?"

"I just don't think the Council will want to take that hard a line with SoCal."

"Then why don't you push them to do the right thing, even if they'd prefer not to? Or do you only bring them recommendations you think they'll accept?"

He glared at her, trying to control his anger.

She slumped, then sat up again. "How about this, Brad? Why do anything yourself right now? If you do anything at this point, you are going to put yourself in the spotlight. Why not let the Planning Commission weigh in? The Initial Study is on their agenda tomorrow night. Let them do their job and provide advice to the City Council."

He felt a jolt of relief over the possibility of kicking the whole tertiary issue to the Planning Commission. Still, he was wary. Megan was the primary staff support to that commission. She had much more access to the commissioners than anyone else, including him.

"OK," he said. "We'll let the commission decide what to do with the tertiary study. But I want you to stay out of it. If they decide to keep with the tertiary study alternative, I want it to be their idea, not the result of your arguments. If you can give me your assurance that you will do that, I'll stay out of it for now, too, and let the commission decide."

Megan cocked her head. "Wait. Are you telling me I can't talk to my own commission?"

"You can talk about everything *but* the water issues. I want Dee to cover the discussion about water supply and demand, including any questions the commissioners might have about the tertiary treatment alternative. I will instruct him that he is to present the tertiary alternative as you've written it in the IS. Let the commissioners decide whether they want to proceed with it without a lot of drama. Agreed?"

It wasn't. Megan objected to yielding the floor on such a significant matter to the public works director, whom she regarded as biased in favor of Green Valley. Further, she thought the commissioners would find it odd to have her make the IS presentation, then turn the water section over to Dee.

Brad held his ground. "Look, some people don't think you are giving the project a fair shake. I want to get you out of the field of fire. Let Dee present the water, and let the commissioners decide it. Don't you advocate on it."

"But, Brad," she complained, "that would be like you just sitting there mum while the finance director presents an annual budget you don't support. Your training and integrity wouldn't allow it. You'd want to give the Council your best advice. I don't think it's fair for you to deny me the same opportunity with *my* commission. Besides . . ."

"It's *the Council's* advisory commission, not yours," he interrupted. "Either way this goes, there will be controversy. I want it to focus on the issue, not the people. You're too politically hot. I repeat, you need to stay out of the water discussion."

"I'm prepared to take that heat," Megan responded, ignoring his admonitions. "Fred and I talked a lot about that over the weekend, too. I know that in the total scheme of things in California, what we do here in Santa Ynez won't even be a ripple. I may not be able to bring much influence on statewide issues, but I can plant a flag for good planning right here, regardless of the personal consequences. It's the right thing to do. Let me do it."

Brad noticed a change in his young department head. The agitation she showed at the beginning of the meeting seemed to have yielded to fatalism. Her pale blue eyes were riveted on his, waiting for him to respond. He broke the contact, stalling for time. For the first time, he noticed that she was wearing a coral pink sweater. He had an image of Lilly in the hospital wearing a housecoat with a similar shade. He thought of the man Lilly called "Dad" and the guilt he lived with for not standing up to power. What a contrast with the young woman sitting before him who had the courage of her convictions.

"I respect you for being willing to stand up for what you think is right, Megan."

"But?"

"But nobody anointed you to be the savior of community development in California. I want the staff to be seen as neutral, objective professionals who dutifully carry out the direction of the councilmembers elected to set policy, and their commission advisers. Staff shouldn't be pursuing their own agendas. Now, the commission may agree with the tertiary alternative, or they may not. Either way, I want the staff role limited to asking the commission about the adequacy of a 12 percent water surplus and whether it wants to study tertiary as a mitigation. Let the commission reach its own conclusion based on the facts Dee presents, not all these other broader issues involving statewide water policy you want to get into."

She looked hurt and uncertain. He felt guilty. "Thank you for sharing your opinions. I know you don't agree with this, but I'm doing what I think is best for the overall organization." He stood at his chair. "Are we clear?"

She sat there, giving no indication of leaving on cue. Finally, she nodded her head quickly, put her notes in her portfolio, stood up, and smiled. "I heard you, Brad." And she walked out.

He watched her leave and thought about calling her back to get the commitment he had asked for. The outer office door clicked shut while he still debated with himself.

He hated bullies. He thought again of Lilly's father getting shut down by William Mulholland. He needed a friend and placed a call to Quinn O'Rourke. He had called the consultant over the weekend to brief him about the tertiary treatment language that had found its way into the Initial Study.

"Quinn, I know I'm rushing you, but I have to make some snap decisions and was hoping you had something for me on the tertiary language. I can't wait for the city attorney to give me a treatise on it."

"I talked to our young geniuses," O'Rourke said. "They said what you'll probably hear from your city attorney, there's no case law on the point. You heard right that the EIR alternatives can be deemed infeasible if they don't achieve the project objectives. That's why studying converting a proposed project from an apartment complex to a park, like all the neighbors always want, wouldn't hold up as being a feasible alternative. Most of the time it's a financial test."

"I get that," Brad said. "What can I do to get rid of the tertiary study language at this point?"

"Well, I can't think of any social, environmental, or physical reasons *not* to do tertiary treatment. It's a cost feasibility issue. The problem is, now that the IS has been circulated to the responsible agencies with the tertiary study alternative in it, my guys say you can't just say you aren't proceeding with that alternative because it's too expensive. You have to prove the point. That means pulling out the cost estimates along with the developer's pro forma with all sorts of information they'd prefer to be kept confidential. Like everything else in an EIR, if you don't do a good job providing a factual basis for your decisions, it can be challenged. Courts usually prefer to send things back for more study rather than taking the position that the public doesn't need more information."

"Oh, crud," Brad groaned. "I can just hear my buddy Jeff Simpson's reaction if he has to disclose SoCal's pro forma, when we aren't even spending any public money to subsidize their project. Even assuming he pencil whips it enough to make it seem like it's a barely profitable venture, the opponents will have a field day second guessing all the costs and income projections. And some of the information that would be critical may not be disclosable without violating some contract. Like the terms of their purchase option with Nettlers."

"I've worked with Simpson before," O'Rourke began, before seeming to choke, and breaking into a coughing spasm. He eventually recovered. "Sorry, wrong pipe. I started to say that Simpson's a tough guy. He may just opt to pull the plug on the whole project rather than let the public in on his numbers."

"I can see he had quite an impact on you," Brad chuckled before becoming serious. "He's already threatened to bail," Brad recalled. "What if we adopted the IS 'as is,' with the language about the tertiary study, but never do the study? Just let it die a silent death?"

"Yeah, we talked about that, too," Quinn said. "My people say you should assume that one of the first things the opponents' experts will do is compare the Draft EIR to the IS, to see if anything was left out. The DEIR will have to have a section called something like Alternatives Considered but Rejected from Further Consideration. That's where you would say that you were planning to study tertiary but later dropped it because it wasn't feasible. Again, you have to demonstrate why it wasn't feasible, so you're back to square one. Plus, you'd still be issuing the EIR scope with the tertiary alternative included. Jeff's probably not going to like that."

"Maybe it would be OK with him if he knew we were keeping the tertiary alternative in the study because we have to, but we assure him we won't require it later as a condition of approval." He felt desperate.

"Think about that one," Quinn advised. "Your Kay Nance and her group file a legal challenge against the EIR. They hire one of the hotshot law firms that makes a killing fighting EIR adequacy. They subpoena everyone. Facts start to come out when people are under oath. You get a deposition notice. Some $500-an-hour lawyer with a bunch of assistants next to him gets handed a piece of paper that he waves in front of you. It might be an email from somebody, 'evidence mail' it's known as to litigation attorneys. Or, maybe it's a transcript of a recorded phone call. You don't know. He says, 'Mr. Jacks, did you ever tell anyone at SoCal not to worry about tertiary treatment, that you'd make sure it never saw the light of day in the final map? And remember, Mr. Jacks, you're under oath.'"

Brad paused.

"Now, I'm making an assumption that you'd still rather sleep with Marie than some burly inmate, right?"

"Scratch that idea. Brain fart. What do you think I should do?"

"You mean besides the one we get all of the time, 'go to plumber's school?'"

"Right," Brad laughed. It was so good to talk to Quinn. He understood and had already calmed him down a little.

"Look, Brad, it's like I told you before. You can't control everything."

"Yeah," he said softly.

"You're all wrapped up trying to manage this Green Valley project. Now, maybe it is the best opportunity your city will ever see. Or, maybe, it's a shit sandwich on raisin bread."

"Huh?"

"It looks good sitting there in the Saran Wrap. But once you open it up for a closer look, you realize it smells."

"God, Quinn!"

"All right, a stupid metaphor. It's what came to mind. All I'm trying to say is you are all worried about bringing this project in for a smooth landing, but it's too big and clumsy to be anything but a bumpy road."

"Hold on a sec," Brad laughed, "I'm trying to sort through all of your metaphors."

"Listen, Green Valley is a huge, controversial project for a small town. Smart, committed people are already lining up. Whatever you do, and however it turns out, you're going to make enemies. Santa Ynez isn't going to be cute and cuddly for a long time. Remember your oath of office. Do your best to be fair and let the chips fall where they will. They will, anyway.

"Thanks, Quinn. One more thing?"

"Shoot," O'Rourke said obligingly.

"Are you hiring?" Brad asked, only partially in gest.

20

"See the paper this morning?" Jane asked ominously, as Brad walked into the office on Tuesday morning.

"No, I went for a jog and was going to read it here. What are our friends in the Fourth Estate up to now?"

"Making trouble for you, I'm afraid," she said, pointing to a front page article. The headline said, "Green Valley EIR Set For Approval."

"What the hell?" he cried.

"I think the article itself is fine. Just the headline."

He stood at her counter and skimmed the article. It noted that the Planning Commission was due to get a briefing tonight on the Initial Study prepared by city staff to determine the scope of the EIR study. Blah, blah, blah.

"Same old problem," he said. "The people who write the stories don't usually write the headlines. The headline makes it look like the whole EIR is up for a vote tonight, not just a discussion of the scope of study. This is really going to stir things up for the Planning Commission tonight."

"Do you want me to get the publisher on the phone for a correction?"

"I guess not. I don't ask for a formal correction every time I see something in the paper that's off. I agree with Mark Twain, 'Never pick a fight with people who buy ink by the barrel.' Besides, the damage is done for tonight. Why don't you at least call the reporter so she can pass out better information if the paper gets calls about this today? I better call the Council to give them the heads up. Will you call Megan and make sure she sees it? She might want to call the commission and prepare them for a big crowd tonight."

*****

The Tuesday staff meeting was uneventful, even jovial. They went over the draft agenda for next week's Council meeting, as usual. Then Brad tried an experiment. He asked Megan to summarize the Green Valley Initial Study and Dee to cover the water section. The other department heads played Planning Commissioners. It was by far the largest project in Santa Ynez's twenty-year history. It warranted spending some time to do a dry run of the IS presentation tonight, especially in light of the likely crowd.

Based on the department heads' questions and comments, Brad gave direction to Dee and Megan about areas to explain more thoroughly and even some exact wording to use regarding water supply. Quinn O'Rourke's warning about over-managing the situation rang in his head. Nevertheless, he re-emphasized to Megan, in front of the entire group, to let Dee discuss any issues related to water supply.

Dee Sharma followed him back to his office after the staff meeting. "I have the report from the independent lab that did the samples that Chip Geis was supposed to be doing. And I have Payton/Carlisle's estimate on tertiary treatment."

"What's the cost look like?"

"Remember, you wanted the best we could get by noon today. They said to use $5.4 million as a rough estimate for now. They could give you a more precise number if you give them time to meet with us to go over the project plans and look at our water quality reports to nail down the treatment process."

"That's not far off what SoCal thought," Brad said. "I was hoping they were blowing this whole thing out of proportion."

"No. I wish I had been consulted about the whole tertiary alternative before she sent out the IS. I would have argued it was overkill. I have to believe Megan knew it would present a big obstacle for the project and put it in there to cause trouble."

Brad didn't take the opening to join in the Megan bashing. Early in his career he had been warned against speaking ill about a department head to another department head. It builds mistrust. He shifted the discussion back to Dee's domain.

"What about the lab report?"

"We dodged a bullet on that one, Brad," chirped the public works director.

"Are you saying that the samples show everything is good? I was thinking about that ridiculous water quality report we have to mail out to everybody once a year. Nobody but a chemist can understand it. Everybody else throws it away and bitches about how wasteful it is to send it out. But if we had to send out a revised version because of some problem, *that* would sure get everyone's attention. So, everything's good, huh?"

"Yes. No problems to report. The test did show a spike in iron at Well #2, the one we bought from Nettlers. But it's below the MCL."

"MCL?"

"Maximum Contaminant Level. It's a health standard set by the feds and state for drinking water. We are below the MCL for iron, so we don't have to do any special reporting or treatment. Iron isn't a health issue, anyway."

Dee's calming assurances didn't seem to match his body language. Brad's BS meter kicked on. "What's the problem with too much iron then?"

"Oh, nothing much, really. We need iron in our bodies. People take iron supplements." His smile was too tight.

"What's the problem?" Brad pressed.

"Oh, some customers closest to that well might get a little metallic taste of it, and, if it gets bad enough, there can be staining on laundry, dishes, and plumbing fixtures. It's common in the unincorporated areas to have high iron in their wells. Water from rainfall seeps through soils and rock with iron in it and gets dissolved into the water table. It's natural. You can't avoid it."

Brad thought for moment. "Have you been getting complaints about iron?"

"A few," Dee said. "We get taste complaints once in a while. Of course, some people imagine things being in the water that just aren't. And we still have people who swear the fluoride we add for dental health is killing them. But our water is very good." Dee leaned back in his chair, as if that should be the final word.

Brad's BS meter started to ping. "What about stain complaints? Are you getting those, too?"

"Some," Dee said vaguely. "Probably associated with that higher iron reading at Well #2. Well #1 doesn't show a spike."

"What could cause that all of a sudden from one well?" Brad asked impatiently.

"The most likely thing is that the water table is dropping from the drought. And, remember that we had to give Nettlers unrestricted connection to Well #2? It looks to me that they have a lot more of their land planted in alfalfa for their cattle business. They could be drawing down the well much more than in the past, and the strata we are now drawing from has some different constituents, including higher iron, than we get at #1."

"What's the worst that can happen?" Brad asked.

"If the well doesn't go back to drawing from a better strata and the iron builds up at our customers' homes, they can experience on-going staining and their dishwashers and sprinklers could clog."

"What can we do about it?" Brad was getting nervous.

"You can treat the wells to remove most of the iron. Right now we just give the wells a little shot of chlorine and fluoride and put it right into the distribution system. Adding an iron treatment process would be expensive. We might be better off just abandoning the well and drilling a new one."

"What if the entire aquifer gets too high in iron and Well #2 is just a harbinger of things to come? We just had these big studies of our water supply and are telling the public we have plenty of water for them and Green Valley. Your comment about the water table sounds like what Megan was worried about. I'm trying to understand if we need to send a different message to the public on water availability for Green Valley based on this."

"I don't think that's necessary at all, Brad. We'd just be inviting more trouble. All we need is some good rain years. That should bring the water table back up to where it was when iron wasn't an issue. I wouldn't abandon a well or spend a ton of money right now just because a few people don't like the taste of their water or see some rust stains in their sink. We'd be better off buying some bottled water and Bon Ami for the hardcore complainers." He laughed, but Brad thought it was a nervous laugh.

He leaned forward and looked Dee straight in the eyes. "Is that it?"

Dee cleared his throat and looked down at the report in his lap. "Oh, the lab did pick up an elevated chromium reading. But it's below the MCL, too."

"That's comforting, I guess. Tell me about chromium."

"Chromium-3 is an essential element in our diet. It's in many of the foods we eat. Chromium-6 is toxic. The chromium-6 did show a jump since the samples taken before Geis was hired and they're higher than Well #1. No big deal since they're still below the MCL," Dee added hastily. "Again, we only have to report it as a problem if it exceeds that."

Brad felt rising panic. "This place leaks like a sieve, Dee. *You* know that." Brad glared at Dee. "The problems at the plant are going to come out once the discipline gets appealed to the Council. If we have a looming problem at the well, especially with something toxic, people are going to freak. We need to get ahead of that."

"The discipline actions won't get imposed and be to the Council for weeks," Dee said, still appearing unfazed. "We have time to study the iron and chromium problem, so we'll be in a better position to address it. If we bring it up now, while the whole Green Valley IS is being hotly debated, without having more facts, it's going to really fan the flames. Both sides will go nuts if it seems like there's a question on the reliability of our current water sources, when it probably will turn out to be fine."

Brad saw the dilemma and frowned.

"Like I said, Brad, iron isn't a health issue and the chromium-6 is within healthy range. I sure wouldn't want *us* to alarm people about it right now. It will just get everyone unnecessarily panicked. That won't be good for either of us."

Brad saw the fear in his public works director. It hit close to home. "I suppose you're right," he said, resignedly. "Stay on it and keep me informed." He thought a moment. "And no sense rushing the Skelly process right now. We have people on paid administrative leave, but that's a cheap price to buy some time on the water quality issues before the appeals hit Council and things go public."

"Good deal," Dee said, clearly relieved when he left.

Brad stood, pondering, then sat down heavily, stewing over what Quinn O'Rourke said about paying attention to his oath of office. Had he just participated in a cover-up of important information the public had a right to know? He thought of the LA aqueduct and the dam disaster, a betrayal of the public's confidence. Had anyone in the Pat Brown administration carried any remorse for the deception used to sell the State Water Project to the public? Or, more likely, given the times, they believed that the project was so vital to the state that getting it built was the overriding public interest; the end justifying the means. Was he putting the Green Valley Village project into that category?

*****

Driving home for lunch, Brad looked up at the Santa Ynez Mountains to the west, toward Ronald Reagan's former home, Rancho Del Cielo, overlooking the Pacific Ocean. From out of nowhere, he recalled the former President's saying, "trust, but verify." It had been one of Reagan's signature lines, describing his approach to the former Soviet Union at the end of the Cold War. He picked up his cell phone and left a message for Quinn O'Rourke.

*****

Brad was dictating a memo to Jane after lunch when the phone rang. She looked up at him, questioningly. He nodded, and she got up to answer from his phone. He hated to have people go to voicemail, or worse, those damnable phone trees.

She hit the hold button and held out the receiver with a questioning look. "Quinn O'Rourke."

"Oh, good," he said, moving to his desk. She started to leave but he gestured for her to sit down again. He covered the receiver and whispered, "This won't take long."

He briefed O'Rourke on the problems at the water plant, the pending disciplinary hearings, and the recent lab reports on Well #2. Jane looked up from her pad with a blank face.

"My public works director wants to keep the problems bottled up, no pun intended, for as long as possible, especially with the Green Valley water studies so much in the public eye these days."

"I can see why he would," Quinn observed. "He's got to be worried about his own neck."

"So am I," Brad admitted.

"What can I do for you, Brad?"

Brad was looking at Jane as he spoke on the phone, seeking cues from her expression.

"Not sure. Maybe just verify what Dee said. He said the iron isn't a health issue. The chromium is, but the reading is within range, whatever that is. He says neither will likely result in having to abandon the well. He thinks some good rain may be all we need to get back to better water quality. At worst, there could be some additional treatment at the well that will be expensive, but can be done. He's got Western working on that scenario now."

"Sounds reasonable," O'Rourke said.

"I just wonder how much of Dee's advice is motivated by his fear of losing his job. If there is a real threat to health or our ability to serve

Green Valley, I don't want to get nailed later for downplaying it. I'll look pretty sleazy if it also comes out that I've directed Megan to stay out of the water discussion at the commission meeting tonight and let Dee handle it. People could make it look like I'm conspiring with Dee to silence her for Green Valley's benefit."

Jane raised her eyebrows.

"Gotcha," O'Rourke said.

"Here's the deal, Quinn. We're about to kick off the Green Valley EIR tonight. I feel caught between a rock and a hard place. If I bring out the water quality issue now, it's instant ammo for the opponents. It might push Simpson over the edge and make SoCal bail. If I don't mention it, and it turns out to be a major problem later, the public will accuse me of a cover-up for SoCal's benefit. Or, maybe even SoCal sues us for not disclosing it before they spent a lot more money on the entitlements."

"Remember my shit sandwich analogy? Looks like that's what you've got," O'Rourke said. "How can I help?"

Brad looked at Jane who had a worried expression. "I guess I'd like you to see what your folks say about iron and chromium. Is Dee right, and the worst thing is having to spend some money to treat it? What range of cost might we be talking about? I'd just like some independent check before I decide whether or not to disclose the well problems tonight."

Brad noticed that Jane was writing on her pad.

"Off the top," the consultant began, "based on what I've picked up around here, I think the iron spike isn't a big deal. But the chromium-6 could be a PR problem for you, even if it's below the MCL. I'm blanking on the name of that movie with Julia Roberts where she played a legal clerk researching water quality problems out in Hinkley, that small town in the Mojave Desert."

Brad knew instantly. "*Erin Brockovich.*"

Jane cocked her head and looked at him quizzically.

"That's it. It's based on a true story. Our firm did some work on that case for PG&E long before I started. Probably shouldn't say too much. But it's common knowledge that the Hinkley residents sued, alleging high rates of cancer resulting from chromium-6 from the cooling water PG&E used at a plant outside of town, then dumped into unlined ponds and canals where it perked into their groundwater. The case settled for $333 million, the largest settlement paid in U.S. history for a suit like that."

"Oh, great! Cancer. So we might be on the verge of poisoning people with industrial toxins?" He shook his head to Jane who grimaced.

"Nah," the consultant said calmly. "My understanding is that there are trace elements of arsenic, lead, chromium, and all kinds of other toxins in drinking water all over the state, and always has been. A lot of it occurs naturally, not the result of industrial pollution. If it's a low enough reading, it's not a problem. That exhausts my knowledge. Let's get the geniuses on it."

Quinn O'Rourke agreed to set up a conference call with his water quality experts and Dee tomorrow to get more facts. He promised to report back to Brad once they had time to consider the issues. Brad thanked O'Rourke for his help and returned to the dictation.

"Sorry about that, Jane. I'm playing whack-a-mole right now."

"So I heard. That *Erin Brockovich* movie was pretty scary. If Kay and her group get a whiff that there's anything wrong with the city water supply, she'll use it against Green Valley. Does Megan know about all of this?"

"I don't think so," Brad said. "It's not like Dee would ever confide in her about *anything*. And, frankly, I suspect if she did know, I'd have Kay calling me about it already." He bit his words. "I probably shouldn't have said that."

"Well, there does seem to be a direct pipeline there," Jane agreed. "What's your plan?"

"That depends on what I hear from Quinn and his people. I obviously won't cover anything up if there's a health and safety matter, or if it is a huge threat to our water supply. On the other hand, I don't want to be perceived as some Chicken Little yelling the sky is falling, if it isn't. I'm leaning toward keeping it close to the vest for now while we get more information."

"Sounds sensible," Jane said. "Green Valley is already controversial enough, so whichever way you go, you'll attract fire. Better to get your ducks in a row first. Are you going to tell Scott?"

"Not yet. No point in alarming him either. Besides, he'd be obligated to tell his boss who's already pissed off about the tertiary treatment study and threatening to pull the plug."

"Ouch," Jane said. "That would come back to bite you personally. And, like I said before, I was just getting you broken in." She forced a smile, but they both knew the truth she had spoken.

"Yes," he said soberly.

"Lean on me," she said. "Let me help you."

"Will do. I got to thinking PD and the fire marshal probably should be told about the headline so they can prep for a big angry crowd with bad information. Can you make the calls and make sure they coordinate their plans for covering the meeting tonight, just in case? I need to call the Council. And, Jane, I don't tell you often enough, but I really do appreciate all you do. Let's catch up soon on how things are going for you."

He finished dictating the memo, called or left messages with the councilmembers, and called Scott about the troublesome headline.

"That damned IS is the gift that keeps on giving," the developer moaned. "We're going to have Kay's people all cranked up thinking we're bypassing the EIR review process and going straight to approval."

"I've called all the councilmembers asking them to spread the clarification to their folks. Maybe it won't be so bad."

"Where are we with tertiary treatment, Brad?"

"Still waiting for a response from the city attorney. Don't know what we'll be able to do before the meeting tonight."

"Jeff's not going to like that," Scott warned. "Between this tertiary business and his perception that Megan is out to get us, he's beyond jumpy about Santa Ynez. I better go ahead with an idea I had to level the playing field and calm Jeff down. It's better if I leave you out of it.

*****

Far too much of the rest of the afternoon was spent straightening people out about the Planning Commission meeting that night. One upset woman called demanding to know how the city could be approving the EIR so soon. She claimed not to have seen the newspaper headline and it was obvious she wasn't too sure what an EIR was, anyway. She declined to say where she had gotten her information. Brad explained the misleading headline and the agenda for tonight's commission meeting. She ended up saying, "Oh. I guess I got worked up for nothing." Brad thought of Rosanne Rosanna Dana, who ended her ill-informed Weekend Update rants on *Saturday Night Live* with, "never mind."

*****

Brad was just getting ready to leave for the day when Jane put through a call from Councilman Landon.

"Thought I'd let you know that I just got back from picking up some tickets from Brian Brando at the Chamber," the councilman advised. "Kerry and Scott were there, meeting in his office. They clammed up when I poked my head in to say 'hi.' I made a little crack about how they looked so conspiratorial. They kinda just looked

342

at each other. Then Scott said, 'just getting ready for the Planning commission meeting tonight. You can bet that the other side is doing the same thing."

"I'm sure he's right about that," Brad said.

"Uh huh. But then Brando made a crack about doing some damage control and 'evening the odds' tonight. Scott said, 'we should probably keep Al out of this.'"

"Hmmm," Brad mused, trying to appear nonplussed. "Wonder what that was all about?"

21

Brad settled back in his favorite family room chair and switched the cable box to channel seventeen, the government access channel, just before 7 p.m. The screen displayed the city logo and announced the City of Santa Ynez Planning Commission meeting at 7 p.m. He killed some time looking through the channel guide for later in the evening.

He went back to seventeen a few minutes later. The sound wasn't on yet. The camera at the rear of the City Council Chambers showed people in every seat, lining the walls, and sitting in the aisles. Some were waving signs. He suspected that the crowd spilled out to the lobby and, possibly, even outside. His pulse quickened. He could see Chairman Parker Fleischman standing behind the dais with Commissioner Jerry Wright, Planning Director Megan Cain, and City Attorney Henry Fitzhenry. The pow-wow eventually broke up and everyone took their seats.

The sound came on, revealing the background hubbub that comes with a roomful of stirred up people. Chairman Fleishmann banged the gavel and called the room to order.

"Ladies and gentlemen, welcome to the Planning Commission meeting. We don't often see so many of our citizens here. Unfortunately, the fire marshal has advised that we have exceeded the room's occupancy limit. However, he will not order a reduction in occupancy, so long as a few rules are observed. First, people are not to block the exit from the Chambers to the lobby and from the lobby outside. Second, picket signs that could pose a trip hazard in the event the room had to be evacuated will be picked up. I'm asking representatives from both sides of the Green Valley issue to gather them up now and pile them on the floor in front of the commission dais so they will be out of the way of the exits. You can pick them up afterwards."

Several people popped up and began collecting the signs. As that was going on, Chairman Fleishmann continued.

"And this point I emphasize, everyone is to exercise proper decorum. No shouting, applauding, or similar demonstration either for, or against, anything that will be said tonight. Anyone who violates this protocol and disrupts these proceedings will be removed."

"Sieg heil!," someone yelled from the back of the room. Many in the audience turned around to see who it was.

Brad stiffened in his chair.

Chair Fleishmann acted decisively. "That's exactly the kind of behavior that will not be tolerated. The police are on the way and will keep order. Now, it's obvious that almost all of you are here for the Green Valley Village Initial Study presentation. And, maybe by now, you understand that the newspaper headline this morning was wrong. The EIR is *not* up for a hearing tonight. We planned to have a staff presentation on the Initial Study only tonight. That just talks about what will be studied in the EIR. I repeat, the EIR is not up for vote tonight. The draft report hasn't even been prepared yet."

The camera showed people in the audience talking to each other. Many held confused expressions. Others seemed angry or suspicious that a fast one was being pulled.

The chairman pressed ahead. "We have people here who have paid and waited a long time to have their projects on the agenda for consideration tonight. My concern is, with so many people here who might want to talk about the Green Valley project, we might not get to the other applicants until very late. So, if my colleagues concur, since you are all here now about Green Valley, we will go ahead tonight with a staff presentation of the Initial Study. I think that will address a lot of the misunderstanding people have from the unfortunate newspaper headline this morning. Rather than opening the matter for a hearing, I'd like to propose a special session for this Thursday to receive public comment before we take action on the Initial Study. That way we will be able to address the action items tonight before our normal 10 p.m. cutoff. Is that acceptable to the commission?"

"We're here now! Don't stall!" shouted another angry voice that apparently came from audience left.

Chairman Fleishmann slammed the gavel. "Can the rest of the commission make it for a special meeting Thursday at seven for public comment on the Green Valley IS?"

With concurrence, Chairman Fleishmann asked everyone to stand and remove their hats as he led them in the Pledge of Allegiance, followed by a moment of silence. After everyone was seated again, the chairman asked the planning secretary to call roll. Everyone was present. The next item was Approval of the Agenda. The chairman said, "The chair will entertain a motion to revise the agenda to move the Green Valley Village Initial Study presentation, item H-1, to item F."

"So moved," one of the commissioners said.

"Second," said another.

"All in favor, say aye." They voted quickly and unanimously.

Brad checked his commission packet and saw that this put Green Valley ahead of the scheduled public hearings and Business from the Floor, the latter being an opportunity for anyone to speak for two minutes about anything not on the agenda. With such a big crowd, and emotions already running high, that would be fraught with peril. Better to thin the crowd out first. He looked up from his packet to see a uniformed police officer enter the room from the rear door behind the dais and walk directly behind the planning director and city attorney, who Brad assumed were briefing him on the ground rules for the evening. Officer Crombie was a perfect choice for this assignment. He was a big, imposing, authority figure with a friendly demeanor.

The chairman noticed Officer Crombie also and seemed to relax a little. "Is there a motion to approve the minutes?"

"So moved."

"Second."

"All in favor, say aye."

"Unanimous," the chairman announced. "We'll now take up item F."

A male voice from the audience shouted, "Yeah, 'F' for fucked up!"

Parker Fleishmann nodded at the officer. The rear camera picked him up walking back to the audience, gesturing to the offender to get up, then walking him out of camera view. The chairman waited for the message to sink in.

"We aren't kidding here, folks. We have a full agenda we need to get through tonight. And we will observe proper decorum. I know some people feel strongly about this project. But this is a democracy and we are all neighbors. Let's respect each other's right to speak without commotion. You'll have a chance to address us on Thursday.

I'll now ask the planning director to present the Green Valley Village Initial Study. Ms. Cain?"

Planning Director Megan Cain conducted a PowerPoint presentation on the staff's recommendations regarding the issues to be studied in the Green Valley Village Environmental Impact Report. The audience sat quietly, except for a few unattributed cat calls. Officer Crombie was back standing behind the staff table scanning the audience from side to side with a businesslike expression. Brad made a mental note to send one of his formal "Atta Boy/Girl" notes to the police chief about Crombie. He had already shown he would respond quickly to a disturbance, while being relaxed, not hard-assed.

Megan started through the alphabetical listing of environmental issues. After touching upon Aesthetics, Agricultural and Forest Resources, then Air Quality, Chairman Parker Fleishmann interrupted her. "Megan, most of this is standard stuff. And, since we are going to be going through it again on Thursday, I'm going to ask you to move through this more quickly so we can get to the other items on the agenda."

"Let her talk!" a woman yelled. The camera operator switched from the shot of Megan to a wide angle view of the audience from behind the dais. The officer was already on his way up the aisle on audience left. A woman stood up and pulled a small picket sign from under her topcoat that said, "Wine Not Houses!" She seemed to be ignoring the officer's command to come with him until he squeezed by a few seated people and gently clutched the woman's arm and whispered something in her left ear. She immediately put down her sign and was escorted out of camera view. Brad thought of the officer in Santa Paula in 1928 who said something that finally convinced the mostly Spanish-speaking crowd on the bridge to take off just before it disintegrated in the flood.

Brad could see people in the audience whispering to each other. The chairman held a somber visage and resumed. "I will clear the audience if we keep having these interruptions. Please continue, Megan."

People whispered to each other.

The planning director picked up the pace on the other issues in the Initial Study. Megan was wrapping up the Transportation and Traffic section. Brad saw that Utilities and Service Systems was next up. He turned up the volume and hit "Record" on his remote control.

Megan quickly covered the wastewater portion of this section, noting simply that there is adequate capacity in the city's wastewater plant to accommodate the estimated demand from the project, as well as the build-out of the rest of the General Plan area. So far, so good.

"Public Works Director Dee Sharma will discuss the water portion of this section," she said, without further explanation. She leaned forward, snapped off her microphone button, and leaned back in her chair, rocking with her arms folded, clearly piqued. Brad winced and turned up the volume.

Dee was seated at a table in front of the commission dais with his back to audience right. He, too, used PowerPoint slides that summarized the Western and Payton/Carlisle reports. The camera behind the commission dais had a wide shot that showed Dee in the center of the frame and also picked up audience members seated behind. Scott Graves was in the shot, in the front row, just over Dee's right shoulder. Brad kept his eyes on the developer who was paying close attention to what Dee said, nodding continuously.

The camera switched from the screen where the slides were projected to a close-up of the public works director. There must have been some audience reaction to his presentation. He could hear Chairman Fleishmann hit his gavel and issue another warning off camera.

Dee wrapped up. "In conclusion, we have enough water to serve the Green Valley Village project and the rest of the General Plan area, and still have an adequate surplus. There's a comment here that asks if the commission thinks it's necessary to keep an even bigger water surplus. If you do, the possibility of requiring tertiary-treated water for the golf course and landscaped areas could also be studied in the EIR. But only if *you* think it's necessary. This is not a staff recommendation to do that."

Brad squirmed in his chair. That wasn't exactly what had been scripted.

Dee went on to give a short description of tertiary treatment. He ended it by noting it was a very expensive process, similar to bringing the city's treated effluent from the end of the wastewater plant up to drinking water standards.

The camera switched to a shot of the full commission. The chairman hit a button in front of him and recognized Megan Cain. The camera operator must have been distracted as the live shot being sent out was still of the public works director, not Megan. Dee, along with Scott Graves, Kerry Smith, and Chamber CEO Brian Brando looked warily in Megan's direction.

Off camera, Megan said, "I believe what the public works director *meant* to say is that you can reach different conclusions about water supply and demand. These two studies showed there *could* be a surplus with this project, but the staff thinks the commission should decide if it's enough of a surplus, and if tertiary treatment should be studied for the golf course, parks, streetscape landscaping, *and* the residential front yards. It's a water conservation measure being done all over the state."

The camera showed Dee Sharma frown and shake his head. Behind him, Scott sat up rigidly, staring first in Megan's direction, then at the back of the public works director's head as if trying to bore into his brain. Brad thought he saw Scott say something under his breath and Dee nod slightly.

Without asking for the chairman's permission to speak, the public works director responded testily, "The water supply and demand figures used in these studies came from consultants who are experts in this field. They rely on their lengthy experience and knowledge of industry standards, just like they did for wastewater, drainage, traffic, and everything else that gets studied in an EIR. Of course, since we are talking about projections, there is always room for some differences in interpretation. However, the point is that both studies showed we have an adequate surplus of water to serve this project."

"Bullshit!" was heard over the microphones. The chairman banged the gavel again. Officer Crombie was back in view moving down the aisle on the audience left as a reminder of his presence. He carried a slightly sterner look that said, "don't mess with me." The camera was still on Dee who stiffened at the outburst and glared in Megan's direction.

The chairman punched a switch on his light panel. "Commissioner Wright?"

Jerry Wright looked out in Scott Graves's direction, above the audience, as if searching. Brad thought it looked affected. "I'm a little confused about what I've just heard," the commissioner began, still looking to the audience. "Ms. Cain, does the Initial Study conclude we have enough water to serve the project, or not?"

The operator switched to the front camera for a side angle shot of Megan Cain sitting there, obviously mulling her response, as the seconds clicked by. "I think that question needs to be directed to the public works director," she said, in a monotone.

Commissioner Wright leaned forward. "I *will* ask Mr. Sharma, but right now I'm asking *your* opinion, Ms. Cain. This commission relies on your judgment all the time. I'd like to know what that is."

More seconds went by. "Go ahead, Megan!" someone yelled. The chairman rapped his wooden gavel on the dais again. The camera showed a shaken Megan Cain. After a few more seconds of painful silence, she looked down at the papers in front of her, as if reading a prepared statement, and said, "I've been directed to turn over questions about water supply to the public works director."

The microphones picked up the background rumbling of the crowd. Brad's gut tightened. He had just been brought onto the battlefield.

"Bullshit!" the same male voice yelled again. This time Officer Crombie could be seen walking purposefully back to the rear of the audience, just out of view of the camera. Heads moved with him.

Commissioner Jerry Wright still had the floor. "Sleazeball!" Brad grumbled to the TV screen. Wright was the reason they had to create the word "smarmy." He was a political operative for hire. He played the big shot at civic events, often making large donations to popular causes on behalf of his biggest client, the local Indian resort casino, as if the money came from his own generosity. He fancied himself as a smooth PR professional. Brad's assessment was that Wright's only skill was cultivating and hyping his own connections to local businesses and politicians. A varied list of clients paid Wright a small retainer, in hopes that by association with his client list, they might pick up a little more local clout. Brad had been delighted to see Wright get his comeuppance in the last Council election when, despite business community backing, he failed to pick off either incumbent, Kay Nance or Gretchen Schmitz. In fact, Gretchen had filleted him at a candidates' night sponsored by the League of Women Voters. Brad had heard that Wright was the originator of the Megan "Cain't" slur.

"Ms. Cain," Commission Wright said, "I can see that you are biting your tongue. And I don't want to put you in an awkward position."

"Like hell, Jerry!" Brad barked again at the TV screen. Wright had tangled for years with Megan. His Council race included slogans like "Let's make City Hall work for people again." Presumably, his clients. It was no secret to his supporters and detractors alike that he had no use for the planning director.

"So, I'm not going to ask you the details about the water issue. I understand that the public works director is the expert in that area, anyway." Wright smiled for the camera. "But you said tertiary treatment is being done all over. My understanding is that it's such an expensive process, it's only being done where the water supplier doesn't have enough potable water. Isn't that right?"

"I haven't done a survey on it, Commissioner Wright," Megan replied. "But. . ."

"Oh?" he interrupted, raising his eyebrows in mock surprise.

"But," Megan continued, "I'll stand by my statement that tertiary treatment is an increasingly common practice to conserve water. I think that's pretty obvious, Commissioner."

The commissioner still looked out to the audience. "But you don't have any facts to support what you're talking about, do you, Megan? And you haven't disputed my contention that the only places using tertiary are those that don't have adequate water supplies; which both you and the public works director have already said isn't a problem in Santa Ynez. That's what seems obvious to me."

The camera switched to the young department head who was staring bullets back at Jerry Wright. "I said I didn't do a survey, Mr. Wright, on how many cities have tertiary treatment. But I know it's a growing trend in a state with so many water problems. Planning conferences often have presentations on what other cities are doing with tertiary, desalination, and recharge basins. As to the expense, yes, tertiary treatment would be considered a major condition of approval if it ends up being required. That's obvious, Mr. Wright," her voice dripping with sarcasm. "The cost estimates would come out of further study if the commission opts for that alternative to be considered in the Draft EIR. I would argue that it's a prudent study to do, given how critical water supply is for our city and the statewide issues that threaten it."

There was a smattering of applause which the chairman gaveled down. Brad slammed the arms of his chair. Stop, Megan!

Commissioner Wright still held the floor. He shifted his attention to Dee Sharma. "Now, Mr. Public Works Director, you are responsible for ensuring that infrastructure like streets, water, and sewer that will be analyzed in the EIR will be sufficient, correct?"

The camera switched to Dee Sharma who appeared to sit up a little straighter. "Yes, Commissioner Wright."

"And I know, Mr. Sharma, that you have been doing this kind of work for Santa Ynez for many years, and for other cities for many years before that. Isn't that correct, too?"

"Yes, sir."

"And, I suspect, Mr. Sharma, that like any other department head, you'd like to have more of everything in a perfect world. Just like the Police Department would like more officers on the street and the Parks and Recreation director would like more parks. You'd like more traffic capacity and water, too, wouldn't you?"

"Of course," Dee said flatly.

"But, it's a matter of balance, isn't it Mr. Sharma? Somewhere in the design of public services, the taxpayers or ratepayers need to be considered. You don't push for unreasonably expensive service levels or facilities if they aren't needed. It's not that you wouldn't love to have more and better, it's just that you have a responsibility to not overburden the people who will pay the bill, right?"

"Yes," Dee said again. "You're right, it's a balance."

"Hmmm," the commissioner said, looking down the dais to his

right and left. "I apologize to my colleagues for these questions. It's just that this tertiary treatment study seems to be the biggest issue we are being asked about. From what I've heard, it is such an expensive option that, if it is required, it could kill the project. Before we even start down that road, I think we should hear from the person most responsible for ensuring adequate water."

"Proceed," said the chairman.

"Now, Mr. Sharma, as I understand what you said a little while ago, after two separate consulting reports, the Initial Study concludes that we can serve the Green Valley Village project and the rest of the General Plan area and still have a water surplus. And I believe that you labeled that surplus 'adequate.' Not 'abundant' or 'excessive', but 'adequate,' in keeping with your responsibility to achieve a reasonable balance. Is that correct, Mr. Public Works Director?"

"Yes."

"Mr. Sharma, as the city expert in these matters, in your professional opinion we have enough water to serve the project and the rest of the General Plan build-out and still have an *adequate* surplus left over. And it's not good public policy to require taxpayers and ratepayers to pay for expensive public services that aren't absolutely necessary. So, I'm confused, Mr. Sharma. Why, then, are you recommending that tertiary treatment even be studied in the EIR?"

Brad heard the background noise spike from angry voices. It seemed to come from both sides of the audience. Commissioner Jerry Wright smiled in a pose reminiscent of a congressman at a nationally televised committee investigation grilling a hapless witness.

The chairman again restored order with a few raps of his well-used gavel and said, "Folks, I'm going to wrap this up. We aren't going to decide anything tonight, and we'll have a public meeting this Thursday when everyone can talk. But since Commissioner Wright asked a direct question, I'll let the public works director respond.

Mr. Sharma, the question was, why are you recommending tertiary treatment be studied if you think the city has ample water to serve the project?"

The camera switched back to Dee who was looking down, reading something. After a moment, he looked up to the commission and said, "To be more clear, the IS doesn't *recommend* that tertiary treatment be studied. It just raises the issue that it is a technique for stretching water supply if the *commission* thinks there should be an even greater after-project surplus."

"Since I haven't yielded the floor," Commissioner Wright pressed, "it doesn't make sense to me, Mr. Sharma, that you'd be asking us that question. You are the professional expert being paid to make that decision, aren't you? Are you asking because you aren't sure? Or is this just too controversial and you want the commission to decide it for you?"

Brad braced himself. This was hitting Dee right in his most vulnerable spot, his professional competence and ability to defend his arguments, without coming unglued.

"No, Mr. Wright!" the public works director erupted. "We will have a large enough surplus of water even after the project without going to the expense of tertiary treatment. The facts support that."

"Thank you, Dee," the commissioner said, with a satisfied smile. Then, as if an after-thought, "Gee, Dee, I guess I'm still confused. As our expert in utility capacities, why did you even include the idea of a tertiary treatment study at all, if you don't think it's necessary?"

"Yeah! Why?" yelled someone from audience right.

"*I* didn't!" exclaimed a clearly exasperated Dee Sharma.

Behind the camera shot of the public works director, Brad could see Brian Brando, the Chamber CEO, nudge Scott Graves with his elbow.

Commissioner Wright affected a quizzical mien. "Well, then, Mr. Sharma, can you tell us how that tertiary idea got in there and why? Who wrote that part, Dee, if it didn't come from you?"

The camera switched back to the public works director who looked like he had just guzzled colonoscopy prep. After a loud silence, he said, "The Planning Department wrote the Initial Study report and added the tertiary treatment study concept. I suggest you ask the planning director."

It sounded to Brad that the noise level had spiked again. There were no shouts this time. The camera showed people whispering to their neighbors in anticipation of the drama that was about to unfold. He also noticed that a second police officer had now joined Officer Crombie.

Suddenly, a tall, thin, bearded, middle-aged man with his hair pulled back on top and braided down his back, stood in the third row of audience left pointing at Commissioner Wright. "You know God damned good and well who wrote that, Jerry. She's trying to protect this city from people like you and Public Works who are in SoCal's pocket!" Brad recognized him as a potter who went by the name "Noble." Noble shared co-op gallery space with Councilwoman Kay Nance.

Brad saw a man he knew was a Chamber Ambassador, but wasn't sure of his name, stand up from the other side of the audience, point his finger at Noble, and say something harsh that the television didn't pick up. It must have been spicy, since other people on both sides of the aisles also stood up. Both officers took up positions in the center aisle, motioned for everyone to sit, and pointed forcefully at Noble and the Chamber Ambassador to come with them. Noble seemed to balk. Officer Crombie put his big left arm around to the back of his Sam Browne belt toward his handcuffs, and held it there a moment for emphasis. Noble left with him without struggle.

From off-camera came the voice of Megan Cain, Planning Director. "Chairman Fleishmann, I would like to respond to Commissioner Wright." She didn't wait to be officially recognized.

"*I* wrote the section about tertiary treatment. That's the 'who.' As to the 'why', it's because of what I said before. Reasonable people can come to different conclusions about water supply and demand. We had one consultant report that said one thing. We got a second opinion that was more conservative. In *my* opinion, even the second opinion was too optimistic. They came up with a 12 percent surplus after the project, which leaves very little room for contingencies. I continue to question several of the assumptions about how much water the future residents and landscaping will use, along with how reliable our current water sources will be twenty-plus years out. The second report that was more conservative didn't even address all of the statewide efforts underway to protect the environment, which will likely result in there being *less*, not more, water for the city in the future."

"But, Megan," Commissioner Wright tried to interrupt.

She spoke over the top of him. "I think that if you were to get an independent assessment of the situation from a consultant who really had their finger on the pulse of all the truly troubling problems facing water supply in California, we'd be much more interested in conserving what we have now. In that light, having tertiary treatment to retain more of our precious potable water is good planning. We don't know what tertiary treatment costs with any precision yet, but it's being done all over, and the developer hasn't presented any concrete evidence that requiring it would be unfeasible. That's why I think it should be studied."

Brad could hear a mixture of loud applause and hoots. His stomach was in knots. His heart raced.

The wide angle from the camera at the back of the room picked up the entire commission dais with the staff table at camera left. Commissioner Wright flicked on his microphone switch. "Commissioners, I think it's clear that there is an agenda being played out here. It's the same anti-development hysteria we have seen before from Planning."

Megan shot forward in her chair and flipped on her own microphone, speaking to the entire audience, not the commission. "*My* only allegiance is to the citizens and businesses of our city, both today, and in the future. If this project goes forward, and we end up not having as much water as some people think, it will impact everyone already here." She swept her arm across the audience. "*All* of you, not just the future residents of Green Valley, are going to suffer the consequences."

She turned her head in the direction of Commissioner Wright with her jaw set and eyes like blue lasers. "So, Jerry, you can try to spin this away from the serious water issues we face in this state and right here in Santa Ynez and try to make this about me. Since that, too, seems obviously to be *your* agenda. I don't care. I'm used to it. But as long as I'm here, I'm going to give this commission and this city the best advice I can, even if it's not what you and your clients want to hear." She smacked off her mic switch, held her head up, and stared straight ahead.

The audience erupted. It sounded at home like the loud applause and cheers of the project opponents drowned out whatever the project supporters were yelling. The rear camera showed Commissioner Wright snarling something back at the planning director that couldn't be heard over the din and the chairman's vigorous gavel-banging. After a few moments of trying and failing to restore order, Chairman Fleishmann shouted into his microphone, "I'm declaring a fifteen-minute recess. There will be no more discussion tonight about the Green Valley project. We will resume our normal agenda in fifteen minutes."

The camera operator was on the ball. He muted the sound in the Chambers as soon as the chairman rose. The rear camera stayed on the dais and front part of the audience. The chairman and another commissioner hustled out the rear door. One stood at her place, surveying the scene. Three, including Commissioner Wright, moved out to greet people in the audience. Brad noticed that Scott Graves and Kerry Smith met Wright halfway and shook his hand.

Brad kept his eyes on the silent screen, seeing what was happening in the Council Chamber. Twenty minutes passed. There were still people milling around talking and laughing. Some appeared to be arguing. The two officers were keeping the peace and ushering people out. After almost thirty minutes, the audience had thinned out considerably. The chairman was taking his seat and apparently calling his colleagues to do the same. Commissioner Wright still wasn't seated or in view.

The chairman banged the gavel as the sound came back on. He looked at his agenda and called Business from the Floor, reminding the audience that there would be no more comment about the Green Valley project tonight. Commissioner Wright entered the picture and took his seat, a contented look on his face.

"Is there anyone who wants to address the commission on any subject that is *not* on the agenda?" asked Chairman Fleishmann. "And, I repeat, we are not accepting any more comment about the Green Valley project. Please state your name, if you come up."

The rear camera picked up a local contractor named Joe Lopez approaching the podium. Lopez was a mainstay at all the Chamber events. He was normally genial but had a chip on his shoulder about government and was boisterous in his contempt for the City of Santa Ynez in general, the Planning Department, in particular, and Megan Cain't, even more specifically. Brad tried to avoid him as much as possible.

"My name is Joe Lopez." He looked ready to fight. "I make my living building in this community. I volunteer as an Ambassador with our Chamber of Commerce to promote bringing more business to the area." He scowled. "Based on what I heard tonight, we might as well abolish the Chamber. How can we possibly promote business, when you have a planning director who is so opposed to it? The Chamber has no confidence in the planning director. We urge this commission to fire her immediately." He spun around and walked off to the cacophony emanating from the audience.

The chairman once again resorted to the gavel. "Mr. Lopez, you are out of order. This commission has no jurisdiction over the hiring and firing of city staff. If anyone else is still here to deliver a similar message, I'd ask you to respect this commission and let us get on with the business we need to attend to. We have applicants who have paid money to have their projects discussed tonight and have had to wait a long time because of an erroneous newspaper article. I'm sure the business community wouldn't want to stand in their way by further delaying our proceedings with something we have no jurisdiction over anyway."

Parker Fleishmann hovered the gavel in the air. "Now, is there anyone else who wishes to address the commission on an item *not* on the agenda tonight and *not* involving Green Valley or the performance of city staff?"

"Yes," a voice boomed from the audience. The chairman glowered as Pat Kirby, the city's unofficial watchdog, rose in the front row, audience left.

As he approached the podium, the chairman asked, "is this an item that isn't on the agenda, isn't about staff performance, or Green Valley, Pat?"

"Yes, Parker," Kirby assured. He put a thick file down on the podium deliberately. "I have been a member of the Chamber of Commerce for twenty years and I denounce the statement that was just made by Joe Lopez. He doesn't speak for me or hundreds of other members. I would ask this commission to send a letter to the Chamber of Commerce asking them to also denounce Joe's statement as not being reflective of the Chamber's position and, further, recommending that they terminate his membership."

Kirby stood there proudly, waiting for a reaction. All he got was a quick gavel and a tired "you're out of order" from the chairman. Deflated, he returned to his chair. Chairman Fleishmann banged the gavel again to close Business from the Floor and called the next agenda item.

Brad changed channels. He had seen enough. The phone started ringing shortly afterwards.

22

"Kay's in there to see you." Jane said, as Brad walked slowly through the outer door Wednesday morning.

He took two quick whiffs and concurred. "Thanks," he said, loudly enough to be heard, "for the warning," he whispered.

Councilwoman Kay Nance was curled up in some sort of yoga position atop one of the chairs next to the window. Her eyes were closed and head upturned to capture the morning sunlight on her back. She had on something akin to a housecoat, or, maybe it was what women called a lounger. It had an oriental pattern, bright red, with big golden dragons. She looked like she had been up all night without bothering to clean up before coming over. Her long gray hair, which was normally tied in a braid, hadn't seen a brush in a while. It looked matted.

"Morning, Kay," he said, breathing through his mouth.

"You know she was set up, don't you?" Her eyes were still closed.

"Huh?"

She let out a long breath that seemed to originate from deep in her core and continued through closed eyes. "I had a little gathering at my house for the meeting. We all thought it was obvious. Last night was an orchestrated plan to get Megan fired. Scott laid it out and that prick, Jerry Wright, was his tool."

"Interesting theory. But why do you think they thought they could get her fired?"

She kept her eyes closed as a smile emerged. "I called Megan late last night. She was pretty down. She knew she was in trouble with you because you told her to stay out of the water discussion. We think Scott, Jerry, and the gang knew you had muzzled her. They hatched a plan to bait her into taking ownership of the issue and facing off against the project supporters."

"How did they know what direction I had given Megan about that presentation?" Brad asked, wracking his brain.

The councilwoman opened her eyes and shifted in the chair slightly so she could make full eye contact with Brad. "That's what we'd like to know." Her eyes locked on his.

He cocked his head and held up his hands defensively. "Wait a minute, Kay. If you are accusing me of talking to Scott and plotting with him to get rid of Megan, you are way off base!"

"We know you are supporting the project and are friendly with Scott. You know how strongly Megan feels and how tough she can be defending her positions. It's hard for us to imagine that you'd really expect her to just sit there quietly while Dee soft-peddles the project impacts. Some of my friends wondered if you were pressured into giving Megan marching orders you knew she couldn't ethically obey last night so you could fire her when she didn't."

"Absolutely not! Just the opposite," he protested. "My direction to her was designed to protect her, get her off the hot seat, not part of some grand plan to get rid of her."

They were both silent for a few moments holding eye contact. Brad was breathing rapidly, getting angrier by the moment.

"I have something for you." She reached over her head with both hands and removed her necklace. It was a leather cord with a piece of metal hanging down.

"It's the Chinese symbol of Forgiveness. I made it for you last night after everyone went home. Sliced my finger open in the process." She showed her bandaged index finger. "Fortunately, I had some pain numbing medicine on hand," she laughed. "I made this amulet to give you if I was convinced you weren't involved in getting Megan. I am satisfied you weren't, and ask that you forgive me for upsetting you."

He took it from her and examined it closely as it lay in his palm. In his nearly thirty years in public service, he'd never received a gift like this from a councilmember. Maybe they felt that approving his annual contract with an attractive compensation package was gift enough. It was even more special because the gift came from Kay's own hands and she had probably stayed up all night crafting it.

"It's very nice," he said. "Thank you."

"I'm sorry I accused you," she said, gathering her bulk and dismounting from the chair. "I didn't think you'd do that to her but I promised I'd ask. I hope the power of forgiveness is in you, for me *and* for Megan."

He sat speechless as Kay reached the door. Kay Nance was a piece of work.

*****

The newspaper story this morning about the commission meeting fanned the flames of controversy between the planning director and business community. He recalled a mentor once describing the press as bystanders who avoid the field of battle and, when the carnage is over, come rushing in to shoot all the wounded. He took the "no comment" route this morning when the City Hall reporter called for more dirt.

Mayor Buddy dropped in shortly after Councilwoman Kay Nance left. He demanded that Brad fire his planning director and call Scott Graves to apologize for her behavior. No, he hadn't seen the Planning Commission meeting himself, yet. Brad suspected that he had all the information he needed from his buddies at the coffee shop this morning. The mayor didn't care if Megan had been baited.

He didn't have to keep a log to know the anti-Megan sentiment was far more vocal than her defenders. "I appreciate you sharing your views, and I promise to take them into consideration moving forward," was his standard, get-off-the-phone response.

Councilman Landon had only heard about the meeting and came in to watch the DVD copy since it hadn't yet been uploaded to the city's website.

He came back to Brad's office afterwards. "It's pretty bad, Brad."

"Yeah, I'm disappointed."

"I hear that Hubie and the Chamber group are patting themselves on the back this morning that they finally got rid of Megan. It must have been what they were cooking up when I was at the Chamber yesterday. Is it true?"

"I think it's probably true they are crowing, but it isn't true she's been fired. I haven't even talked to her yet."

"If you do have to let her go, how does that affect tomorrow night's carryover meeting on the Initial Study?"

"I haven't thought about that yet," Brad said. "Other things on my mind right now."

Landon didn't attempt to influence Brad. Before he left, he simply put a hand on Brad's shoulders and said, "Remember, God is with you as you struggle with this difficult situation."

He felt himself relax slightly and thanked his boss. Two gifts from councilmembers already this morning.

Chamber CEO Brian Brando called later in the morning. "I hear you are thinking about letting Megan off the hook."

"Now where did you hear that, Brian?" These constant leaks and gossip were truly annoying. "Here's a deal, you tell me your source and I'll tell you the secrets behind the Warren Commission report on who killed Kennedy."

Silence in the receiver.

"Look, Brian, you know this is a personnel matter and I can't talk to you about it, right?"

"Yeah, I know. I just wanted to make sure *you* know that a lot of people have been frustrated dealing with Megan for years. Now she's really gone over the line. And people are watching *you* to see what *you* do."

"Thanks for that, Brian," Brad said, insincerely, and gave him the noncommittal response of the day, even though he considered the Chamber CEO a friend.

"While we're sharing rumors, Brian, I heard one about last night being a plan that you and Scott and Jerry Wright played out to get Megan fired." He waited.

"All I'll say is that you know she has been a pain to the business community for years. We aren't going to lower the flag to half-staff if you, in your awesome power, were to decide to send her packing. Hell, you'd probably be a lock for Grand Marshal of the 4th of July parade."

"You just helped me decide, Brian. I'm giving her a 10 percent raise. Thanks for the call."

Vice Mayor Tim Mullikin stopped in next. That, by itself, was unusual. Mullikin was a frequent visitor to the Police Department, where he would have coffee and chat it up with dispatchers and sworn staff where he used to work. But he seldom came to City Hall, unless he had to. Even though his position on the City Council stamped him as part of "the city," instead of "the Police Department," he still felt more comfortable hanging around with the PD. It was a recurring problem. After complaints by the Sheriff Department lieutenant designated as the city's police chief that Mullikin was undercutting his authority during his visits, Brad repeatedly had to gently counsel his boss.

The vice mayor was apparently tasked to deliver today's message, "All eyes are on *you*, now, Brad. Fire her!"

*****

Brad didn't want to listen to any more unsolicited advice. He called Megan and asked her to come over. He could hear her greet Jane as she walked in. Her head was held high as she strode a little too confidently into his office to her usual chair. They exchanged hellos, keeping up the pretext that this was a normal meeting.

Early in his career, he had to fire his secretary, after trying in vain for a year to get her performance up to snuff. He was nervous and tried to make it as painless as possible for her. He had hemmed and hawed so much that he heard from the personnel director later that day that the secretary was shocked when he called her to set up an exit interview. Lesson learned.

He came out from behind his desk and sat across from Megan. "I suppose you know I have to let you go."

"You 'have to' or you 'want to?'" she asked.

"I don't want to have to do this, Megan. I wish you had done what I asked you and this wouldn't be necessary. You chose to put yourself at the head of the storm. And now your objectivity is irreparably damaged."

"Brad, do you really think that what I said was wrong?"

"Not completely. As I told you before, I don't disagree with a lot of what you said about the need to preserve our water supply. Where you went wrong was disregarding what I told you about staying out of the water issue. I like and even admire you, but I can't let any department head get away with disobedience."

"I get that. You could give me a letter of reprimand or, maybe a week's suspension, to make that point. But I suppose that wouldn't appease the bloodlust out there for my hide."

"Megan, I've taken a lot of heat about you whether you know or care about that. I've counseled you when I thought you needed it, but generally felt you were keeping things between the lines. Last night you obliterated the lines. Like I told you before, I want Green Valley, and every other matter that comes before Planning, to get fair, objective treatment. If there's going to be arguments, they should be about the merits of the project, not the director's objectivity."

"Fred recorded the meeting last night and we watched it when I got home. It was all planned. I got fed up with Dee's misrepresenting the IS and sweeping the Green Valley impacts under the table. Oh, and, by the way, by *his* disobedience of what you told him to say. Seeing the signals passing between Scott, Dee, and Jerry Wright, I guess I'd

WITHOUT PURPOSE *of* EVASION

just had it. I've been fighting with some of these people since the day I started my planning career here."

He nodded his understanding. "I've always told people that the planning director's job is even more difficult than mine. You get it from both sides of a development application."

Seeing that as a tangent from the main point, he recovered. "Like I said, I am letting you go, but don't like having to do it. I'll give you the opportunity to submit your resignation. You can talk about how much you've enjoyed the experience here in Santa Ynez, the only planning job you've had, but now you want to pursue other interests. That sort of thing. I'll do a press release accepting your resignation, thanking you for your dedicated service to the city, and wishing you well in your new endeavors. *I* don't have a bloodlust to fire you."

"It won't fool anyone. Everybody will know I've been fired."

There was no denying that. He sweetened the pot. "I would also be willing to have a separation agreement, giving you three months' severance pay and continued health benefits, until your successor is on board, in exchange for your full liability release and assistance to staff on an on-call basis during the transition. But, if we are going that route, everything needs to be done by five today. I'm not going to get into a negotiation with some attorney over this. And, frankly, I don't think you want people on the Council getting wind of that offer, or I'll withdraw it."

She sat there quietly for a while until speaking softly. "It's like I told you Monday. Fred and I feel strongly that community development in California, and water policy, in particular, needs to change. We want to be change agents, not just go along with the same type of development that is spoiling this state. And, like I also told you, we are prepared to take whatever personal consequences come with that."

"I understand," Brad said solemnly. He thought again of Lilly's father who had made the personal decision to stomp on his principles in order to retain his job.

"I don't want to get an attorney. Look, it's going to take you a few months to get a replacement on board. And I don't need to keep the health benefits. Fred and I are getting married, and his health plan at the college is better than ours. How about five months' salary, no benefits?"

"Congratulations. I'm sorry if it took this situation to finally get him to the altar," Brad said.

"It was a contributing factor," Megan said. "I'm pregnant."

*****

City Attorney Henry Fitzhenry was at first reluctant to even work on the termination agreement without consulting his clients, the City Council. Brad painted a scenario that caused the barrister to see the value in an amicable separation even if it cost the city the five months of pay for the liability release. A young, attractive, and either very pregnant or nursing mother, her entire career spent with the City of Santa Ynez, annual evaluations that cite her work ethic and dedication, pushed out in what appears to be a conspiracy that likely involved members of the City Council. Even if the city prevailed in a wrongful discharge action, the attorney fees would be far more than the severance payment that was in the budget anyway. Fitzhenry went along.

Just before 5 p.m., when the resignation and agreement were executed, Brad started calling councilmembers to tell them what he'd done and to expect a press release in tomorrow's paper. It was a done deal. His decision to make. He wasn't asking their approval, just letting them know.

The Council's responses were all over the map. He took their feedback respectfully and argued his action as best he could. The most troublesome response came from Councilman Landon who said how unfortunate it all was. He said he would pray for both Megan and Brad. Then he added, "Maybe there's a lesson in this for you to exert stronger control over your department heads so things like this don't happen."

He slammed his receiver down.

*****

Weary and bone-tired, Brad suggested dinner at the Hitching Post in Buellton. He gave Dillon money for delivered pizza. He needed some private time to talk with his wife. On the way over in the car, he brought her up to date on his decision to terminate Megan and allow her to resign, in exchange for a separation agreement.

"She really gave me no choice. I hated to do it. But one good thing came out of it. I've united the Council. They're all mad at me, either for terminating her, or being too generous with the terms."

Over a glass of Chardonnay, Brad warned his wife that the war drums he had heard before in his career were beating again. The future of Green Valley Village project was uncertain at best. A lengthy entitlement process lay ahead, likely followed by intense political discord and legal battles. Even if it does get built someday, could he hang on long enough to retire as city manager and move in? What if he couldn't? With Kris still in grad school, and Dillon so excited about going to a college where they'd have to pay higher out-of-state tuition, he couldn't make it work by retiring as early as he was hoping. They might have to move, yet again, to a new city manager job.

They talked a while, trying to handicap the different scenarios. It passed time but was as futile as the golf analysts arguing passionately for Phil's, Jordon's or Rory's odds of winning the next major.

The conversation was interrupted by a cute, young waitress, whose nametag said "Kierra." She was carrying a tray holding two glasses of red wine.

"These are from that gentleman over there," she nodded to the booth area on the opposite side of the restaurant. Brad looked behind and to the right to see Hank Nettler smiling at them, a glass of red in his raised hand. He was with his father, Hubie. Brad thought of a favorite line for such times, "And I was all out of hand grenades."

"It's Vitus 2009 Reserve Cabernet," the waitress said with reverence. She looked at a piece of paper in her hand. "He said, 'here's to better days ahead.'"

Brad had several thoughts. He was cautious about not accepting gratuities to the point of being considered prudish by his colleagues. He might occasionally accept offers to join other public officials for a golf outing and nice dinner to follow, sponsored by the local public utility company, but he would hand over a personal check with a reasonable estimate of the value when he arrived. He knew others didn't. In this case, two glasses of wine didn't ping his ethical radar screen. On the other hand, he didn't feel like celebrating or accepting anything from a Nettler right now.

"What the hell," he said, quietly, taking the glass from the waitress. He raised his glass back at the Nettler table with the type of forced smile that comes from waiting too long for the photographer to click the shutter.

"Didn't take long for the word to get out about Megan, eh?" he said in disgust, holding his glass as if it contained hemlock. "I should have thrown it on the floor. The Nettlers must have been in on setting up Megan."

"Take it easy," Marie warned. "You said yourself that she brought this on herself. You did what you had to do. Besides," she smiled, swirling the glass in her long, thin fingers, "this is *really* good."

"It might as well be Two Buck Chuck, as far as I'm concerned," he snarled, still forcing a smile across the room through clenched teeth. Seeing the Nettlers at an out-of-town restaurant was unfair. There was no escape from his anxieties. His mind drifted to tomorrow night's public hearing on the project, which he had to staff himself.

Marie asked him a question that brought him back to the present.

"Sorry, hon, I wandered off for a minute."

"More than a minute, Brad. Heads up. Here come the Nettlers."

"Thanks for the wine," Brad said, half-heartedly, as the two men stood at their table.

"My pleasure, Brad," Hank replied, his rough voice contrasting with his smile. "I figured you finally earned your pay today. That woman has been a problem since she got here. We're all glad you got rid of her. Green Valley can move along now."

"It was not a fun day, Hank. I did what I had to do, that's all."

Hubie placed his massive hands on his hips. "Hey, buck up there, pardner. You look lower than a snake's belly in a wagon rut. It's just business. You had an injured animal on your hands."

Brad glared up at him.

Hank jumped in. "Listen, we just wanted to say hello. We don't need to talk business right now. Come on, Dad, let's leave these nice people alone." Then to Brad, "Let's get together for lunch sometime, Brad. Outside of Rotary, I mean. Are you sure I can't drop off a case of steaks and roasts for the family to try?"

Marie rescued him. "I'm sure we'd love them. Too much, I'm afraid. We need to eat lighter." Brad laced his hands over his plate, trying to block their view of his 15-ounce prime rib.

Marie raised her glass and added, "Thank you for this, though, it was lovely. Have a nice evening." She put her glass down and looked up.

The Nettlers got the message and said their goodbyes.

"Well played," he said, toasting her with Nettlers' wine.

23

Brad was reviewing a long letter from the boutique hotel developer Thursday morning when he heard Jane greet Scott Graves. He continued to read but kept one ear on what was happening outside his door. He strained to hear their muted conversation, interspersed with what sounded like bawdy laughter. Hmmm. He listened harder then threw the letter down and went to the door.

"Morning, Scott. Here to see me?" Brad asked.

Scott, who was leaning over the counter, straightened up instantly. "If you have a minute," the developer said. He had a manila folder in his hand.

Nobody ever took just a minute. "Come on in."

"Sorry, Brad, I couldn't warn you fast enough to get out through the window," Jane joked.

"You're fired," he teased and led Scott into his office.

When they were seated, Scott opened the folder slowly, pulled out a two-page letter, and reached across the table with it. "I'm glad

I was able to catch you rather than just dropping this off."

Brad was on guard. "Doesn't sound like fan mail."

"Not quite," the developer said. "This is a letter from Jeff Simpson. We went back and forth on it. I think it's a lot harsher than he means it to be, but he's the boss."

Brad was even more guarded. "What's it say?"

"It's addressed to the mayor and City Council directly. It just makes official what we've said before. Our engineers have penciled out the cost of tertiary treatment. They say it's closer to six-and-a-half million, with inflation, rather than the five-something million Dee used at the commission meeting. There's also some discussion and data about how the draft Development Agreement was predicated on the cost estimates from the project designs that were, in turn, based on the unit types and price points from the market research. The letter should give you what you need to find that tertiary doesn't qualify as a feasible alternative under CEQA, so that you can drop it from the EIR scope right now."

"That *could* be useful," Brad said neutrally.

"I thought you'd like *that* part of the letter, at least," Scott said. "I think the numbers on costs and the market are good. The part I wanted to warn you about is where Jeff talks about how we got into this project trying to do something of high quality for the community. He says we started down the road with the belief that we could make it work, if we had the full cooperation of the city. He says the tertiary study threatens the economics and, because of the way staff sprung it on us, he's disillusioned about the partnership with the city we need to make the project successful. He says that if the commission doesn't kill the tertiary language tonight, he is asking the Council to hold a special meeting to do it. Failing in that, he will conclude that they have neither a feasible project, nor a willing partner."

"Ouch!" Brad responded. "Is he saying he's going to bail on the whole project if the tertiary study stays in?"

"That's his message. But, after thinking about it this morning, between you and me, I really think that if you limited the study to the golf course only, and committed to pulling back on some of the costly community benefits in the DA to offset the cost, he'd probably go along with it. He's a numbers guy and has to produce, but you should know he's never been that sold on Green Valley. And he has a short fuse if he feels like he's getting jerked around. He doesn't understand why tertiary is even on the table, except for some personal agenda Megan had. I suspect that if we didn't already have so much money into this thing, he'd tell me to drop it right now and go somewhere else nearby with a bigger project."

Brad pondered that a moment, making a steeple with his fingers. "I see why you'd be nervous about the letter. This sounds like an ultimatum to the Council. Elected officials don't like getting ultimatums."

"Frankly, I argued that your taking care of Megan improved our partnership. I told him that you and I have a close working relationship, and I wouldn't want the Council majority to go after you if they got this letter and felt you were obstructing the project."

"I appreciate that," Brad said. He dropped his head and rested his lips on his fingertips as he mulled what had been said. After a brief silence, he raised his head with a smile and looked straight at Scott. "I don't believe for a moment that you intend to send this letter out. You know that you have maybe a 3-2 vote right now. If you push Landon into a corner with this ultimatum, he could just as well make it 2-3. So the letter is garbage."

He paused to study Scott's face and saw a twitch.

Brad continued. "But I like the compromise of studying tertiary for the golf course only. I'd like to be able to announce that tonight at the beginning of the meeting. It should help it go smoother. What do you have in mind for the cost offset in the DA?"

Scott chuckled. "I won my bet. I told Jeff you were too smart to bluff with that letter. But he really does hate the whole idea of doing tertiary, even if it's just for the golf course and comes with a cost offset. He thinks tertiary's a waste, pardon the pun."

"Then why would he go along with even a more limited study alternative?"

"Business, Brad. Jeff wants to position SoCal as a sustainable development company. Using some tertiary water for the golf course, along with the low-flow and energy- efficient appliances, the photovoltaic panels at the community center, and everything else we are doing will help us on two RFP's in other cities we are working on. These are much larger projects on former redevelopment sites. The cities are looking for a green developer. We'd be getting some street cred with this project."

"Maybe we can throw in a kumbaya party for Jeff and Kay and see if she'd write a letter of endorsement, too," Brad joked.

"Well, the PR value is one thing. The lawyers are what really sealed it for Jeff. They said we'd have to disclose all our financials if we claimed we weren't doing tertiary because of financial impact. Jeff said he would walk before he would open his books on a private project, and I think he meant it. He was pretty worked up. The lawyers said that by doing some tertiary alternative analysis as described in the IS, and providing some financial data in this letter to justify scaling it back a bit, we'd be defensible for scaling back the study."

"God bless the lawyers," Brad said. "But you said Jeff wants an offset for the cost out of the DA. What do you have in mind?"

"That's where I was afraid I was going to lose him again. He went off about how stupidly wasteful it was to add that extra water treatment cost when the city has plenty of water for our project. He wanted to cut the nonprofit building. Make it hurt."

"Yuck!"

"Yup. And maybe the community room, too, depending on how the cost estimates come in for the golf course tertiary."

"Perfect! Target the part of the DA that people are most excited about. Smart move," Brad said sarcastically.

"Yeah, well, like I said, Jeff wants it to hurt if the city is really going to insist on tertiary."

"Uh huh," Brad said, stalling for a better comeback.

"I hammered on him about not making that linkage. I told him that would likely come back against you personally, Brad. The nonprofit building and community room are really popular with a lot of influential people who might make life tough for you if they're suddenly in jeopardy because you didn't block your planning director from injecting tertiary into the discussion. You could be blamed for snatching defeat from the jaws of victory. I didn't want to put you in that position. We need you."

"I appreciate that, too," Brad said honestly. "I'm getting it from both sides over the whole tertiary thing. So, you talked Jeff out of cutting the nonprofit building?"

"He is leaving it up to me to find the comparable cost savings. I really went to bat for you and told him we'd work it out. He's assuming that if tertiary is studied for just the golf course, it will end up being imposed as a condition. I think he'd accept your personal guaranty that you will make it work for us in the DA, if it is."

"He's probably right about it being imposed. What do you figure the golf-course-only tertiary will run?"

"It's probably going to be in the $2 to $3 million range. The easiest way to deal with it is with impact fee credits."

"Yeah, I figured that's where you'd want to go," Brad said. "You know I had a hard time selling the Council majority on the partial credits we already included for the street improvements. Landon argued both sides in closed session and finally went along when I reminded him your streets are going to be private and the city won't have to maintain them. If I have to go back and ask for more fee credits in the DA, I'm going to need solid facts to support it. I can't do it just on my own charisma, you know."

"You could make the case for some water credits because of the new tank and how that's improving water pressure outside our project, or park credits because we are building our own parks. We'll give you everything you'll need to make the case to the Council. But remember, Jeff isn't going to open our books for public review. He'll walk *you* through the numbers, but he's not going to make our pro forma a public debate."

"Wonderful!" Brad said sacrcastically. "When the DA goes to Council, I'm supposed to tell the public that we are subsidizing your project from your impact fees because the project doesn't pencil out for you if we don't. I tell them I've looked at the numbers myself but can't share anything with them. Sort of like, 'I'm from the government, trust me?'"

Scott mulled that. "I sure wouldn't argue you are subsidizing anything. We'd be fairly sharing project costs and community benefits. You know how to make that go down smoothly. You've been around the block. The problem is our three-piece-suited lawyers say we can't give you, or some consultant you hire, any written materials or you'll be legally obligated to produce them as part of the public record."

"I understand that, but can't you see how that puts me out on a very flimsy limb? I'm not a construction manager or development consultant. I'm not qualified to say, with any credibility, that crediting back some impact fees is necessary."

"We actually talked about that, too, Brad. Our lawyers had a suggestion for getting you off the hot seat. You could select a qualified consultant to come to our office and go through the numbers with us.

We just can't let them leave with hard copies of anything. You'd have the testimony of an independent expert."

"That's a little better, I guess," he said, warming to the suggestion. Then he frowned. "Except then the argument will be on the consultant's quality and objectivity. How long until somebody brings up all the consultants who looked the other way on Enron and subprime mortgages? No go, Scott. Look, you refuse to give the public information they think they should have and you're asking for trouble."

Scott looked exasperated. "Wait, maybe there's another option."

Brad thought of those infomercials that promote some miracle, life-changing product for $19.95. "But wait, act now and we'll send you two for the same low price of $19.95. . ."

"Free shipping and handling?" Brad teased.

"Huh?"

"Never mind."

"What if our attorneys send the data to Henry Fitzhenry and use the attorney-client privilege to avoid having to disclose it. We'd need Henry to sign our standard Non Disclosure Agreement. Henry would be able to validate what we are saying and tell people he'd been given all the data to review. He just couldn't share it."

"That's the worst idea yet, Scott. You want Henry to be your credible independent authority? Even if you could talk him into taking that responsibility, which he never would do, he has even less background than me when it comes to analyzing a developer's pro forma."

Scott slumped. Brad continued. "The people haven't trusted government since our Constitution was adopted. It's even worse now. Polls show the public doesn't trust *anybody* anymore, even their doctor and minister. People will demand to see the information themselves, even if they can't understand it. Whether it's a city official, or a consultant, who tries to validate your position without providing hard data, the public will assume we are on the take."

Scott threw up his hands. "I don't know where that leaves us. Help me here, Brad. Jeff is bending over to find a compromise on this thing for tonight that doesn't hurt you. He'll go ballistic if you are saying you aren't willing to sell the cost offset in the DA to cover the tertiary hit without giving up our confidential data. It's not going to happen. We might as well know that now, before we spend a bunch more money on the entitlements. He'll pull the plug and it won't be pretty."

"I don't know either, Scott. I'll try to catch Henry right away to see if he has any suggestions, but, knowing Henry, he's not likely to give me anything useful before the meeting tonight."

The developer sighed heavily. "I think Jeff will be OK going forward with the tertiary study limited to the golf course, if I can at least tell him that you have personally committed to doing your best to sell the Council on the fee credits to offset the costs without independent pro forma review. Like I said, we have faith in you. And I think that, with you on our side, I'm not worried about getting the votes for the final DA when the time comes. That gets the EIR launched now and buys us some time to work on handling the cost if the city imposes tertiary for the golf course. Can I count on you for that much?"

"Tell you the truth, Scott, I'm not comfortable committing to anything just now. I want you to be able to count on my word, and I just don't know where we are legally with all of this. And, let me remind you that we don't need your concurrence for what we include in the EIR. It's the city's call as lead agency."

"Now who's bullshitting who, Brad? Don't make me go over your head with this. It's a fair compromise."

Brad exhaled deeply. "You can tell Jeff I'll recommend pulling back from the full tertiary to just the golf course and that I understand you want a cost trade off if we impose the requirement. I just have to think more about how to make that happen considering legalities and political ramifications."

"That's good enough for me, Brad. I know we can count on you. I'll get back to you after I talk to Jeff. I've got to get going on calls to commissioners before tonight. I'm eager to get this compromise in place with Jeff."

"All right," Brad conceded. "Looks like we have a plan, but don't over-commit me."

They stood up and shook hands. "We'll work through this, Scott. I appreciate you coming in. Your project is dividing the whole city and I think I have everyone on the Council pissed at me for different reasons. I'd love to be able to bring forward a reasonable compromise for reducing some of the tension tonight."

"Me too, Brad," the developer seconded. "I enjoy working with you."

Brad accepted the compliment silently. He felt an urge to brief Scott on the water plant problems and the additional studies being conducted on water quality, but held his tongue.

After Scott Graves left, Brad felt a little excitement over the idea of a compromise on the tertiary issue that could defuse things a bit. His sense of dread about staffing the commission meeting tonight diminished, a little.

He assembled the city attorney, public works director, and Associate Planner Elaine Shelley to brief them on the golf-course-only compromise. Brad would introduce it tonight. Dee would be prepared to answer how much this would reduce the project's water demand. Elaine would cover the rest of the IS details.

The planner sat quietly through the meeting, but seemed agitated. She finally spoke up. "Doesn't SoCal have to prove justification for scaling back the Initial Study?"

Brad made a face that caused the young planner to sit rigidly like a deer in the headlights, unaccustomed to mixing with the mucky mucks. Brad stifled his impulse to strangle her. She acted like the kind of government staffer his dad hated, too hung up on process and too scared to cut a deal. He thanked her for her "concern" and asked City Attorney Henry Fitzhenry for his opinion.

Bond, James Bond, was his normal, cautious self. He hadn't had time to do thorough research. Off the top of his head he didn't know of any case law on what constituted adequate disclosure of financial impact to warrant a modification of an EIR alternative. It was an obscure issue. There might not be anything on point.

Under the pressure of the night's meeting, the consensus was that Brad would pitch the compromise to the commission using Dee's data. Brad would get SoCal to beef up their arguments demonstrating why the full study wasn't a feasible alternative. He'd reference the letter but not distribute it tonight. If there were a legal objection to the reduced study, the city attorney would delve into the matter more carefully later, and they'd make adjustments to the EIR consultant's scope of work, if necessary.

He spent the rest of the day with normal duties. He reviewed a half dozen draft staff reports for next Tuesday's City Council meeting. He took some pride seeing how much better the staff reports were than when he first came to the city. He had brought in a retired English professor from nearby Hancock Community College, who volunteered to do writing seminars. He and Brad worked out a template to standardize Council agenda reports. Today, he was happy to see that there wasn't anything in the drafts that needed to be sent back.

He met later in the afternoon with the police chief and fire chief to go over their operational plans to control what could be a raucous Planning Commission meeting tonight. He was anxious about it, but knew he was as prepared as possible.

*****

Councilman Landon phoned around 4:30 p.m. "Just had a meeting at the Chamber with Brian Brando and Scott Graves."

"Oh, what'd they have to say?" Brad asked.

"It was a positive meeting. Sounds like you and Scott have figured out a good compromise on this tertiary treatment issue, limiting it to the golf course? He was telling me that his boss was all worked up about it and going to drop the whole project if there's a threat that we might impose that tertiary thing on the housing areas, too."

"That's what he claims."

"Based on what I understand from you, and that section of the Initial Study I read, I can see his point. It appears to be overkill to use recycled water on the houses. Reducing the study to the golf course may make sense."

And that was as clear a message as Alan Landon ever issued off the Sunday pulpit. Brad wanted to probe further but was interrupted by Jane at the door with a note in her hand. He motioned for her to come over. The note said, "O'Rourke on line 2. . .?"

"Excuse me, Al, I have an important call about all of this that I've been waiting for. Can I put you on hold a second to talk to Jane?"

With Landon's concurrence, he put the councilman on hold and addressed Jane. "I'm running out of time, here. And I want to talk a little more with Al. You know about the iron and chromium issues I talked to Quinn about yesterday. Would you talk to him about their conclusions and shoot me an email with bullet points so I can have it before the meeting tonight?"

She nodded and left quickly. He watched her leave and reminded himself how lucky he was to have such a competent, trustworthy assistant.

"Sorry, Al. Back with you. Did Scott tell you that they want an upfront commitment that if tertiary is studied and later made a condition for just the golf course, we'll give them relief in the Development Agreement to cover the cost? Probably through more fee credits?"

"He touched on that. He said Green Valley would be paying us over $20 million in impact fees, so there was plenty of room to give them some credits and still build the capital projects we need. He thought the two of you could work that out, but didn't go into details. What do you think?"

"I think it has merit, Al. It keeps things moving while we work on the cost issues. What do you think?"

"I sure don't want to see the project killed at this stage. There are a lot of good things in the DA," Landon replied.

"Thank you, Al. I'll keep that in mind." He noted that the councilman again avoided an absolute commitment of his position.

They strayed to a few other city issues. When they hung up, Brad mulled the call. Scott wanted to give him a little prod by letting him know the Council majority wanted him to make the deal on the reduced tertiary study. He was probably more eager to use his remaining time to line up votes on the Planning Commission.

Scott called just before 5 p.m. "Looks like we are good to go with what we talked about. Jeff is fine with you presenting the golf-course-only study tonight. He's trusting me that, with your help, we can manage the cost issues."

"You've been busy," Brad said. "Al Landon called. He was trying to tell me to pitch the golf-course-only study tonight, without telling me to pitch the golf-course-only study tonight."

Scott laughed. "I know what you mean. But he was much clearer about that at the Chamber with Brando. I think we have five, maybe six, votes on the commission tonight. Jerry Wright is ready to run with the tertiary compromise as soon as you present it."

"See you tonight," Brad said, aping Councilman Landon's knack for noncommittal commitment.

*****

Brad's neighbor, Lee Andre, was changing a light bulb at the front of the garage when Brad pulled into his driveway. They exchanged hellos.

"How is Lilly doing?" Brad asked.

"She is walking much better now," Lee said. "I'll see you at the meeting tonight."

"Really?" Brad asked. "I don't recall ever seeing you come down to a meeting."

"I got a call from somebody named Kerry from the Friends of Green Valley Village. She asked me to show my support for the project by attending the meeting."

Brad nodded. His stomach clenched, thinking about the packed house awaiting him.

"I'm in hopes that I get some priority when it is time to pick a lot," Lee said winking.

"I am sure they will reward your presence," Brad smiled back.

"Now that I think about it, I shouldn't have to go. We are moving over together and you'll get a first pick. I just need to take care of you," Lee said, conspiratorially.

"Long way off, I'm afraid, Lee. I may not make it to the finish line. You better do your own kissing up. See you there."

After a hurried dinner, Brad stretched back in his chair and closed his eyes, his mind racing. Despite his best efforts, things just happen. If he hadn't missed the draft Initial Study language about tertiary, it wouldn't have been the problem it had become. He wouldn't have had to push Megan out, thereby displeasing the entire City Council in one way or the other. Scott expected him to support his compromise. Kay and her group won't take his word that it's necessary for them to subsidize the tertiary when it came to that. What would he say tonight?

He remembered that he had asked Jane to summarize the water quality report from Quinn O'Rourke. He grabbed his laptop next to the recliner and pulled up her emailed notes:

- *Confirmed iron and chromium below Maximum Contaminant Levels at Well #2…good news*
- *Not enough info to predict if probs are recent anomaly or signaling trend indicating sharper decline?*
- *Reverse osmosis to treat chromium ±$1 million per well*
- *Can't tell whether treatment of new well better, need more longitudinal data, drill test well?*
- *Pub notice rqd if contaminant exceeds MCL, doesn't apply, (yet)*

He sighed with relief seeing confirmation that there was no legal requirement to disclose the iron and chromium readings at this point. He had time to get more information and develop a thoughtful strategy.

Marie came over with a cup of coffee and a plate of his favorite Owl Eye cookies she bought at Madsen's Bakery in Solvang. "Here you go. This is just a reminder of the good things life has to offer. There will be more cookies waiting. And, I rented *Midway* for you to watch when you get back. That gives you two things to look forward to afterwards."

"Thanks, Hon. You know, the Battle of Midway was the deciding point in the Pacific Theatre. It could have gone either way. Admiral Spruance knew he was going to be known forever as the man who won, or lost, the war. That's kind of how I feel about tonight's meeting."

"Go get 'em, Admiral," Marie cheered. "I love a man in uniform. There, that's three things now," she smiled flirtatiously.

24

Brad got back to City Hall at 6:30 p.m., leaving plenty of time to get what he needed from his office prior to the Planning Commission meeting. The parking lot was already filling up. A fire engine and rescue, along with four police cars, were parked near the front entrance. Brad wondered where they dug up all the police cars, since they normally had only two circulating at any given time, but he endorsed the showing of strength to set the right tone as people arrived.

He unlocked the door to his office and went to the bank of filing cabinets behind Jane's desk to retrieve the LAFCo Municipal Services Review, in case he needed good background on water and other city services for the meeting. The cabinets were locked. He opened the top right drawer of Jane's desk to get the key and made a mental note to tease her about her hiding place, the equivalent of putting a door key under the mat.

The files were organized alphabetically. He couldn't find the report under the "M's". He tried the "L's" for LAFCo and "W's" for water, and struck out. While he avoided calling Jane at home, the clock was ticking. He placed a call. No answer. He opted to not leave a message on her machine and tried her cell.

"Hi, Brad," she answered on the second ring. "Did you decide to run away or are you at the meeting?" She seemed in a good mood.

"I'm at the office, damn it. I'm looking for the Municipal Services Review report but don't know where you filed it. Help!"

"That's a LAFCo report, right?" she said instantly.

"Yeah, but I didn't see anything under the 'L's'."

"Look under the 'S's'," she advised.

"You're saying 'S' as in 'Sam?'"

"Sure," she said. "It should be under SBCLAFCo for Santa Barbara County LAFCo. That *is* their official name, you know."

"Naturally," he said sarcastically. "Why not under the P's for 'potential annexations.' Look, you're already my right arm. I wouldn't know what to do without you. You don't need to engage in such obscure filing for job security."

"Hey, a little extra security never hurt a girl," she said.

"I see your point. I could use a little security myself about now."

"Well, from what you said this afternoon, it looks like the Council majority is with Green Valley. You shouldn't get any heat from them if you get the commission to compromise on the tertiary study. You're still going to propose that, right?

"Yeah, it makes sense and keeps the Green Valley project moving forward. I gotta get to the meeting. Thanks for the email on Quinn's report and for the fascinating insight into your filing logic."

"Do well."

"Sorry for interrupting your night out or whatever else you're doing."

"Just dishes," she said quickly. There was something funny in her voice. "No problem. Good luck. I'll be watching."

He wondered why she hadn't picked up her home phone, but let it pass.

As he walked up to the front door of the Council Chambers, he touched base with Sergeant Heather Mahnken who was in charge of the police detail. She seemed less perturbed about the job ahead than he was. He then cornered the volunteer who ran the cameras at public meetings to give him instructions not to turn the camera on any commotion in the audience, just keep it on the staff, commission, or screen. He made small talk with Chairman Fleishmann, trying to keep each other relaxed as the Council Chamber filled up. It looked to Brad that the pro-project folks outnumbered the opponents again.

He stood at Parker Fleishmann's position chatting, trying to appear casual. The whole time his eyes scanned the audience. He recognized many of the people even though he didn't know all their names. The factions were self-segregating with the supporters again on the audience right behind the staff table and the opponents gravitating to the left side of the center aisle. Friends of the bride or the groom?

His neighbor, Lee Andre, walked through the lobby door and waved at Brad as Kerry Smith veered him to the right. Brad's son, Dillon, was on his heels. He remembered Dillon was there to cover the hearing for his term paper and had offered to give Lee a ride since the ninety-year-old hated to drive at night. Brad felt his stress rise having to perform under his son's watchful eyes.

The Chambers buzzed with the normal background crowd noises of laughter, squeaking folding chairs, and yells like "over here, Sheree." A scream and angry shouting from outside pierced through the background ruckus. Sergeant Mahnken put her hand to her earpiece, signaled to Officer David Williams to come with her, and left the Chambers, briskly signaling Officer Crombie to stay put inside.

WITHOUT PURPOSE *of* EVASION

People in the audience didn't want to give up their seats but many were standing in place trying to see what was happening outside. More raised voices. Officer Crombie shifted his weight from side to side, eyes on the Chamber entrance, ready to move.

A few minutes went by without anyone else coming into the Chambers. Then the flow resumed, led by Megan Cain and her partner, Fred Buderi, who went directly to two seats that were being saved for them at audience front left. Fred's sweater was ripped and his long black hair disheveled.

Brad heard the door behind the dais open and saw Sergeant Mahnken in the alcove beckoning him over.

"We had a little fracas outside. Hubie Nettler got into a shouting match with Ms. Cain and her friend. Supporters from each side started to face off, but we jumped into the middle of it and separated everyone. A couple of people got shoved, and there might be some torn clothes, but no punches were thrown. We ordered one person from each side to go home or they'd be arrested. It settled down. Nothing serious enough to warrant an arrest. All the same, I think I'll stick around through the meeting with Officers Crombie and Williams. We'll keep an eye on outside, also."

"Good idea, Heather. Thanks," Brad said. He felt his stomach tighten as he took his place on the semi-circular dais to the commission's right.

When he was settled in and had organized his papers, he looked up to see that his son was directly in his line of sight, sitting in the middle of the "pro" side with Lee. Dillon caught the eye contact. He dangled a Ziploc bag of Owl Eye cookies and gave his father a thumbs up, no doubt on Marie's instruction. He was calmed even more when City Attorney Henry Fitzhenry took his seat next to him. A friend in the foxhole.

At 7:10 p.m., Chairman Parker Fleishmann rapped the gavel and brought the special meeting to order. He started with the same admonitions about decorum and the consequences for those who don't observe it tonight. He acknowledged the city manager who was there tonight to advise the commission. He didn't have to say why. He asked Brad to lead them in the Pledge of Allegiance, after which he asked everyone to remain standing to observe a moment of silence.

The chairman pushed ahead with the agenda, asking the planning department secretary to call roll. One absent. The chairman then asked for a motion to approve the agenda with the only change being to move up the Green Valley Village IS presentation as the next item, ahead of Business from the Floor. The motion was made, seconded and approved swiftly. The commissioners wanted to get this meeting behind them, also.

Chairman Fleishmann, following the process that had been discussed with Brad and the city attorney, called the Green Valley item and asked for the commission's concurrence with the evening's procedures. Unlike the previous meeting, where the public was not allowed to talk, this meeting would be devoted to hearing the public. The city manager and staff would make some introductory comments but not repeat the point-by-point summary of the Initial Study that had been given by the staff last time. Following the staff comments, the applicant, SoCal Communities, would be given ten minutes to address the commission. After that, people would be asked to line up along the center aisle.

Everyone would have three minutes. The secretary had a timer with three lights. It would show green for the first two minutes and turn to yellow, warning the speaker to wrap up. When it went to red, the chair would interrupt and ask the speaker to be seated.

Noble, Councilwoman Nance's artist associate, seated in the front row, audience left, suddenly blurted, "How come the developer gets ten minutes? He's only here for the money. This is our town. Let us have ten minutes of rebuttal, too." A couple of people near him clapped, while others nodded their heads vigorously.

Officer Crombie started toward the man. The chairman intervened. "I'm going to ask the officer to hold back this time. Hear me, people, that's the only freebie tonight. We are serious about keeping the peace and won't tolerate any other outbursts. As to why I'm giving the applicant ten minutes, it's common practice for this commission to let the applicant go first with introductory comments since they are paying for the privilege. Nothing special here."

He reminded everyone to keep themselves under control and added that the increased police presence here was not to stifle public expression but to make sure *everyone* had the opportunity to speak, without being disrupted. The vibe in the room calmed a little. Officer Crombie went back to his spot at the front of the audience.

Chairman Fleishmann continued. "Folks, as far as I'm concerned, I'm willing to be here all night, if necessary, so that everyone who wants to be, can be heard. But there are two caveats. First, I remind everyone that the *only* issue for discussion tonight is the Initial Study for the Green Valley EIR. The speakers *must* keep their comments to what should, or shouldn't, be studied in the EIR. The project itself is not up for a vote yet, and may not be for a year, or more. It's premature to have people conclude that this proposal is either the best or worst thing to have hit Santa Ynez. All we are doing tonight is considering what should be in the scope of the EIR study, not whether any of us like or hate any aspects of the proposed plan. So, please, focus your comments only on the EIR scope of study. If you stray from that, I will gavel you out of order, as a warning. I'll allow you to continue, but if I have to gavel you out of order a second time, the secretary will move the timer to a red light and you'll be told to sit." He nodded to Officer Crombie and let that sink in a moment before moving on.

"Second, please don't repeat something someone else already said, or we really could be here all night. For what it's worth, having served on this commission for many years, I can tell you that you will be more impactful with a factual, crisp argument than by trying to wear us down or being emotional. Besides, I'm self-employed and, unlike many of you, I can sleep in tomorrow. Think about it."

There was a little laughter in the audience. "Good job, Parker," Brad thought.

The chairman asked for, and received, his colleague's approval of the ground rules. As that went on, Brad glanced at the audience and saw his son writing on a tablet. He turned his head right and saw his former planning director staring back at him. It wasn't a nasty, threatening look. But it was still unnerving to have her there.

Brad heard his name called and realized the chairman was turning it over to him. He snapped to alert and looked at his prepared outline. He thanked the chairman for the introduction and told the commission it was nice to be here with them tonight. Insincere, polite, bureaucratic throat-clearing.

He assured everyone he had only brief comments and, as the chairman had said, he wouldn't be repeating the same summary of the Initial Study that staff gave at the last meeting. However, for the benefit of those who weren't there at the last meeting, he took five minutes to describe the Green Valley project and the review process that lay before it. He touched on the benefits being negotiated with the Development Agreement, then introduced Associate Planner Elaine Shelley who summarized the purpose of the IS and a few of the more obvious environmental factors that would be studied in the EIR.

The associate planner looked extremely uncomfortable but got through her portion of the meeting with only a nearly imperceptible quiver in her voice. He remembered how his guts turned over before and during his Council budget presentations as a young administrative analyst in the City Manager's Office. Brad thanked her and took the floor again.

"The scope of the EIR, as described in the Initial Study, will be comprehensive and meet the requirements of state law. One area the staff identified as needing some policy input from this commission is the project's water demand as it relates to available supplies. I'd like Public Works Director Dee Sharma to summarize this issue. I know he covered this at the meeting the other night, but it's a key issue so I'd like him to hit it again. Dee?"

Brad shut off his microphone and nodded to Dee. His eyes made contact with Scott Graves, seated once again behind the staff table in the first row, audience right. Scott gave him a slight smile and nod. He looked up a few rows to see Dillon still leaning over writing. Or, was he already bored and checking scores? He peeked right and saw Megan Cain still looking at him, not at the public works director who was running through his short PowerPoint.

The public works director's presentation was succinct. There were no questions from the commission. Brad flicked on his microphone switch.

"As Dee showed, we believe the city has adequate water sources to serve the build-out of the current General Plan area, as well as the amended General Plan to include Green Valley Village."

He paused, still uncertain where he was going. He looked again at Megan Cain. Was she going to testify? Was this going to get ugly? Should he go ahead and talk about scaling back the tertiary study to the golf-course-only? Someone coughed and he was aware everyone in the room was waiting for him to continue. He cleared his throat, stalling for time. Or divine intervention. Or something. He saw a path forward.

"As the public works director described, we have two independent studies concluding we have sufficient water for the project. I emphasize that these are estimates. Hopefully, conservative estimates, to ensure we don't run out of water."

He paused again, looking up at Scott Graves, who looked back expectantly. He glanced over to Dillon, who was watching him closely. His son caught his eye and gave him an encouraging nod, as if to say, "go for it, Dad." What did that mean? He felt hot and tense.

"That said, given the uncertainties in forecasting water supplies thirty years or more out, we are asking the commission to consider studying the potential of tertiary-treated water for the project in order to provide an even greater margin of surplus water for the future. Since tertiary treatment was described at the last meeting and, I know the commission wants to hear from the public on the EIR scope, I'll stop there."

He shut off his mic and looked across at Megan. She cocked her head and exchanged quizzical looks with her partner, Fred. What was that about? He quickly replayed his words in his mind. And panicked. Did he just veer off his own script by recommending the tertiary study, instead of simply asking the commission to discuss the adequacy of the water surplus, and whether they thought tertiary should be considered? He looked back to his left at Scott Graves, almost apologetically. The developer raised his eyebrows and opened his hands in a gesture that conveyed "what the. . .?"

Brad noticed Scott exchange looks with Commissioner Jerry Wright. Wright did the same with Fleishmann.

Chairman Fleishmann turned to Brad and cued him. "Is there anything else you'd like to add, Mr. City Manager?"

He was lost in thought, staring ahead at his son. The next generation. Water. The Delta. His promise to be a good steward of natural resources. Dillon was still smiling back calmly. Could his son possibly understand the nuances and ramifications at play here? What was he trying to say?

"Brad?" Chairman Fleishmann prompted again.

"Oh, sorry," Brad said self-consciously. "No, Mr. Chairman, I have nothing further at this time."

The chairman looked puzzled. He glanced to his left, down the dais at Commissioner Wright, who was looking in Scott Graves's direction. Resignedly, the chairman invited the applicant to come to the podium and directed the secretary to put ten minutes on the timer.

Scott Graves gave Brad a look like a batter getting off the dirt after a brush-back pitch. He wore a periwinkle blue blazer, camel-colored slacks, and white shirt with blue pinstripes open at the collar. He managed to pull off cool, calm, and friendly, despite the scores of citizens over his left shoulder who would love to smack him with a tomato. Thankfully, there were no boo's or similar taunts as he came forward. No doubt the enhanced security was having the desired effect.

The developer took off his large gold watch, set it on the podium, and pulled his notes from his blazer's breast pocket. He walked everyone through a PowerPoint overview of the development project, emphasizing the high quality design and community benefits it promised. He completed the last slide, looked at his watch to see how much time he had left, and transitioned to his next bullet point, letting everyone know that SoCal is an environmentally responsible company. He described some of the practices they typically follow to reduce their projects' environmental footprint.

"Our company is in nearly complete agreement with the scope of the environmental impact report. There is, however, one alteration to the scope that I wasn't sure if the city manager wanted me to address, or if he was planning to later." He looked at Brad for a signal. Brad hesitated and motioned for Scott to proceed.

Scott Graves looked uncharacteristically flustered. He looked at the still-green light on the timer and said, "Since I have a little time left, I just wanted talk about the water impacts."

The developer started by praising the city for its foresight in securing multiple sources of high quality, potable water. What an enviable position that put Santa Ynez compared to other California cities. He mentioned a city on the coast that is opening a new desalination plant, at considerable cost to the water ratepayers, because *their* city officials hadn't done as good a job tying their growth to their water resources. He applauded the city staff for calling for two water studies from well-qualified firms, to be certain of the conclusion written in the IS, that the city had an adequate supply of water for Green Valley.

The light on the timer turned to yellow. Scott saw it and appeared to adjust his presentation on the fly.

"Of course, as the city manager noted, there are always uncertainties when it comes to forecasting anything. Most of us are better at 'post-casting.'" He waited for a laugh that didn't come. He looked nervous and began talking faster.

"We have provided staff with documentation showing the cost estimate of tertiary treatment for the golf course, landscaping, and home front yards, and the costs for all of the community benefits SoCal is prepared to bring the community under the draft Development Agreement. It is clear that the tertiary treatment alternative study will not meet the project objectives. Therefore…"

Ping! The timer went off as the light turned to red.

Scott was jolted. "May I finish, Mr. Chairman? I only need another minute or two. I really thought the city manager was going to cover this last part."

"Time's up, Graves!" Noble shouted. "Tell him to sit down, Parker."

Brad saw Chairman Fleishmann's quandary. If he gave a time extension to SoCal, how could he deny it to anyone else? The chairman apologized to Scott, saying he needed everyone to abide by the ground rules that had been set. No exceptions. Somebody patted Noble on the shoulder.

Scott looked shocked. He looked urgently at Commissioner Jerry Wright who was on the job and and hit his light switch, requesting to speak.

When he was recognized, Commissioner Wright thanked the chairman and asked him to confirm that commissioners would be permitted to ask questions of the speakers after they have finished their comments. The chairman agreed.

"Thank you, Parker," he said. "Now, Mr. Graves, I understand there is an alternative suggestion for the tertiary treatment study that you wanted to propose. A win/win alternative. I think this commission would like to hear that."

Scott loosened his grip on the podium. "Yes, Mr. Wright. Thank you. With the commission's indulgence, I just want to take a moment to say, again, that we are very sensitive to the environment. And, while the city has done a superb job of managing its water, and will have a large surplus even after our project is built out, we endorse studying the feasibility of using tertiary water for the golf course as one of the required EIR alternatives but not for the houses and other landscaped areas which wouldn't be feasible."

Commissioner Wright seized the spotlight again. "Thank you, Mr. Graves. Can you or the public works director give the commission an estimate of how much that would reduce the project's water demand?"

"Nearly 50 percent, Commissioner Wright," Scott said happily. There was a murmur in the audience.

"Really?" the commissioner gushed.

"Yes, it is a significant savings," Scott said, apparently going for a deliberate underplay for credibility. "Like I said, we are very environmentally-responsible developers."

"Wonderful," Wright fawned. "I'm sure we all appreciate your commitment, not only to Santa Ynez, but to the environment. I know that treating the water from the sewer plant to the equivalent of what we drink out of the tap will be very expensive. I salute you for being willing to consider that alternative for the golf course."

"Oh, brother," Brad thought. It's up to the *city*, not SoCal, to decide what should be studied in the EIR. Wright was pouring it on. Brad thought, "why don't you ask how the golf course tertiary will be paid for, Jerry?"

Brad surveyed the audience. The "pro" side seemed impressed by the reasonableness of the revised tertiary proposal. In contrast, he noticed Megan Cain and Fred Buderi in a whispered conversation, fervently flipping through materials on Megan's lap and writing. Brad was sure they weren't going to let Scott or Jerry Wright get away with giving the public the impression that the city would have an abundant surplus of water, or that SoCal was proposing to bear the burden of bringing tertiary water for the golf course as some charitable act.

One of his favorite words came to mind, "eleemosynary." It meant "a charitable act." He learned it the same time America did, from Senator Sam Ervin, who chaired the Senate Watergate hearings in the 70s. Brad felt a twinge of sadness, remembering watching the hearings on the family room TV; his father, Spike, in his recliner, puffing his pipe and regularly evincing his disgust for politicians and government bureaucrats. And yet, here he sat tonight, a government bureaucrat. Brad could almost smell the sweet pipe tobacco smoke hanging in the still air.

Chairman Fleishmann broke the mental tangent by thanking Scott Graves for his presentation and asking those who wanted to speak to begin lining up in the center aisle. He again reminded them of the ground rules. It was 7:40 p.m. already. Let the fun begin.

His friends sometimes asked Brad how he could do it; sit there passively and listen, sometimes late into the night, as the Council meeting droned on. They were surprised when he admitted that his attention span went in and out. They'd say, "But we watch the meetings and sometimes the camera is on you when somebody is at the podium. You're even writing notes as they speak. How can you focus like that?"

He'd explain that he might not have been taking notes. He might have been counting. He had a running $1 bet with the city attorney about who could come closer to guessing the number of "O's" appearing on the agenda handout. Each would write their guess on a slip of paper, then begin filling in the "O's" to make them easier to count. He and the city attorney might be seen "conferring" during the public testimony. That probably involved comparing each other's "O" tally as they went from page to page resolving any discrepancy. Brad found that having something mindless to do as the hours droned on kept him alert. He looked attentive and easily tracked the testimony.

It didn't take one's full concentration to get the gist of the debate. After thirty years of attending public meetings, Brad could predict the arguments that would be raised for or against a development proposal. Sometimes there were surprises. Years ago, a Native American spoke, nearly in tears, about the pending loss of native flora and fauna on a hilly, tree-covered development site. He reached into his coat pocket and pulled out a live baby squirrel, telling the Council that its spirit doesn't want the area bulldozed.

He'd never top the story told by a city manager colleague about a Council hearing on a small residential infill subdivision. It was only a three-acre plot of flat, barren land, completely surrounded by urban uses. One of the neighbors was bemoaning the loss of the habitat and begging the city to buy it for a wildlife sanctuary. She hit the Joanie Mitchell button, "Take paradise, put up a parking lot," concluding that what was being called improvements for the site weren't really.

"Man can't improve on nature," she pronounced with finality as she spun around to take her seat.

A contractor's boisterous, busty, bleached-blond wife, with fun-loving notoriety, had groaned and snickered all the way through the lady's habitat arguments. When the protestor finally sat down, she bolted to the podium next and said, "Who says you can't improve upon nature?" With that, she pulled her t-shirt up to her shoulders and said, "a man sure improved these!"

Brad didn't expect anything nearly so titillating tonight. He sighed watching as the line of speakers stretched from the first row, just behind the podium, to the lobby. More would likely join them when the line went down. Henry Fitzhenry slipped him a piece of scrap paper with "10:30" written on it. Game on.

Brad thought for a moment, wrote "10:45" on the scrap and handed it back. There was another buck riding on who could come closest to predicting the meeting adjournment. It was Fitzhenry's turn to go first. The rule was, once the first person picked a time, the second person's time had to be a half hour earlier or fifteen minutes later, his choice. Brad's experience told him the "under" wasn't a good bet tonight. He saw the city attorney shake his head regrettably. Henry would gladly give up a dollar to have Brad win with a 10 p.m. bet. Brad sighed and thought about the cookies, bourbon, and movie that seemed so far away.

The next two-and-a-half hours followed a predictable pattern. Usually the pro and the anti-development groups had a plan and people designated to carry it out. These people would rush to the podium to try to get their licks in early, before human nature overcame the commissioners and their attention span waned. Their job was to lay the foundation for their side's key points, others would be slated to pound the arguments into the ground later.

Chairman Fleishmann was doing his best to keep things

moving. He wielded his gavel with a surgeon's precision in a valiant attempt to keep people on point, the scope of the EIR, and snuffing out spontaneous applause or taunts. Brad penciled in the "O's" on the commission agenda as he listened, looking up to the podium occasionally. He made some notes based on speaker comments that he planned to address at the end. Commissioners, seeing the large number of people lined up to address them, self-policed by not asking questions of the speakers along the way. Occasionally, Chairman Fleishmann or another commissioner would simply flag something that had been said and ask staff to address it later. They were eager to get to the end of the public portion of the agenda.

Brad was eager, too. His former planning director's presence in the front row, and her constant huddling with her partner, Fred, made him anxious. Was she going to attack him personally?

As the line began to dwindle, Fred Buderi stood up and walked solemnly to the rear. There were still three speakers in front of him.

Seeing Fred get up, Brad noticed Scott Graves whisper to Kerry Smith of the Tourism Bureau, who got up and, in turn, whispered to others on their side of the aisle who nodded and joined the line.

Brad stopped filling in "O's" and paid more attention.

The current speaker said he was a golfer from Solvang who was interested in moving to Green Valley Village. He worried about tertiary water on the course. "Am I going to have to wipe my balls before I handle them?" he deadpanned. The audience giggled. The chairman played it straight and said he had already asked staff to address the health issue of tertiary water.

Brad knew the next speaker was active with the Chamber and had talked to her at functions. He wrote down her name when she introduced herself, in hopes he would remember it next time they met. She said a few words about how this is such a dream project for the community and she hoped we didn't lose it to another city that saw its true value. The chairman gave her a first gavel, warning her to talk about the EIR. She suddenly turned angry. "I've had to sit here and listen to *those* people," she jerked her head back and left, "threaten to recall anyone who supports this project."

Chairman Fleishmann raised his gavel for the second time saying, "You are out of order. Please be seated."

She didn't move. "I'm telling you right now, I've got a lot of friends."

The chairman kept slamming the gavel.

"And we will recall anyone on the Council who *doesn't* support this project."

The chairman was smashing the gavel so hard Brad feared it would break. Officer Crombie was in motion.

"You people are just like all the other no-growthers," she said, pivoting left. "You got your house, but nobody else should get theirs."

The officer grabbed her forearm lightly as the chairman continued banging. She allowed herself to be led away from the podium and the Council Chambers.

The last speaker before Fred was good old Pat Kirby. He started by welcoming everyone tonight, as if he were hosting them at his home. The chairman already had his gavel in his hand. Kirby saw the threat and hurried to make himself relevant.

"Commissioners, there have been a lot of good questions and comments raised tonight about the EIR," the watchdog began. Chairman Fleishmann lowered his gavel, keeping it at the ready.

"This is a very big project, the biggest we are likely ever to confront." Kirby often said "we" to include himself as a decision-maker. "And the EIR is probably the most important document we will be reviewing. I know it's getting late and you want to whiz through this meeting. I suggest that another meeting be set so that we can hear the responses from staff, and have another opportunity to address the commission, before you start the EIR."

People on both sides of the audience groaned with the mere thought of another round of this drama. Brad recalled a C. Northcote Parkinson quote a favorite mayor often cited, "delay is the deadliest form of denial." The law didn't even require a public meeting on the Initial Study. It was approaching cruel and unusual punishment to even consider a third such meeting.

The commissioners allowed Kirby's suggestion to evaporate into the ether.

Fred Buderi approached the podium. "Good evening, Chairman Fleishmann," looking from side to side along the dais. "Commissioners? Staff? As some of you know, I'm a bio-chemist. I have a PhD and considerable training and experience as an environmental scientist. I have a lot to contribute to your deliberations, but I can't do it adequately in just three minutes. We ask that you extend us the same courtesy that you gave to the applicant, and give me ten minutes."

The chairman stepped in immediately. "I explained the ground rules upfront, Dr. Buderi. We are following our customary practice." He looked to his left and right down the dais. "Is there anyone on the commission who wishes to discuss changing the rules of procedure we previously set?" No motion was forthcoming. The chairman said, "You have three minutes, Dr. Buderi. And, let me remind you, that you are free to send in a letter with any comments you have about the environmental assessment, even if you can't get it all in tonight. I will ask the secretary to move the timer back to the beginning. Please continue."

Brad felt himself tense. What did Fred and Megan have up their sleeves? A sudden jolt of fear coursed through him. Were they tipped off about the problems at the water plant and the chromium spike at the well? He began to formulate his response to that threat.

Dr. Fred Buderi's testimony ended up being a nonevent, at least in Brad's mind. Fred covered the same ground Megan had in Brad's office about the threats to the city's current water supply delivered through the State Water Project, worsening water quality in the Delta, particularly increased salt and nitrates, loss of endangered species and their habitat, and threats of saltwater intrusion from earthquakes and rising tides from climate change. He cautioned about selenium build-up, over-pumping of the Central Valley groundwater, and attempts by big ag and Southern California interests to pull even more scarce water out of Northern California, which would exacerbate the crisis. He talked authoritatively, but hit so many points in such a short time that Brad sensed he'd overwhelmed people. The timer light switched to yellow.

"What I'm trying to explain, in the all-too-brief time you've given me, is that California has huge water problems. We who live in a semi-arid climate are living in a fool's paradise if we think we will be getting more water from major state projects. It's far more likely our current supplies will continue to be cut over the long term. The responsible thing would be to include in the EIR a realistic assessment of the city's current deliveries from the State Water Project. There are a lot of people who are experts on the issues that should be consulted before the city launches the EIR study using the water analyses that have been cited here. Our water supply is far less certain than is being assumed. The people involved with those reports have their heads up their. . .well, in deference to decorum, let's just say they are part of the establishment who are motivated to bury their heads in the sand."

The timer light went to red. Dr. Buderi got in a final lick. "Please, commissioners, this sprawl and waste of natural resources must stop." He looked over his left shoulder in Megan's direction. "Some people have made personal sacrifices to expose the myriad problems in California water policy and community development being brushed aside to promote the moneyed interests. Listen to those brave enough to speak truth."

The anti-side exploded in applause and hurrahs. Chairman Fleishmann pounded his gavel. Angry voices countered from the "pro" side.

The bio-chemist persisted. "Don't give in to the status quo. It's driven by corporate greed. It's bad for California and bad for the citizens of Santa Ynez."

"Please be seated, Dr. Buderi," Chairman Fleishmann ordered.

Buderi grabbed his papers from the podium and turned with a parting shot. "Include a fair and impartial review of our State Water Project supplies in the EIR. You are public officials. Protect the *public* interest, not the *corporate* interest."

"Sit down!" Hubie Nettler yelled from audience right.

Officers Williams and Crombie moved toward the middle of the room under the protective fire of the chairman's gavel. Things settled down, but the queue suddenly grew, mostly from project supporters.

There were two more anti-project speakers next. One woman talked about the loss of view when the hills and grazing land become developed. This was an unavoidable impact, and, in her mind, the suggested mitigations didn't diminish the impact. She asked that the water tank being proposed on a ridgeline be undergrounded. Dee was asked to comment on that suggestion and responded that at least partially burying the tank was likely for water quality reasons. The woman wanted it completely buried for aesthetics.

Another man from the anti-side spoke in favor of using tertiary treated water in light of what the doctor had said. However, it was clear he wasn't an expert on the matter and was just attempting to endorse Dr. Buderi's comments, whom he twice called "Dr. Berry."

The "pro" side was much better armed. Speaker after speaker endorsed aspects of the project or lauded SoCal as a responsible developer. When the chairman reminded them to confine their comments to the Initial Study, most of them had nothing further to say and sat down.

Commissioner Wright assisted with softball questions for some of the proponents, like, "The IS indicates there will be an improvement in public services from the project, including two firefighter/paramedics to be stationed at the development 24/7. Where would you rate that project impact relative to seeing a partial water tank on a distant ridgeline?"

As the final speaker was finishing up, Brad looked in Scott Graves's direction and saw the look of betrayal in his eyes. Brad looked down guiltily. He stole another glance at his son who was still locked on him. Was Dillon thinking about his father's vow that day on the Delta?

Chairman Parker Fleishmann tapped the gavel to end the public portion of the meeting. Staff spent a half hour responding to commissioner questions arising from the testimony. Brad still hadn't weighed in. His brain was in warp speed, searching for a landing zone in the fog of his conflicting thoughts, emotions, and values.

"Mr. Jacks, is there anything final you wanted to say?" he heard Chairman Fleishmann ask. It sounded more like the priest on Death Row asking him what he wanted for his last meal.

He had to choose a side.

25

City Manager Brad Jacks felt all eyes turned to him, expecting a thoughtful recommendation. He still wasn't sure where to go.

"Mr. Chairman, and members of the commission," he began and looked down, appearing to study his notes. Stalling.

Dillon couldn't possibly understand. Public policy issues are complicated. There are good arguments on all sides. He'd have to explain his role to his son again. He'd tell him that his first obligation is to carry out the wishes of the Council majority, even if he disagreed with them. In the real world, you often have to go along to get along.

"I agree with those speakers who noted that this state has some serious water issues that are in need of reform. But this is very complex stuff, and smart people on all sides of water policy have been fighting about it for a hundred years. I think it's unreasonable for the City of

Santa Ynez, or a specific development project, to take on the burden of sorting it all out in an EIR."

He looked directly at Scott Graves to see if he was scoring points. The developer seemed to be studying him.

Brad would remind his son of the higher cost of out-of-state tuition; unaffordable if his father is unemployed. This will be a good life lesson for him. An adult has to make tough choices and sacrifices.

"We've heard a lot of good comments tonight, some about the potential benefits and impacts of the Green Valley Village project. And while the chairman has said it many times, it bears repeating one last time. Tonight is only about discussing some preliminary information about the project to determine which issues should receive further study in the EIR. There will be numerous opportunities for the public to stay involved in the long process ahead."

"Now except for floods, when it comes to water discussions in California, more is better. We can't predict with any certainty what's going to happen in the future. The best we can do is to deal with what we know today and make some reasonable contingency plans in case there is a glitch. I emphasize *reasonable* while recognizing that's a loaded term. The city attorney here will tell you that what's reasonable in every situation depends upon perspectives and facts. He might want to comment on this, but it's my understanding that the courts have ruled it's not reasonable to study an EIR alternative that doesn't meet the project's objectives. An alternative that is so expensive as to make the project infeasible would not be deemed reasonable."

More stalling. He heard restless crowd noises. Jump.

"However, I do think that some additional safety margin for the city's long term water supply would be prudent. Therefore, I recommend the commission adopt the Initial Study with the inclusion of the potential of using tertiary-treated water for the proposed golf course only. Staff estimates that would reduce the project's water demand by 45 percent, at a cost that's only about 25 percent of the full tertiary option. In short, it's a good bang for the buck and worth considering."

He waited for some reaction from the audience. Nothing. Scott and Brian Brando were whispering. Megan shook her head sadly when their eyes met. He pushed back an impulse to mention the potential water quality problems that might have a bearing on the discussion. He opted to throw a different bone to audience left.

"If the golf course tertiary ends up being imposed as a condition of approval, the staff and consultants will be reviewing the cost of that mitigation. I'm sure SoCal will want to negotiate that cost in the context of the Development Agreement." He just couldn't let Jerry Wright get away with implying the extra treatment would be an eleemosynary gesture by SoCal.

"But the golf course tertiary concept would add only about a thousand dollars to the home prices. I wouldn't expect the city to lose much ground on what we already have in the draft Development Agreement with SoCal to make it feasible. I'd rather focus our energies on doing something that will be an effective mitigation, because it can be reasonably imposed, versus a loftier goal that likely won't make it beyond the study phase and just creates discord."

The meeting ended with the commission approving the Initial Study for the Green Valley Village EIR, with the golf course tertiary language, on a 5-1 vote. People filed out of the Council Chambers. Brad stood at his position, fiddling with his papers to give an opportunity for people to come up and shake hands.

Scott Graves was the first visitor. "You gave me heartburn, Brad," said the developer. "I was wondering if Kay and her crowd got to you and you weren't going to support the compromise we talked about. I had the votes for it, anyway. Jerry was all set to lead the charge if you bailed on me, but if you had, I don't know what Jeff would have done. He really trusted me that you were committed to the compromise and to helping us with the cost if it gets imposed. I hope he doesn't see the video of this meeting. Your last-minute endorsement and suggestion that the whole cost can be loaded on the house prices, was, let's say, disappointing."

"I know, Scott. I was just trying to put a positive light on all of this. You know, frame the debate as wasting money on another grand and glorious government study, versus doing something that will actually be useful. Downplaying the cost issue and implying it could be loaded on the houses was part of selling that. I'm still there with you on working out a trade-off in the DA. You can tell Jeff."

They chatted in a businesslike, rather than friendly, way for a few more moments. As Scott walked off, Brad replayed his actions and words. He had tried to be statesmanlike, reconciling competing perspectives and pitching a deal that would work for the developer and could be sold to the opponents. Why was he feeling devious? His tactics weren't anything like Mulholland, Pat Brown, or the promoters of the Delta tunnels.

His reflection was broken by the sight of Megan and Fred walking over. "You had me going for a minute," Megan began ruefully. "I actually thought there was a chance you were going to do the right thing and recommend the full tertiary study. I'm not surprised, just discouraged. You had a chance to do something important for the future of this community, Brad. Something that might have reverberated beyond this region. You only went as far as SoCal was willing to go. Too bad."

"Yeah, well, I've got to consider a host of factors that you don't have to acknowledge, Megan. I don't think the Council majority would have kept the full tertiary study you wanted, and they sure wouldn't have imposed it later. But we should get the golf course tertiary done. Forty-five percent of the loaf is better than starving in my book."

Megan's soon-to-be husband shook his head vigorously. "Nice rationalization. But this isn't over," Fred warned. "It's only starting. There are people here in town and all over the state demanding that their public officials start putting more emphasis on protecting our natural resources, and less on doing the bidding of the corporate interests."

Brad looked past Fred to see who else was nearby.

"Sure, you can blow us off, Brad," Megan grumbled, "but I think that deep down, you know we're right. Maybe someday you'll take a leap of faith and join us. Let's go, Fred." They both turned and walked off.

He stood there a while feeling the sting of the dressing down, then turned to Henry Fitzhenry to settle their bets.

"See you at home, Dad?" he heard Dillon ask.

He looked up and saw his son standing by the podium. Lee was leaning on a chair at the back of the nearly-vacant chamber.

He snapped out of his funk, forcing a smile. "You go ahead and take Lee home. I'll be home in a few." He gave Lee a little wave.

Dillon's expression gave no indication of what he thought of his father's performance. He watched his son leave wishing he could talk to him now. He sighed, shook his head, and gathered up his papers.

He thanked Sergeant Mahnken on the way out, locked the front door panic bar, and gave the door a good tug, mainly to get everyone's attention that it was time to leave. He stood outside by the door, pretending to read the top paper on his stack, hoping some of the Green Valley supporters, his friends, would come over and shake hands. He looked up after a moment to see a large cluster of project proponents in a circle by the parking lot listening intently to Scott Graves. There were several smaller groups of opponents nearby, laughing. Nobody came up to him or beckoned him over. He felt like a man without a country.

He faked a nonchalant air and headed to the car slowly, hoping anyone from either side would befriend him along the way. A few did say "good night." They just weren't the people who understood and mattered.

As he neared his car, he felt his cell phone vibrate. He pulled it out of the holster and saw the screen announce it was his assistant, Jane Stanar.

"Glad you called, Jane," he said, "I can use a little propping up right now."

"...have been worse," Jane said.

"You watched the meeting?" Brad asked.

"...screwed the pooch" he heard a man in the background say. There was something familiar about that voice.

"Jane?" Brad said.

There was muffled conversation he couldn't make out. He pulled the phone away and stared at the screen, confused. It was Jane all right. He put the phone back to his ear and heard a man's voice, but it was too noisy outside to pick out all the words. He figured it out. She had pocket-dialed him by mistake.

"Jane!" he yelled.

He heard her say, "At least he finally recommended that compromise. And he fired Megan."

His heart raced. She was talking about him! Who was she with? He jammed the phone hard against his left ear. A small group, several cars away, erupted in laughter. He glared at them, inserted his key, hurried into the car, and closed the door softly. He missed a little of the dialogue in the process. He thought he heard the male voice say "wimp."

"He's getting pressure from both directions," Jane said clearly.

He picked up bits and pieces of the man's response. He thought the man said something about "the well." He distinctly heard "iron

418

and chromium." Who is that?

He strangled the steering wheel with his right and pressed the phone in his left hand so hard against his ear that it began to hurt. The man was doing most of the talking. His tone was harsh but Brad couldn't track it all at first. Then there was some rustling noise coming through the phone, and the man's voice suddenly became louder and clearer.

". . . take that off and let's celebrate," the man said.

Brad gasped and immediately poked the red circle on the phone, ending the call.

It was the unmistakable, gravelly voice of Hank Nettler.

26

Brad sat in his car under the dim yellow light from
the pole just above him. He'd never felt so alone in his life. A few
diehards still yucked it up outside, their levity fueling his misery. His
chest pounded. Hank Nettler knew about the iron and chromium!
Jane had sold him out. All those leaks. Thought it was Dee. He'd
trusted her with the confidential information about the water quality
problems. He even had her talk to Quinn O'Rourke and write him a
report about it. The betrayal burned through him as if carried by his
blood to every part of his body. He'd trusted her. How blind could he
have been? Jane and Hank Nettler! Never imagined it. Maybe Scott,
but Hank was a married man.

A shiver brought him back to the present. He started the car,
turned up the heater, and drove slowly from the parking lot, his brain
nearly frozen with anger, edging toward panic. He remembered a
pleasant conversation with Hank's wife, Patty, when they ended up

seated next to each other on a Rotary Mystery Trip. It turned out to be a polo match outside Carpinteria, south of Santa Barbara. He didn't know anything about polo or horses, but Patty was very nice to explain things to Marie and him. It was much more interesting to watch once he knew what was going on. They talked about their children. He remembered that brat, Jenny, who had bushwhacked him in Dillon's government class. He felt guilty for feeling revenge. The poor kid. She was smart and cute. Her upbringing wasn't her fault.

By the time he'd made the short drive from City Hall to home, his primary emotion was gloom. He hadn't felt this much pain since finally releasing his mother's cold, pale, bony hand for the last time after her final, shallow breath. Betrayal from his trusted confidante. What did it mean?

Marie was in bed and Dillon in his room when he got home. He poured himself a tall bourbon on the rocks and turned on *Midway* in a futile effort to distract his mind.

"That's kinda loud," Marie complained, coming down the stairs, pulling her floor length blue velour robe tighter.

"Sorry," he said, reaching for the remote. He muted the volume on the TV and took a big swallow of bourbon.

She spotted the distinctive brown bottle on the kitchen counter. "Must have been a doozy of a meeting."

"You didn't watch?" he said, with amazement.

"Bridge at Lilly's tonight. Remember?"

He nodded like he did and took another swallow.

She sat in the black leather couch across from him and threw on the comforter draped over one arm. "Tell me about it?"

He summarized the commission meeting and the inadvertent call from Jane afterwards. Marie was as shocked as he was.

"So you think she's been feeding Hank information all this time?"

"I don't know how long she's been seeing him. You know I'm the last to hear the local gossip. I know for sure that she told him about the problems with the city well field. I heard her say it." He looked down at his drink. "I never would have believed she would do that to me." He rattled the ice and took a swallow.

"What are you going to do?" Marie asked.

"I've been wondering the same thing. I'm so blown away by Jane's treachery that I haven't processed what it means for the Nettlers to know about our well problems."

"Maybe I can be your sounding board," Marie offered, tucking the comforter around her. "Using your normal way of looking at the world, what's the worst that could happen?"

He slapped the chair and snapped, "I told you! I don't know!"

"Simmer down," she said. "Let's work through it."

He took a deep breath. "Sorry." He gathered his thoughts before continuing. "Jane told Hank about the iron and chromium problems at the well. We don't know ourselves how serious that is, so she couldn't tell him what we don't know ourselves. All he would know is that we are investigating water quality at Well #2, and that could affect their deal with SoCal."

"That doesn't sound bad," Marie said encouragingly.

He started to relax then stiffened. "Oh, crap, she probably told him about all the slackers at the water plant, too."

"What could he do with *that* information, again, in a worst case scenario?" Marie prompted.

He threw up his hands and shrugged. "I don't know. It sure wouldn't seem like he'd want that information out there. He'd know it would reflect badly on city management. Maybe he wouldn't care if it hurts me but they'd realize Dee would take the first bullet and they probably want to keep him around. Besides, with SoCal already diccy over the whole tertiary water cost, I wouldn't think Nettlers would want anything negative about the city getting out. They'd want predictability."

The mantel clock broke the temporary silence, its histrionics taking forever to simply announce it was 11 p.m. Annoying. Get rid of that damn thing.

"Unless…." His voice trailed off, as he stroked his chin.

"Yes?" Marie urged.

"What if Nettlers are planning to use the information as leverage against me? They could say something like 'I know all about the scandal at the water plant you've been covering up but you can count on me to keep it quiet,' with God-only- knows what kind of quid pro quo attached. Or, maybe they didn't like the termination agreement I made with Megan or how I handled the tertiary compromise tonight. Maybe they're going to expose the water plant problems to get me fired."

Marie shook her head. "Your first thought makes more sense. It doesn't seem like Nettlers benefit by having problems with the water plant circulating. I can see him buddying up to you with what he knows, like he's doing you a big favor."

"Yeah, probably. Why do I keep thinking of the scene in *The Godfather* where Don Corleone tells the undertaker he'll take care of his troubles, but there may be a time when he'll be asked to return the favor?"

She chuckled. "It's not like he's going to ask you to rub out Kay."

"No," he agreed, taking a sip of bourbon. "I just don't like surprises. It can't be good for the Nettlers to think they have something on me."

"So, just talking out loud. . ." she started.

"Thinking," he corrected.

"What?"

"Just *thinking* out loud. You always screw that up."

"Look, buster, my bed and book are a lot more appealing right now than Hank, *Midway*, and your bourbon." She was smiling but he got the point.

"OK, pleeeeease finish your thought."

She smiled. "So, even if Hank does buddy up to you and try to extract something for keeping it quiet, so what? Isn't that information going to come out at some point soon, anyway? He really doesn't have that much leverage."

"Hmmm. Maybe my only problem right now is that I've got a confidential assistant I can't trust anymore."

"I just can't believe Jane would sell you out like that," Marie challenged.

"I heard it myself. I can't have someone in that job I can't trust. I'm going to have to let her go."

"Oh," she cried. "Do you? Really? Can't you just be more careful not to give her access to information that you want kept confidential?"

"I can't do it, Marie. I trust my staff until they prove to be untrustworthy. Then I can't use them anymore. Especially my own assistant. I tell her everything so she can be more help. And to sell me out for Hank Nettler? I couldn't imagine a worse person. Well, except for Hubie."

"But if you fire her, won't you have the Nettlers all over you, in addition to losing a top-notch assistant?"

"Geez, that's right. I'd be making two problems out of one." He stroked his chin again. "If this were a TV show, the good guys would figure a way to use the secret information the bad guys know against them."

"You're not that conniving," his wife said. "I don't think you should play that kind of game with the Nettlers. They're experts at it."

"Probably right. Better not say anything about what I heard. Let it ride for now but be careful going forward. I sure don't need to have the Nettlers even more pissed at me."

"Right, keep your powder dry for the time being," she agreed, standing up and throwing the comforter aside. "I'm going back to bed." She headed for the stairs.

"Night, hon, thanks. I'm calming down already." He swirled the bourbon around the glass, as she started up the stairs. A sudden jolt. "Wait!"

Marie turned instantly on the stairs. "What? What?"

"I just thought of something. Maybe playing it cool isn't an option. What if Jane already discovered that she pocket-dialed me and told Hank I might have heard them? He may already be planning to strike."

She came back to the couch. "How would she discover that?"

"I hung up after just a couple of minutes when she pocket-dialed me. But she didn't. She never ended my call. Her line stayed open the whole time until whenever it was she saw the open call and hung up. That could well have been after an all-night push-up session with Hank, for all I know. She'll think I heard a lot more than I did. Oh, God!"

Marie weighed that a moment. "Slow down. I don't think it works like that. I think that as soon as you hung up, you disconnected on her side, too. She doesn't have to hang up to disconnect with you. It's not a problem."

A wave of hope fluttered in his chest. "You sure?"

"I think so," she said, with less certainty than he would have preferred. "Do you know what kind of cell phone she has?"

"iPhone, like mine. We sometimes talk about new apps we've found."

"Perfect. Let's do an experiment."

They simulated the pocket dial, from Marie's phone and demonstrated that Jane's phone would have disconnected when Brad did. She showed that even in the unlikely event Jane looked at her "Recents" screen, then hit the little "i" circle to get more information about the inadvertent call with Brad, all it would show is the time and duration of the call.

"Look," Marie concluded triumphantly, "at the worst, she may figure out she accidentally called you, and that the call lasted only a couple of minutes. No big deal. She doesn't know if you heard anything at all, and, looking at the time, she's not going to have any idea what she and Hank were saying or doing at that exact time."

"You're right, Sherlock!" He put down his phone, picked up his glass, and toasted her. "She won't know what I heard even if she digs into it. I don't have to do anything when I see her in the morning. I can play this out how I want to. Not that I know what that is yet." He twirled the tumbler admiring the amber liquid swirling around the tinkling ice.

"Thanks, hon. Finding out Jane has been the source of all the leaks coming out of City Hall has really put me in a tailspin. I wasn't thinking clearly. I'm glad you came down and helped me sort it out."

"Helped *you* sort it out?" she snickered. "Left to your own devices, you were headed for another night of falling asleep in your chair. Now come to bed."

"Pretty soon. I want to relax with the movie."

She got up and dropped her comforter at his chair, just in case, and gave him a peck on the cheek.

He waited for her to get upstairs, finished his last swallow of bourbon, and headed to the kitchen for a refill.

"Go light on that," she warned from the top of the stairs. "You'll need your wits about you tomorrow."

"Love you," he replied from the kitchen.

27

It was a morning like too many others lately. Brad hit the alarm, more tired than when he went to bed. He pivoted to the side of the bed with a groan, put his feet on the ground, and rubbed his head. Too much bourbon last night. He thought about calling in sick. A lot of people did that on Fridays. He had so much sick leave on the books, he could stay home until Easter. He teetered on the edge of the bed, trying to decide which way to lean, then swore to himself, and trudged to the bathroom. He got himself ready, popped two aspirins, drank a smoothie, and left for the office about six minutes later than normal.

He felt a wave of relief approaching the glass panels of his outer office seeing that Jane wasn't at her desk. All the scenarios he had played out about how he would greet her this morning might be for naught. Maybe *she* would call in sick. He walked slowly to his office, plopped his briefcase on the credenza, hung up his sport coat, and went back to the outer office to make coffee.

He bit open the coffee packet and took a moment to enjoy the deep roast aroma. Maybe today would be all right after all. He stood by the coffee maker, listening to it gurgle and pop, inhaling the pungent steam. Looking out through the glass wall, he saw Jane coming through the City Hall entrance, uncharacteristically late. His impulse was to make a hasty retreat to his office, but the coffee maker was taking an eternity to produce a cup of the elixir. He pivoted quickly to avoid eye contact, and grabbed a water conservation brochure from the rack next to him, pretending to read it. The door opened behind him.

"Good morning," she said quietly. He knew instantly she wasn't herself. He didn't care.

"Good morning," he replied coolly, without turning around. He kept his head bent to the brochure while glancing impatiently at the coffee pot. Out of the corner of his eye, he saw Jane go to her desk, retrieve the filing cabinet key from her not-so-imaginative hiding place, unlock the master latch and begin opening the doors, her back to him.

He saw the opportunity, quickly poured a cup, and walked briskly through the swinging door by her desk into his office, without a further word. He knew already that this wasn't going to work. How could he ignore her? He sat at his desk, staring out the door to the corner of Jane's desk, wondering what was going on with her.

He knew Jane was seated at her desk, but there were no sounds. No phone calls, shuffling of papers, or computer pings. Nothing. What was she doing? After a few minutes, he heard her chair squeak and saw her come around the desk toward the outer door. He heard the lock on the door clank in place. She was at his door a moment later.

"Got a minute?" she said.

She looked terrible. Her normally perfect hair was in disarray and her eye make-up smeared. She looked tired, like she'd hardly slept. Her face was puffy and her left cheek a little red. Had she been crying?

"I guess," he replied guardedly. He stayed in his chair behind the desk, watching her take a seat at the coffee table.

She looked down at her folded hands for a moment before breaking the silence. "Something happened last night. I wasn't sure if I was going to talk to you about it, or not. It's embarrassing. But I have to tell you."

"Uh huh?" He rested his chin on his pointed index fingers and waited.

She gathered herself and looked up at him through bloodshot, hazel eyes. "The Nettlers know about the problems with the well. You know, about the chromium and iron. They know all about it."

"Well, of course they do," he exploded, "you told them!"

"What?"

"Oh, save it, Jane. I know all about it."

She shook her head and seemed on the verge of tears. "But…"

"How do I know?" He leaned back and smirked. "You ought to be a little more careful with your cell phone."

She cocked her head and stared at him.

"Look, you accidentally called me last night on your cell. I didn't listen long, but long enough to hear you tell Hank about the wells."

"No!" she protested.

He picked up a paper clip and began pulling it apart. "Come on, I heard what you said to him. I wish I hadn't. I didn't sleep at all last night because of it. I never thought you'd betray my trust."

She sat rigidly, shaking with a look of shock. A tear escaped down the side of her nose. "No. I didn't. You have it all wrong. What did you hear?"

He clenched his jaw, threw the paper clip into the waste basket, and smacked the top of his desk so loudly that the picture frame of his family fell over. "I heard you tell Hank about my going along with the tertiary compromise and firing Megan, and then you talked about the well problems."

"No," she cried, shaking her head slowly.

"I *specifically* heard Hank talk about the iron and chromium. Where do you *think* he got *that?* God only knows how much you've been telling him." The burning betrayal that had coursed through his veins the previous night now reignited. Jane was about to become a burn victim.

"Hank Netter?! God, Jane, of all people. How could you do that to me? To yourself, for that matter?"

"I've been asking myself that for the last eight months, Brad."

"Eight months?! You've been seeing him for eight months? I've never even heard any rumor about you two." His mind raced back over all the confidential information he had given her during that period that was now compromised.

Jane wiped her face with her hand. "We've known each other since school days, but the relationship changed at a party Scott threw last spring. Hank and his wife had separated. In fact, he moved out of their house and into the main house on the property with Hubie over a year ago. He keeps talking about divorcing, but I haven't pushed it."

"You don't push the Nettlers," he acknowledged.

"Well, Hank's not the same as Hubie. Sure, he has some rough edges. But he's been very sweet to me and the girls. Very generous, too. We kept it quiet because we didn't want people to assume what you are assuming now...that I'm some kind of snitch for the Nettlers."

"It's an easy assumption to make."

"I've told myself over and over to break it off. Alex has been gone for two years now. And there's not a lot to choose from in town. I don't have much time away from work and raising the girls to look around, anyway. I wasn't about to do the bar scene. It just kind of happened with Hank. The companionship has been nice. But, you have to believe me, I never told him anything I shouldn't have."

She was looking at him directly, pleading with her eyes. "I'd like to believe you, Jane, but I haven't recovered from the shock of learning my trusted confidante has been sleeping with the enemy."

She slumped, dropped her head into her hands, and sobbed deeply. He checked his impulse to comfort her. He'd been made a sap by a woman's tears before. Someone jiggled the locked outer office door. Neither made a move to open it. His right foot tapped the floor as he waited for her.

Her face was a mess of tears and smeared mascara. Her left cheek looked different, puffier, redder. He sighed, got up, and handed her a small square box of Kleenex in a green floral pattern from his credenza. The lotion scent of the tissue reminded him about teasing Marie over her purchase. Do we really need to have a scented tissue in a special box with color-coordinated patterns?

She wiped her face and blew her nose. His mind strayed back to "the great tissue analysis," when he demonstrated to Marie the per sheet price of the lotion-laced tissue in the special box compared to plain old white, from the normal, rectangular box. He still caught hell for that. He sat back behind his desk and waited impatiently for Jane to compose herself.

She wadded up the tissue and looked down at her lap. "I never revealed any confidential information, Brad. Not to Hank. Not to anyone. Sure, he sometimes asked me about you and things at work. But it was a line I never crossed, and he knew it. It was never a problem until last night."

"Jane, I heard you two talking about the iron and chromium at the well. Do you really expect me to believe that he didn't get that information from you?"

"Yes!" she exclaimed. "Because it's the truth! I don't know what you heard last night. Hank is the one who brought up the well, not me."

He moved from his desk to a chair at the coffee table across from her. "Hank?" he replied suspiciously. "Tell me about it."

"Well, Hank came over for dinner and brought some nice wines. I couldn't get a sitter, and he wanted to watch the commission meeting, anyway. So, we just stayed home, drank wine, and watched the meeting. A lot of wine. I don't remember everything word for word, but it was fine until he started getting really mad...at you."

He tensed. "Me?"

She nodded. "Hank said you were supposed to propose the change to having the study only look at tertiary water for the golf course. When you didn't do that at the beginning of the meeting he started getting really mad. He told me the family gets a half million dollar option payment from SoCal once the EIR is launched. He was afraid SoCal would pull the plug if they thought the full tertiary requirement was even a possibility. He said Scott was OK with the golf-course-only study because they thought they'd get you to give them a credit on the Development Agreement."

"That tracks. I know I disappointed Scott by not coming out with that compromise right off the bat. I had a lot of things swirling around in my mind at the time."

"I told Hank not to give up on you," she said. "But as the night dragged out with all of those speakers, and you still not supporting the compromise, he got even madder. Drunker and madder."

"Didn't he calm down after I recommended the reduced study at the end of the hearing, and especially after the commission approved the IS that way?"

"A little. He was pretty drunk by then. He called you a wimp, waiting to make your recommendation when you knew it would be safe. He kept going on about how you almost cost them a half million dollars and, forgive me, how you didn't have the balls to push the project along?"

"I see."

"The more I tried to defend you, the madder he got. It was like he was jealous. He started bragging about how they could get you fired anytime they wanted."

"Probably right. I didn't make any friends on either side of the project last night. But how did the well water quality come up?"

She crushed her tissue and looked up to the ceiling a moment. "He said something about using SoCal's option payments to plant alfalfa and expand their cattle business into dairy, also. He said they have been taking their own water samples at the well and knew about the chromium and iron increases. He laughed about how they got the city to give them unlimited water when they sold that well site. He said the water quality isn't a problem for cows."

"Hmmm," Brad mulled. "Hank said something about getting into dairy operations at Rotary a while back. I assumed he was talking about doing that on other land they own. Was it your impression he was talking about having a dairy business on the Green Valley Village site?"

"I don't know, for sure," she said, still shredding her tissue. "He started to get pretty ugly by then. He started laughing. I kept asking him what was so funny. He finally said, 'paybacks are hell.'"

"What was he talking about?"

"I wasn't paying close enough attention at this point. I had too much wine myself. But I was getting a little scared by how he was acting. He said something about sticking it to the city again."

He leaned back in the chair and rested his lower lip on the steeple of his raised index fingers. "Let me sort this out. The Nettlers have been doing their own samples of the well and know about the iron and chromium. They are worried that SoCal won't make their option payment if they don't get the tertiary compromise deal and bail on the project now. But they must know that the water quality problem at the well is going to come out, eventually. And when it does, it's likely going to require us to implement expensive additional treatment at a minimum, and maybe even force us to take the well offline entirely, if the same problem shows up in test wells elsewhere in the aquifer."

He tapped his chin with his fingers, deep in thought. "Nettlers are smart. They know we aren't going to want to stick that treatment cost on our current residents and businesses, especially if we can show we have enough water for the existing customers without that well. We'll be more likely to impose the obligation on Green Valley to pay for the treatment. Given how nervous SoCal already is about their pro forma, that condition might kill the whole deal."

He stared out the window. "The family likely makes a killing with the land sale to SoCal. Why would Hank not care more about the well problem? And what's that got to do with a dairy?"

"I don't get it either, Brad. At that point in the night, I was more interested in getting him out of my house than trying to understand their motives."

Lost in thought, he let her statement pass. He suddenly straightened up wagging his right index finger in the air. "Hah!" was all that came out.

"What, Brad?"

He nodded his head slightly and turned to face her. "Unless they never intended to sell the 550 acres at all."

"What?" she protested. "But you said yourself they probably will make a killing selling that land once the project is approved."

"True, but we don't know how much they stand to net from that sale after taxes. Their basis would be like zero."

"I don't follow you, Brad."

"Maybe, after taxes, they are better off long-term expanding into a dairy operation. Besides, have you ever known Nettlers to sell the family's land? I remember Scott telling me about how convoluted their option agreement was. It had all kinds of nonrefundable progress payments tied to milestones in the approval process. You said they are getting a half million dollars once this EIR gets underway. Approval of the IS launches the EIR. Maybe that's their whole scheme. Just string the city and SoCal along and collect as much as they can in progress payments. Even if the water issues turn out to be serious enough to scuttle the project, they keep their land and SoCal's progress payments to invest in the dairy operation."

Jane sat back in her chair. "You think?"

"Just a theory. I can see why a large dairy on the Green Valley site would appeal to them. It's close to public streets for the truck traffic and the power grid. They would still have unlimited water from the city well. If they stay in the unincorporated area, a dairy would be allowed by county zoning. Plus, maybe they like knowing that the smells, noise and other nuisances from such an intensive land use so close to the city limits will cause us all kinds of citizen complaints. That would sure 'stick it to' us if that's what Hank was referring to."

Jane looked skeptical. "But what about all the disappointment from everyone trying to push the project along. They'll sure be mad at Nettlers if the land becomes a dairy instead."

"Uh huh," he agreed. "There are a lot of people counting on things in the Development Agreement or the additional business. Even if Nettlers keep the option money and do their dairy, they still have to live in this community. They won't want to make the Green Valley collapse their fault. They…" his voice trailed off.

Jane picked up the thread instantly. "They would want the city staff to take the fall for killing the project. Maybe because of the water quality problem. Is that what you're thinking, Brad?"

"Exactly! God, here's a horrible thought. What if Nettlers know about all the goings on at the water plant? They must know we are going to have to reveal the problems with the well pretty soon. What if they plan to take this half-million-dollar progress payment from SoCal, and leak the water plant and well quality stuff themselves, right after they get their money? City staff, and me in particular, look even worse for covering it up, like we are just lackeys of SoCal. The public is outraged against the city and turns on the project. SoCal bolts. The Nettlers are publicly shocked about losing the project but commit to preserving their land in agricultural use. They keep their pro-development backers, since it wasn't their fault the deal collapsed, and they win some points with Kay and her group for committing to keep ag and not pursue development with somebody besides SoCal. Heck, that way, they might end up getting support from both sides when they go after the use permit for a dairy. The city ends up with nothing but complaints while Nettlers come out smelling like a rose."

Jane groaned. "You might be right. And I hate to say it, but from what Hank said about you, I think they believe that you won't say anything about the wells until you don't have any choice. Hank kept talking about how you'd count the votes and not want to rock the boat until you had to come out with it. I don't know how far down the road that would be, but maybe they figure they can collect even more progress payments from SoCal before you finally let the cat out of the bag."

"Hmmm. So they are counting on me to just keep everything percolating along on Green Valley, huh? Quinn and Dee both said it could take six months before we drill test wells and know where we stand with our well field. Nettlers may well get more money out of SoCal during that period. From what you're saying, they are counting on me not to do anything until after that. Nettlers may push Scott to talk to councilmembers today, since they saw me waiver a little last night on the tertiary compromise. Get the Council majority to put some back pressure on me to expedite the processing."

"Hard to say what they'll do next," Jane said. "But muscle is their go-to tactic. I could see them and the Green Valley supporters brow beating the mayor and vice mayor, and maybe even Al Landon, to be tougher with you to push the project forward, just to hit another milestone or two before it unravels."

"And none of them will suspect what we do. For all we know, once they've milked all the progress payments they can, Nettlers might start a whisper campaign to get people jacked up about chromium in their water, like in *Erin Brockovich.* People will want to hang on to their other water sources. They'll be less willing to give any to Green Valley."

Jane nodded, going along with the scenario. "And you and Scott will take the heat from your bosses if the project can't get enough water, or you have to load the project with extra treatment costs. Some people will celebrate if it goes down, but like you said, there are a lot of others who want the project."

"Yeah, I may get four, instead of three, people holding the rope for my lynching if we lose some of the goodies in the DA."

Jane looked pensive. "Of course, we don't know if this is Nettlers' strategy, but it all fits, based on things Hank said last night. I remember him saying something like you'd end up holding the bag on the water issues. I complained that wasn't fair, given how hard you were working to get the project approved. He got jealous again, and told me I should care more about him, and what the family stood to make, than for how it would affect you or Scott. We had words and he slapped me."

"Oh Jane, I'm sorry."

"Me too." She caressed the red spot on her left cheek. "It wasn't a hard blow, but it was enough to knock some sense into me. I threatened to call the cops and kicked him out."

"Good for you."

"Before he left, he threatened that I better keep my mouth shut or they'd make sure you and I were both gone."

"I don't know if he could pull the votes to get me fired. Maybe. But he's got more to lose than you if word gets out about your relationship. He's still the married one. So he's not going to come after you."

"I'm not so positive about that. He said, 'nobody ever took on the Nettlers and came away from it good.' He went on about how everyone knew he was separated, and he'd get macho points from his buddies when they learn he's been sleeping with me. He didn't stop there. He said he'd tell everybody I was his spy at City Hall. He said I'd be ruined in this town and not able to get another job anywhere around here. He was slurring his words at this point, but I believe he meant what he said."

"He's a bully. We better keep this conversation between us, Jane. If Hank knows that I know what he said last night, he's likely to do something rash before we have a plan ourselves. I don't know if I'm going to come out of this whole Green Valley thing intact, but that is how it is for city managers. There's no sense in your going down, too. You have your kids to consider."

"Thanks, Brad. I'm a big girl, but you're right that Nettlers are liable to be more dangerous if they feel threatened. And they'd be threatened if they knew you are onto them."

She had a sudden thought. "What about Scott? He deserves to know what's going on, especially before he makes a big payment to them."

"Yeah, I have to figure out how to warn him without telling him so much that Hank will figure out you said something to me. And fast, before he makes that half-million- dollar payment."

Somebody was jiggling the outer door again. It was unusual for the office to be closed at this hour. She raised her eyebrows and nodded toward the door. He agreed, and she left to open the door. He needed some alone time to think.

He recognized the sweet, grandmotherly voice of Connie

Fenton coming from the outer office. She must be making her mail run. Mrs. Fenton was one of the city's community volunteers but had become more than that. She donated her time in the morning to distribute the US and inter-office mail to all the city offices. She dispensed good cheer, recipes, crochet tips to novices, and home remedies to those in need along her route. People loved her. Brad enjoyed her caring personality also, but usually stayed holed up in his office until she left in order to avoid time-consuming mothering. Yes, Connie, he was as tired as he looked. No, Connie, he wasn't getting enough sleep. Yes, Connie, he'll try freshly squeezed lemon in the morning to ward off colds.

He heard Jane talk to Mrs. Fenton a short time, then the outer glass door open and close. Jane appeared at his office door with the mail. She pulled the door knob toward her. "Hold calls and visitors a while?"

"Yes, thanks. You read my mind, Radar. I need some thinking time, and a bigger thinker. And Jane, thanks for coming to me with this. I'm sorry I doubted you. I appreciate you."

"Likewise, boss. I'll be right here if you need me." She smiled and closed the door softly.

He picked up another paper clip and began bending it to different shapes, as his mind processed the situation. After a few minutes of accomplishing only a fair likeness of a right triangle, he tossed the clip on the desk. There were just too many factors to hold in his head at the same time. He made a list:

- *Iron/chromium below MCL, no disclosure legally required…yet*
- *Won't know for months if it's getting bad fast*
- *Expensive treatment more likely worst case than losing entire supply; who pays?*
- *Can we serve GV without the well, with full tertiary?*
- *Can we serve city, not GV, without well?*

- *Nettlers playing SoCal/city?, warn Scott, protect Jane*
- *Majority favors project and good DA*
- *Kay/Megan, Delta, Dillon, protect the water*
- *Ethical responsibilities*

He looked over the list several times trying to formulate a strategy. He thought about some of the pros and cons and technicalities of the notes. Each time, his pen lingered over the last item and added another underline to it.

Since he wasn't getting anywhere anyway, he turned his chair to the wall, leaned back, put his feet on the credenza, and stared at the photograph of Mt. Shasta. He closed his eyes and concentrated on his breathing. It didn't take long before he recognized what was bugging him. "Ethical responsibilities." St. Francis Dam disaster. Lilly's father. LA water grab. Deceiving the voters. Ruining Owens Valley to promote sprawl. The State Water project. An amazing political and engineering feat, but state management so fraught with deceit and private interests over public good. The beat goes on with the arrogant Delta twin tunnels project. Community development driven by money and power; environmental preservation takes a back seat. Am I part of the problem or part of the solution?

He slowly opened his eyes and found himself looking at a plaque just below the Mt. Shasta photo. The International City/County Management Association's Code of Ethics sat largely overlooked, where it had for years, in a frame on his credenza. He scanned it now; twelve tenets calling members to the highest ideals of public service. The profession was constantly revisiting the tenets, adding guidelines that helped members apply the code to real life situations. Anyone could debate the interpretation of the language in a given set of facts. But, clearly, protecting the public interest was the cornerstone of the Code and the value professional city management adds to local government.

His eyes were drawn to Tenet 4: *Recognize that the chief function of local government at all times is to serve the best interests of all of the people.* Interesting. He read it again. That's odd. Typically, when facing a difficult policy recommendation, he was swayed by what he thought the Council majority would want. He read the tenet again and had an "ah ha!" moment.

Somewhere along his lengthy career path, he saw his role morph from protecting the public interest to doing the bidding of the Council majority. Maybe it was the pressures of a mortgage, retirement planning, kids' college, and getting along with the local power brokers. It was certainly less complicated and safer to count three votes than really reflect on the public interest before making a recommendation. Was he, after all, no different from Lilly's dad, or anyone else who sees his main role as satisfying the boss, even if that means suppressing their own sense of integrity?

He closed his eyes again to let this new insight settle in. The fear was palpable. He sat with it a while, breathing in and out fully, to see where it would go. He felt the familiar tension in his gut, chest, and arms starting to give way to a tingle. It felt good. He stayed with his breathing and continued to feel an internal tug of war between fear and excitement. The excitement won out and yielded to a sense of power and resolve. He sat calmly, absorbing the sensation. He knew what he had to do, and knew that he could.

He opened his eyes, said "namaste" to the mountain on the wall, and got up to open his door.

"Jane, what time will the packets get delivered to Council today?"

"Connie usually picks them up around three. But you know her, if you need something different, just tell her."

"Hmmm," he said. "May not give me enough time. Can you ask if she can come later today, like around five?"

"Time for what?" she asked.

"Something else I need to do today."

He closed the door and placed a call.

"All right, Quinn," he snickered, "you know how you wanted me to pay attention to my gut?"

"Yeah," O'Rourke said warily.

"Well, I may end up getting it nice and tan. I may be on the beach soon. Got your crying towel dry cleaned?"

They spent a few minutes talking about the prior night's commission meeting. At Brad's request, O'Rourke hung up to track down the woman at his firm's Ventura office who had done the peer review report on water and set up a conference call. She was sharp and quickly provided answers to Brad's questions. Quinn O'Rourke served as a sounding board, helping Brad brainstorm his options. O'Rourke's biggest contribution was reminding Brad that, even if the worst happens, there is no stigma within the profession from getting fired. In fact, going down over an ethical stand was a red badge of courage. Brad was ready to act.

*****

"Jane, bring your pad, would you?" Brad said firmly.

She settled in at her normal spot at the coffee table, as he got into his dictating position, pacing.

"This is a Council agenda memo. Subject: Reconsideration of Planning Commission Approval of Green Valley Village EIR Initial Study," he began.

"Oh, Brad, are you sure you want to do that?"

"Hell no, I'm not sure! I hear a voice saying 'prepare three envelopes.'"

"But it's so unusual for you to appeal an action by one of the Council's advisory commissions. And you'd be appealing your own recommendation to the commission. You're really going to make yourself the target."

"I know, but, if Scott makes that progress payment to Nettlers, relying on the Planning Commission's approval of the IS, and it later comes out that the city staff knew there were potential problems that could affect the water supply, I think we'd have some liability to SoCal."

"Don't you want to talk to Henry before you bring this down on yourself? Maybe he could send SoCal a notice, or something. Or, why don't you have Dee do the memo?"

He picked up the right triangle paper clip and twirled it silently a while. He smirked and nodded his head, contemplating something. He shifted his gaze to the family portrait on the desk, and his expression turned resolute. He tossed the clip aside and looked squarely at Jane.

"As appealing as it is to have someone else carry the water on this, hey, that's a pun. . .," his voice trailed off as he shifted his eyes to the family photo on his desk.

She looked at him, expectantly.

He resumed, "I finally realized I have a responsibility that I've been evading. Liability and politics aside, I have an ethical obligation to disclose to the public that there are some potential problems with our water supply, before we proceed with the EIR. I have to level with them that we may be looking at needing to pick up some, or all, of the additional treatment costs to serve Green Valley."

Jane looked up at him sadly. "I'm so sorry that my relationship with Hank brought you to this point. You know it's going to be tough for you if you agendize this."

"It's all right. There's a potential upside. Maybe Hank will give me one of his juicy t-bones to nurse the black eye he'll give me."

"That's not even funny."

"Gallows humor. Remember? An occupational hazard."

"Well, I'm sorry for anything I may have done to put you

into harm's way."

"An ironic comment, Jane. That's the name of a war movie that reminds me of my favorite movie. It's time I acted like Admiral Ray Spruance and turned the aircraft carrier into the wind."

"Huh?" she said, not getting the *Midway* reference.

"Never mind. This is now about doing my duty, it's not about you. I put myself in harm's way when I chose this career and took the oath of office. I'm going to call it like I see it now."

She looked alarmed. "Why do *you* have to be such a Boy Scout?"

"I don't know. I guess I've had my eyes opened lately to a few things. I suppose everybody finds forks in the road that cause them to question their sense of right and wrong and personal responsibility."

She broke eye contact and looked down sadly. "Some of us didn't take the right road."

"Don't beat yourself up, Jane. I'm not proud of some of the decisions I've made in my life, either. But I'm reminded about my poster in high school. Do you know the poem *'Desiderata?'*"

"Not sure," she said.

"It's old, but became popular again in the 60s and 70s. There's a line that says, 'And whether or not it is clear to you, no doubt the universe is unfolding as it should.' I've been getting more nudges in that direction lately that make me think that's true. I'm open to the idea that this is all happening for a reason we can't fathom. I can tell you this, if it hadn't been for your relationship with Hank, the accidental cell call last night, and our talk this morning, I might well have ignored my conscience, and felt bad about it later. What I'm doing now feels right."

Jane's look told him she understood.

"Don't beat yourself up, Jane. I'm just grateful for getting a second chance to do what I should have done before." He paused, an image of Lilly's father passing through his mind. "I may suffer from this short-term, but I'm going to be able to look in the mirror the rest of my life."

"You're quite a guy, Brad."

"Not really. Just another flawed human being who's trying to get better. Let's finish the memo before I get cold feet."

He labored over the words as he paced around the room, making constant revisions.

"Sorry," he apologized. "I think I'm saying more than I need to right now. I'm not trying to cover up the problems at the water plant, or minimize the potential ramifications on Green Valley, but the disciplinary stuff is a personnel matter that's likely to end up at the Council for appeal. And we truly don't know how big a deal this is going to be for the city's water supply yet. I should be more general. Let's start over."

He finished dictating the memo with his recommendation to the City Council and returned to his desk.

As Jane got up to leave, he said, "Oh, let's keep this confidential for the time being, right?"

"Sure, Brad. I've never let you down."

"I know. Now. Would you go ahead and finalize the memo but don't send it for copying just yet, in case I decide to make some changes? Oh, and please ask Dee to come down."

*****

Brad briefed his public works director on his decision to ask the Council to reconsider the commission's action on the Initial Study because of the water quality issues. Dee Sharma attempted to talk him out of the appeal by repeating his prior worry that it would bring immediate controversy to them both and quite possibly prove to be an unnecessary alarm.

Brad held the course and cut the meeting short, telling Dee he needed to get on the phone immediately to inform the Council about his revised recommendation on the IS before the packets went out.

He busied himself the rest of the morning with paperwork and returned phone calls, but couldn't keep his mind from mulling how events might unfold.

He went home for lunch and caught Marie up on his misreading of the situation with Jane, and his decision to appeal the commission action to the Council.

"You are doing the right thing," Marie said consolingly. "They have golf courses up by Stockton, too, I hear."

28

Back in the office after lunch, Brad put the finishing touches on his counter-proposal to the boutique hotel developer and gave it to Jane to prepare for his signature. He looked at his watch. Nothing yet.

He picked up the Police Department's year-end crime report and thumbed through it, killing time. His eyes caught a paragraph heading in eighteen-point bold type, "Auto Theft Up 50%." He looked closer and grinned. Three last year. Gotta love living in Santa Ynez! How much longer would he have the pleasure? He saw that property crimes were up 16 percent, but the totals were still small. Violent crime was down. He knew what to expect in the text and found it. The drop in violent crime was tied to the Police Department's aggressive community policing initiatives, while the property crime increase was blamed on broader economic and social trends. He smirked and tossed the voluminous report aside.

He looked at his watch again and checked through his emails. After a half hour of half-heartedly going through the in-basket, he was relieved to hear his phone buzz.

"Scott Graves," Jane announced.

He grinned and swept up the phone. "Scott! You beat me to it. I was just getting ready to call you."

"Afternoon, Brad. It sounds like we need to talk."

"About what?" he said coyly.

"About your revised recommendation on the IS, of course."

"Boy, do you have a bug in my office, Scott? I haven't even sent the memo out yet."

"You know how politicians talk. You should be glad people worry about you doing something you'll regret."

Brad sniggered. "I'm grateful to have that kind of support. Who should I call to thank? Buddy? Mullikin?"

"Nice try, Brad. The important thing now is for us to talk this through before you go ahead."

"Talk away. I owe you that much, Scott."

The developer seemed to be searching for the words. "You should know I've spent a lot of time defending you since the commission meeting. People aren't so sure they can count on you to drive this project over the finish line."

"Oh?" Brad responded, matter-of-factly.

"Yeah. I told them you did what you thought was best to get out of the full tertiary study gracefully, even if you hedged on the cost offset and weren't as forceful as we'd hoped. But now, if you change course and recommend the full tertiary study, I don't know what to tell people anymore. And, Jeff Simpson? You have to know he'll be pissed at both of us."

Brad savored his victory.

"Brad, are you still there?" Scott asked.

"I'm here, but you also should know something. First, there are only two people who know about my revised recommendation. And I told them different things. I haven't even called the Council yet. Second, despite what Dee told you, I'm not recommending the full tertiary study."

There was a long silence in the receiver. "Busted," the developer finally admitted. "Don't be hard on Dee. He didn't call me. I was calling him about turning over maintenance at the soccer field and we got to talking about last night. He sounded upset and I dug it out of him. I think he was hoping I'd have some influence on talking you out of it. He was protecting you from yourself."

"I suspect he was more worried about protecting himself," Brad cracked.

"So, you're not asking the Council to change the commission's decision?" Scott asked hopefully.

"No. Postponement of the IS while we figure out what, if any, impact the well issues will have on our water supply."

"Postponement of the IS? Damn it, Brad, that's even worse! I thought we had a good enough relationship that you would have consulted me about this first."

Brad took note that the developer didn't ask about the "well issues." "I had your interests in mind, Scott. You should want to know if our water quality will affect your project before you spend more money for. . ." He caught himself before warning Scott about further option payments to the Nettlers.

"If you're talking about the iron and chromium," Scott said, "we know all about that."

Brad was stunned by the revelation, but didn't want it to show. "Then, why are you worried about a little delay? Don't you and Jeff want to know the lay of the land before you commit much more on this project?"

The receiver went silent a moment. "I guess I shouldn't have expected you to understand," Scott said glumly. "You live in a world that puts the emphasis on process and risk management. If a developer did that, we'd go broke. You have to take chances to make real money."

"I get that, Scott," Brad said. It was a theme he'd heard from his father all his life and his friends in the private sector. "It even drives me crazy sometimes. I'm more like the old school city managers who want to see things coming out of the ground. But I've come to understand that sometimes running roughshod over public processes hasn't turned out well. I may not like it either but I think it's best to have a little more process in this case before we jump ahead."

Scott continued. "As I started to say, we don't often have the luxury of time and doing things sequentially to minimize risk. We have to run concurrent processes, make educated guesses, and take big chances."

"But you'd be running a helluva risk proceeding without certainty about our ability to supply your water."

"Sure, it's a risk. Everything we do is a calculated risk. And, by the way, Dee didn't tell me about the iron and chromium problem. Nettlers did. Nearly six months ago. We brought in our engineers. Their assessment was that it's very unlikely it will be bad enough to take the entire well field out of production. It may eventually require some additional treatment, but it's doable."

It took a moment for that to register. "Wait, you've known about this for six months?" Brad exclaimed.

"Sure. Nettlers' lawyers probably warned them that it would likely come out eventually that they had done their own testing, so they better disclose it to us, or we could nail them big time later. Nettlers may not be nice people, but they have good lawyers who cover their butts."

"You guys were bitching so much about just tertiary treatment for the golf course. Aren't you worried about a big bill on additional treatment for the chromium? Reverse osmosis is expensive, I hear."

Scott sighed again. "It didn't serve our interests for there to be any question about water supply just yet. And as for the cost of the additional treatment, that's a cost you'll have to spread to the entire customer base, you can't just stick it on our project. The water quality problems are an existing condition. We didn't cause it, and we won't be the only ones to pay to fix it. Our pro forma includes a contingency for our fair share of the problem, but nothing for tertiary. Despite what you said last night, we can't just add that to the house prices. The studies show we are already pushing the market as is. We usually don't get this far in a new project without projecting a much higher return. Jeff's been willing to keep going because I've convinced him we had solid cost estimates, and lots of local support to get everything done quickly to minimize our risk. That's why I needed you to come out strong for the tertiary compromise and cost offset."

Brad's victory lap from finally exposing the City Hall leak had been cut short. "I see," he said remorsefully.

"Look, you manage a city. Most of the time, it doesn't matter that much if some decision gets made now, or months later. Or if a capital improvement project is built now or next year. In our business, timing is critical, like money. We have Green Valley programmed in our plans to begin construction in two years. To do that, we have to hit our schedules. If you are talking about putting everything on hold until after there are test wells and other steps taken to fully resolve the water issues, we miss the construction season we've targeted."

Brad felt the recurring demon of self-doubt rising up.

Scott continued his lecture. "And, if we miss that construction window, *everything* is up in the air. We always have other projects moving through the stages competing for our time and money. I've told you before that Green Valley isn't a big homerun for the company. It's a small project with barely adequate returns. It's been left in the pipeline to keep our people busy. If the delay you want puts us off schedule,

Green Valley goes back into the pot to compete with other projects we thought would come online later. And I know it won't compete well."

"I see," Brad said again.

"I know you were trying to do the right thing by your job and to protect us at the same time. But, to be honest, I'd rather you had just proposed the full tertiary, like I thought you were doing, rather than a postponement. I can get the votes to kill the full tertiary, but how do I mobilize against a city manager who says he's suddenly worried about his water supply and wants more information before committing to such a big new development? Where you come down makes or breaks this project."

"I can see your point, Scott. And yes, I wasn't intending to make this more difficult for SoCal. Just the opposite."

"But, it's not too late, right?" Scott said hopefully. "You haven't talked to the Council yet, and you said the memo hasn't gone out, right? Don't bring everything to a grinding halt. Let the commission decision stand. We'll deal with the water stuff later."

After a long silence he shrugged. "I appreciate that, Scott. And I hope we can keep things together. But you said it yourself. You and I have different drivers. My primary responsibility is to support the public interest, not expedite private interest. I almost forgot that. It's not always easy to ferret out what is in the overall public's best interest. I personally think Green Valley has a lot to offer the public. The public itself should weigh in on that, based on the best information I can bring forward. I'm not comfortable withholding information from them. And I also don't want to set the city up for a lawsuit from SoCal later if the water problem ends up killing the project."

"Oh, come on, Brad. We're not going to sue you if you agree to keep processing our application like we ask you to while the water stuff is analyzed. Maybe we could have our attorneys work with Henry Fitzhenry on a hold harmless agreement to that affect. If it stays private."

"Don't know if that's possible, Scott."

"Let's look into it if it's something you think you need. You're more worried about this water problem than we are. Like I said, our engineers say the worst case scenario is adding some expensive additional treatment at the well. We're prepared to pay our fair share of that. We'll also do the golf course tertiary, if you give us some relief on our development fees to offset it. There's no risk to the city if you keep going with the entitlement processing."

Brad felt a moment of exhilaration that quickly disappeared. "Not quite, Scott. I see another option for the public. I confirmed with Payton today that if we end up exceeding the MCLs for iron and chromium at the well, we could take it offline entirely, rather than paying for the extra treatment. We'd have enough remaining supply for the existing General Plan area. But not with Green Valley added. We might have to jack up our water rates a bit and institute tougher conservation measures to live with the reduced supply. I don't know yet what that would look like, but it's one of the alternatives I'd want studied during the postponement period. Then, when we have better information, the public can comment on the alternatives and the Council can decide."

"Oh, God, Brad. Jeff is going to freak if he hears you are recommending postponement of the IS. If you even hint that taking the well offline is a possibility, he'll shut us down today."

Brad thought a moment. "I can recommend the postponement without mentioning the possibility of taking the well offline. I was going to be vague on the details anyway, since we really don't have all the facts yet. No point in throwing out all sorts of doomsday scenarios at this early stage. I'd need you to say publicly that you prefer to continue at your risk. That meets my sense of ethical responsibility. And, of course, if you can get three votes to defeat my recommendation and proceed with the IS, so be it. No hard feelings."

They wrangled a few minutes longer about the subjectivity of the terms "ethics" and "public interest" without agreeing to a definition or how the terms applied to the Green Valley controversy. Brad pulled the receiver from his ear, closed his eyes, and leaned back in his chair, waiting for the developer to finish.

"Maybe we can continue this discussion over a beer sometime, Scott. Right now, I have work to do. And I intend to do it in a way that meets my own sense of responsibility. I intend to agendize a recommendation to notify the responsible agencies that we are postponing circulation of the IS. Let the Council decide it."

Another pause on the line. "I can see your mind is made up, Brad. I wish it weren't. I better tell Jeff in person so I can peel him off the roof. Assuming he doesn't fire me on the spot, I'll try to get him to allow me to commit we'd hold you harmless if you keep the EIR going while the water study proceeds. With that, I'm confident I can get at least three votes to overrule you, if you aren't too aggressive in what you say, that is."

"I don't plan to be," Brad assured him.

"My problem is still Jeff's nervousness about where *you* are. Suggesting the postponement, rather than working in partnership with us to expedite the project, is bad enough. So, this is important. I need your absolute commitment that you won't talk about taking the well offline on Tuesday, and, if we get the votes to proceed, you won't include that in any study of alternatives."

"Like I said, I don't feel compelled to say anything about that option at the Council meeting next week. It's premature. Besides, didn't Chicken Little get eaten by a fox? If pressed, I can say that we are aware of the potential need for additional treatment at one of our wells and just need some time to be sure about the alternatives before we proceed with the IS. That's honest, and shouldn't spook the public, or Jeff, for that matter."

"And you won't plant the option of closing the well with somebody else to bring up Tuesday? Right?"

The question jolted him. "Of course, Scott!" He hesitated. "But you know that if the study concludes we have to spend millions of dollars to treat one or both wells and increase water rates to do it, somebody is going to ask what happens if we just close them or use the well water for irrigation and other non-potable uses."

It was the developer's turn to deliberate. "I suppose somebody might ask that. And we should be prepared with a strategy for addressing that if it comes up. We can work behind the scenes with you on that. We'll demonstrate that if the wells come offline, people will have to cut back their consumption, maybe do some things they won't like: browning out their lawns or not washing their cars or hosing down their patios. If they want to keep the wells and avoid all of that, they'd have to pay even higher rates, if and when the additional treatment is needed, if they don't have Green Valley Village helping to shoulder the burden."

"Quite likely," Brad acknowledged. He recalled Kay Graves' worry about people opting to pay more for water to protect their property values and lifestyle rather than suffering big cutbacks.

Scott's voice reflected encouragement. "In fact, we can probably get people to see that supporting Green Valley Village is a way to offload a big chunk of that pending cost and not have to kill their lawns. And they can keep all the other benefits you've squeezed out of us in the DA. We can sell it, even if the extra treatment becomes necessary and somebody raises the well closure question."

Brad scowled. "A good PR firm could sell a bladeless jackknife without a handle. Look how much money and garbage is made because they convinced us to buy bottled water at an outrageous price per ounce that's really no better than what comes out of the tap. Sorry, that's a pet peeve."

"I can tell. Anyway, back to Jeff. I have your commitment that you won't bring up the well closure option Tuesday night and will stay general on the details behind the postponement. Yes?"

"Yes, certainly," the city manager said firmly.

"And whether or not we get three votes to overturn your recommendation on the postponement, you'll work closely with us to sell the additional treatment cost, if that's what has to be done?

"Yes."

"And you won't have the study include the impact of closing the wells versus adding more treatment? Yes?"

Silence.

"Brad?" Scott said anxiously.

"Not so sure about that last part, Scott. Developing facts for the Council and public on a legitimate alternative, like closing the well or wells, is part of my job. It's called 'completed staff work.' I insist on it from the staff. I'm uncomfortable committing to working clandestinely with you and some PR firm you'll hire to help us sell the public on the alternative that best serves SoCal's interests, without putting all the options on the table."

Brad felt like the moment just before mustering the nerve to jump off the high board for the first time. "Now, it may be that we'll never have a problem with iron and chromium that requires us to do something. And if we do, the Council and public might support paying for the extra treatment rather than closing the wells and rationing their water use more. I'd just want all the facts and options on the table. As much as I like you, Scott, and support your project, I'm not going to conspire with you today, or any other time, to evade my responsibility. There's been too much of that in this state, especially with water."

"Be careful what you're saying, Brad. I've told you how tenuous our commitment is to Green Valley right now. We helped you get rid of Megan. I convinced Jeff that with her gone, the biggest obstacle to hitting our schedule was removed. What you say or do from this point forward can make or break the project. Don't make yourself a new obstacle."

Scott Graves, Vice President of So Cal Communities, tried everything he could think of to talk the city manager out of the postponement recommendation. The conversation was polite but no minds were changed. It ended with the developer ominously saying, "I guess we'll both have to do what we have to. Good luck, Brad."

*****

Normally, Friday afternoons were quiet. Not this one. After hanging up with Scott, Brad placed calls or left voice mails with the councilmembers and Planning Commission Chairman Parker Fleishmann to inform them of his decision to place the Initial Study on the Council agenda, with a recommendation to postpone circulation, pending further water study. They all, of course, wanted to know the reason behind such a turnabout in his recommendation from the night before. He alluded to personnel issues at the water plant that he wasn't at liberty to discuss at this time.

Mayor Buddy was livid, nearly panting when he stormed over from his real estate office. The mayor insisted on knowing the sordid details. Brad gave him a little more about the investigation at the water plant without getting too graphic about all the goings on or talking about chromium and iron levels rising at one well. He had to keep the mayor's independence for the disciplinary hearings to come, and didn't want anyone spooked about water quality prematurely.

The only supportive call came from Councilwoman Kay Nance late in the day in response to the voice mail he'd left her.

"So, you're still there," the councilwoman joked when she called back later in the day. "They haven't run you out of town yet, huh?"

"No, but I think I smell hot tar and it's too cold to resurface the parking lot today." He gave her a little more background on why he was recommending the postponement, being careful not to tell her more than he did the mayor.

"You earned some points today," Kay said. "Don't be surprised if, when all the information gets out, you'll have more support than you're getting right now. You haven't told me too much, but I appreciate that you are trying to do what's right, and are likely taking shots over it. Speaking of shots, if you and Marie are looking for a place to hide out tonight, come on over. I can probably dig up another bottle of Mezcal for you."

He laughed. "Yeah, Kay, hanging out with you is really going to help my image right now."

Kay's suggestion about hiding out hit home. He called Marie who went to work on it.

He gutted through nasty phone calls and imagined plots until 5 p.m. When he got home, Marie had already packed a cooler and made arrangements for them to spend the weekend with her sister in Burbank.

29

Brad was standing in line at Universal Studios in Hollywood getting tickets for everyone late Saturday afternoon when City Attorney Henry Fitzhenry called.

"Henry! What's the good word?" he asked sarcastically.

"Hi Brad. Sorry to bother you on the weekend."

"I imagine you've been pestered a lot since yesterday. Everything copacetic back home?" He felt an instant twinge of guilt for relishing the thought of the city attorney having to work Friday night and Saturday on the mess Brad left behind. The City Council's only other appointee was paid about the same as Brad for far less personal toll in terms of hours, stress, public visibility, expectations about after-hour community involvement, and political buffeting. Plus, Henry was a master of staying above most of the tough frays. When there was a really hot issue, he regularly advised Brad and the Council that the smart move was to retain a firm with specialists in that field of law. Brad liked Henry, but couldn't help being a little resentful of his colleague, especially at a time like this.

"I just wanted to let you know that the Council asked me to notice a closed session for Tuesday evening, just before the Council meeting, to evaluate the city manager's performance. They want you to be available in your office on stand-by. And, when the press calls you about it, just say that annual evaluations are part of your contract and it's a good practice to do them at the start of the year. Nothing else."

"Oh, I see. Was the meeting called by Buddy alone or are you following a majority of the Council?"

"I'm afraid the majority, Brad. Sorry to have to call you like this." He sounded sincere.

"It's OK, Henry. I'm not exactly shocked by the news. Thanks for the heads up."

"Oh, and Brad," there was hesitation in Fitzhenry's voice. "You didn't hear this from me. I'm sticking my neck out here. OK?"

"Sure Henry," he chuckled, imagining the city attorney's angst compared to what he was going through. "I promise I'm not recording this."

"All I want to say is that just because a majority went along with setting a meeting, it doesn't necessarily mean there is a majority agreement. I don't read it that way. So don't go driving off a cliff or anything. Good luck, Brad."

He ended the call and wiped the grit and sweat from the creases in his neck. Weird to be so hot and miserable in late January. Seasonal Santa Ana, "devil winds," were blowing hard, scouring Southern California with hot, dry, sandy air from the deserts to the east. Fire departments worked to exhaustion trying to prevent localized flare ups in the hills from becoming conflagrations. Fine sand found its way into every crack and orifice. Skin crawled. Nerves fired. Tempers flared. Not a good time to get bad news or be in a ticket line with scores of other grumpy tourists and their kids trying to keep things nonviolent. He looked up at the colorful, cool, blue sign above and smirked at the irony. He hoped the WaterWorld venue wouldn't turn out to be another Southern California mirage.

*****

Driving back home to Santa Ynez Sunday evening, Marie and Brad veered off the Ventura Freeway and headed north, up I-5 to Santa Clarita and the Highway 126 West turnoff toward Ventura on the Pacific Ocean, just below Santa Barbara. The anticipation of seeing the path of the dam disaster was a welcome distraction from what lay at the end of the trip.

He was in surprisingly good spirits, considering the front page stories about the closed session he read online that morning. There was a short article simply announcing the meeting with a quote from the city attorney that it was common practice for the Council to conduct performance evaluations at the beginning of the year. Brad snickered reading that the reporter asked the city attorney when he last received *his* Council evaluation. Henry was quoted as saying, "I don't remember exactly."

The bigger article was speculation on the true purpose of the meeting, replete with unattributed, off-the-record statements. Councilmembers were officially "no comment," although Brad could tell some of them were the unattributed sources. Councilmembers had to take care of their relationships with the local press, after all. The article quoted a couple of his friends saying good things about his character and accomplishments. The most surprising support came from "veteran City Hall watchdog" Pat Kirby, who called the city manager "competent and fair." The most disappointing comment came from his friend, Chamber Exec Brian Brando, who said that, while the Chamber has had a good relationship with the city manager in the past, even if they haven't always agreed, the Chamber stays out of city personnel issues as a matter of policy.

Overall, the press got it right. The story said that City Manager Brad Jacks did not return repeated phone calls to comment. He had decided to avoid the calls rather than lie, as he'd been directed.

Calls from Lee and Lilly, a few of his Rotarian friends, and several other well-wishers buoyed his spirits. He was especially warmed by the four phone calls from his colleagues, both in the area city manager group and from different parts of the state, who had been tipped off.

"Looks like Quinn's been busy," Marie observed.

"Yeah. I can't describe how good it feels to get that kind of support from people who know what it feels like to be in the barrel. I feel bad about all of the times I heard about a friend being in trouble and not taking the time to call. I'm going to be much better about that in the future."

Marie added hopefully, "It was nice of Kay and Gretchen to call. From what you said, it sounds like they are busy getting public support for you."

"Yes, it was nice," he agreed. "But, frankly, I wish it had been Al Landon who called. He'll be the swing again."

He had his iPod hooked up to the car's USB port, playing his 60s playlist. Judy Collins came on singing about looking at clouds from both sides now. He reached out to hold his wife's hand. She smiled back.

They drove on, hand-in-hand, listening to the music and enjoying the scenery along the undivided Highway 126. He looked at his navigation screen and noticed that they were approaching the imaginary line separating Los Angeles and Ventura counties.

He saw the train tracks. "Right about here, I think," he said, pointing out his side window. "This must have been about where Lilly was when the flood hit their camp."

Marie looked left and right. "Just imagine that wall of water and debris barreling through here in the dead of night."

"Yeah, nearly ninety years ago, Lilly was clinging for her life on those hills over there, as her parents washed out to the ocean. Think of it."

He held her hand tighter as they drove on toward Fillmore and Santa Paula. Looking to his right over a field he imagined his father, Spike, as a child, playing cowboys and Indians with Lilly. Little Spike had a homemade wooden rifle like the one he made so many years ago for Brad. Lilly was galloping through the dusty construction camp astride her trusty steed, Brownie. Spike was smiling and waving at his son. Brad took it as a sign of his father's approval and felt the blessed relief of an old pain leaving his body.

"I know you're out there somewhere" came through the car speakers. He recognized the song instantly. The progressive rock band Moody Blues was a favorite of his and his cousin and lifelong best friend, Ed. Ed died from cancer a few years ago. Every time the Moody Blues came on the radio, it reminded him of their times cruising in Ed's El Camino, listening to their tape. He thought of Ed. Would he ever see him again? Was there some sort of afterlife?

He'd never paid much attention to the lyrics of this song. He just assumed it was another love song about a guy looking to reunite with a lost lover. But, for some reason every time it had come on since Ed died, the song penetrated his core. He had always dismissed the emotion as sadness from missing his best friend. Now, he felt there was something more to it. He took his eyes from the road and saw Marie smiling back at him.

"Listen to the words, hon," she said, as if this had all been staged.

He heard about the mist lifting, promises, beauty, soul, truth, and eternal love. He felt the back of his throat beginning to tighten, straining to hold something back. Marie was looking straight ahead, still smiling like she held some secret.

He listened more and felt his concentration yield to a sudden charge. "Wait a minute! This is about God!" he exclaimed. "I've heard this song a thousand times and been moved by it, but I never understood why. Hit Replay, will you? I want to hear those lyrics again."

"Yes, listen again, but don't analyze, listen with your heart," she said softly.

She leaned over to the iPod and hit a button. The song began again. He took a deep breath and exhaled slowly as the song engulfed him like a warm bath. When it was over, he drove on silently, basking in the calmness.

"That line, 'none so blind as those that will not see,' goes back hundreds of years. We just had a sermon about it, remember?"

Marie nodded.

"It was about how much easier it is for children to accept things before their egos take control of their lives and demand answers within their logical understanding. That's a message I need to hear. I've always complained about why God makes Himself so hard to understand."

"I know. Maybe *you're* making it too hard," she said. "And, besides, would you want a God that was only as omnipotent as your own understanding?"

He glanced up at the early moon above the darkening horizon and his mind drifted to the vastness and order of the cosmos. He didn't understand that, either. But neither did he deny it. He felt open to the possibilities.

"It's so beautiful!" he said solemnly. "I mean, the view and the message."

Brad marveled at the precision of the dark green rows of orange and lemon groves passing by. The quartering moon made its appearance in sync with the vast universe, as it had from the beginning of time. The strong, bare sycamores trees swayed gently in the winter breeze, sturdy limbs silhouetted against the clear, purple sky. No denying that the world was still an uncertain, scary place, even for a competent 54-year-old, just like it was when he was six. Yet, as he had been in the Delta, he was again reminded that it was also full of love and beauty for those who aren't too blind to see it.

He let himself relax into the comfortable driver's seat. "I don't know what we are going back to, but I'm glad you're with me." He reached over and squeezed his wife's hand.

EPILOGUE

I understand now that the saying, "may you live in interesting times" is a curse, not a blessing. Brad and I would have gladly opted for our predictable routine over what we came home to that Sunday evening. Our answering machine was full of reporters pestering Brad for a comment on his potential termination and friends offering good wishes or ideas to help him. He didn't call the press back, but did call his friends thanking them for the support. He declined to say anything bad about anyone or to join in with any plans being cooked up.

We both attended a seminar at an ICMA conference a few years ago dealing with getting fired, or, as ICMA euphemistically refers to it, "being in transition." The session was offered to city managers and their spouses. The panelists were city managers and spouses who had experienced "transition." They candidly discussed the anger, embarrassment, financial dislocation, and strain on their marriages that came from such a life-altering event. I had saved the hand-outs and badgered Brad into going through them with me when he finished his calls. I think it helped.

I have to give Brad credit. By the time we went to bed, he wasn't nearly as upset as I expected him to be. I suspect much of that was because of the supporting phone calls and the advice from the ICMA session. But I think it also reflected some spiritual growth, letting go a little, trusting.

Following the advice, he kept to his normal schedule. He went into work Monday and Tuesday, as usual, even though it was awkward, to say the least, with the closed session scheduled for Tuesday evening. He kept his nose to the grindstone and tried his best to stay out of the drama playing out around us both. I was never prouder. Neither was Dillon who seemed to draw closer to his father since the duck hunting trip, and closer still, when Brad started taking fire.

Brad called me right after the closed session that night. He was never called in, but City Attorney Henry Fitzhenry told him all about it. From what Henry said, there were harsh words exchanged. Buddy and Kay really went at it, apparently straying into arguing their positions on Green Valley with Henry trying to keep the meeting legal. In the end, Councilman Al Landon refused to support the mayor and vice mayor in firing Brad. Brad said that the entire council was tense when they came out of the closed meeting to open the regular council meeting. Kay gave him a wink, but both Mayor Buddy and Vice Mayor Mullikin were very cool to him.

Lilly and Lee came over to sit with Dillon and me that night. We opened a bottle of my brother's Zin after Brad called. They stayed to watch the Council meeting with me. Lilly is doing so well.

The Council meeting was interesting. It started with Henry announcing that the Council met in closed session regarding the city manager's performance evaluation and that there was nothing further to announce. You could tell that the people in the packed Council Chambers weren't sure what to make of that. When the mayor banged the gavel, and Brad was still seated at his spot, they must have caught on quickly enough. There seemed to be a mixed reaction.

The Council revised the order of the agenda to take up the Green Valley Village Initial Study issue early, since that, and Brad's status, was obviously why most people were there. Brad summarized his memo recommending a continuance because of further studies being made on the City's water supply without going into much detail. The public testimony droned on for a couple of hours. It was mostly about the pros and cons of the project, not Brad's recommendation.

When the public portion was closed, Gretchen picked up Brad's recommendation as a motion, which Kay quickly seconded. It went down 2-3. Mayor Buddy argued against, then moved to strike, the tertiary treatment language in its entirety from the IS. It, too, went down 2-3. Kay moved to revise the IS to include a comprehensive, neutral assessment of the state's capability of delivering the City's water entitlement through the State Water Project. That motion died for lack of a second.

It was becoming quite comical, really. Every motion was met with some reaction from the audience: hoots, applause, and even laughter. The audience was getting restless for a conclusion. Finally, Councilman Landon got the floor and moved to circulate the Initial Study with the tertiary study for the golf-course-only, the option Brad originally supported. To everyone's surprise, that motion passed. Unanimously. Kay whispered to Brad later that night, "see, I listened to you, I compromised to get what I wanted." He was stunned. Little did he know that the advice he gave her about compromising would end up saving his job. At least for now. He didn't want to ask any questions about how all of that got worked out.

It's been a few months since the eventful Council meeting. Word finally got out about the mess at the water plant and the water quality issues, even before the first of the disciplinary appeal hearings got to the City Council. Brad declined public comment on the disciplinary matters pending the hearings, but made sure staff was ready with fact sheets about the rising iron and chromium levels at the well when that hit the front page. Having a neutral engineering firm emphasize that the water quality still met all state and federal health standards and that there were alternatives to treat the water if that situation worsened, calmed most people down.

The anti-Green Valley Village group went into hysterics, of course, trying to stop the project because of uncertainty over the City's water supply. Fortunately, Brad had pushed Public Works and the consultants, so they were also ready with a contingency plan addressing public health, water rates, and the impact on the Green Valley project. I thought it was logical, neutral, and well-presented.

The study concluded that adding additional treatment for the site was the best option *if and when* the water quality at the well field declined into the unhealthful range. There were no guarantees that drilling new wells in another location wouldn't just yield the same problems, now, or later. The time it would take to go down that path jeopardized the Green Valley schedule. While expensive, adding the additional treatment at the wells was determined to be the best long-term fallback position. And, yes, much to SoCal's chagrin, the study included the impact of closing the wells entirely.

Brad and the staff concluded that if more treatment became necessary at the well, some of the cost could be shifted to the Green Valley project and the balance could be loaned by the city's Capital Improvement Fund with repayment over time. The fairly modest, phased-in water rate increases that would be required didn't seem so bad to most people compared to the hardships they'd experienced if the city closed the wells.

The meeting about the contingency plan was also very contentious. I guess that's just the way it's going to be in Santa Ynez for a long time. Anyway, Brad's recommendation went through on a 3-2 vote, with Kay and Gretchen dissenting.

Despite the Green Valley project plodding ahead and some clarity on the water issues, Brad's status is still shaky. Candidates are already lining up for the next Council election. The EIR and all the other votes on Green Valley will be held off until after the election. Mayor Buddy, Vice Mayor Mullikin, and Councilman Landon are up this time. Rumor had it that Planning Commissioner Jerry Wright wanted to run with the mayor and vice mayor, but the pro-development group thought he was too polarizing and they really wanted to elect a more predictable supporter to replace Landon. They talked Planning Commission Chairman Parker Fleishmann into joining their slate. The Green Valley opponents countered with a ticket that included Dr. Fred Buderi, artist Paisley Menezes, and master gardener Kalo Debevec. Both sides were officially neutral toward Councilman Al Landon. Who knows how it will all shake out and what it will mean for Brad or Green Valley?

In the meantime, we keep taking it a day at a time. Brad doesn't spend as many nights in front of the TV working on our family finances spreadsheet. That's progress. I don't nag him about it when he does, because it's infrequent and you can only expect so much change at a time. Giving up drinking as the transition advisors suggested was big enough. Besides, doing his spreadsheet seems to give him some extra reassurance. I don't know the details, but I trust him when he says we'll be fine regardless of what happens. That's a relief to Dillon who is so excited about starting Colorado State.

As for me, I'm taking golf lessons at the local public course. Brad tried to help me get started, but it was too much like our wallpapering adventure early in our marriage. I don't know if there will ever be a course at Green Valley or if I'll be around to play it. I have to admit, I'm enjoying the game and looking forward to being good enough someday to not embarrass myself or Brad when we start playing together. I've met some nice ladies on the course and even gotten Jane to join me on Saturday afternoons. I don't know how long that will last since she is reaching her second trimester. Brad and I have become very close to Jane and her girls.

Like I said, Brad and I don't know what is going to happen in the election a few months from now. But, after all, we don't know what could happen in the next minute. I have my faith, and that's good enough. I'm always reminding Brad about my cousin, Joan, in Coalinga who copes so positively with setbacks. I still let him vent a little bit about his anxieties. Some of that is probably a good release for him. Then, like Joan, I get him to focus on all our blessings, especially family, friends, and our good health, which are so much more important than whether we retire in Santa Ynez or do something else.

Brad's coming along. After thirty years of marriage, I'm beginning to think he's trainable.

ACKNOWLEDGMENTS

Big thanks to Kevin O'Rourke, city manager colleague and friend, for his encouragement to devote this book to the real life issues and challenges faced by local government professionals. He exemplifies the commitment to the profession and to good government that is true of so many men and women who have chosen the city management field.

In addition to Kevin, I'm indebted to the other friends and colleagues who also read the manuscript drafts and offered their suggestions: Stephen Harding, Kalo Heldt, Debby McGuire, Dr. Elizabeth Moulds, Sean Quinn, Nat Rojanasathira, Jack Simpson, Diane Thompson, and Dr. Gordon Wolf.

Peyton Goodman, a student at Centre College in Kentucky, served faithfully as my research assistant on state water issues. David Tompkins and Jackie McCall were especially valuable contributing technical water quality information and story ideas. Fred Buderi and

Ron Rowland helped me with community development entitlement questions. Dr. Jim Gemmer, Al Lavezzo, Jack Kelly, Tim Mullikin, and Michael Wright contributed other technical advice.

Leon Worden of SCVHistory.com, Alan Pollack of the Santa Clarita Valley Historical Society, and graduate student Ann Stansell provided background information on the St. Francis Dam Disaster.

The dialogue regarding the flaws with the Bay Delta Conservation Plan, now California Water Fix and Eco Restore, was assisted by the work of attorney Dante John Nomellini, Sr., Dr. Jeffrey Michael at the University of the Pacific, staff members with the County of Solano, and Assemblyman Jim Frazier's office, in addition to numerous websites and newspaper accounts.

I'm so glad to have discovered Tiffany Colter's website giving fledgling authors practical writing tips. Her coaching and editing throughout the writing process were especially valuable. http:// writingcareercoach.blogspot.com/.

The talented staff at Hillcrest Media, Inc. did an outstanding job ushering me through the publishing process. I'm grateful for their expertise, responsiveness, and patience.

While this is a work of fiction, it draws on my fulfilling experiences as a city manager. I'd like to thank some of the people who put me on that career path and served as mentors along the way. Dr. Elizabeth Moulds was my Government instructor at California State University, Sacramento in the late-60s. She made government and politics so interesting that I changed my major to Political Science. Dr. Alan J. Wyner, one of my political science professors at University of California, Santa Barbara, and my faculty adviser, was the first person to suggest a career in city government. He arranged an internship for me with the City of Santa Barbara Finance Department, which gave me an early interest in city finances. Paul Nefstead, then Santa Barbara's Budget Director, gave me interesting assignments and insights into organizational dynamics. David Sibbet and the Coro Foundation provided eye-opening experiences on the role that business, labor, media, non-profits, and other groups play in public policy. Most importantly, I'm grateful to have worked for excellent city manager role models: Tom Dunne, Robert Christofferson, Walter Slipe, Bill Edgar, and Walter Graham. I learned from all of them.

Finally, thank you to my wife, Diane, for supporting me in this undertaking, as she has with everything else for 40 years. I promise to take at least a month off before launching into something else.

SUGGESTIONS FOR FURTHER READING

St. Francis Dam Disaster

> *Man Made Disaster: The Story of St. Francis Dam* (2003) by Charles F. Outland is a thorough, factual, and unbiased account of the dam disaster written by an eyewitness.

> *"PRIVILEGE AND RESPONSIBILITY: William Mulholland and the St. Francis Dam Disaster"* by Donald C. Jackson and Norris Hundley, Jr. is an article appearing in *California History* (Volume 82, 2004). The authors reviewed transcripts of the Coroner's Inquest and engineering studies of the dam disaster. They firmly lay the blame for the disaster on William Mulholland, the chief architect of the project.

> The Santa Clarita Valley History Society has a treasure trove of articles, photos, and video interviews of survivors. http://www.scvhistory.com/scvhistory/stfrancis.htm.

California Water & History

> *Managing California's Water: From Conflict to Reconciliation* (February 2011) by -, Ariel Dinar, Brian Gray, Richard Howitt, Jeffrey Mount, Peter Moyle, and Barton "Buzz" Thompson is a well-researched book published by the Public Policy Institute of California. It does an excellent job describing the historic and current legal, environmental, and political factors surrounding California water policies. It includes some recommendations for reasonable reforms that seek to balance competing interests.

> *Water Heist: How Corporations Are Cashing In On California's Water (2003)* by Public Citizen, a national, nonprofit consumer advocacy organization, is a disturbing report on the power the large water contractors have wielded on statewide water policies.

> *Cadillac Desert: The American West and Its Disappearing Water, Revised Edition* (1993) by Marc Reisner is a very well-written, fascinating account of the economics, politics, and ecology of the massive water projects that made development of the American West possible.

> *Water and Power: The Conflict over Los Angeles Water Supply in the Owens Valley (1983)* by William L. Kahrl dispassionately tells the story of the City of Los Angeles' actions to secure the water rights of Owens Valley and build an aqueduct to bring the water 230 miles to spawn the incredible growth that city saw in the beginning of the 20th Century. It is both an amazing feat of engineering and government achievement and an example of the role that power and arrogance have played in water projects.

> Those interested in the development of the Los Angeles Aqueduct, as well as the history and politics of broader statewide

water developments in California, should obtain *The Great Thirst: Californians and Water: A History*, by Norris Hundley, Jr.

> *Battling the Inland Sea: Floods, Public Policy, and the Sacramento Valley* (Reprint Edition) by Robert Kelley is the account of how the 100-mile sea that once formed in the Sacramento Valley from winter rains was tamed by thousands of miles of levees and drains to become the highly productive area it is today. Kelley addresses not only the public and private works that made the transformation possible, but also the historic and still-current relationships between politics and environmental policy.

> *California: A History (Modern Library Chronicles) Reprint Edition* (2007) by Kevin Star is a favorite nonfiction source for background on the Spanish, Mexican, and early statehood eras of California.